Empower

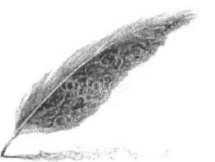

Publishing

Also, by Percy Kepfer, M.D.
and *Empower Publishing*

The Daughter of the General

A Homeless Veteran

The Smell of Power

by Percy Kepfer, M.D.

Symbiosis

By

Percy D. Kepfer, M.D.

Empower Publishing
Winston-Salem

Empower

Publishing

Empower Publishing
302 Ricks Drive
Winston-Salem, NC 27103

First Empower Publishing Books edition published July, 2025
Empower Publishing, Feather Pen, and all production designs are trademarks.

For information regarding bulk purchases of this book, digital purchases and special discounts, please get in touch with the publisher at publish.empower.now@gmail.com

Cover design by Pan Morelli
Manufactured in the United States of America

ISBN 978-1-63066-621-7

To Alli, my most avid reader,
And to all my family.

—Percy D. Kepfer, MD

One

They called him "the Cuban." Not only because his name was Andy Garcia, like the Cuban movie star, but also because he came from Miami. However, he was neither Cuban nor resembled the famous movie actor. In fact, Garcia was a third-generation Mexican American.

His birth certificate read Andres Garcia-Rosales (as it was the Spanish custom; the last was his mother's maiden name, which he dropped for the simpler Andy Garcia).

He was born in El Paso, Texas, and raised in Miami. Although handsome and taller than his movie actor counterpart, he was dark-skinned and curly-haired. Yet, his light green eyes could pierce the soul of those looking at them and inspire tenderness, as they did in most women, or fear, as in some men.

Andy Garcia used both to his advantage in performing his job because he was a detective with the Sheriff's Department of Saint Lucie County, Florida.

He hated his nickname and had a strong dislike for all Cubans and everything Cuban. Everyone in the department knew it, so nobody dared say it to his face, and only very close friends, all of whom were still in Miami, were permitted to call him by that name. Yet, he knew that behind his back, many of the guys—especially those not very fond of him, referred to him by that nickname.

Anyway, Andy, "The Cuban," was sound asleep when the cell phone sitting at the night table rang; at first, he tried to ignore the ringing and covered his head with his pillow, but the woman lying naked next to him picked it up and handled it to him.

"You better answer, sugar…it is your job, remember? besides, I want to go back to sleep," she said.

Cursing, he picked up the phone.

A tired voice came from the telephone; he recognized it as one of a rocky deputy who was covering "the graveyard shift" that night.

"Hello boss, sorry to wake you up at this hour, but we have a dead Mexican here, and you know that investigating that belongs to your department."

Andy loved his job and had been a policeman for several years but was not a morning person. He did not mind staying up till the wee hours of the night doing a stake up or working on a case, but to be awakened in the early hours of the morning pissed him off very, very badly, and everyone in the department knew it.

"Were?" he asked while looking at the clock on the nightstand; the red numbers indicated it was 1:30 a.m.

"Orange Avenue North, between 31st and 32nd"

"Be there soon, do not touch anything, do not let anyone touch anything, and send someone to see if someplace is open to get me a cup of coffee, but you stay put right where you are. Have you called the CSI team? I do not want to be the only one awakened at this awful hour."

The cop understood very well and answered in the affirmative while readying himself to face an angry, not-a-morning-person detective. He sent his partner for coffee.

The dead man was lying face down on the sidewalk while the rest of his body was partially hidden by tall grass and bushes growing next to the sidewalk. There was a bullet hole in the middle of his back and his pockets were turned inside out.

Garcia arrived at the scene before the CSI team, so he grabbed a digital camera from the car's glove compartment and put on rubber gloves before getting out of his car.

Two officers were waiting on a patrol car with the red and blue lights working. One of them got out and handed Andy a plastic cup filled with hot coffee.

He grabbed the cup, took a sip, spat some out while uttering a curse word, and then, after blowing into the steaming brew, he carefully took another sip. Then, after snapping a few pictures of the death scene, the detective kneeled beside the body and turned the corpse over.

Taking a meticulous look at the dead man, he took more pictures and asked, "Did you notice anything weird about this officer?"

The young cop did not answer right away; he took a good look at the dead man, then at the surrounding area of the place where the body was positioned, and said:

"Well, sir, this man is probably an illegal alien, probably Mexican. He must have been drinking and got robbed at gunpoint while walking home; he may have tried to fight his assailants and was shot and killed."

"That is brilliant, son. However, your crime scene theory can be easily destroyed. First of all, you said the man had been drinking. Did you smell him? Does he smell of alcohol, mezcal, or tequila since you think he is Mexican?

"Second, where is the blood? If this man was shot in this spot, there should be blood in his shirt, on the sidewalk, and in the grass. I see no blood in any of those places, do you? This man was shot elsewhere, possibly after he was already dead.

"Oh, you could tell me that someone took the time to wash the body and the clothes, but then why is there a fucking bullet hole in the shirt still with a gunpowder rim on it?"

Without waiting for an answer, the detective continued: "Also, I do not think he is Mexican, although, to you guys, all Latinos seem to be Mexican. This guy is shorter and darker; I believe he may be a Guatemalan, or

Honduran, or Peruvian, although I may be wrong, I am betting on the first one. But I think I am right; it says here on his shirt mark, 'Made in Guatemala.' Of course, only that does not make him a Guatemalan. Nowadays, everything is made in China, Taiwan, the Dominican Republic, and a thousand other countries, so why not Guatemala?"

At that point, the Crime Scene Investigation van pulled over, and several members of the team got out.

"Here is the CSI team fresh like a morning breeze. I bet you guys took your precious time to shower and have breakfast, didn't you?"

A petite blonde wearing tight jeans responded: "Do not be sarcastic, Garcia. We are as happy as you are about being up early. You are an ass hole most of the time but more so in the mornings, do you know that?"

"So, I have been told, darling, you should go out with me one of these evenings so you can see how sweet I can be at night."

"That can be construed as sexual harassment, Detective," she said with a flirting smile.

Then she turned and looked at the dead man's body and said, "Did you move this guy?"

"I just turned him over. He has a bullet hole going through and through."

"So I see," she said. "By the size of the hole, it was caused by a large caliber weapon—perhaps a Magnum—but where was the blood? It should be a puddle and splattered all over."

"That's my point exactly. See, everything you've been hearing about blondes being dumb is just a fallacy."

She did not know how to respond at that remark, but she took it as a compliment, yet she retorted, "Fuck you, Garcia."

TWO

Melvin Bright, (aka "Melvin Not-So") Bright, MD., was happier than a pig in creamy shit. Not only had he laid his first job after finishing medical school—and a very brief residency, but he also thought that he had found his life, true love.

It was not that he had never been in love before, although the subject of all his previous passions were not aware of it. This time was different, stronger than ever before. This time, he promised himself he would not keep his sentiments buried deep in his heart; this time, somewhat, sometime, he would have the courage to express his feelings to the subject of his affection.

Never mind that he had met her for the first time less than one hour before and was not sure she even noticed him.

It was a beautiful morning, with the sun bright and shining. Although it was hot, it was not yet humid. Of course, it was still early in the morning, and at that time of the year, in sunny Florida, he knew very well that it would get hotter and as the day progressed.

Melvin Bright could not ask for anything more. Well, perhaps not having hurricanes would have been nice. But even those—which were the only thing that he disliked about Florida—he could live with, especially since hurricane season was almost over now. It was the middle of October, and the weather had been cooler than usual for at least the last three weeks.

God only knew how much he hated and feared hurricanes. Of course, there was a good reason for that. He had been through "Andrew" when, as a child, he lived in Homestead with his family, but he also had gone through a couple of them while he went to medical school in the islands. Then, shortly after returning to the US, he had to go through "Frances" and "Jeanne," the two strong, back-to-back Hurricanes of 2004.

Melvin just finished a residency in an Orlando Hospital, which he needed to fulfill the requirements of the Florida Board of Medicine and obtain a license to practice in the state.

He had failed the Board exam but did not want to think about that because, even without a Florida License, he was going to have a job. Never mind that his father, a prominent Neurobiologist, had pulled some levers to get him the job.

Melvin did not care too much about being a doctor; he did not care too much about anything. Except for video games, food, and beer, actually in that order. He was far from being an alcoholic, leaning more towards hotdogs, hamburgers, pizza, and any junk food, which was evident to most people as soon as they saw his portly figure and prominent abdomen.

During his high school and college years, he learned that in order to make friends he had to be respected or admired for something. Since he was fat, slow, and not good at sports, despite being over six feet tall, he took on playing video games and drinking beer, which his large and portly frame allowed him to consume in large quantities without getting drunk before everybody else did.

He was gifted at playing video games; none of his friends or foes could beat him at on-screen games. In fact, he participated in tournaments with kids from other schools and beat them all.

Unfortunately for Melvin Bright, he was not too bright as far as books, learning, and academics were concerned, and that earned him the nickname of "Not so" Bright," a name that followed him from high school to college and eventually to medical school, even though he attended a foreign medical school in Mexco, a school he attended only because his father insisted that he followed in his footsteps and those of his grandfather and great-grandfather before him, and because, even with his father's connections and influence in the scientific and academic medical community, he did not have the necessary qualifications to enter a medical school in any university in the United States of America.

Melvin Bright had been and still was a nerd, although his physical appearance had changed somewhat since high school when everyone thought he resembled a fat version of Napoleon Dynamite, including his braces and curly hair. Now that the braces were gone, and although still portly, he had slimmed down some, yet the glasses remained, so he resembled a fat and tall Woody Allen.

Melvin did not care much that this new job at the brand new neurobiological institute located in Indiantown, Florida, was given to him thanks to his father, who indeed honored the family name by being super bright and well known for his work in neuroscience all over the US and the world.

After all, it was to please his father that he had gone to medical school to follow the family tradition. Melvin loved his father as his father loved him, so he was used to the fact that his father made decisions for him and also that he paved the way of life ahead of him. It has been that way even when his mother was alive, but when she died in a car crash when he was only a boy, his father and older sister cared for him and provided him with everything he wanted.

Yet Melvin had been a good kid. Even under this strong family shadow, he never became the spoiled brat that most children under similar circumstances become. However, he became highly dependent on his father and sister and, to a lesser degree, on the influence and opinion of his peers, who—to his good fortune—were primarily good kids and geeks like himself.

So, after finally accepting the fact that his child was not medical school material—at least not USA medical school material, the senior Doctor Bright persisted and found Melvin a place in a medical school in Mexico. In Mexico, and somewhat to his father's surprise and pleasure, he obtained a medical diploma and became fairly fluent in Spanish.

During the year of his internship in Orlando, Melvin became interested in interventional radiology. Perhaps due to his skills as a video game player, he was very good at it. "It," however, was that he became very good at inserting needles and following them through CT scans, MRIs and ultrasounds, but his failure to dominate the uses and side effects of different contrast media, as well as the need to be coached as to where to place the needles and wires, because of his poor knowledge of the human anatomy, excluded him from being a candidate to continue in the program.

So, after the one-year mandatory internship at a US hospital, which is required for United States citizens graduating from foreign medical schools, Melvin Bright was ready for his first job as a Doctor.

This job was at the newly built, state-of-the-art Neurological Institute in Indiantown, Florida, where he had just met the woman of his dreams.

THREE

The scientist sat around a long, shiny, U-shaped table in the well-lighted, ultramodern conference room.

The mood was not festive.

Ten men and two women, all wearing long, white lab coats, some of which were clean and starched while others were stained with strange fluids, were chatting very fast among themselves. Some spoke to each other in foreign languages, others in English. Most had grey hair or no hair at all, indicating that they were all either approaching middle age or beyond it.

The leather-padded, elegant, large chair at the head of the table remained empty, and most of the individuals present in the room occasionally glanced worriedly at it and at the mahogany door behind it.

When the door opened, all conversations stopped, a complete silence came to the room, and all individuals stood up as one when an old man in a battery-powered wheelchair made his entrance. He looked probably older than he really was because the blue eyes behind the spectacles he wore looked bright, alive, and full of energy, with a hint of cruelty.

Behind the old man and standing like a soldier on guard was a man who, disregarding the fact that the chair was battery-propelled, had pushed it into the room. This man seemed to be about forty or forty-five years old. His dark and well-combed hair was graying at the temples, yet his face was young and his build was that of a bodybuilder or a well-trained athlete. His height, probably over six feet, added to the handsome looks of the man. His blue eyes, however beautiful, were cold and cruel, his face was expressionless.

Both of them wore tailor-made, expensive-looking dark suits.

All the men in the room were younger than the first man but older and much smaller than the second. Their expensive suits seemed cheap in comparison.

The women could not take their eyes off the tall, younger man and dreamed.

All of them appeared subdued in the presence of the first two men.

"Good morning, doctors. It is a beautiful day, isn't it?" the man in the wheelchair said, without any indication in his tone that he really wished the others anything good or that he cared whether the day was good or bad.

"Good morning, Mr. Mellon," they answered in accord.

"Ivan and I have flown here from New York because I would like to hear from the lips of everyone present about the progress of your work."

After a short pause, the man named Mr. Mellon said: "Also, we are here because I have been informed that there have been some accidents during your work and that the team of my chief of security and good friend, Ivan,

13

here, and his team has been forced to clean the mess you produced."

"With all due respect, Mr. Mellon", one of the men in lab coats replied, "there is always a chance that something that is supposed to go right fails or turns left. Medicine is still, even in this day and age, not an exact science but an art. Accidents do happen, medications can produce unforeseen and sometimes unknown side effects, and this is in everyday medical care; we are dealing here with something different, something that has never been done before, something that can change the whole human race."

"Spare me the gibber jabber professor. I am well aware of the facts of what you are saying, and that is why I have been tolerant of those accidents, but six accidents in a month—eight in less than two months—are totally inexcusable. I am surprised that the police have not been sniffing around our way yet. If this keeps up, sooner than later, they will be knocking on our doors. And guess what? I am not going to risk my ass to protect yours. We will not let you jeopardize this project because of the stupidity or clumsiness of a few of you. I can assure you that Ivan here shares my views on the subject. Is that clear?"

The last words delivered a subtle warning that produced a chill in the spine of most of those present and a forced smile in the face of the man named Ivan.

Mr. Mellon continued without allowing the professors to speak: "the other matter is no less important and, to me, more urgent than that of the accidents. We are running out of time, gentlemen. I will turn seventy in three months, and I would like to see the Symbiosis project finished and functional before I either die or lose my bloody mind.

"You are supposed to be the fucking most bright scientists in the world in your respective fields. I am paying you millionaire salaries. I have built this facility for you to work in secret since the type of research you are doing is not seen with good eyes by our president or the religious right. I had let you hire the people of your choice to research other areas that had little or nothing to do with Symbiosis, and guess what? Their research has produced more results and even some profits, while you—the brightest of all—have done nothing. Therefore, I would like to know exactly what you have so far. Let's see who can speak for all...Professor Bright."

Professor Bright sat beside his older partner and friend, Dr. Paul Bernstein. Being the younger of the two, and a pupil of the older doctor, Bright was somewhat surprised that Mr. Mellon addressed him instead of this senior partner. He thought, "The old man knows; I am sure of that."

"Well, Mr. Mellon," he addressed the man with as much authoritarian and self-confident tone as he could muster instead of the meek and apologetic tone that his colleagues generally used when addressing their boss. "Symbiosis is going well. Regrettably, there have been those accidents that you mentioned. Doctor Linda Porter has done wonders with the chimps. She has some of them actually talking."

Mellon interrupted, "You mean that her monkeys are speaking? Like speaking English?

"Well, actually, most of them speak Spanish. As you know, most of the donors speak Spanish, but she also has a couple who speak English."

"Whoa, that is wonderful! Tell me, Professor Bright, how many Doctor Porter's chimps have suffered accidents?."

"None, Mr. Mellon. All the accidents have occurred on either the donors or the human transfers."

Mellon used a sarcastic tone. "So the veterinarian lady doctor is doing better with her monkeys than the two famous professors are doing with their patients?"

A smile broke out in the face of one of the female scientists around the table. An attractive woman in her forties with black hair down to her shoulders, usually worn in a large curl on top of her head. One could sense that there was a nice body under the long laboratory coat. Thick glasses covered her dark green eyes. She came from the Middle East to work at the institute, and nobody knew much about her past except that she was or had been married to an American last name Porter.

"As far as that, yes, sir, Doctor Porter is an excellent scientist. However, on our side, we have succeeded in transferring personalities, memories, etc., from one subject to another and some of our volunteers are now speaking fluent English without even an accent."

"Don't most people speak English in this country?"

This remark from Mellon caused a smirk that could pass for a smile on the stone face of the man referred to as Ivan. Otherwise, he remained silent and stood as a soldier on a parade.

"These people are Indians from Guatemala. They barely speak Spanish; their language is Kanjobal."

Mr. Mellon's expression softened as he said, "Oh, Guatemala. I was there a few times in my younger years when I had full use of my body. Pretty country. Too bad we had to mess it up in 1954."

That comment did not surprise anyone in the room. Although everyone knew of Richard Mellon—the billionaire, entrepreneur and playboy—very few people knew the man, his background, and much less how he had made his enormous fortune. Rumors abounded, but the most widely accepted was that he came from a small town which he left at an early age, joined the armed forces and then became either CIA agent, a mercenary, a high-price assassin, a drug dealer, an arms dealer or that he had befriended a rich old woman, who died in mysterious circumstances and left him a vast fortune. Richard Mellon was aware of the rumors, and although he never gave an interview to the media, he did not bother to dispel any of the rumors about him.

Most of those in the room believed every word of the rumors, especially since many of them had met him in foreign lands from which he lured or extricated them to come to work on this project at the institute.

Mr. Mellon continued addressing the speaker for the doctors. "All that is well and sounds promising, Dr. Bright, but how far do you think you and your colleagues are from completing symbiosis to the point that I can safely use it?"

Dr. Bright responded, " I think I speak for all of us here when I tell you that we are very close, Mr. Mellon, but it is not a simple task to combine nanotechnology with stem cell research and neuroscience. We have to combine the work of each one of us, which is most important, so the nanoparticles could act like a computer programmer and tell the stem cells what to do after implantation."

"That sounds fascinating and exciting, professors, but this is why you have been hired, you are the best of the best in your fields, and I have brought you here at great expense and at great risk; therefore I want to see Symbiosis completed before I die."

Professor Bright asked, "What about the recipient from the main subject, Mr. Mellon? I believe you may not want to use a Mayan, a Mexican or a homeless person for that, and we will need to run hundreds of tests on him before the transfer is done."

Professor David Bright's words tried to put Mellon in a defensive position. As he suspected, it did not work.

"Let Ivan and me worry about that. When you are ready, the subject will be ready, I am already ready, I have been ready since before you guys started symbiosis."

Everyone in that room was aware that Richard Mellon did not have any children as heirs and that he hated every single one of his four wives. So who could be the subject?

Professor Bright thought he knew.

Mellon said, "Gentlemen "And with this he pushed a button and the wheelchair started to move with Ivan behind. Before they reached the door of the conference room, Mellon turned around to ask:

"I heard that the Institute has two new hires, who are they?"

"One is my son, Melvin. The other, I believe, is Professor Porter's daughter."

"Oh, I see. We are all a happy family. What will they be doing, if I may ask?"

"Melvin will be working in implanting and extractions. He is very good with his hand dexterity—" He did not mention that he had acquired that playing video games. "—Dr. Porter's daughter is a veterinarian like her mother. She is a Harvard graduate, *cum laude*, and took some convincing from mom to bring her to work here—" He did not mention either that Dr. Porter, being from the Middle East, wanted to keep her daughter close to her to protect her, as she was becoming too westernized.

"I hope, for the sake of both of you professors, that neither one of them is yet aware of Project Symbiosis."

Both of the professors answered almost in unison, "No sir, she is not."

"He is not, we did not think it was wise to."

"Very good, ladies and gentlemen, very good. The least number of people to know about the real aim of Symbiosis, the better we all will be."

And with that, they left.

FOUR

Detective Andy Garcia was still tired but feeling much better than earlier. It was almost seven thirty when he got home and took a long shower.

The woman who had been with him the night before was gone. She had fixed coffee and scrambled eggs before leaving, but they were cold by the time Garcia got home, so he only drank a cup of black coffee. After getting dressed, he got into his car and went to have a hearty breakfast at the local Waffle House on Okeechobee Road: coffee, orange juice, steak, and eggs. That was his fourth cup that morning, but he needed it because his brain still resented that it had gotten up so early.

He also began to feel guilty about his behavior towards the two young cops and the CSI people. Why in the world was he like that? He thought most people should be happy in the morning. It should be considered a blessing that one could wake up, be able to come out of bed, walk, hear, and see when there were so many people crippled, lame, blind, deaf, stricken with cancer or other deathly diseases, or worse yet, dead, like that poor fellow that morning in Orange Avenue.

But again, he tried to rationalize. It had not been technically morning. One thirty a.m. is one hour and a half into the next day, but it is not a morning with the sun still four to five hours from appearing, and most people do not wake up until six or seven anyway.

Nevertheless, he should have behaved better and remembered how much his partner Frank Glisson used to help him in this regard. God only knew how much he missed his partner Frank, who was now on vacation and recovering from a wound sustained in the line of duty.

Frank Glisson was an okay guy, older, more mature, and totally his opposite, but he was much more. He was his best friend, confidant, and advisor. Above all, Frank was a morning person and one nice enough to take all the early morning calls and not to bother his friend at all at those hours unless it was strictly necessary. And then he had the magic of being able to calm him down and have a cup of coffee ready for him upon his arrival to whichever crime scene.

Yes, Frank was a wonderful guy, and Garcia was thrilled that it was not during one of those calls alone that Frank got shot. It happened when Frank was off duty, buying something at a convenience store when some punks decided to rob it.

Frank got one of them, but one of the others shot him in the leg, severing one artery and breaking a bone. Garcia made a personal quest to track down the shooter, and the guy died in a shootout with the cops who went to arrest him. Never mind that more than ten bullets hit the suspect, Garcia knew that the one that killed him had come from his gun, and he had aimed for the head. He wanted to make sure that no soft-hearted judge or ambulance-chaser lawyer was going to let that bastard get out of jail with only a slap on the wrist.

Yet it seemed that more than two guys were involved in the robbery. One may have been the driver of the getaway car and that person and the car were never identified.

Unfortunately, Frank was still several weeks away from returning to work, and Sheriff Ken Mascara had not been able to find him a substitute partner, someone who was willing to work with Detective Garcia. The department was short on personnel, that was true, but both Garcia and the Sheriff were aware that most people did not want to partner with him.

After finishing breakfast, he drove to the Sheriff's office to write the report of the case. There was not much more to write about, but he was bothered by the whole thing; it did not make much sense. The simplest explanation would be the version that the young cop who was at the scene had described: a lonely man who, either after having had too much to drink or spending the night with a woman, walks home late at night in a desolated, crime-ridden area of the city and someone robs and shoots him. Happens all the time.

The problem was that there was no blood, and the guy did not smell of alcohol. If he had sex recently or had consumed drugs, that would be found after performing an autopsy and toxicology exam. Another strange thing was that no one in the nearby Latino community living in the vicinity of the crime scene recognized the man. Granted, a Polaroid photo of a dead man's face, taken at night, was not easy to identify... but still.

As Garcia walked into the sheriff's department building in route to his desk, he spotted Sergeant Karla Colles of the CSI division working at her desk. She still wore the same tight jeans she was wearing before and it was obvious that she had not been home yet. Garcia initially thought of avoiding her and turned around, but then, the guilt returned. And, with an effort, turned around and walked towards her desk. "Good morning, Sergeant Colles. It looks like you've been working straight through since last night."

She lifted her head from the computer screen, glanced deceptively at him, and said, "Unlike some. But, if you do not mind me correcting you, it was not last night. It was earlier this morning"

Whatever you say, Sergeant Colles, I want to apologize for my behavior. You are right, I am an asshole. And would you please forgive me?"

Without lifting her head from the computer monitor, she said, "I'll have to think about it. Let you know tomorrow."

Garcia did not know what to say and babbled, "Would you please really let me know? I am truly sorry. I feel terrible towards you and those two young cops."

She did not answer or look at him again. She just continued working, so

Garcia entered his office and started typing his report. Fifteen or so minutes later, Sgt. Colles knocked at the door of Garcia's small office and, without waiting for permission, she entered. "I am still thinking about accepting your apology, and I think you first should apologize to those two officers. But that is not why I came here. I want you to look at this." She showed him several pictures of the crime scene. "I figured you do not have yours developed yet," she said.

Garcia blushed and scrabbled for words, finally coming up with: "I was going to stop at the lab to have them develop. Then, I will go to the morgue to see if the docs are finished with the post-mortem. What you got?"

"Look here, at his left arm. Do you see anything there?" Karla said, pointing to a picture she had put on the desk in front of him.

"I do. It looks like a small tattoo, certainly not professionally made, maybe a bird of some type. There is also a couple of tiny letters, maybe initials," said Garcia.

She pointed at the picture, "I had it enlarged. Look at it again. What do you see now?"

Andy said, "It is definitely a bird, but I am not sure what kind. Certainly not a common one. And the letters are pretty badly written, but they seem to be an I and a T."

"You are right, Garcia. It is a bird and not a common one. It is a Quetzal. Do you know what country it is the National Bird of?"

"I know Mexico's National Bird is the eagle, so I am going to guess Guatemala."

"Final answer?" she said emulating the tone of the host of a popular game show.

"Final answer," Garcia responded.

"So you win a million dollars," she continued, mocking the *Who Wants to Be a Millionaire* TV show. "You were right in thinking that our dead man was a Guatemalan. And there is more to it. I called Doctor Raymond, the Medical Examiner and his assistant told me they have another Guatemalan in the freezer there. The police found him over a week ago. The Medical Examiner is waiting to ship the remains back to Guatemala, and that may happen today. However, this fellow was not shot. They found him floating in one of those channels in Port Saint Lucie. It was assumed he was drunk and drowned. The funny thing is they found very little water in his lungs. And, although there was much rum in his stomach, the blood alcohol level was almost nothing."

"So he did not drown and he was not drunk. What in heavens did he die of?" Garcia asked.

"They do not know yet. But, so far, all the toxicology has been negative except for some hard-to-identify substance that they expect to get a report of later today from a referring FBI laboratory. I requested the good doctor to return to that corpse with a fine tooth comb and to do the same with our Juan

Doe, or perhaps Ignacio T. or possibly It can't be Thomas, actually Tomas, in Spanish," Colles said.

"Thank you, sergeant. You have done a great job. Congratulations," said Garcia. "Unfortunately, 'I.T.' could be the man's initials, those of his wife or girlfriend, or those of one of his children—if he had any—or perhaps the place of his birth. Maybe his favorite soccer team or who knows what."

"True, but he does look very Guatemalan from what I've seen around here. You should be able to figure it out. You speak Spanish and you are Latino," said Sgt. Colles without any hint of malice.

"I am an American, born in the good old USA, for your information. But wait a minute, I know a place where many Guatemalans live, and many of them go by last names that sound like first names. Like Pedro Pedro, Pedro Juan, etc. Maybe our guy's name is Ignacio Tomas or something like that," responded Garcia.

"And where is such a place?" asked the CSI officer.

"The name of the town is Indiantown. In the past, the Seminole Indians lived there. But, oddly enough, during the seventies and eighties, when there was a bloody civil war in Guatemala and the Guatemalan Army thought that the best way to control the guerrillas was to prevent the peasantry from helping them, the army started a bloody campaign terrorizing and killing everybody and anyone in the countryside who could even remotely provide help to the them."

"Whoa!" Colles said. "I heard something about that war, but I do not know much about that piece of history. If I remember correctly, that war ended sometime at the end of the nineties, correct?"

"You are correct, but the war lasted over thirty years, and thousands were killed or simply disappeared. The Guatemalan Army massacred entire villages, killing men, women and children, often in the most horrific ways. It seems the idea was to make the peasants so afraid that nobody would dare to help the guerrilla fighters. However, that did not work, as many survivors or people from neighboring villages joined the guerrilla movement.

"Somehow, many Guatemalan Mayan Indians managed to escape their country. They walked across Mexico and appeared in Indiantown, Florida, USA. At first, a handful were protected by the Catholic Church. Then family, friends, and relatives started coming. Now, they are probably the majority of inhabitants of that town and have spread to Stuart and even West Palm Beach." Garcia stopped to catch his breath after the long talk, then added, "What do you think if we paid a visit to the morgue and then let's go have lunch in Indiantown? The lunch is on me."

"I hope you are not trying to buy my forgiveness, impress me with your knowledge of history, or make a pass at me, Detective. However, I may feel more inclined to forgive you and go to lunch with you if the lunch is good and not at McDonald's or Burger King. Besides, you must keep your best behavior and reverse the schedule: go to Indiantown, have lunch and then visit the medical examiner. Split-open dead bodies are not the best appetite stimulants. Additionally, you have to promise to do something about that personality problem. I am referring to your mood changes."

"What personality problem are you referring to Seargent?"

"The Doctor Jekyll and Mr. Hyde problem of yours. Actually, I know a couple of good psychiatrists that would be glad to help."

Garcia listened with a contrite expression and responded, "Fair enough. I will behave. I will take you for lunch to a nice place. There is a small hotel in Indiantown. I think it is called the Seminole Inn. I had lunch there once. It was perfect. Oh, and I will certainly keep in mind your advice about seeing a shrink. Meanwhile, we need to see another kind of physician. Do you think that Doctor Raymond will be able to hold the body of the guy who you said appeared to have drowned? At least until after we get back from Indiantown?"

"Yes, I have already told the Doctor to keep the body until we get there and until we get back and after he gets that toxicology report," responded Karla.

"You are really on top of things, sergeant. That is great. Thank you."

"Depending on your behavior this afternoon, I may let you eventually call me Karla. But for now, let's continue being formal. Agreed?" she said with a coquettish smile.

"Agreed," Garcia responded," however you can call me Andy."

"I think we better stay formal, and let's go inform the boss where we are going to be for the next few hours, especially since we are going to leave the county," Colles suggested.

"Good idea, you do the talking," said Garcia.

Sheriff Kenneth Mascara was a pleasant fellow, about six feet tall and heavy set, with curly black hair and a mustache. He wore silver-rimmed glasses. He was actually a chiropractor but had been a great sheriff and was now on his third term in the office. After hearing the full account of the case and their reasons for visiting the neighboring town, the sheriff had no problem authorizing the trip. However, he warned the officers that if they found a suspect or had to make an arrest, they would have to contact either the Indiantown Police Department or the Martin County Sheriff's Department.

As they were leaving the office, the Sheriff said to both of them, "Since you seem to be getting along so well and both are working in the same case, you, Sergeant Colles, will be Detective Garcia's new partner until Detective Glisson is fully recovered and back to work."

As she tried to protest, the Sheriff added, "Seargent Colles, do not be alarmed. This is a temporary assignment, at least until this case is solved or Detective Glisson returns to full duty. Understood?"

Sgt. Colles was going to protest, but Garcia grabbed her gently by the arm and led her out of the office while whispering: "I guess you are stuck with me, Sergeant Colles. For once in my life, I am beginning to wish that this case takes a long time to be solved and I know that Frank is still several weeks from coming back."

"You may change your mind after this afternoon. Perhaps you will be sorry, Garcia," she said in an obviously insincere tone.

"Something tells me that I won't be sorry at all and that it is going to be fun working with you Colles."

"We shall see," was all she replied, and then asked, "Are we taking your car or mine?"

"Do you know the way to Indiantown?" asked Garcia.

"Never been there, but I am sure it would not be hard to find the way " she said.

"Then let me drive. Do you want us to take US 1 or go the scenic route?" he asked.

"I did not know that there was a scenic route. How about we drive up taking US 1, then return by your scenic route? That way, we may avoid rush hour traffic if it takes longer than expected. I am assuming there is no heavy traffic on the scenic route," the girl said.

"You are absolutely right. But we have to get back at least by three-thirty at the latest. Otherwise, we may not find the good doctors at the Medical Examiner's place."

"It is only ten-fifteen AM. If it takes half an hour to get there, a couple of hours to snoop around and ask questions, another hour for lunch, and another half hour to get back, we should be back by three thirty or four o'clock."

Garcia's car was a black Mustang. It was a special edition hard-top convertible. He was single and his family in Miami was not wealthy, but was well off enough that they did not need any economic help from their kids. So although he did not make much money as a detective, he figured he should treat himself to an expensive car. Actually, he had his heart set on a Corvette, but unless he could afford two cars—which he could not—a Corvette would not have been the ideal car for going around doing his work. Even the Mustang, although he actually would have gone for a red one, was too visible. Still, he figured that he needed something less conspicuous, so he settled for a black one with the convertible hard top, up only rarely—and always when he was not on duty—he would put the top down. Yet, he felt like doing it that morning.

It was a beautiful day and not too hot. Still, he felt compelled to ask her if it was okay to convert the car.

"I see you want to impress me, Garcia, but do not try to be a smart ass. Not all blondes are dumb, as you should have realized by now. This is not a date. Besides, I do carry a gun, and I am a blackbelt in Karate."

Garcia did not know if she was serious or joking, but he felt stupid and mumbled an apology. "Sorry I am so stupid. I guess I was trying to impress you. Please forgive me."

"Don't be silly, Garcia. I think it is a great idea to put the darn top down, but let's do it after we are a few blocks away from the station. I do not want those folks to start any rumors. Okay? And in that case, let me go to my car to get some sun protection cream. I do burn easy. Most dumb blondes do."

Garcia wanted to say that she was not even close to being a dumb blonde, but said nothing. He, just looked at her walking away towards her car, in those tight jeans that molded what definitely was a gorgeous body. She was wearing a jacket over a pink blouse and had little makeup. She was petite, with her blonde hair down to her shoulders—which she mostly wore tied in a ponytail—all of which made her look like a teenager even though she was twenty-four years old. Her eyes were of turquoise blue, and the color changed to light green depending on the light. They were turquoise at that moment.

He continued watching as she returned to the car. Meeting her gaze, he turned and looked the other way. She saw that he was looking at her and smiled. She was fully aware of the effect she caused in most men ever since coming to work for the sheriff's office from Gainesville. She avoided personal involvement with department members, and her behavior had always been strictly professional. She did not intend to change that.

Garcia got out of the car and opened the passenger door for Karla to get in, not being sure if she would accept that gesture with grace or if it would get her upset. Some women, especially those who work in what some would consider a man's job, take offense at chivalrous gestures.

She just smiled and, putting her sunshades on, got into the car.

The Sheriff's office was located on Midway Road, next to the main post office, and was actually closer to the "scenic route" to Indiantown—Route 709, also known as Glades Cut-Off Road, that Garcia had mentioned. That would have been to the right, so instead, they drove left on Midway towards US 1.

It was indeed a beautiful morning, not too hot for October but sunny enough that after Garcia brought down the top of the convertible, Karla Colles had to take her jacket off, revealing her tanned and perfectly round arms. The blouse she was wearing was sleeveless, saluting the shape of her breasts, small but pointy, under the cover of a tight bra. She applied sun protection cream to her arms, forehead, and nose, and for a while, they drove in silence.

Karla was the first to talk, "I do not think that I had the opportunity to tell you how sorry I was about your partner's being shot and all. I guess having to work alone can make you depressed and crabby."

"Frank will be okay. He will be able to return to work in a few weeks. He is out of the hospital and undergoing physical therapy. The bullet shattered his femur, and the doctors had to put a graft in the bone, metal plates, and screws. But he is tough, he is okay." And after a long pause and without looking at her, he added, "I miss him a lot, though."

"Well, I guess that you are human after all," she said.

"I guess I am," he retorted.

After another long period of silence, she said, "I heard you are from Miami. Your name is Andy Garcia—like the actor. Were you born in Miami or in Cuba?"

Garcia hated that kind of questioning. Normally, he would give a snappy answer or an insult, but coming from her, he felt like laughing at the question.

So, he answered with surprising naturality. "Neither, I was born in El Paso, Texas, third generation Mexican-American. My father was in the grocery business and owned a couple of stores in El Paso. My mother had some relatives in Miami, so they moved there and opened the same kind of business. I was only eight when we moved. An older brother and a sister took care of the stores in El Paso. They are still there, and my parents and younger brother and sister still live in Miami. Andy Garcia, the actor, was unknown to them when I was born. My correct name is Andres Garcia, and actually, there is a famous Mexican actor by that name. But everyone here seems to think that I am Cuban. And to be honest, I hate that, and I do not like Cubans much either. How about you?"

"Me?... I do not have anything against Cubans, or Mexicans for that matter. Andres, I like that name, it has a nice ring to it. You want to know about me? There is not much to talk about me. Born and raised in Sarasota, I went to the University of Florida on a volleyball scholarship. My dad was a cop and I admired him very much. So I wanted to follow in his footsteps. Both mom and dad were worried about me being in the field, carrying a gun and going after the bad guys, so I settled for forensic investigation and pathology. Therefore, I consider myself a lab cop. After graduation, I worked in Gainesville until someone told me about an opening in Saint Lucie County with better money.

"I miss Gainesville, which is a fun-filled college town and the home of the Florida Gators. I miss going to the football games and I miss my parents a lot as well. It was hard to get used to this small town, but now I love it. And I love my job. Dad is retired now and they own a small condo near the beach here. So they visit often. I have a sister who still lives in Sarasota. She is married with two small, adorable kids."

"So you were kidding when you said you carry a gun and are a blackbelt in Karate?"

"No, I wasn't. Do you want to see the gun?" She pulled a Beretta from her purse. "And I know how to fire it, too. My dad taught me how. In fact, according to him, I am a very good shot. As for the karate part, that is true too. I took lessons while in Gainesville, and, yes, also, I am a blackbelt."

"What you are is an amazing girl, and I mean in every which way you look and with all due respect," said Garcia.

"Well, thanks. That is nice of you. I suppose that it is Dr. Jekyll speaking now. Do you think Mr. Hyde will appear any time soon?" she teased.

"I do not think Hyde is anywhere near here. I heard he only comes out when Jekyll is awakening too early in the morning," Andy answered jokingly.

And then, more seriously, he went on to say, "Honestly, I am not sure why I am that way. It's been like that since I was a little boy. My mom tells me how hard it was to get me up to go to school in the morning and that most of the trouble I got into in school was in the first couple of hours of the day. Only my mom and Frank have been able to cope with me at those hours."

"Well, sure, moms usually have the power to control their kid's behavior, but your partner must be a saint," Karla said.

"My mom is also a saint," Garcia said.

"I am sure she is," Karla replied, keeping her mouth shut for the rest of the trip.

Five

Melvin did not have a very good night of sleep. He had spent the night at his father's beach front condominium in Hutchinson Island because after driving back from Indiantown the day before, he had stop to eat at "Taps" where he had a lot to eat and several beers.

Then, on his way to the condo, he was stopped by the cops, who almost took him to jail because he smelled of beer. Thank God he was able to weasel his way out by requesting a breath analysis, which revealed a reading below the illegal level.

He got a $200 ticket anyway.

Then he stopped at a convenience store to buy beer, chips, nachos and salsa. He knew that his father would have none of that in the fridge at the condo. The clerk refused to take his credit card, so he had to go looking for an ATM machine to get cash.

Finally, after he got to the condo, he found that his father had changed the lock the last time he was in. He had to go see the building administrator—who fortunately recognized him—to get a key.

To top it all, he discovered that he did not have the proper cables to connect the Xbox video game to any of the TV sets in the apartment. Afraid to go out again and be stopped by the cops, he went to the beach, but he was unable to get in the water because there was an invasion of Portuguese man-o-war. So he went back to the condo to drink beer, eat chips and watch TV.

He hoped that all those events would not be a bad omen for the start of his job the following day, but the thought made him quite nervous. So he decided to dream instead about the woman he had seen the day before.

Despite having slept poorly and restlessly, he woke up before the alarm clock went off. After shaving and showering, he ate breakfast consisting of three Twinkies and twelve ounces of Coke. He dressed in lead-colored pants, a navy-blue blazer, a white shirt, and a striped blue and gray tie.

Thereafter, he went down to the parking garage where his father's silver sport Mercedes was parked. Although that was not his car—he drove a Blazer SUV—he had his dad's permission to drive any of his cars. So, after retrieving the keys from a magnetic box underneath the car's passenger door, he drove away, hoping that today would be a better day than the last half of yesterday.

Most of all, he hoped that she would be there, and perhaps this time, she would look at him or, better yet, smile at him. At this juncture, he was not even sure what she looked like. He was sure that she was tall and slender, with long, dark, silky hair. And her eyes—he was not sure—maybe they were green or blue, but with the dark hair probably were hazel or dark.

Her lips were red and her mouth small with a smile to die for, her face was elongated, a perfect picture for the frame of her hair. She was maybe twenty-four or twenty-five years old...hopefully not married or engaged.

SIX

The soldiers had been dropped from a helicopter several miles away. Now they hunkered down dressed in camouflage fatigues that melted with the barren and rocky landscape.

Light snow was beginning to fall. They knew that an equal number of their comrades were waiting at the other side of the ravine and constantly looking at the narrow dirt road that ran between the two groups of soldiers.

The year was 1980, the place was Afghanistan. About one and a half year earlier The Soviet army had invaded the country in support of the Kabul government who was being threatened by a religious guerrilla movement called "The Taliban."

As soon as Washington learned about the Soviet invasion, it started a covert operation to supply the "mujaheddin"—or holy warriors—with weapons and logistics in their fight against the Russians.

Despite Washington's denial, Moscow was fully aware of the role that the Americans were playing in that war and obviously were not very happy about it. Yet, so far, they had not been able to prove it before the United Nations and the world. They needed badly such proof.

Of course, the CIA did not use regular operatives to help the rebels and instead hired adventurers, smugglers and bandits as mercenaries to do the work. And since Afghanistan was one of the world's largest growers of poppies, the flower from which opium and heroin are extracted, these mercenaries profited. In spite of the danger, they were willing to risk their lives to become rich in this trade.

That particular day, acting upon secret intelligence information, an elite KGB unit of the Red Army was waiting for a supply convoy that was supposed to come through that road.

The plan was simple: hit the first and last truck with bazookas and then shoot the men in the trucks one by one. Their orders were not to take prisoners but to keep them alive until they gave information about their suppliers, routes and names of those who sent them and those who were to receive the weapons.

The cold did not affect the Russians, who were quite used to it, but they had been waiting for several hours, and the soldiers were showing nervous strain. It was beginning to get dark when they heard the noise of the engines, and shortly thereafter, the first of five trucks appeared.

An American man was in the passenger side of the first truck. He had done this several times before, and—so far, he never had a problem—he delivered the weapons. He was paid handsomely by both the CIA and the rebels, sometimes with money. Other times with opium or heroin which, although he had to carry it back through Afghanistan and then across Pakistan, actually yielded him a much higher profit, even after the many bribes he had to pay to Pakistani officials.

He had enough money, a lovely apartment in Manhattan, and a couple of legitimate import and export businesses in the United States that were rapidly extending to Asia and Europe. He was good-looking, and his name was becoming known in the USA and elsewhere as a millionaire and playboy. Still, it was hard to leave this weapon supply business. This was not because he gave a damn about the cause he was helping, as he had worked often for both sides, but simply because it was fun and stimulating. He felt it gave him a purpose in life besides being extremely profitable.

He promised himself that after each delivery it would be the last, but his ambition was insatiable and he came back. Besides, he loved the adrenaline rush that he felt every time he crossed this rugged terrain to make a delivery.

He had been trained by the CIA but was fired when they found that he was involved in drug trafficking and—although they never were able to prove it—also in the murder of an Interpol agent. Yet they did not mind him being hired for these weapons jobs, as they knew that he was very good at them.

He first spotted the setting sun's reflection on the binoculars and then saw the steam coming out of the mouths and noses of the soldiers hiding.

Yelling at the driver to stop the truck because there was an ambush, he jumped out of the vehicle before it came to a complete stop. In doing so, he twisted his right ankle and fell on the ground, hitting his head against a large rock at the side of the road. Although he lost consciousness momentarily, it may have saved his life. In that same instant, the truck he had been in was blown away by a massive explosion.

The last truck on the convoy wasn't yet at the point where the Russians wanted it, but they were very accurate in their aim. The truck was destroyed by a second explosion only seconds after the first one.

Needless to say, nobody who was on those two trucks survived, but the Afghanis who were in the other three trucks came out firing their weapons while trying to find cover behind the rocks along the road. It was a useless effort; they were caught in the gauntlet made by the Russian soldiers. One by one, the natives fell as the Soviets came down from the slopes towards them, firing their weapons. Most of the Taliban were wounded, and many were dead.

The Russian Captain ordered his men to cease firing and yielded: "Sergeant Ivanovich, you are our expert in languages and also our medic. Come down here and see what you can do. Do not let anyone die before we can get information from them. Understand, Sergeant?"

As he came down, a tall and handsome Russian officer responded," Yes, sir, I shall do my best."

It was snowing heavily by now, so the captain said. "This storm is going to get worse. We were supposed to call for a helicopter to get us out of here with the prisoners and with whatever weapons were still usable. But in this storm, no helicopter can fly and get us. I saw a cave on our way here; it is about half a mile away, so let's just carry a couple of prisoners with us—the ones who can be able to walk. Shoot the others and blow the trucks off."

As the Soldiers carried their orders with the utmost efficiency, Ivanovich was caring for few and pointing at the unfortunate wounded that in his opinion were harder to carry, meaning they should be shot.

Then he saw the American.

The right foot of the guy was bent in the wrong direction, and he had a nasty-looking gash in the head from where much blood was coming. As Ivanovich pointed his gun to the man's head, ready to fire, he yelled, first in Russian, then in English: "Please do not shoot; I am an American."

Ivanovich hesitated and at that instant the other three trucks of the convoy exploded in balls of fire, sending fragments of trucks and weapons all over the place. One of those pieces of steel hit Ivanovich in the right thigh, which prevented it from hitting the American in the middle of the forehead. However, another smoldering piece of metal fell on the same leg that he broke upon jumping off the truck.

Ivanovich stoically pulled the piece of metal off his leg and threw some snow over the hot metal that was burning the American leg; then, walking straight as if he was never wounded, the Sergeant went over to his captain.

"Sir, there is a guy there. He cannot walk, but you probably want to keep him alive anyway. I think he is important."

"And why do you think so, sergeant?" The captain responded with a sardonic smile.

"Because he is an American, Sir," Ivanovich said without a change in his expression.

"An American? Are you sure?" the Soviet captain asked.

"I have not seen his birth certificate, captain, but he speaks English without an accent, and he does not look like an Arab. I am pretty sure he is American."

"Good job, Sergeant. If you are correct, this mission may prove much more valuable than just destroying a weapons delivery to the enemy."

Then, noticing the blood stain on the sergeant's leg, which was getting larger by the minute, the senior officer said, "You are wounded, Sergeant Ivanovich. Is it bad? We can't afford to have you wounded. You are our medic as well."

"It is just a scratch, sir. A piece of shrapnel hit me in the leg. I should be fine. The American is wounded worse."

"Nevertheless, we can't afford to lose you, sergeant; I'll order some men to help you and the American until we reach that cave. The storm is getting worse and it is getting darker. I hope we will be able to reach that cave before we can't see anything. Let's get going"

Ivanovich ripped his pants with his knife and looked at the wound in his leg. The metal had cut the skin and the muscle but did not go as deep as the bone. He applied some antiseptic and closed it with metal staples without using any local anesthetic. Then returning to the side of the American, he did the same with the wound on his head and immobilized the fractured leg with an inflatable splint. Two soldiers carried the American on a stretcher while the Russian sergeant insisted on walking by himself.

It was pitch dark, and the snow was now a blizzard when they finally reached the cave. It was one of many caverns that crisscrossed the barren landscape of the Afghan mountains where rebels, shepherds, and smugglers often hide from the elements or surprise their enemies.

This cave was relatively spacious, so all the men fitted in it comfortably. There were signs of an old fire there and some logs to make one again. There was even a stack of old clothes, probably used by the cave dwellers to change after they had been caught in the rain or snow. The captain posted guards at the gate, although it was improbable that the Mujaheddin would attack in that weather. You never could be too sure.

The storm lasted all night, and into the next morning, the American had been coming off and on out of consciousness and could not be interrogated. Although the bleeding from the large cut on the scalp had stopped after Ivanovich stapled it, he was in pain and started to run a fever. The burn in the leg was probably getting infected, so the medic had to administer antibiotics and several shots of morphine.

Around noon, the storm started to calm down, and the Russian captain informed Sergeant Ivanovich that he would try to contact the base and see if a helicopter could pick them up. He knew that if they had not been attacked yet, the improvement in the weather conditions would most certainly bring up an attack from the enemy.

After several attempts at the radio, they were able to contact their base and were told that a helicopter would be on the way within half an hour. Unfortunately, they had to walk down from the cave to a slope and then into more plain terrain. It would be about two hundred yards from where the helicopter could land.

The captain and Ivanovich scanned the terrain without detecting any movement. They also sent four men to search in all four directions for any sign of enemy activity. They reported none. It took more than half an hour before they got a radio message that two helicopters were nearby and that they would be landing in a few minutes.

The captain ordered the men to leave the cave and to stay prepared in case of an attack. They could hear the motors of the Helicopters now, and the order was given to start coming out and down.

Ivanovich's leg had been throbbing all night, and the last time he looked at the wound, now bandaged, he noticed that the leg was quite swollen and red. He had to be assisted to walk by one of the soldiers. The American was being carried on a stretcher, and all five were, therefore, at the rear of the group.

The snow was light now, and the terrain was totally covered with a white coat. There was a timid sun that caused quite a glare and bothered the eyes. The Russians, of course, had goggles to protect their eyes. They could see the two metallic birds approaching and getting low and ready. The Captain and some men were ahead and only about one hundred yards from the landing spot.

Then it happened.

First, they heard the hiss of a rocket, and one of the helicopters received a direct hit and exploded before it could even land. The other helicopter was able to maneuver and avoid a second rocket while directing machine guns and rockets to the spot where they had seen the fire come.

The fire from the helicopter must have been effective as no other rocket was launched. However, small arms fire could be heard from several sites. The Russians returned fire while running towards the helicopter that by now had landed farther away. The men inside it spread the landscape with heavy machine gun fire.

Many of the Soviet soldiers fell to the ground, hit by the bullets, including the captain; only about ten made it to the helicopter, which took off without waiting for anyone else.

One of the two men carrying the stretcher was hit in the head and died instantly, dropping the stretcher with the American in it to the ground. Ivanovich and the man who was helping him also fell to the ground, though they were not wounded. They crawled back to the Russian with the stretcher and yelled for them to return to the cave.

The helicopter had taken off and was flying high now, still firing at the probable positions of the enemy. They heard some screams, so probably some mujaheddin had been hit, and the others were perhaps taking cover or changing positions. Therefore, there was a momentary cease-fire. These few minutes allowed Ivanovich and the other three Soviets to drag the Americans and themselves back to the cave. They heard the helicopter making one more sweep and then leaving.

The two Soviet soldiers could not hide their disappointment and rage for being abandoned. Sergeant Ivanovich tried to calm them down and reassured them that the helicopter had to leave. Otherwise, everyone would have died. Their duty now was to die fighting, as the chances of another helicopter coming to their rescue were rather slim.

Ivanovich, now the highest-ranked officer, took command and ordered the two other surviving Russians to take positions by the entrance of the cave and not open fire until they could see someone coming up toward them

The American was awake and spoke in perfect Russian: "Yeah, sergeant, tell them not to fire until they see the blank of their eyes. However, I believe nobody has to die. I think all of us can survive this."

Ivanovich responded by telling him to shut up, but the soldiers asked him to hear what the American had to say.

"We are listening."

"As you may be fully aware, those guys out there hate the guts of everyone who does not share their religious beliefs, but they loathe especially the guys who invaded their country. So they probably would prefer to catch you alive and then kill you little by little. They probably hate me as well, but they need me to supply the weapons they use to fight you."

"So?" interrupted the Russian.

"So that they would spare my life but certainly not yours,"said the American.

"We realize that American, but that is why we are going to kill you before we die, so you do not bring weapons from America to kill Soviet soldiers."

"I figured you would do that, and this is why I am going to offer you a deal," said the American

"I do not think you are in a position to offer us a deal, American," said Ivanovich.

"Oh, but I think I am in such a position. You see, those men out there know me and need me; they also know that I usually bring other men with me when I make a delivery. All you have to do is take off your uniforms. See if you can fit in any of those civilian clothes that someone left here. When they come, I shall tell them that you are some of the friends that came with me. After all you, sergeant, are wounded the same as I am.

"By the way, I have not thanked you yet for saving my life. Thank you, sergeant! My name is Richard, Richard Mellon. "Yours is Ivanovich. Am I correct, sergeant?"

"It is Peter Alexandrovich Ivanovich, sergeant of the Red Army KGB unit."

"Well Sergeant Ivanovich of the Red Army KGB Unit…can I call you Peter, or better yet Ivan? What do you think of the plan?" asked Richard Mellon.

"Those people out there are not stupid. Fanatics, yes, but stupid, no." They saw four people coming up here, three wearing Red Army uniforms. They would expect to retrieve at least three corpses," responded Ivanovich.

"Maybe they did. Maybe they didn't. You guys were wearing blankets over your head. It was snowing. They were not very close to us, and they were busy trying to shoot your people and avoid being shot themselves. I bet you they did not pay much attention to how we looked like," explained Mellon.

"Still, they would become suspicious if they did not see that we left at least one man guarding you," the Russian said.

Switching to English, the American said to the Russian, "That is a problem that you can resolve. Do any of your men understand English?"

"Yuri does a little; why do you ask?" inquired Ivanovich.

"Because we should kill your comrades. Of course, that would have to be done before they attack or soon after they start coming.

Ivanovich did not respond; he was pondering what the American had suggested.

At that moment, the two Russian soldiers guarding the cave's entrance reported that some Mujahedin were beginning to climb the slope and approach them.

Contradicting his prior order, he commanded them to open fire.

While the Russians fired upon the guerrillas, Ivanovich took off his uniform, threw it in the fire, and, picking up some of the old, dirty clothes that were piled up in the cave, he put them on. Then, going towards his comrades in arms, he shot both in the back of the head with his pistol.

Returning to the side of the American, he said: "No tricks now, or you be next and remember that I understand perfectly the language that these people speak."

"Do not worry; a deal is a deal. Richard Mellon may be many things, but he sticks by it when he makes a deal. By the way, you can be court-martialed and hanged for what you just did. "

"It is the survival of the fittest and the smartest. Besides, I am not planning to go back to my unit. Now, you go to the cave entrance and start yelling to them who you are." said the Russian

Oddly enough, the trick worked, although the Afghanis were a bit suspicious at the onset, they at least agreed to take them to their leader and carried them through rough terrain, to another cave, about three miles away, where they were introduced to their commander.

The commander was one of the tallest Arabs both men had ever seen; he was even taller than the Russian; he also had a beard longer than most of the other men in the group. The Afghanis introduced the man as Sheik Osama bin Ladin. The sheik was obviously educated. He spoke to them in English and said he had traveled and studied in the USA and England.

Mellon introduced the Russian as a fellow American named Ivan Peters. Osama believed their history, especially when he learned of the two dead Soviets in the cave, so he ordered his men to take the Russians and the Americans to a village several miles away where they could be taken care of and cured of their wounds.

Because of their injuries and the particularly harsh Afghan winter that year, the two men had to become guests of the guerrillas for almost two months. Although Mellon's ankle did not heal correctly, despite the care of the local healer and that of the Russian, it did heal eventually, albeit slightly crooked.

During those two months, the two men established a firm bond. Mellon looked at the Russian as a man he could trust to become his henchman, and the Russian looked at Mellon as his ticket to the West, to wealth and to freedom.

When they eventually returned to Pakistan, it was not difficult for Mellon to obtain a birth certificate and an American passport for the Russian, who officially became Ivan Peters, born in Detroit, Michigan, USA.

SEVEN

The scientists got up and started leaving the elegant conference room of the neurological institute one-by-one or in groups of two.

Only one, Professor David Bright, remained seated and held the arm down of the man sitting next to him, gently forcing him to sit again as he was also about to leave the room.

"We need to talk, Paul. Please stay after everyone leaves."

Professor Paul Bernstein did not argue. He sat down and then poured himself a cup of coffee from one of the silver kettles placed earlier around the conference table.

"What do you want to talk to me about, David?" Dr. Bernstein asked, while calmly sipping his coffee.

"You know darn well what I want to talk to you about, Paul. Did you hear what Mr. Mellon said?"

"Well, yes. He knows about the accidents. Things like those do happen in medicine, and more so when one is doing research. Besides, we did report those incidents to him and they were written down. Those things are no secrets, David."

"Paul, dear Paul, you know that I have a lot of respect for you. You have been my teacher, my mentor. I consider you my older brother. But do not take me for a fool. So far, I have been willing to share the blame with you, but both of us know very well that all those 'accidents' happened only to you. And you also know darn well what the reason for that is. All you have to do is accept it."

"I refuse to accept your idea that I have Parkinson's disease, David. You are a great neurologist, but just because I have a little tremor in my hands occasionally, it is no reason to—"

"'A little tremor once in a while,' you said? Maybe I could accept the 'a little' part of it, but the 'once in a while'? Just now, see it for yourself: You are holding that cup with both hands to keep them from shaking, and you spilled some of the coffee when you poured it into your cup."

"That fellow Mr. Mellon and his crony Ivan, or whatever his real name is, made me nervous. And now you are telling me so seriously, 'We need to talk, Paul.' A lot of people would have a bit of tremor under those circumstances."

"Do not try to be funny with me, Paul. Human lives are involved in this. You have to stop draining and injecting subjects and also should agree to have yourself tested and treated. Remember that right here at the institute we are close to curing Parkinson's."

"Sure, David. Let everyone who works in this institution know that Dr.

Paul Bernstein has Parkinson's and is no longer able to do his work."

"I promised that only you, me and a selected few of those involved in the research for the cure of that condition—and only when the right time comes—will know about it. Besides, I am sure that I am not the only one who suspects it. Moreover, I am almost sure Mellon and Ivan know that all eight mishaps happened to you."

Now, for the first time during the conversation, Dr. Bernstein started to show concern. "Do you really think they know David?"

"There is no way that I can be sure, Paul, but you noticed the way Mellon talked to us and the way he threatened us with the police and with his friend Ivan taking care of things," responded Dr. Bright. He continued, "I do not know how or who handled the aftermath of those incidents, but I suspect they were turned over to the chief of security, who responds only to Ivan. Perhaps they gave money to the families. I do also know that they have hired a prominent local lawyer to handle business down here for them."

"I do not want you to do all the work for the two of us, David," said Bernstein.

"I don't want to do it alone either, Paul," responded Professor Bright. There is no way I or anyone else is going to take you out of the project. After all, you had the original idea and you did the first bit of research."

"Yeah, but I could not have done anything without your help, input and countless hours of work," retorted Paul. "Besides, you were the one who contacted Mellon and got him interested in the experiments when the government refused to permit this kind of research."

"I cannot take credit for that either. As you recall, they heard somewhere about our work and, although they came to see me because they knew I was doing work at the University of Miami, they wanted both of us from the start," continued Bright.

"Okay, David, what do you have in mind?" Paul Bernstein asked.

"Here it goes: We continue doing our research like always, except you and me do not do patient procedures. Also, you should agree to submit to testing and treatment," Bright proposed.

"You put it simply, but if neither you nor I will do the procedures, then who? And forget about the test and treatment for now. Perhaps later," shrugged Professor Paul.

"You are more stubborn than a mule, Paul, but I am fine with that for now also. As for the first part of your question, we will have to train someone to do it. We hired a guy today for that. You heard Mellon asking and you know him. Remember my son, Melvin?"

"Your son, but David, you know that Melvin is not... Well, he is not..."

Bernstein hesitated, and Professor Bright completed the sentence: "As smart as us? As knowledgeable as everyone here? As bright as other Bright family members or most members of the staff? I know that Paul and believe me that I will take personal responsibility for him, I shall be his shadow. You may not believe it, but Melvin is extremely good with his hands. And he is great with handling all those new electronic devices. He can put a needle in the nucleus of a cell. I am sure of that."

"I know that, David. Melvin is a good kid. I've known him since he was a little boy. I did not mean any offense...." said Bernstein.

"None taken, Paul. So, it is settled. No more brain taps for us two, right?" answered the senior Doctor Bright.

"Yes...it is settled," a somewhat reluctant Doctor Bernstein responded. And then asked, "Is Melvin already here at the institute this morning?"

"He is indeed. In fact, I am supposed to meet him at the office of human resources to give him a tour of the facility," said Bright.

"Mind if I come along, David? I have not seen your son Melvin in quite a while, since before he left for medical school. I bet he has changed."

"I have not seen him either in about six months. As you know, he was doing his American Internship and then a residency in interventional radiology at Orlando Medical Center, in Orlando."

"But of course, David, I believe you told me that. In fact, I was going to accompany you to see him when my wife took a course for the worse." Dr. Bernstein tried to say it with a straight voice, but it became hoarse at the end of the sentence.

"It still hurts, Paul. I know. Belinda has been gone for more than ten years and it still hurts." Dr. Bright responded.

"Life must go on, David. At least you have two wonderful kids."

"I am very fortunate with that, although I do not see much of them, and I haven't through the years, because of my work...our work," said Professor Bright.

"You have been a wonderful father to those kids. You should have no regrets, David. What would you think if we tried for a while to forget the past and concentrate on the future? Let's go see that son of yours. Shall we?"

The two professors stood up and proceeded to leave the conference room.

EIGHT

The two detectives were talking over lunch at the "Seminole Inn" in Indiantown. It was an old hotel that still lodged transients and visitors and whose restaurant was famous locally and in the surrounding areas. The lunch was not only delicious but abundant. They both had crab cakes for appetizers, grilled lemon chicken for entrée, and key lime pie for dessert.

They were now talking over coffee. The woman had refused the invitation to drink wine because they both were on duty.

Sergeant Karla Colles said, "You were right about this town, Detective Garcia. It is pretty small. I bet that it does not even stretch a whole mile over Route 710. And then it is only a few blocks deep. There is not even a McDonald's here, and the only large building is that institute at the entrance of the town."

"But you have to admit, Sergeant Colles, that our trip has been so far worth it. First of all, I am having lunch with the prettiest CSI officer in the state of Florida. Second, we obtained a positive ID on the dead guy. And third, we have a very possible motive for the crime," said Detective Garcia.

"Flattering will take you nowhere with me, Detective. This is a work-related trip, and I hope you understand it well," Sgt. Colles said seriously.

"I do, I do. But considering that up until this morning you would not give me the time of the day, I am thrilled about having lunch with you now," said Detective Andy Garcia.

"Besides, we should celebrate that we were lucky that Sister Imelda, who works at Holy Cross Church and the Hope School here in Indiantown, was able to ID our corpse. "Said Karla.

"Don't forget, Detective, that we must confirm that identity. Besides, she told us that that guy showed up in Indiantown a couple of years ago, claiming to be from Guatemala and giving the name Ismael Torres. He told the people here that those were his initials in the tattoo below the Quetzal on his arm.

"He was very active in the church and in the community. The sister remembers him as a very nice and willing-to-help-everyone guy. The sister also recalled that the town's folk called him 'Indiantown' because of the I.T. tattoo. Of course, that was until one night at one of the church's gatherings, an Indian woman started screaming that she recognized him as one of the soldiers who came to her village in the jungles of Guatemala and started killing everyone. And then she went as far as accusing him of being the soldier who raped her pregnant daughter and then killed her by splitting open her belly," concluded Garcia.

"It was pretty horrible stuff what the Guatemalan military did to their very own people." Added Karla.

"War is hell, sergeant, and civil wars are said to be bloodier and crueler than wars against other countries," said Garcia. "Did you hear that the Indian mother told the nun she was hiding in the jungle with her two-year-old grand-daughter and that to keep her quiet, she covered her mouth so tight that when it was all over, and the soldiers were gone, she realized that she had suffocated the child?"

"Yes, indeed, a terrible history. It is hard to believe that such things are still happening in the twenty-first century."

"Anyway, it must have been true because when that woman recognized him, the man ran away, not to be seen ever again. So the history must have been true," said Sgt. Colles.

"Well, there is also the possibility that he became afraid to be lynched. According to the sister, there was a very irate mob at the place after the Indian woman told her history," added the Detective.

"Possible but not proven; we have yet to confirm the man's identity with the Guatemalan consulate in Miami, right?" asked Sergeant Colles.

"Yes, but I am willing to bet either we do not find anything out because the guy probably came illegally to the US. And if we go to the Guatemalan military, it may take weeks—if not months—to get an answer from them," said Garcia.

"Just like with our military here," joked Colles, adding, "So, we are to think that this guy was recognized again by someone from here in Indiantown or by someone from Fort Pierce, and he or she killed him," said Colles.

"Well, the Indian woman has an alibi. She was at an evening function at the Catholic Church, and many people saw her there. Besides, she does not know how to drive, and her husband does not own a car. So, unless she can teletransport herself, she did not do it," Garcia said.

"Well, we think that he was not killed at the scene, that he was killed elsewhere. So why not here in Indiantown?" Karla asked.

"And then drive the body in someone else's car to Fort Pierce? "There are a lot of canals, wooded areas and pastures between this town and ours. Don't you think that if they killed him here, they would have dropped the body in one of those places?" Andy said.

"You are right. It is just that we have to consider all possible scenarios," Karla said.

"You are correct, and your statements are true, very true. Now, let's finish this coffee and get back to Fort Pierce to see if we can learn something else from the coroner. Although, if our theory is correct, I am afraid that we are not going to learn much from the good doctor" Detective Garcia replied.

"You never know, detective, you never know. But it does appear that our guy and the drowned guy the coroner had before do not belong to the same club," said Karla.

"Yeah, it is hard to believe that those two deaths are related in any way, but—like you said—we have to consider every possible case scenario."

After asking for the check and leaving a good tip—mostly to impress the woman, who pretended not to notice it—Garcia added, "Let's go back now. You finished your coffee, right?"

"Yes, I am done. Let's head back."

And with those last words, they walked back to Garcia's car.

Although they took the route that Andy had called scenic to return to Fort Pierce, they talked very little on the way back, both thinking about what they had learned from Sister Imelda about the dead guy. If the story was true—and they both felt it was—the guy got less than what he deserved. Still, there was something strange about that murder, something that did not quite fit into the simple revenge scene. They continued to think about it until they arrived at the coroner's office precisely at 3.45 pm.

The Medical Examiner's office was located on the campus of the local community college. To the unfamiliar, it would have been difficult to find, but both detectives had been to the place far too many times before. They walked straight in.

The place was modern and state-of-the-art, but it still had that peculiar smell that all morgues and mortuaries have: a mixture of antiseptic, formaldehyde and the aroma of flowers and perfumes, which are supposedly there to disguise the smell of death.

Doctor Ray Raymond, the County Medical Examiner, looked more like a door-to-door encyclopedia salesman than a physician. Of course, most people think that doctors should look something like those on TV shows or daytime soap operas: tall, handsome, with thick black hair graying at the sides and a deep, melodious voice.

In contrast, Doctor Raymond was short, chubby, and partially bald, with the few hairs that he had left white as snow and poorly combed at the sides and back of his scalp. However, despite what he lacked in appearance, he made up for with charm and knowledge. He appeared always happy, and his smile came very easily to his white teeth and chubby face, illuminating his deep blue eyes.

He came from Mississippi and could not hide his thick Southern accent or his southern charm. Dr. Ray, as he was known to his friends and fellow workers, had the best of his smiles to greet the visiting detectives.

"Good afternoon, Sergeant Colles, Detective Garcia. I have been expecting you. I have some interesting information about the two deceased individuals the beautiful sergeant called me about."

Karla smiled and thanked him for the compliment as the three of them walked towards the doctor's office.

"You know, Sergeant Colles," Dr. Ray was saying, "it was good that you called me personally this morning because in most of these cases, when the cause of death seems so obvious—such as a big hole made by a bullet in someone's chest—we do not bother to perform a full body autopsy. And it is done most times by one of my assistants—under my supervision of course—

but this time you piqued my curiosity with your phone call and guess what we found."

"What did you find, doctor?" the two detectives asked immediately.

Dr. Raymond continued: "Well, for one thing, I agreed with your impression that the man did not die from a bullet to his chest. He had been dead already when he was shot. There was almost no blood in the chest cavity even though the bullet blew the heart almost in half."

"So, what caused his death?" asked Garcia.

"We are still running the routine and not-so-routine toxicology analysis, but when we opened the man's head we found a hemorrhage in the posterior part of the brain at the base of the head, the part some people call the cisterna Magna or cerebromedullar cistern. It seems someone put a pointy instrument in that place. It caused him to die instantly."

"But in order for someone to do that, the man had to be either restrained, drunk, or drugged. I did not see any scratches, bruises or signs of struggle when I looked at the body," said Karla Colles. "Did you find any of those?"

"No, we did not. What is more interesting is that I went back to review the autopsy findings of the other guy we had before. The one they found floating in a canal in Port Saint Lucie but did not have hardly any water in his lungs, and guess what?"

"You found the same type of injury on him, right?" said Colles

"You are a brilliant woman, sergeant. Indeed, we did. Come take a look," the Doctor said, as they walked into the autopsy room where two naked bodies, with their scalps pulled over their faces and the top of the skull having been removed, exposing the brain.

Doctor Ray put on some rubber gloves, gently slid his gloved hand behind one of the men's brains, and pulled the encephalic mass forward, exposing the posterior part of the brain. "See the blood in there and those tiny punctures in there? That is the Pons; it was punctured with a small tool, maybe a needle."

Garcia spoke: "There seems to be only a tiny bit of blood there, and the wound in that pond appears almost microscopic. Can that kill a man?"

"Are you a country boy detective? Have you seen cattle killed?" asked the doctor.

"No, doctor, I am afraid I have been a city boy all my life," responded Garcia

"Well, then maybe you have been to a bullfight, south of the border or in Spain."

"That I have seen," said Garcia.

"Well, then, unless you went to a bullfight where the Matador was exceedingly good, most times the bull is not killed with one stroke of the sword, so the Matador or his aides have to go back and give the bull 'the *Puntilla*,' which is a short dagger that they stick at the base of the animals head, it collapses instantly, has a short convulsion and dies within seconds.

That is what happened here, my dear detectives."

"Sounds awful," responded Garcia. "I guess the matador must have been really good because the only bullfight I went to see with my father in Mexico City, they dispatched the bulls with the sword. Let me ask you this, doctor, in the case of a bull, he is wounded and charges with his head down, so it would be not too hard to stick the *Puntilla* in the brain, but we humans have a relatively short neck, and it does not seem easy to do that to conscious person."

"You are correct again, detective. You two are so smart. I feel safe knowing you are working to protect all of us in the community."

Dr. Ray had been smiling and cheerful all this time, so the detectives were not sure if he was making fun of them or being serious. They decided on the latter, so they gave him a polite smile and thanked him for the compliment.

Dr. Ray continued, "Remember, sergeant, that this morning when you called me, I told you that the toxicology in the 'floater' had been negative for most substances of abuse: narcotics and barbiturates. But that there was something we were unable to identify here and we sent to the state lab? Well, I am pleased to announce that we have the results back....It is Versed."

As he looked at the faces of the detectives, Dr. Raymond realized they had no idea what Versed was, so he explained. "Versed is a widely and commonly used intravenous anesthetic, used mostly for simple and or fast surgical procedures, endoscopies, etc. It works fast, is very safe and produces retrograde amnesia. In other words, you not only do not feel anything that is being done to you, but you do not remember what was done after it is over. Our floater here, lady and gentleman, was put to sleep with Versed before someone stuck a needle in the back of his brain.

"Moreover, I am willing to bet that we will detect the same chemical in our hole-in-the-chest guy. Unfortunately, it would take several days before we get the analysis results from the state lab on that one."

"Doctor Ray, you are a genius," said Karla Colles with a sincere smile.

"Yes, you are a genius," Garcia confirmed. "Unfortunately, and with all due respect, those findings shake our prior murder theory, so now we may have to return to square one."

"If you want my advice, I will start by asking the police of the neighboring counties to see if they have found something like this. I, for one, will call my colleagues in the coroner's office in Martin and Okeechobee Counties. Even if they do not have any bodies now, they may have saved the blood of some suspicious deaths and can have them tested for Versed," said Doctor Ray.

"Are you saying that may be a serial killer on the loose, Doctor Raymond?" asked Garcia.

Before the Doctor could respond, Karla intervened and said, "Thank you, Doctor Ray, that is excellent advice, and we certainly appreciate your input and help in this matter. We would appreciate any help and advice you can give us in the future. Please let us know what you find as soon as you can. Would it be okay if one of us calls you tomorrow?"

The doctor was extremely pleased that the detectives seemed to let him play cop along with them. He told Karla he would call her as soon as he knew anything, but if they did not hear anything from him, they could call his office or cell phone in two days.

As they were walking out of the coroner's office and towards Garcia's car, she asked, "You do not think that there is a serial killer of Spanish immigrants on the loose, right?"

"I don't know yet; after all, that Vesicle, or whatever the name of that anesthetic is, was only found in one dead guy and not in our guy. He could have been anesthetized for something, and then without being fully awake, he wandered off and fell in the canal."

"That is a possible and logical case scenario. I guess we just have to wait for the toxicology analysis in our dead guy. Meanwhile, asking our friends in the neighboring towns does not hurt, as the good doctor suggested. By the way, the name of the anesthetic is not Vesicle; it is Versed Midazolam."

Garcia was about to argue, but Karla stopped him by saying, "Don't worry. I do that myself. Your bedside manners probably have not earned you too many friends among our neighboring colleagues."

With that, they arrived back at the sheriff's office.

NINE

At about the same time that the two detectives were talking with Sister Imelda at the Holy Cross Parochial School in Indiantown, Richard Mellon and Ivan were marching towards the helipad, where a company helicopter was waiting to take them to the West Palm Beach International Airport to board the private jet that was going to take them back to New York City. The two had stopped to make a quick tour to the facilities. Also at that very same time, Doctor Bright was in his way to meet his son Melvin at the institute's cafeteria.

After the conversation with his colleague Dr. Paul Bernstein, he had forgotten if he was to meet his son at his office, the institute's reception area, or the office of Carlessa Williams. A quick call on his cell phone to Mrs. Williams gave him an answer. His son had gotten tired of waiting in her office and had requested directions to the cafeteria for some lunch.

Dr. Bright consulted his watch. It was only twelve-fifteen, but he knew his son suffered from hunger episodes quite often. So he directed his steps toward the cafeteria with a sight of resignation.

Like the rest of the building, the Cafeteria of the Neurological Institute was very modern, well-lit and state-of-the-art. It resembled more the cafeteria of one of the resorts at Disney World than that of a scientific institution. Besides, it was probably too big for the number of people who normally ate there. But then, again, he remembered that Richard Mellon had a flair for the grandiose and enough money to do whatever he wanted.

There were very few people in line for the food and fewer yet sitting at the tables, so it was not difficult to spot his son Melvin seated at the far end of the room, accompanied by two women.

The Doctor stopped briefly before being spotted to contemplate the beauty of the women, one older than the other and wearing a lab coat over her dresses. Despite the age difference, there was an unmistakable resemblance between the two. Doctor Bright immediately realized that they were mother and daughter. However, he knew the older of the two and was aware that, without the professional dress, the lab coat, the hair not pulled up and the thick-rimmed glasses, the two could perfectly pass as sisters.

The women had their backs turned towards the approaching Doctor and his son Melvin was sitting right in front of them, yet Melvin's concentration was one-third on the food he was consuming and two-thirds in contemplation of the two beauties he had before him. He did not notice his father's presence until he greeted them.

"Well, well, son, I see you are fast getting acquainted with the best of the best around here." Then, addressing the ladies, he said, "Linda, I see you met my son Melvin. And this beautiful lady must be your sister, right? It is obvious that beauty runs in the family."

"Get out of here, David. You know this is my daughter and, although I appreciate your flattery, I am unsure if she does. It is not nice for a young lady to be confused with the sister of an old bag like me," responded Dr. Linda Porter. "This is my daughter Jasmin. You knew she was coming to join our team, but I am unsure if you have met her.

"Jasmin, this is Doctor David Bright, the second in command here. Who is also know the person responsible for your new friend, Dr. Bright Jr., here."

"Melvin hates to be called 'Junior,' but I am sure coming from either one of you—even if you call him 'asshole'—it will feel as a compliment. So you can call him anything you want."

Melvin's face became red as a tomato and he felt his ears getting hot, but then Jasmin got up and, stretching toward the father's hand, said, "It is a pleasure to meet you, Doctor Bright. Your name is known in most academic institutions, and it is an honor. As far as your son, he appears to have inherited your charm, so I would call him Marvin if that is okay with him."

"*Touché*, and my apologies to you and my son; sometimes my sense of humor is slightly off the mark."

Almost choking on a piece of baked potato, Melvin took a big gulp of Coke from his glass and responded, "As my father said, you can call me anything you want. But Melvin would be fine. Thanks."

"Okay. You can call me Jasmin, deal?"

"Deal," answered Melvin.

David Bright did not easily feel embarrassed, but he had to admit that the young lady's response took him off guard. He recognized that he not only had been out of line but had probably offended his own son in front of these women who were bound to work along with him at one time or another.

So he said, "Well, since I am here and it is lunchtime, I am going to grab something to eat. Do you ladies want something?"

"No, thank you," they responded in unison and then giggled, listening to themselves.

Their laughter was music to Melvin "Not-So" Bright, MD's ears, and his excitement made him eat more.

Dr. David Bright could not help but notice his son's extra-large plate of food and compare it with the two small salads that the women were eating. Also, the women had no soda. It was bottled water for the younger woman and hot tea for the other one. David wished his son would eat less. He noticed that he was fatter than the last time he had seen him.

When he returned to the table, he had a small steak, a baked potato with sour cream, and a cup of coffee. The women were almost finished with their salads. They had a short conversation and then excused themselves because the mother would have to give her daughter a tour of the institute and introduce her daughter to her coworkers and her future work.

Doctor Bright stated that he planned to do the same with his son, and once alone, the older man did most of the talking. He informed his son first that he would be working under the direct supervision of Doctor Paul Bernstein and himself and that the work he would be doing involved "mostly the use of his technical skills" without going into details about which skills he was referring to.

Then he went on to describe the anatomy of the institute. He told Melvin that the building was E-shaped and that, at the base of the E, the main entrance and the lobby were located along with the reception area, the business offices, human resources and patient registration.

The radiology, medical, and research laboratories were in the long arm at the middle of the E, while the mid branch was used for patient observation and hospitalization. The animal research laboratory was located at the top arm of the E and it included "a small zoo." That was the area where the two women who were sitting at the table with them did their work.

Dr. Bright informed Melvin that the institute employed over 300 people, including many locals, for office and menial work but also employed some of the world's most renowned scientists and researchers.

He answered the question of what kind of work they were doing by simply saying, "You will know in due time, and of course you have to understand that the work we are doing here is top secret. No one, outside some of the scientists, should know about anything we do here. That is a promise you have to make and I am sure you already made it in writing when you signed your contract early today, right?

Melvin answered in the affirmative, though, of course, he had not the slightest idea of what he had signed earlier. He only remembered Jasmin Porter's green eyes. He only half heard his father saying something about the great danger to them if word about their work filtrated into the outside world and then something about a dammed Russian guy before his dad got up and ordered him to follow him on a tour of the institute.

They exited the cafeteria, which was located in the main body of the E between the business section and the rest of the building. Dr. Bright skipped that business section and walked along the long corridor flanked by many doors. He used his ID card on one of the doors that read "Radiology," then punched a number code on a keypad. As the door opened, they found themselves in a spacious suite divided into several smaller rooms. A couple of men, obviously Latino, were sitting on small waiting room chairs, talking in a language that was neither English nor Spanish.

Moved by curiosity, Melvin asked, "What language are these people talking, Dad?"

"I believe it is called Kanjobal, son. They are Indians from the Highlands of Guatemala who flew their country's Civil War and somehow ended up here, in Indiantown, Florida."

At the sound of their voices, a very tall, balding man of indefinable age—

perhaps fifty-something—with flecks of white hair sticking out from his temples like awnings dripping snow, emerged from one of the rooms surrounding the small waiting room to greet them.

He was one of the tallest men Melvin had seen outside of the NBA. Thick-rimmed glasses covered a pair of light blue eyes, which were also protected by bushy eyebrows as white as the few hairs remaining on his head. In spite of his imposing stature, the man had an aura of benevolence that made him likable at first sight.

His father introduced him to Melvin as Doctor Raj Ramsjold from Finland, one of the top radiologists in the world and the inventor of multiple innovations in radiology, ultrasound, computerized scanning and MRI.

Doctor Ramsjold was thrilled to meet Doctor Bright's son and expressed his pleasure by a warm handshake that almost broke all the bones on Melvin's hand. But despite the pain, he could hear his father announcing that Melvin would also be working in the radiology department. He was going to be "our youngest interventional radiologist." As his father announced, "he happens to be very dexterous with his hands and has some previous training in interventional radiology." Of course, he omitted mentioning that his dexterity came mostly from playing video games.

The Finnish radiologist appeared to be sincerely excited and with a voice that probably could be heard to Lake Okeechobee, should they have been outdoors, he called:

"Sarah, please come here to meet our new assistant." Before the person named Sarah appeared, Doctor Ramsjold informed Melvin that he was referring to Doctor Sarah Schneider, originally from Israel, who also happened to be one of the top radiologists in the world.

It took a couple of more yields from the tall doctor for Sarah Schneider to appear. Junior Doctor Bright hardly could keep himself from laughing when he saw her, not because she was odd or unpleasant looking, but because of the sharp contrast that she offered with the gigantic Ramsjold. She was petite, maybe four ten, probably size 2, and about the same age as her colleague; her hair was curly and dyed red, as a carrot; gold-rimmed glasses covered a pair of vivacious brown eyes, and her nose gave her away as being a Jew. She was so vivacious and talkative that one could almost think of her as hyperactive. Also, like her partner, she was extremely friendly and easily likable.

Her handshake was firm and strong for a woman of her size, but of course, not near as strong as that of Dr. Raj—as she referred to her colleague and partner.

Both Doctors spoke English well but with a strong foreign accent that, although different to those with a trained ear, it sounded similar to Melvin Bright.

"It is a real pleasure to meet you, young Dr. Bright," said the woman. "Has Dr. Raj shown you around our facility jet? Have you seen what our machines can do? Have you met BANBI yet?"

"Not yet, Sarah," Dr. Raj interjected, "the doctors are just getting here."

"BAMBI. What is BAMDI? Is that a dog? Do not tell me that you are experimenting with cute little deer here," Melvin asked.

His father laughed, along with the other doctors, as he said, "BANBI stands for Behavior Analysis Neurological Brain Imaging. It is a wonderful machine, a truly revolutionary innovation in the field of radiology Imaging. Do you mind showing us BANBI doctors?"

"Of course not. Dr. Raj and I are very proud of having contributed to developing it. Please come this way," said Dr. Schneider as she led the way into a short hallway and opened the door to a room.

"Doctor Schneider is being very modest, son. She and Doctor Ramsjold developed this machine, which is almost ready to be launched into the market and will make both of them not only famous but also very rich."

"What does the machine do? It looks like a regular MRI scanner," said Melvin.

"That is basically what it is, but it goes much farther than an ordinary MRI machine," said Doctor Schneider. "Not only does it show the anatomy in full color rather than black, white and grey—and with much higher resolution—but also the computer makes color changes when it finds pathology. We have those machines for the whole human body. Then, we can detect pathology that the regular MRI cannot, as well as detect smaller tumors and, with quite a good degree of accuracy, differentiate benign versus malignant pathology. We have those machines here in the other rooms. Our sponsor is already making them available for commercial use within a year or so. We expect that those machines will revolutionize the way physicians practice medicine."

Doctor Schneider could not hide her enthusiasm and barely stopped to take a breath before continuing: "BANBI, however, goes beyond that; BANBI is capable of detecting human emotions, behavior, personality, criminal tendencies, mental illness, whatever goes on inside the human brain."

"But that is impossible; I am aware that some people have developed MRIs that show changes in the brain on certain mental illnesses, but are you saying that this actually can read minds?" asked Marvin.

"Well, not quite," Doctor Raj said, being allowed to speak for the first time since the arrival of Doctor Schneider. But what it does is show areas of the brain in different colors and shades of color. After analyzing thousands of them from our own countries and here in the US, we now have a computer program that can predict the given pattern of behavior and what it could represent."

Dr. Schneider spoke again: "Red, for example, indicates rage, aggression, the potential for violence and even for criminal actions such as murder, depending on the areas of the brain involved, the intensity of the shade of color, and the amount of cerebral matter involved."

"Let me show you two studies done here recently", she said as she pulled a computer disc and placed it inside a computer.

Soon, the monitor's screen showed a human head, with the most precise view of the brain and other surrounding anatomical structures that Melvin had ever seen during his medical school and subsequent training at the Orlando hospital's radiology department, which was proud to have the latest in radiological technology. His father remarked that he had never seen such clear pictures taken by any machine before. The brain scan had extensive areas of red covering the brain, with few spots of white, blue and other colors.

Doctor Schneider explained, "You know what the red means? This man was a murderer—as we have since learned from Doctor Alicia Rodriguez, our PhD, psychiatrist who interviewed him."

Dr. Schneider continued: "This man was, or is, from Guatemala. He was an officer in the Military there and was in charge of fighting the guerrillas in the mountains of his country. He told Dr. Rodriguez that he ordered the massacre of people of entire villages, and he did that with untold brutality and gore. Moreover, he confessed that he enjoyed what he did. It made him feel powerful and very manly.

"He escaped his country after the government and the guerrillas signed a peace accord, fearing reprisals, but he felt very little remorse until he met the priests of the Catholic Church here in Indiantown. Yet, as you can see, there are very few white areas indicating remorse. There is still a lot of evil in this man's mind."

"This man can be really dangerous. I am sure that you turned him over to the police, right?" Melvin asked.

The three Doctors exchanged a glance that went totally unnoticed by Melvin. It was his father who answered for them. "We were certainly about to do that once Doctor Rodriguez informed us what she had learned from this man. But before we could do it, he disappeared without leaving any trace. I am sure the police are looking for him because our security reported to them."

Doctor Bright wished that Doctor Schneider's enthusiasm would not have led her to show his son those particular pictures, but he did not want to say anything further about the subject. He suggested they show him some other study.

Dr. Raj ejected the first disc and Dr. Schneider pulled another one and put it into the computer. Another head popped into the screen. This one also had some red areas but many grey, green and black areas. Doctor Raj explained that the pictures were those of a homeless man who came to the institute high on drugs and alcohol. Although he had some rage on him, the black and grey areas represented parts of the brain that were dormant because of the use of alcohol and drugs, the gray areas were those that were not so heavily loaded, and the green indicated some traits of schizophrenia. There were other colors as well, but those were the predominant ones.

Melvin asked if this guy was a criminal as well. He was informed that he was a drifter who came to the institute looking for a job. Although he had been in jail numerous times, it had been chiefly for drunkenness, drug use and petty crime. They were not sure, however, if the colors of the black and grey areas would change as he got cleaned of the substances he abused. And yes, he was still an inpatient at the institute. He was only known as "Homeless Tony," and he was in the process of being cleaned both of body and mind.

After the radiologist showed the Doctors Bright a few other studies and the other imaging machines, the older Bright asked the two doctors if they would have any objection to his son helping him and Doctor Bernstein to perform "some of the procedures, after a week or so of further training."

The doctors, of course, agreed. They honestly liked the Bright Doctors. But even if they had not, they would not have dared to refuse since they were aware that Bernstein and Bright were really the heads of the Institute.

After Mellon and Ivan, of course.

Once they left the Radiology Department, the older Doctor Bright lead his son into the next area, which was several yards down the main hallway from radiology. They had to put plastic, astronaut-like, suits over their clothing and pass through an area lit with red lights, where they were sprayed from devices in the ceiling and walls with some disinfectant. There, after a stream of warm air dried their suits, the red lights turned green and a door opened automatically. Only then did the two men step into a room as large as the lobby, which was divided in two by a half wall, and at the end of the room were three doors leading to what Melvin assumed were offices.

The place was busy with people dressed in white, most of them wearing hoods on their heads and gloves in their hands, inclined over a myriad of test tubes, probes, incubators and machines similar to those that Melvin had seen in the laboratories of the hospitals were he had done his training. Except that these were newer and, he guessed, probably much better and probably capable of doing incredible things.

His father was talking now: "This is our largest laboratory and the core of the whole institute. On the left side is the Stem Cell Research, on the right is the Nanotechnology Laboratory, and at the end of the room, next to the offices of the doctors who run the place, is where we combine the two technologies. I am sure you heard about stem cells and nanotechnology son. Have you?"

Melvin knew what stem cells were and was aware of the controversy between the right and the left wings of the US Congress about funding such research, as well as the fact that President Bush had cut the funding for such research altogether. As for nanotechnology, he did not know if it was something edible or something that made videogames more real, so he decided to play it safe and just said, "I thought the government did not approve stem cell research because it kills babies."

"That is totally moronic. Stem cells are taken from embryos that were never meant to become kids in the first place. The argument is ridiculous and hypocritical because it comes from the same groups that do not quarrel with sending other people's sons and daughters to die in stupid and unprovoked wars in faraway places. Anyway, we do not get money from the government. We are privately funded and the embryos are shipped frozen to us. We have no idea where they come from."

"I get the picture, Dad," said Melvin.

"The men in charge of stem cell research are Doctor Ching Chong from North Korea and Doctor Celin Cho from the People's Republic of China. The ones in charge of Nanotech are Doctor Majikh Sing from India and Doctor Charles B. O' Mitt from the good old USA. They both have doctorates and PhDs from MIT. I will introduce you to them as soon as I can find them. Everybody looks the same under these hoods. And to complicate matters, we have many other foreign doctors here, mainly from the Orient and India."

Melvin wanted to respond that hood or no hood, all Oriental people looked the same to him, but he guessed—probably correctly—that his father would not have appreciated that remark. So he just said, "A proverbial United Nations, right here in Florida."

Before they could single out the doctors Dr. Bright senior was talking about, a man came forward to greet them with great enthusiasm and, in a loud voice, said, "Doctor Bright, what a pleasure seeing you here, sir. What can I do for you, sir?"

The man's excessive politeness sounded very fake and out of place. Melvin could tell that his old man was not very pleased to see such servitude. He never liked Brownnosers, and he seemed to have a special dislike for this guy. Yet, Doctor Bright was a gentleman and stretched the hand that was extended to him while saying, "It is good to see you too, Kevin. But I am not sure why you acted surprised. I come here every day."

"Well, it's a pleasure to see you every day, sir. I see you have company. Are you giving a tour of our facility to a friend, sir?"

"This is my son, Melvin. Actually, it is Doctor Melvin Bright. Melvin, this is Doctor Kevin Nielsen. He is doing an internship here for the summer after finishing medical school last fall. He is a helper to all the doctors here."

Kevin forced an exaggerated smile and shook Melvin's hand with the same enthusiasm. "Well, I am a kind of a helper-doer, doctor. I want you to know that it is a great pleasure and an honor to meet the offspring of such a bright and wonderful scientist as your father. I am sure you will measure up to him."

Melvin profoundly resented that last remark because that had been his only sore spot all his life, being compared to his father and not hoping to ever measure up to him. He had reconciled himself to the idea but hearing it from other people really burned him up. So he took Kevin's stretched hand and squeezed it as hard as he could. Both men were wearing gloves, but he knew that his squeeze had hurt the guy. Smiling, he said. "I certainly hope so. That is why my father brought me here to work with him."

"Oh, is that so, Dr. Bright?"

"Yes, Kevin, Doctor Bright, Jr. will be working with Dr. Bernstein and me, first learning the ropes and eventually performing the procedures."

The change in Kevin's attitude was so drastic and obvious that Melvin could not help but smile as he said, "I was under the impression that Doctor Bernstein had plans for me to perform the procedures eventually. As you know, his hands do shake a little."

Doctor Bright ignored Kevin's last remark and proceeded to walk inside the lab, saying, "I am afraid that Doctor Bernstein has not mentioned that possibility to me, but I shall discuss it with him. Now, if you excuse us, we have a long day ahead, and it is getting late."

"Nice meeting you, Kevin. I'll see you around," said Melvin, turning his head towards the man as they walked forward. Kevin's expression of hate was detectable in spite of the hood partially hiding his face.

At this point, several men came to greet the Brights from various areas of the extensive laboratory. Four Oriental fellows genuflected in front of them and introduced themselves as Doctors Chong and Cho, which David Bright had mentioned before to his son; with them were Doctor Takaka Tehiede and Doctor Manejatu Motto from Japan, all involved in the stem cell project. In another group were Doctor Singh and Dr. B.O. Mitt of the nanotech research. They were all glad to meet Dr. Bright's son and eager to show them around as they explained their work to Melvin.

As far as he understood, they were harvesting stem cells from human tissue cells to grow or repair human organs. The implications and possible uses were enormous: from new pancreas tissue for diabetes to regenerating severed spinal cords, repairing damaged hearts, etc.

Then Melvin learned that nanotechnology was a new science that aimed to create computer chips of microscopic size that could be placed into the human body or instructed to join together in groups of a few to several hundred and run a regular computer program. But what was new, more exciting, and somewhat frightening was that the nano scientists were making microscopic computer chips that, when incubated with stem cells, could instruct such cells to do what the computer chip was programmed to tell them to do. Moreover, if those microchips were previously incubated with human adult cells, they were capable of absorbing and storing information from those cells and later transferring such information to stem cells.

Obviously, Melvin was flabbergasted by all that information, and most of it was above his level of understanding, so his father would have to patiently repeat it more than once to his son during the next few weeks.

When they finished touring the laboratories, it was almost five in the afternoon, and some of the employees were already leaving to go home for the day. The elder Bright was tired, and he knew that his son would be too, besides being aware that Melvin was not capable of processing all the information he had received that day and remembering it all.

He was not going to embarrass his son by asking questions about what he had learned. So, after they removed their gowns, he simply confessed that he was tired, that he had enough for one day—although he was going to stay in his office for a little longer to review the mail and check few other things—and told his son that he could go back to the condo on the beach or, if he preferred, he could stay with him in the house that the company had built for him on campus where he spent most of his days and nights.

Melvin thanked his father but declined his invitation, admitting that his head was hot from so much he had learned, that he needed fresh air and perhaps a dip in the pool or the ocean to try to process all the scientific information he had received that day.

His father did not press the issue. What Melvin had said made sense. Besides, it was only Monday. He expected Melvin to be there before eight the next day. They still had to tour the hospital and the animal research area. Plus, he would show him where his office was going to be.

The older doctor walked with his arm around his son's shoulder to the lobby of the institute.

Melvin embraced his father, kissed him on the forehead, and said, "Thanks, Dad, you are the greatest. I will not let you down. See you tomorrow at seven so we can have breakfast together."

"Good night, son; God bless you! I'll see you tomorrow for breakfast. Call me on the cell as soon as you get here. We meet at the cafeteria. "

They could have a more private breakfast at his home, but he had noticed the spark in his son's eyes upon looking at the pretty Veterinarian girl, Jasmine. He knew that if they were to eat at his residency, Melvin would be uneasy thinking that the woman was at the cafeteria. Besides, perhaps he himself could resume an old friendship with the young lady's mother.

Almost at the door, Melvin turned around and yelled to his father: "Don't trust that fellow Kevin, Dad; I am pretty sure he hates you."

And he left to get his car.

TEN

She arrived early the night before and stayed the night. However, Garcia wished that she had not come. Not only had he not been in the mood to make love to her, but he had been tossing and turning in bed all night, unable to sleep.

Stranger yet, it was too early, only 6 am, and he was not only up and awake but had already shaven, taken a shower, and had fixed a breakfast consisting of scrambled eggs, pancakes, freshly squeezed Florida orange juice and steaming hot coffee.

It was the smell of the coffee that woke her up. She sat in the bed rubbing her eyes as if what she was smelling and hearing was not possible. She was butt naked and she walked that way into the kitchen, where she saw him reading the morning paper and drinking his coffee. He did not even turn to look at her, but simply said, "Go put something on and come to have breakfast with me."

In all, in the almost two years that she had been visiting him, this was the first time she remembered that he had gotten out of bed before her. He had never, ever fixed breakfast before. In fact, she was not sure if he was able to cook. Therefore, she did not know what to say. She simply walked back into the bedroom, grabbed one of his bathrobes and covered herself up.

"What is the matter, Detective?" she asked. "Is the world coming to an end? Has hell frozen over? What are you doing up so early in the morning? I did not hear anyone call you."

"Nobody called me, sweetie. It is just that I could not sleep, that is all."

"You could not sleep, you are up early, I lay down naked next to you, and you did not even touch me. What the heck is going on with you, Andy Garcia? I do not look attractive to you anymore. Perhaps you are seeing another woman. Is that it? If it is so, I want to hear it from you right now."

Andy had not seen her acting that way ever before. Yet, more than concerned, he was amused. Women have such a sense of perception, perhaps a sixth sense. No, he was not seeing another woman, he said. "Maybe I am becoming gay," he joked. But what he did not mention was that he had been dreaming about Karla Colles all night and that she had been in his mind ever since he left her the previous afternoon at the sheriff's office.

Now he was feeling as if he was the naked one and this woman was capable of looking at him and somehow reading his innermost thoughts.

He gently kissed her and assured her that there was no one else. It was just this new case that had been bothering him. He then told her to go ahead and eat her breakfast before it got cold. His words and the hearty breakfast—

which she decided was actually quite tasty—changed her mood, and she apologized for her outburst.

"Well, thank you. I have to admit that that was a good breakfast, although it was barely enough to compensate for my sexual frustration of last night," she said.

"If I am not turning gay, maybe I am developing a case of erectile dysfunction, and instead of screwing, I will be cooking for the rest of my life," Andy said.

"Very funny!" she said, and then, looking at the clock over the microwave oven, she put her cup of coffee down, saying, "Jesus, I did not realize that it was so late. It is almost seven, and I am on the seven-to-eleven shift at the hospital. I am going to be late."

"If you hurry, we can get you to the hospital in ten minutes or less. I'll drive with blaring sirens and police lights. But go ahead, hurry up!"

Andy really felt bad about the woman. He knew that she sincerely loved him, but he could not help it. He simply was not in love with her, and he had been honest about it from the start of their relationship.

It was supposed to be an all-physical, friendly, uncommitted relationship. He had told her that he wanted to see other women and that he wanted her to see other men, and she had been ok with that at the time. But the fact was that, over the last year or so, she had not seen anyone else.

As for him, well… let's say that he had cut down drastically on his dating other women, and in fact, for the last several months, she had been the only woman in his life. The rationality was that he felt safer that way. She probably took it as a commitment on his part.

Her name was Annie, and she was an emergency room RN at the Lawnwood Medical Center, a hospital in Fort Pierce.

She was divorced and a single mother of two kids over 15 who chose to go live with their father after they learned that he had remarried to a wealthy woman and lived on a ranch in California.

It started as a friendship between the cop who comes to the ER to interview the crime victims or to arrest the suspects and a lonely soul in search of love and companionship; the truth is that she had been tremendous support when Andy's partner was shot. Then she started coming over to his apartment and staying the night.

The sex was good, and she was also a great cook and housekeeper, yet he had balked every time she mentioned the possibility of moving in with him.

That morning, as Andy was driving her to the hospital at 60 miles an hour in the city—where the speed limit was 30—he realized for the first time that she was more a friend he loved than a lover he befriended. Still, he had no desire to give up the sex part of the relationship. Plus he did not want to hurt her. Besides, she seemed to understand him and tolerate his moods…. But then there was now Karla Colles.

Andy stopped to see his partner Frank on the way to the office, mostly because he did not want to appear too obvious, showing up unusually early at the sheriff's office. His friend was recuperating ok and, although he still had to walk with a cane and was not allowed to drive, he was coming along better than expected. Frank announced that he was planning a trip to upstate New York to see his folks and spend the holidays there, probably visiting Niagara Falls,

Then, perhaps, he would go to Canada and return, hopefully to work again at the end of the winter—that is, of course, if he could tolerate the cold up north for that long.

Thereafter, Andy stopped at the medical examiner's office with little hope to learn anything new about his case and mostly to kill some more time. He was informed that—of course—the doctor was not there yet, but had worked late the night before. He had phoned a message for the detectives to one of his assistants. The man informed him that the doctor had received unofficial word from the laboratory that the toxicology analysis on the dead allegedly drowned guy, although far from complete, had detected an "unusual chemical compound" in the man's blood. The doctor had said he was willing to bet it would be the same chemical found in the Guatemalan's body.

Armed with this information, he drove to the sheriff's office. Upon walking in, he found that Sergeant Karla Colles was already at her desk. And upon seeing him, without getting up, he signaled him to approach.

Detective Garcia's heart sank when she failed to show the enchanting smile he remembered from the day before, the one he had been dreaming about. She was again all business when she said: "Good Morning, Detective! You are early for a change. Guess what I found out?"

Her attitude irritated him and without responding to her greeting he blurted: "I know. I am just coming from Doctor Raymond's office. He said that the lab found some chemical in our man's blood, which the good doctor believes it is going to be the same compound found in the other guy, but he can be sure because that is pending further analysis."

"Didn't your mother tell you that it is atrocious manners to interrupt when someone is talking? I was not aware of that information. I was waiting to call the doctor later, but thank you for passing along such delicate information, even if it was done indelicately."

"I am sorry, Sergeant Colles; I just thought we had the same information. I did not mean to be rude. Please tell me what you have."

"Hmm... It looks like you are going to keep apologizing as long as our partnership lasts or until this case is solved because you tend to put your foot in your mouth quite often," Colles said.

"Once more, and for the last time, I am very sorry," Garcia responded, feeling irritated with her attitude. And since—whether you like it or not—we are supposed to collaborate until the case is solved, would you be so kind as to give me the information you were about to give me before my rudeness prevented you from doing so?"

"Sarcasm is not—" She could not finish the sentence as the telephone on her desk started ringing. She picked it up.

She listened carefully for a few minutes, interrupting only briefly to ask questions while at the same time making signs to Andy Garcia to wait until she finished. Finally, she hung the receiver and looked at the detective, pointing to a chair and saying, "Please sit down, Detective."

She continued, "That was Sister Imelda from Holy Cross in Indiantown; I called her earlier. She gave me very interesting additional information right now, but let me start from the beginning, and then we can go back to the nice sister."

"Last night—while you were sleeping or whatever it is that you do at night to make you so crabby in the morning—I spent several hours in the computer accessing files from the Police and Sheriff's Departments of Okeechobee, Indian River, Saint Lucie, and Martin Counties. Found exactly forty-six cases of either legal or illegal aliens, homeless individuals, and drifters who died in ways other than natural over the last 6 months."

"Of those, there are seventeen whose deaths were somewhat suspicious because there were no witnesses of the event nor apparent motive. There were four motor vehicle accidents, three drownings, three drug overdoses—all in American-born fellows, two stabbings, three alcoholic intoxications leading to death and two shootings—one of them our guy. In none of the murder cases was an arrest was ever made, and they are still open.

"Of the latter, two were found in Saint Lucie, one in Okeechobee, and one in Martin County. The others are almost evenly distributed between the five counties. Then, I emailed the list to Doctor Raymond to see if he could obtain more information about the autopsies, especially about the toxicology reports in all seventeen cases."

"I see that you have done excellent homework, Sergeant. My sincere congratulations. You are a good detective."

"Thanks, just doing my job. However, I have not revealed the information that sister Imelda gave me. I called her this morning and ran the names of the victims by her. She seemed to recognize some of them, and requested that I fax or e-mail the list—and, if possible, any photographs that I may have. It took very little time for her to view the information and get back to me. She was able to identify at least four of the fellows, including our victim. None had family locally. At least two of the four worked at that Neurological Institute there in Indiantown, which in itself is not strange because the place is huge and, I bet, employs a lot of people. But what was somewhat odd is that in all four cases, a well-known lawyer from Stuart, paid for the funerals of all four and took upon himself to send the remains back to their home countries. She said the guy is very good with the migrants. She even thinks that this lawyer sends money to the families of the deceased, all out of goodwill. Apparently, he is wealthy."

"Sorry to be skeptical, but I have never known a lawyer with a good heart. Did she give you a name?" Garcia asked.

"His name is Gary Williams. Everybody around here knows him. He has won multimillion-dollar lawsuits against giant corporations and is known as a philanthropist," responded Karla.

"Lawyers can never be truly philanthropists. I bet you a dinner that there is something behind this lawyerly philanthropism. My dad told me never to trust a lawyer and, believe me, that has proven to be true during most of my life experiences. Let us pay this philanthropist a friendly visit, don't you agree?" said Detective Garcia.

"Agreed," she said, "and while we are at it, we probably should also pay a visit to that Neurology Institute in Indiantown" .

"It is back to Martin County. Then let's notify the boss and ask for his ok to take the car out of the county," Andy said. Although he noticed that Karla had not made any comments about the dinner bet, she appeared to be a bit friendlier than earlier. Perhaps he still has a chance to patch up things with her, to have a fresh start. The way things were, he had not only not gotten to first base. At this point, he did not have a chance to bat. Heck, he had not even left the bench!

Meanwhile, at the Neurological Institute, "Not-so" had shown up a few minutes past seven and had breakfast with his father at the cafeteria, with the disappointment that neither Jasmin nor her mother were eating there.

By ten a.m., Doctors Bright had almost finished the tour of the place. After brief visits to the radiology and stem cell labs—where they had met again this time an unfriendly Kevin—they were walking towards the veterinary section of the facility, which was located at the far end of the building.

"Tell me about this guy, Kevin's dad; what is up with him?" Melvin asked.

"Well, son, as far as I know, he is the son of an Ob-Gyn father and a Pediatrician mother, both of whom are excellent and very busy doctors. They have been practicing in the Tampa area for several years. I met them through Paul Bernstein, who was a professor of one of them, a charming couple. They only had one son, Kevin and because they were too busy in their professions and could not dedicate enough time to him, they tried to compensate by providing him with all the material things his heart desired, cars, boats, best schools, you get the idea."

Melvin thought that his dad had done pretty much the same thing to him, but he decided that it was best to keep his mouth shut as his father continued talking.

"It seems that the kid did not do well in school and got into all kinds of trouble, from which the parents always bailed him out. He is very ambitious but does not have the drive to achieve his goals. Paul gave him a job here only until he starts his internship in few months in a hospital somewhere."

"He definitely likes it here, Dad. Besides, can he be that dumb if he is able to become a doctor? Where did he go to school?" asked Melvin.

"It was his idea to become a physician. Perhaps he wanted to follow in the footsteps of his parents, or maybe it was just another thing that he wanted his parents to give him, I do not know. Paul says that mom and dad actually tried to discourage him from becoming a doctor, because they believed that he does not have what it takes. But he insisted and mom and dad, as usual, gave junior what he wanted. They send him to med school somewhere in a Caribbean Island. It took him 8 years to graduate, but here he is now, a medical doctor."

"But do you think that Paul really offered him a job, as he said?" asked Melvin.

"I do not think Paul wants him to stay here, and I certainly do not either…this was supposed to be only a temporary job, a learning experience for him, nothing else."

"He appeared very convinced that Dr. Bernstein was going to keep him here and let him do what you all call ' the procedures.' Perhaps Dr. Paul has not told you yet about it Dad, or perhaps he misunderstood him."

"Or he is lying through his teeth," Dr. Bright said.

"One thing is for sure: He was very upset when he learned that you brought me here and will let me do those procedure things," said Melvin.

"I certainly will ask Paul about it, but I bet he will tell me that he did not tell that young man such a thing. If he did, he would have told me about it for sure."

At this point, they had reached the Animal Research Laboratory, and Doctor Bright put his ID card in a pad at the door, entered a numeric code, and opened the door.

The Animal Research Laboratory was huge. The place did not look much different than the Stem Cell lab, except that the people working there did not wear isolating suits, only lab coats, and some surgical masks. Further down, there were several machines and tubes, as well as incubators and cages of different sizes containing mice, guinea pigs, and rabbits; there were veterinarian tables for examination and surgery for small and more significant animals, but Melvin did not see any of those in there; he did not see Jasmin nor her mother there either.

The two doctors had to walk to the back end of the laboratory and go through a tinted, sliding glass door to find a huge cage, like the one in most modern zoos, which extended almost all the length of that part of the building in which several chimpanzees were seen playing, eating or hanging of ropes or from several children's playground equipment sets. Only half of the cage was inside the laboratory; the other half opened to the outside but was hidden from people walking around the grounds of the building by a wall that was as high as that of the edifice.

Melvin and his father had to walk in front of the cage and towards the far end of it before the younger of the two realized that there was a partition in the large cage, making a smaller cage separated from the main one. In those, there were four chips; the women doctors were inside that cage examining the apes with great attention.

Melvin was not a veterinarian, and although he liked dogs somewhat, he was more of a cat person. Yet he was able to notice that there was something different and unusual about those chimps. For one, their eyes looked brighter and more intelligent, and their faces had almost a human expression. What was obvious was that those monkeys were not playing like the others. Each had untouched food containers in front of them, and looked very sad.

Upon seeing the newcomers, one of the chips got up and walked towards the bars of the cage as if to meet them. Much to Melvin's surprise, the monkey did not walk like a chimp but straight like a man. Standing to face him, the monkey uttered a strange, fragmented, and intelligible sound: something like "*Nochangohuma. No chan go.*"

At this, the women noticed the visitors' presence and came out of the cage to greet them. Melvin, of course, as soon as he saw the younger one's face, forgot about the monkey and everything else.

After the usual greetings, Melvin asked about the monkeys. He thought the four in the smaller cage were sick, and because of that, they had been separated from the others. He was informed that those four were "recipients" and were being carefully observed 24/7, subject to testing on a daily basis and that a video camera recorded their every move.

"Are you sure they are not sick?" he asked. "They do look sick to me," said Melvin.

"They are very healthy; I can assure you, Melvin," said Doctor Porter. "They only appear different because of the changes that usually occur after the transference; that is all."

"Transference? what kind of transference?" said Melvin.

At this point in the conversation, his father intervened by stating

"You doctors have to forgive me. I am afraid that My son is not yet familiar with the process of transference, but that is, in part, what we will be doing here. Meanwhile, would you be so kind, Linda, to give him a brief explanation?"

Doctor Porter asked, "Has your son been at the laboratories?" As the answer was positive, Linda Porter continued, "So you know that what we do there is try to program nanoparticles by incubating them with mature stem cells of a living being and then transferring them to be incubated with very young stem cells in the hope that those young cells would absorb the information provided to the nanoparticles by the adult cells.

"Thereafter, we transfer or implant the young cells into another living organism, again hoping that they will grow and transmit the information they learned to the new organism. Do you understand the process, Melvin?"

"So, what you are saying is that you are trying to transplant the features of an animal into another?" responded Melvin.

"Something like that, but it is not the features we are trying to transfer; it is the traits, the personality, the abilities, perhaps the intelligence of one being to another. Just think about it we may be able to cure cerebral palsy, mental retardation, Alzheimer's disease, mental illness, etc. The possibilities are limitless…" said Melvin's father

"My God, Melvin says, this is fantastic, but have you been able to achieve any of it?" asked Melvin.

"You saw it yourself, son. Those four chimps there have received transfers of human cells, and as you pointed out, they are already behaving differently than their peers," said the senior Doctor, Bright.

"But they do not look as active and happy as the other chimps; perhaps they do not like being smarter than their friends. If they were humans, I would say they are either sick or depressed. They even make different noises than the monkeys in the next cage," said Melvin.

"I have to agree with Melvin on that," –said Jasmin Porter -who had just come out of the chimp's cage to greet the Brights. "They do look depressed to me, but my mother insists that they may have a headache, even though they do not seem to improve after we give them an analgesic." "Also, they seem to be talking or trying to talk to us; my mom thinks it is language and maybe Spanish, but so far, we have not been able to make any sense of what they are trying to say."

"Maybe I can help. I speak Spanish, went to medical school in Mexico. Did you record those sounds? Do you have a sound splitter?" said Melvin.

The older Bright would have preferred that Melvin did not boast about having gone to a foreign medical school.

He was aware that everyone in the medical profession was aware that those Americans graduating abroad did so because they did not have the qualifications to be admitted to a school in the US, but he kept his mouth shut.

"Let's step into the laboratory, next room, and see if our new friend can help us decipher the sound riddle," said the older Doctor Porter.

Jasmin Porter carried the tape to a soundproof room, where a young man greeted her with enthusiasm. Melvin felt a surge of jealousy and immediately disliked the young fellow.

After the four of them entered the room, the man gave them audiphones and sat in front of a state-of-the-art and rather sophisticated sound system. He put the tape in the machine, and they all listened. Melvin became intensely involved, and his attention went one hundred percent into listening to the sounds. He wanted to be able to help; he wanted very badly to impress the beautiful Jasmin.

"Nochangohuma ... nochango, no changohuma ...nochango ... nochangohuma ... no chango"

The tape played the same sound repeatedly by one of the chimps.

"That is George; he is the only one who does that gibbering," Linda Porter said.

The same sounds were repeated over and over, and after several minutes, Melvin said to the technician.

"Can you slow it down and perhaps split the sounds?" asked Melvin

The young man responded proudly: "I can not only do that but make the sounds appear on that computer screen," he said, pointing to a large monitor in front of a computer.

He pushed some buttons, pressed some keys, and adjusted some levers and as the sound continued playing words appeared in the screen

NOCHANGOHUMA...NOCHANGO.

After looking carefully at the words and listening to the sounds, Melvin yielded loudly, "Whoa! I think I can solve the riddle! The monkey is actually talking. He is saying, '*No Chango, human.*' In Mexico, they call monkeys *Changos*. He is trying to tell us that he is not a monkey. He thinks he is human!"

ELEVEN

The detectives couldn't travel to Martin County, as planned, for the next three days. A Hispanic family of four—two small children included—had been murdered, execution style along the Florida turnpike between Fort Pierce and Port Saint Lucie, and every officer from the police department of both towns, as well as the sheriff department, had been very busy in the investigation of such heinous crime.

Fortunately for Karla and Andy, the DEA and the FBI got involved, as it appeared to have been a drug-related crime, and four suspects were arrested, most of them related to the deceased.

The hypothesis was that the father and mother of the children, who belonged to a drug ring run by their family, had recently moved to Port Saint Lucie, perhaps in an attempt to expand the family business into the area or to hide from them. As it was hypothesized that the adults may have been stealing money and drugs from the rest of the family, and they were punished and killed to set an example. The other theory was that this new family was invading the territory of some other drug lords, and they did not like the competition.

In any event, the solving of those murders was the FBI and the DEA's problem now and the local detectives could go back to their routine work.

On the bright side, by then, the coroner had the toxicology analysis results, which proved that the doctor was correct; it was the same compound found in the other body: versed.

The first body had been shipped to the family in the home country, and the expenses had been paid—as they had been informed before—by a Stuart law firm. Nobody had claimed the body of Ismael Torres –if that was indeed his real name-.

The Guatemalan Consulate insisted that they had not been able to find any relatives of the deceased in Guatemala. The Guatemalan army was investigating but so far only hinted that if the man ever served in the armed forces there, most likely was either discharged or was a deserter. They were not interested in reclaiming the body.

So, as the two detectives were busy with their problems and their trip to Martin County had been delayed, interesting events occurred at the Neurological Institute in Indiantown.

After completing the tour of the Institute, Melvin had only a very basic idea of what they were doing there. His father, as well as Doctor Bernstein, had taken pains to emphasize to him not only the importance of the work being done there and therefore the importance of absolute secrecy, but mostly they had shown to him the great benefit to mankind that the research being done there represented for this and future generations.

They spent a good deal of time in the area they called "the hospital wards," in which individuals supposedly ill with diseases considered incurable by modern medicine were being cured or experienced marked improvement of their illness as they were treated with stem cells, nanoparticles or a combination of the two.

His questions about why some of the patients were in very plush rooms and others (mostly Latino-looking) were in small, double, or triple rooms were answered by proudly proclaiming that the former were paying patients, and the others were charity patients. However, only the rooms were different; the care, food, etc., was similar for both.

Melvin, of course, believed everything, and he was bewildered by what he was being shown and prouder than ever of his father and "Uncle Paul" – as he referred privately to Doctor Paul Bernstein.

Two or three rooms were sparely furnished with only a bed and a bench bolted to the floor. Such rooms had padded walls and thick one-sided viewing glass. Only one of those rooms was occupied by a young, white man with a shaved head, which may have been covered before the shaving with reddish hair. That young man was pacing the floor nervously, while a young woman wearing a lab coat was sitting on the bench obviously asking questions— which the man sometimes answered rapidly and angrily, and other times between sobs and tears.

"Those there are Doctor Alice Rodriguez, a psychiatrist with a degree from Harvard, and the young man is only known to us as 'Homeless Tony.'

"He is our newest client; someone found him passed out on the railroad tracks and brought him here. He was so high on drugs and booze that we are not sure if he got there, to the railroad tracks, accidentally or was trying to kill himself.

"Doctor Raj showed us his scan the other day, remember? Tony is a drug addict and a small-time crook. He also, of course, has multiple psychiatric problems," explained the senior Doctor Bright to his son.

"We hope to cure him soon," added Doctor Bernstein.

"And perhaps learn his full name, we called him "Homeless Tony" because the locals call him that way; apparently, he is a drifter and comes to Florida every year, or every other year, fleeing from the winter up north," said Dr. Bright.

Melvin had spent three days with his father and "Uncle Paul," and he had learned to perform cisternal taps under CT scan, first on a very realistic plastic model and then on a couple of patients, both of them Latino men. He was learning so fast and was so successfully that the staff of the radiology department and the staff of the laboratory were almost unanimously impressed by the young Doctor Bright's skill.

That is with one exception: one Doctor, Kevin Nielsen, who found it very hard to disguise his frustration and disappointment at Melvin Bright's success.

Needless to say, the two people most satisfied with Melvin's performance were, besides himself, his father and Doctor Bernstein.

In spite of his "good ratings," There had been one great disappointment for Melvin. It was because of being so busy that he had had no time to see Jasmine Porter. In fact, the first and only time that he had seen her was earlier that morning over breakfast, actually just over his breakfast because she did not eat. In fact, she did not come to the cafeteria to have breakfast. She came down there actually looking for Melvin.

She was obviously upset and crying. She said that she had a big argument with her mother and that "George" was dead.

Of course, Melvin did not remember who "George" was, so Jasmin had to remind him that "George" was one of the chimpanzees—the smartest one, the one who appeared to be saying words in Spanish.

They found him that very same morning when their keeper went to his cage to feed him, he was hanging from the neck with the rope they had in the cage to swing and play with.

Melvin did not mind that she was crying on his shoulder, but he was afraid to hug her, so he just let her cry as he tried to find the right words to console her. At first, he thought of saying that he was just an animal, but somehow, he realized that that would not go very well, so he said, "It sure was a fine monkey, but you have to realize that you only knew him for about a week."

"You do not understand, Melvin!" she said between sobs. "It is not just that. It is that I am sure George killed himself! Have you ever heard of an animal committing suicide? It does not happen. It just does not happen. Animals do not deliberately kill themselves. This chimp did. This chimp committed suicide, Melvin! My mom denies that it happened, but I saw it with my own eyes. That chimp tied the rope around his neck and jumped off the branch of a tree! She says it was an accident. There was no accident, by God. Melvin, what are these people are doing here? What are we doing here?"

"Maybe your mother is right. It could have been a freak accident," said Melvin, still holding her.

"Oh yeah," she said, "then explain this to me. I was the one who was supposed to perform an autopsy on George and, although I could not bring myself to do that, I did find this in his hand." She said this pulling a piece of paper from the pocket of her lab coat and putting it on Melvin's hand.

The paper was wrinkled and dirty and smelled of animal feces and urine, but it was written in large, crooked letters: "*NO CHANGO....HOMBRE.*"

Melvin was so surprised did not know what to say, and before he could react, he noticed that Jasmine's mother and the lady psychiatrist were standing next to them.

Dr. Porter said: "Thank you, Doctor Bright; as you can see, my daughter is terribly upset over the death of that chimp. You see she is a tenderhearted girl and becomes very attached to the animals. Not a very good thing for a veterinarian. Don't you think so, Doctor?"

Before Melvin could answer, she continued: "That poor animal died of natural causes. You yourself pointed out the other day that he looked ill. Afterward, maybe someone with a poor sense of humor tried to play a sick joke by writing that note. But do not worry, doctor. We shall get to the bottom of this. I assure you of that, Doctor Bright."

The two women were gently but firmly pulling Jasmin away from Melvin and out of the cafeteria when the older Doctor Porter turned around and said to him, "I shall take that piece of paper with me if you don't mind, Doctor Bright; it may help with our investigation."

Melvin handed the piece of paper back to her, and soon, the three women disappeared through the door. For the first time since he could remember, he could not finish his breakfast and instead headed back to the laboratory.

Later, upon commenting on the incident to his father, he also dismissed it as regrettable because of the girl's reaction but otherwise inconsequential. He stated that he shared Doctor Linda Porter's opinion about someone trying to play a tasteless prank.

Talking while walking, they headed towards the radiology department, where Dr. Bernstein was also waiting. He announced to Melvin that he had another spinal cisternal tap to perform, except this time, instead of withdrawing spinal fluid, he was to inject some into the patient.

This was great news to Doctor Melvin, but they were a great cause of disappointment to the young intern, Doctor Kevin Nielsen who evidently was there, in the radiology department, involved in a conversation with Dr. Bernstein, obviously trying to talk the old doctor into letting him participate in the performance of the procedures. Or at least to perhaps to put a word for him to the Senior Dr. Bright, so they allow him to work on the patients.

As they walked in, Bernstein was saying, in a not-very friendly tone: "I have told you many times, Kevin, these are very delicate procedures, and you are simply not ready to do them. Finish your medical school, go to post-graduate training, and then David and I will be most willing to review your performance and, if we are satisfied, we will let you work on patients. Is that understood, Doctor Nielsen!"

"Yes sir," Kevin answered while his face reddened and his eyes became narrow with anger and with his fists clenched so hard that his fingernails almost pierced his hand, he added, "It is very clear, Doctor sir. Now, if you excuse me, I shall go back to the lab."

With this he left, and if the door would not have a mechanism to close slowly, without noise, it would have made a noise to be heard all through the institute, yet, before the door closed, he was able to hear Dr. Bernstein greeting Melvin while saying to him "We shall see how you do today, Doctor

Melvin Bright, if all goes well, tomorrow or the next day, we will let you inject "Homeless Tony"; he will be officially your first patient here and you will assume full care of him from today until he leaves the institute."

"Yes…. Thanks a lot, Uncle Ben. I mean Doctor Bernstein," Melvin said as the door of the department closed behind Doctor Kevin Nielsen.

Once in the hallway, Nielsen almost broke in tears. Swearing in a low voice, he took off his lab coat and stopped in the small place that had been assigned as his office. He took his car keys and bolted out of the room. He then headed hurriedly down the corridor towards the lobby, with the intention of leaving the campus of the institute forever.

Kevin was not used to being denied anything he wanted. His parents had always fulfilled all his wishes and desires, and he took the doctors' refusal to let him work on patients as a humiliation and a personal offense.

TWELVE

Detective Karla Colles and Detective Andy Garcia had not had a good day either. They had gone to Stuart in the hopes of talking to Mr. Gary Williams at the prestigious law firm of Williams, Stern, and Suarez, only to be told that none of the lawyers were available or present at the office at that moment—which was very hard for the detectives to believe since there were at least fifteen names of lawyers listed for that firm. This made them suspicious that the lawyers were unwilling to talk to them, perhaps because they were hiding something and promised to return.

After grabbing something to eat for lunch at Wendy's they headed for Indiantown and the Neurological Institute.

It was another sunny, humid, and hot day in Florida. Never mind that it was October; snow may have already fallen in Minnesota, so they thanked God for the Florida weather and put the top of the convertible down to enjoy it.

After the gate guard checked their credentials, they parked the convertible near the institute's entrance. Garcia raised the top of the car with a brief "You never know when it's going to rain in Florida."

"That or if a raccoon may decide to get inside it," said Colles humorously, pointing at the scraps of French fries on the seat and floor of the car. Then, she walked towards the entrance.

Just as she crossed the doorframe, a young man came almost running and, without paying attention, crashed into her. The impact almost knocked Karla down to the floor. In fact, the only reason she did not fall was that Garcia was coming just behind her and was able to prevent her from falling.

The young man, instead of stopping and apologizing, kept walking and semi-turning around, said, "Some people are so stupid they don't even know where they are going. They must have their eyes in their ass."

Garcia heard those words, and after making sure that Karla was okay, he went after the man who had kept walking and was already outside the door. Grabbing him by the neck, he made him turn around.

"You know, I could easily break your ugly face, but I think it will hurt more if I throw you in a cell with four or five bikers so that they can have fun with your sorry ass. You know that you just assaulted a police officer, pal?" Andy said, fire coming from his eyes and spitting every word in the face of the man.

"Hit me, and I will sue you for police brutality," the man said.

"Oh yes, pretty boy, you want to sue me? Are you sure you want to sue me? Because if that is so, I am going to give you a fucking good reason to sue me."

As Andy said this, he lifted his fisted hand and was ready to hit the man in the face when Karla grabbed his arm and spoke. "Let it go, Detective. I am ok, it is not worth it"

"Yes it is worth it, however, if you ask me, I'll let this bastard go. But before I do that he needs to apologize to you. Go ahead, man, apologize."

The young guy was terrified and he said with a squealing voice: "I am sorry, lady. I apologize."

"Is that apology satisfactory enough to you, Seargent?"

She said yes and to let it be. Still, before Andy let the guy go, he took one of his business cards from his breast pocket and said, "There. Here is my card, so you remember who your manners instructor was." Andy put his business card in the guy's breast pocket, while at the same time, he hit him with his knee in the crotch. As the guy bent over in pain, Karla Colles came after them and pleaded again for Andy to let it be.

Ok, big boy, go home and put some ice on those balls," he said and walked away from the man who was still holding his crotch in pain, much to the amusement of the security guard at the gate, who was obviously enjoying the scene and approaching very slowly and in a carefree way.

"Do you hear the lady, pal?" Andy said. "She wants me to let you go unharmed and free. I may be willing to do that, but first, you have to give me your name in case I change my mind and decide to press charges later."

"It is Kevin Nielsen, actually Doctor Kevin Nielsen," the guy said. "And yes, I do sincerely apologize. I am very sorry. I had a bad day. Please forgive me, lady. I am truly sorry. Can I go now?"

"Okay, you may go, but do not let me catch you again, even if it is for a minor traffic violation, because my lady partner would not be there to save you. And you have my card, so you will remember my name…right?'

"Yes, sir. Thank you, sir," Kevin said, trying hard to straighten up. He succeeded only partially. He limped slowly towards his car, a brand-new yellow Hummer of the latest model.

The gate security guard was standing next to them and said, "You should have taken him in, or at least hit him harder. He is an arrogant son of a bitch. Nobody likes him here. He is not even a doctor, just an intern waiting to go back to school. Can I help you guys?"

"We are police officers from the Saint Lucie County Sheriff's Department. We are investigating the murder of somebody who may have worked here. Have you ever seen this guy?" said Karla, while showing a computer-corrected photo of the diseased man.

"Can't say I have, can't say I haven't. To me, all these Latino, Mayan, Indian guys look alike. But I can tell you that in this place, there are a lot of people like him working. What happened? How did he get wasted?"

"We found him in Fort Pierce with half of his chest blown up by a bullet from a magnum 44."

"Do you guys carry those around here" – asked Andy.

"No sir, we all carry Berettas, like this one," the security man said, showing his gun in his holster. "You may want to talk to Mrs. Williams. She is the head of human resources. I bet she can tell you if your man ever worked here. She keeps files of every one of us in her computer. You folks go inside the lobby, and then ask Gladys. She is the receptionist. She will be able to get you to talk to Mrs. Williams, I am sure."

"You sure are very helpful sir. What did you say your name was?" Karla said in spite of the fact that the man was wearing a name tag that clearly said "Smith."

"It is Joe madam, Joe Smith, at your service"

"Well, thank you, Joe. Thanks a lot; I am Sergeant Carla Colles, and this is my temporary partner, Detective Andy Garcia."

"Nice to meet you both," the security guard said, returning to his gate post as the detectives walked towards the institute's lobby.

"Do not ever do that again," Karla said in a low voice when they were alone.

"Don't do what?" said Andy.

"Fight for me, like I am a kid, or a price to win. For your information, I am perfectly capable of defending myself. It was rather embarrassing what you did back there," said Colles.

"Is that so? I did not see you defending yourself very well back there. In fact, if it was not for me, you would have a sore ass now."

"Well, I do appreciate that you are keeping me from falling on my ass; what I did not like is that you fought with that jerk afterward, which was not called for; once again, you have to learn to control your temper, anger, whatever it is that pisses you off."

"Fine, they have said that a good deed never goes unpunished, I take your diatribe as my punishment. Let's see if we can talk with Mrs. Williams."

"Maybe she won't want to see us; perhaps she is related to attorney Williams of Stuart, and he forewarned not to talk to us; after all, they have the same last name."

"Perhaps, but Williams is a prevalent name in most parts of this country."

"True" she said.

Gladys was a well-endowed woman in her mid or late thirties who must have had a terrific body. Though fat was beginning to gain on her, she was still attractive. She had red-dyed hair and enjoyed wearing mini-miniskirts and tight-fitting outfits.

She was now walking ahead of them and did not hear their conversation as she ushered them along the long corridor to the office that read at the door: "Human Resources, C. Williams, Executive Director."

As if it were necessary to verbalize it, Gladys said, obviously flirting with the detective, "This is Mrs. Williams's office. I believe she is in. I'll go to announce you now. Please have a seat while I go tell her secretary."

As she walked into the back office with an exaggerated swing of her hips,

Karla said to Andy, "It is obvious that she likes you. Are you going to ask her for her phone number?"

"Seems to me she likes anything that wears pants or shorts; why are you asking? I bet you are jealous."

"Don't flatter yourself to make me laugh, detective," Karla said.

At this point, they got up as Gladys, accompanied by Clarissa Williams, returned.

She was an imposing woman who radiated authority and elegance. In a navy-blue pantsuit, she looked very executive. With her high stiletto heels, she towered over the detectives, a fact that she obviously enjoyed.

Her smile showed the most perfect white teeth that the Detectives have seen, except in the movies. She was wearing long earrings with a string of at least three diamonds and a white pearl at the end. The bosom showed a discrete but sexy cleavage, and a pearl necklace completed the attire from her long and slender neck.

She was courageous and formal when stretching her well-manicured hand to shake the detectives and saying, "Welcome to the Neurological and Medical Research Institute of The Treasure Coast. "Gladys here informs me that you are detectives from the Saint Lucie County Sheriff's Department. What concern does the Saint Lucie Sheriff's Department have about the institute?"

"It is very nice to meet you, Mrs. Williams. I am Sergeant Karla Colles from the Saint Lucie County Sheriff's CSI department, as you have been informed. This is my associate in this case, Detective Andy Garcia."

Garcia could not help but notice that she had not said, "My partner, Detective Andy Garcia." For some reason, he felt hurt and angry. He felt compelled to say, "Unfortunately, my regular partner has been wounded in the line of duty, so Ms. Colles was assigned to accompany me."

"We are currently investigating the murder of a man whom the department believes used to work at the institute."

"Oh, that is so awful! Are you sure that man worked for us? I have not been informed of anyone not showing up for work today." Seeing Gladys still standing there, listening to the conversation, she said to her, "I am sure you have something to do, Ms. Franklin. Don't you think it is unwise to leave the reception desk alone for too long?"

Gladys' face reddened, and she hastily excused herself, leaving so fast that she forgot to swing her hips in the sexy fashion that she usually did.

"This man, whom we believed worked here, was killed a few days ago, so he won't be among those who did not show up for work today only." "But would you mind if we go to someplace more private, your office perhaps, to discuss this matter further?." Sergeant Colles and I have several questions we hope you can help us with."

"I am so sorry, detectives; I was so shocked by the news that one of our workers had been killed that I forgot my good manners. Please, do, by all means, come into my office," said Mrs. Williams.

She led them into a spacious office with wood-paneled walls, sparsely furnished but very elegantly decorated. What was most impressive was the neatly polished giant mahogany desk and the wall-size picture of Reverend Martin Luther King, accompanied by a young girl about 10 years old.

As she offered drinks after the detectives were conformably seated, and they declined, she noticed their glances at the picture, so she said. "That is me, with Dr. King. I was only eight years old, and the picture was taken only a few days before he was killed. My parents were very active in the civil rights movement."

"A memorable picture of a memorable moment with a remarkable man," Sergeant Colles said.

"Amen!" added Garcia, standing up and approaching the desk while pulling a picture out of his breast pocket, which he handed to Clarissa. "But I am sure you are busy and have many things to do, so we do not want to take too much of your time. This is the man we found dead in Fort Pierce four days ago. He was killed by a bullet in his chest from a heavy caliber weapon. We think his name was Ismael Torres, although he was probably an illegal alien. He could have given a different name here."

"We do not knowingly hire illegal aliens to work at the institute, Detective Garcia. However, as you know, sometimes it is impossible to be certain that the papers they show us are fake or real. Why do you think he worked at the institute? Did he have any papers indicating so?"

"No, ma'am. Our investigations led us to Indiantown, and some of the locals have identified him and hinted that he may have worked here," said Karla.

"I cannot seem to remember him from this picture or from the name you gave me. Let me see if we have something on the computer." Clarissa Williams swung her elegant desk chair and pressed some keys in her computer, the screen lifted up, and the Detectives could see by the reflection on the glass of the Martin Luther picture that pictures of individuals were showing. After a few minutes, she swung back to face the detectives and said, "Sorry, I see no matches for Mr. Torres name, nor anyone's picture that resembles him. Unfortunately, I have a previous commitment and have to leave the institute very shortly. However, I will instruct my secretary to continue the search for you. If she finds anything, I will personally call you tomorrow."

"If you do not mind, Mrs. Williams, we can wait a little longer while she does the search. Meanwhile, we could look around the institute and ask some workers if they remember Mr. Torres.

Mrs. Williams did not seem thrilled about the idea, so she hesitated before saying yes and told them that although they could get into the offices, cafeteria, kitchen, and outside grounds, the laboratories, research areas, and patient areas were off-limits. And—oh yes—her secretary would have to

73

print temporary passes for them. With this, she stood up and walked towards the agents to shake hands and walk them to the door.

"Oh, Mrs. Williams, before we leave, I want to thank you for your help and ask you one more question. Are you related to Gary Williams, the attorney?" Andy asked.

Mrs. Williams stopped, obviously annoyed by the question, and responded, "Williams is not an uncommon name, and I do not understand the reason for your question."

"I am sorry, it was just curious; it seems that Mr. Williams has taken upon himself the expenses of sending the bodies of other foreigners who died recently back to their home countries, and some of those men may have also worked for the institute." said Andy.

"Attorney Williams is known to be a philanthropist and is involved in many charities, so I am not surprised if what you said is true." "And no, I am not a blood relative of Mr. Williams, but I am related to him by marriage. He is my brother-in-law. I was married to his brother."

"We are currently in the process of getting a divorce. He was cheating on me. In fact, the reason I have to leave now is because we have a preliminary hearing this afternoon," said Clarissa Williams, fighting tears.

"We are sorry," said Karla. "In this job, sometimes, we have to ask questions that can bother people. We are just doing our job."

"I understand," she said, and with this, she walked away, stopping only to tell her secretary about the computer search and the passes.

Clarissa Williams' secretary, Ms. Wanda Sherman, was an attractive blond woman in her mid-thirties, who, unlike Gladys Franklyn, dressed much more professionally in an apparent attempt to emulate her boss. She was dressed in business-like fashion, but instead of a pantsuit, she was wearing a skirt, which, extending barely above the knees, allowed her to show gorgeous legs. She wore wire-rimmed glasses, and her hair, which was probably at least shoulder length, was held in a ponytail. She appeared more than glad to help the detectives, especially Andy.

She already had the same program on the computer screen, with photographs and data of the workers that Clarissa Williams had started researching when they were in her office. Very politely and with a pretty pleasant voice, she told the detectives that it would take her a couple of minutes to type the ID cards for them. Andy said it was okay to wait there, but Karla decided that it was best for them to wait in the small waiting room outside her office.

Once seated there, Karla told Andy, "These people are lying to us. I am not sure what is going on, but I saw the reflection of the computer screen in the glass of Doctor King's picture. I tell you that Clarissa was only pretending to be looking on her files for our guy. I am willing to bet that that attractive secretary there will not be very helpful to us either. But I do have an idea. However, for it to work, you need to get that bitch out of her desk. I have in my purse a computer program called PCAnywhere, which I can put into their computer—in case they don't have one on it already—and with it, I can transfer all their data to the computer in my office."

"But that would be illegal, and even if we find something, we won't be able to use it against them because it was obtained illegally," responded Andy.

"I know that Detective, but at least if we find something, then we could get a court order to subpoena the files," said Karla.

"Supposing that you can do that, how do you propose we get her off her desk?"

"Oh, that shall be your job. The girl likes you; I am sure of that." You could ask her to accompany you around or to drink a cup of coffee; it may not be that hard. Clarissa probably instructed her to keep an eye on us anyway. I shall need about twenty to thirty minutes, less if they already have that program installed on their computer. "Go get her, Detective!" Karla teased him.

Andy got up from his chair, walked into the next room, and approached the secretary's desk, smiling the most charming smile he could muster as he said to her, "I hope that you won't mind if I sit in front of your desk while you type our ID cards, do you, Ms. Sherman? My associate seems to be fascinated with an article in one of your magazines, and she is not providing much of a conversation."

"Oh, not at all, Detective. In fact, I am just finishing with the ID cards," the secretary answered, pulling them out of a printer and placing them inside a plastic cover.

"Oh, shut up!" he said, pretending to be disappointed. "I was hoping for a longer time to admire your beauty."

"You are a flirt, Detective," she said, pretending to be annoyed. "I am a married woman and mother of two teenage kids."

Andy said, "And I am willing to bet you look like their younger sister when you go out together."

"That is enough, Detective. Flattering will take you nowhere. Besides, you are not very good with lies," Mrs. Sherman said.

"Ok, but you have to admit to yourself that you do not look like the mother of teenagers and that you are a very attractive woman, too."

"If you say so, Detective." She smiled.

"I do say so, and I apologize if my words sounded like a pickup line. It must be the Latin on me. I cannot help but say a compliment whenever I am in front of a beautiful woman…oops, sorry! Here I go again. It's best to keep my mouth shut and take those cards to my partner out there. Thank you very much." Andy's words sounded sincere.

He was rewarded with another smile from the woman—this one a more coquetteish one—as she handled the ID cards for him. Then he left to go back to the waiting room, where Karla was waiting, pretending to read a magazine.

"I do not think she likes me," he lied to her. "It would be hard to make her leave her desk. Besides, she is a married woman."

"You are the biggest liar, Detective Garcia," said Karla. "I saw you talking to that woman, and she almost threw herself on the floor in front of you. Go tell her something to get her out of that office. I have the PCanywhere program here with me. Now go. We do not have all day!"

"What about you? What should I tell her about you?" Andy responded without challenging her perception of things, even though Karla appeared to be more amused than anything else.

Andy approached Wanda Sherman's desk again. She did not seem surprised or annoyed. She was showing that gorgeous smile of hers.

"Mrs. Sherman, I am sorry to be a pest, but my partner is not feeling very well. I think she suffers from irritable bowel syndrome or something like that and needs to use the lady's room. And, with your pardon to be so graphic, when she gets an attack of that, it takes her a while to get out of the lavatory.... If you know what I mean. So, would you be kind enough to accompany me on the tour of the institute?"

"But I have work to do. Besides, Mrs. Williams does not like us to leave our desks unattended," Wanda said with an unconvincing accent.

"I am sure Mrs. Williams won't be back again this afternoon. She told us that herself. Besides, she said that there are areas of the institute that we are not supposed to enter, and who would be better than you to keep me away from those areas?"

"Would your partner come also?" Wanda asked.

At that moment, Karla Colles walked in, looking very pale. (Andy knew it must be the makeup she was wearing, but she scared him. It was not until she winked an eye that he was reassured that she was only pretending to be sick.)

She said to Wanda: "I am sorry Mrs. Sherman, but I will join you shortly, right now, if you could please direct me to the closest restroom, I would appreciate it very much."

"There is one in this office, just behind that door; I am sorry you feel sick," Mrs. Sherman said without sincerity.

"Thank you. I will be Ok in a short time. These attacks do not last very long. I have some medicine here in my handbag," Karla said while walking in the direction of the restroom. She added, "I will call you on the cell to see where you are. Ok?" Without waiting for an answer, she disappeared behind the door.

"Well, I guess it is you and me only; please do the honors," Andy said while showing his arm to Wanda Sherman. She grabbed it and walked out of the office hanging off his arm.

Karla peered through the crack in the restroom door and prayed silently that Wanda would not turn the computer off.

Wanda Sherman did not turn the computer off.

THIRTEEN

After Doctor Kevin Nielsen left the Neurological Institute, he drove his yellow Hummer South in the direction of West Palm Beach; he was crying because he was in pain and also because of the humiliation, without being sure which hurt him more, the words of Dr. Bernstein or the knee in the crotch by the policeman.

He was doing almost 90 miles an hour on a road marked 55 MPH. and it took him a few minutes to realize that he was breaking the law by doing that. Not that he ever cared too much about respecting the law, but he remembered the words that Andy had said to him, and as much as he hated the guy, the idea of being thrown in jail with a bunch of drunk bikers did not appeal at all to him.

Slowing down to about 76 MPH, he grabbed his cell phone and dialed a number in the West Palm area. It was his lawyer's cell phone number. After a voice on the other end responded to his call, he proceeded to inform him that he had been the innocent victim of police brutality and described his version of the incident while requesting the lawyer to sue both detectives – although he only had the name of one-, the County Sheriff Department and the Neurological Institute for as many millions as he could possibly sue.

His lawyer informed him that he would look into the matter and ask if there were any witnesses to the incident. He mentioned the gate guard and the receptionist, and no, he did not know their names; it was not his policy to socialize with minor employees.

The lawyer informed him that if what he had told him was a fact, he may have a case against some, perhaps all, those people, but he would have to go down there and talk to the witness. He promised to do that first thing tomorrow morning and proceeded to inform him that his bill had already started to run, that he charged for over-the-phone consultations and thereafter by the hour, plus traveling and expenses, and that he was not a cheap lawyer.

Kevin said that money was not an object; all he wanted was, "—to get that son of a bitch cop out of the streets because he is dangerous. You know, it is not about money. It is about protecting the people from bad cops like him."

"Sure, sure—said the lawyer—it is never about money. People always have much higher and cleaner purposes when they sue. They all want to make this world safer for others."

Of course, Kevin failed to grasp the irony of the lawyer's words and felt very reassured that justice was on his side, and he would prevail… He was calmer now. Oh, revenge was so, so sweet!

Then he thought about Melvin's father and Doctor Bernstein, who—he sincerely believed—had betrayed him by failing on their promise to make him their assistant. "The bastards! But it may not be entirely their fault. If that guy Melvin hadn't come to the institute, they would have made him their assistant for sure."

"Perhaps they still would if this son of a bitch Melvin messes things up bad," he thought.

Kevin slowed down further; his original idea was to go to West Palm, get into a strip joint, get as drunk as he could possibly be, and perhaps, might get lucky and have a good fuck with one of the stripers. One thing was for sure: he planned never to go back to that blasted Neurological Institute, which he hoped would one day soon be blown up to kingdom come.

He continued having those thoughts repeatedly, but gradually, they were replaced by another, more sinister idea that started to take form in his head.

What if, instead of leaving the Institute, he could take Melvin down by making him screw up so badly that even his father would not want him to stay on board?

He parked on the side of the road, as the idea was taking shape and becoming increasingly feasible—at least in his mind.

After thinking hard for fifteen minutes or so, he turned the Hummer around and headed back to Indiantown and to the Institute.

Doctor Kevin Neilson, upon returning to the Institute, parked the yellow Hummer in a parking space he had painted with his name. As he walked through the lobby, Gladys, the receptionist, said to him, "Be careful, Doctor. Those detectives are still inside the building."

"They won't be around too long. My lawyer will get them out of here, out of town, out of the county, perhaps even out of the state," Kevin said, stopping for the first time since coming to the Institute a few months earlier to talk to the receptionist. "He would be here tomorrow, and you and that guard out there were witnesses of the way those cops treated me; you will tell him what you saw. Right?"

"Of course, Dr. Nielsen, of course," Gladys answered with some irony that the Intern did not catch.

Kevin Nielsen was not a hard-to-look-at guy; although thin and fragile, he was almost six feet tall, yet, because he had the habit of walking with his head down, and back bent, as if he was looking for something he had dropped on the floor, he gave the impression of being much shorter. His eyes were green behind gold-rimmed glasses, but they seemed cool and expressionless; his hair was honey-colored and always appeared to need combing. His face was elongated, and his mouth was small with thin lips, and perfectly white teeth, unfortunately, the cuspid teeth were a bit too long in comparison with the other teeth and that made him look like a vampire, a fact that he enjoyed but which combined with the expressionless eyes, gave him a bit of a sinister appearance.

Nevertheless, he enjoyed an estranged appeal to those of the opposite sex, an appeal that he was aware of and took quite a bit of advantage of. Oddly enough and unfortunately for him, this appeal did not work with Gladys Franklin, the woman to whom most men had an appeal.

Perhaps it was because that special sixth sense that women are said to possess warned her that the young Doctor was not only a coward and a spoiled rich brat but also an egomaniac and a user of people who could never forget a real or perceived offense.

Such was the man's who returned that afternoon to the Neurological Research Institute of Indiantown, with a desire for revenge in his heart.

Of course, Kevin did not want to encounter the detectives again, so before walking into the hallway, he made sure they were not around. With a fast pace—almost running—he reached the door of his office.

Once inside, he put on his lab coat, walked into the restroom, washed his face with cool water, combed his hair, and, exiting through a side door, entered the bio-research laboratory.

Kevin faked his best smile to the Korean scientist to whom he first ran and excused himself very politely for having left for the last two hours. However, he informed the oriental he was not feeling well and thought that he needed to go home and rest for the remainder of the afternoon. Now he felt better, and his sense of duty and desire to learn from such illustrious teachers as he—the Korean—was, made him return to work.

The Korean responded with equal courtesy and suggested that he go to see one of the physicians in the patient area or that, as far as he was concerned, he could most certainly take the rest of the day off.

"Oh no—Dr. Chong—I shall never do that. My stay here at the institute is only a few weeks long, and I want to take advantage of every minute of it. Thank you very much for your concern; I really appreciate that, thank you Sir," said Kevin and added: "In fact, I would like to make up for the time I took, so- if it is ok with you- perhaps I could work few extra hours in the evenings. I had in mind to ask you or your colleague Doctor Cho if it is ok with you all if I did do that."

"It is fine with me Kevin, and I am sure Celin—I mean Dr. Cho, would not mind either"

"Thank you, Doctor Chong, thank you very much," said Kevin while bowing to oriental style in front of the Korean. "Is there anything you want me to do right now, sir?"

"We just got a new batch of cisternal fluid from one of the patients, it needs mixing with the stem cells of another patient, and then later, perhaps not until tomorrow, either myself or Doctor Singh will add the nanoparticles, you can add the stem cells and place the mixture in the incubator, make sure the temperature is not higher than 96 degrees" .

"Yes, Doctor, right away! Is that specimen by any chance that of the man they call "Homeless Tony?"

"Oh no, I do not think we will get a specimen from that patient until tomorrow, probably. Why do you ask?" said Dr. Chong.

"It's just scientific curiosity, Doctor Chong. Everybody seems to be very excited about that case, but I am not certain why," said Kevin, pretending great interest.

"Well, it seems that the man is a drug addict and has used every drug you can imagine since he was about 12 years old. We are hoping to cure his drug addiction by injecting him with the cells of a person who has never used drugs, and Dr. Sing and Dr. Mitt have been programming their nanoparticles to make the man forget about his habit…Just imagine, if we are successful, we may be able to free mankind from drug addicts."

Kevin, who had smoked marijuana and used cocaine off and on, with the good fortune of not being addicted to either, thought that the drug lords of Latin America and Asia would not be glad if they were aware of those experiments; perhaps there was some money to be made there…if he knew any drug lord. Perhaps Tony, the Cuban from whom he made his purchases, knew the person to talk to; it seems that luck was on his side; he had found another way to consume his revenge, but that one would have to wait.

As the Korean Doctor walked Kevin toward the incubator where he was supposed to be working, they passed in front of three or four incubators labeled with red tags. He knew what those were but found it reassuring to remark, "Why do we keep the cells of the bad guys here? Would not it be best to discard those?"

"Scientific curiosity, my good Doctor, scientific curiosity, none of us wants to discard those specimens. You are right; they belong to some bad people, but maybe we can also correct that one day." With those words, Doctor Chong left Kevin at the incubator where he was supposed to work that afternoon after giving him careful instructions on performing a procedure he had already done several times.

Kevin enthusiastically took to his task and took special care in performing it. He did not want to mess up, not now that he was so close to his revenge.

FOURTEEN

Meanwhile, Detective Garcia and Wanda Sherman, Carlessa Williams's attractive secretary, were making the rounds, starting in the further portion of the outside grounds.

Andy had done this at Karla's suggestion, who wanted to keep the secretary as far away from her office as possible and because he felt that the groundkeepers were most likely to be Hispanics. He could talk to them in Spanish without Mrs. Sherman's interfering or understanding.

Andy had already find out that Wanda did not speak Spanish and also that Sherman was her married name, her husband, a native of Illinois, probably being a descendant of the infamous Civil War General: William Tecumseh Sherman, to whom the Southerners, to this day blame for the burning of Atlanta GA, and Columbia SC, when in reality he did only burn about a third of Atlanta—primarily the railroad and military installations—and in South Carolina he never actually ordered the burning of that city, true, it was his men who did the burning but they were not acting on orders of the general.

Oddly enough, Wanda's family came to Florida from South Carolina, but Andy soon realized that although the woman had some education, it did not include much knowledge of history.

After the couple walked out of the institute and into the well-manicured grounds, Andy spotted two dark Latinos working on trimming a hedge and he approached them to show the photo of Ismael Torres.

At first they hesitated to talk to him but Wanda gave a nod of encouragement and they started talking: *"Creemos que si hemos visto a este hombre, pero no es de los que trabajamos afuera, parece que es de los Erre-Eses, que son los que trabajan adentro y como que no hacen nada y les tratan mejor que a nosotros. Ya hace rato que no lo hemos visto, pregúnteles a aquellos que están jugando futbol allí, son Erre-Eses también y a lo mejor ellos le pueden informar algo más."*

TRANSLATION: "We think that we have seen that man, but he is not of the ones who work outside; we believe he is an R-S. Those people work inside and, as far as we know, do not do too much. Yet they are treated very well, much better than us. However, we have not seen him lately. Why don't you ask them? They are playing soccer right over there; all of them are R-S, and perhaps they can tell you more," the men said, pointing to a group of about ten guys playing soccer further down the field.

Andy thanked the men in Spanish and started to walk towards the soccer players. Wanda, pulling him by the sleeve, made him turn around as she asked, "Where are you going?"

"To show the picture of my murder victim to those guys, and ask few questions, of course."

"Sorry, you can't do that; those are patients and Mrs. Williams was clear to me that you could not go into the inpatient area, nor talk to the patients."

"They do not look sick to me, Mrs. Sherman. Are you sure they are patients?"

"Positive, Detective, I work here, remember, and I have everyone who works—or lives in the compound–on my computer."

"Of course you do, Wanda. That is too bad. I love to play soccer with them, but I guess that would have to wait." Andy did not want to upset her and was wondering how Karla was doing with that very same computer of hers. She would have to call soon so the secretary would not become suspicious, and he would have to continue using his charm.

"One question, and it is ok if you do not want to give me an answer because really, it probably does not have anything to do with my investigation. What do the letters R-S on those Soccer players' shirts stand for?"

"You are right, and I am sorry. I am not in liberty of answering that question either; perhaps you can ask Mrs. Williams on another occasion."

"Yes, of course, no hard feelings," Andy said, forcing his best smile. At that point, his cell phone rang.

It was Karla, she was into the computer, and she had installed "PCanywhere" into the institute's computer and was in the process of start transmitting all the files to her computer.

Although the process did not require her continuous physical presence, it may take a while to transfer the files, and she would prefer to be able to uninstall her program before leaving the institute. She asked Andy to tell Mrs. Sherman that she was going to interview the people in the offices, janitors etc., while they worked at the other end of the building and please to take her to have a cup of coffee and make sure it takes long time to drink it.

Detective Karla Colles was perspiring heavily. She had installed the program on the Institute's computer and was in the process of transferring the data to her own home computer.

She preferred to do it that way for two reasons: first, she knew that what she was doing was illegal and did not want to implicate the Sheriff's Department in case she was discovered. Second, she would have more time to look through the data without anyone at the office looking over her shoulder.

She planned to uninstall the PC-Anywhere program after she finished transferring the files. But just in case someone walked in while she was at the computer, she was careful to remove the program icon from the desktop of the institute's computer. Since the computer was able to do the job without her being in front of it, she called Andy on her cell phone.

She proceeded to do as she told him, interviewing the reception offices, business office employees, janitors, security guards, etc. Some people seemed to recognize the person in the picture, but no one appeared to have known him or even be sure that he ever worked there. She found it surprising that the security people claimed to have never seen the man, especially since she was able to walk into their offices and saw that they have surveillance equipment much more sophisticated and modern than the one they had at the Sheriff's office.

Karla knew, or at least hoped, that the "Cuban" detective had enough sense not to call her on the cell phone because if she was still using the computer at Wanda Sherman's office, the ring of that phone could certainly give her away, and then all hell would get loose. So, as she was heading back to Carlessa Williams's office, she dialed Andy's cell phone.

It took a few rings before he answered, and when he did, he informed her that he was still with Mrs. Sherman, having a cup of coffee at the cafeteria, and that she was welcome to join them.

For some reason, it bothered her to hear the woman's laughter at the other end of the line; it sounded as if they were enjoying each other, Andy and Mrs. Sherman.... Was she jealous? She dismissed the idea as stupid and informed the Detective that she was going to the woman's office to see if the program had finished being transmitted to her computer.

Then, she regretted calling for another reason: her call had made Wanda aware that she had been away from her office too long, and she had told Andy that she had to return.

Karla walked in to the office and glanced at the computer, it was still transmitting data but it was now on the letter W. Realizing that there were a lot of English last names starting with that letter, she did not know if she should stop the transmission at that point or continue to the end, after all they were interested in Spanish names, she could not remember any that started with W and same for those starting with X,Y or Z., so she pushed few keys on the computer key board and stop the transmission, leaving the program installed but with the Icon hidden. Then she walked out of the office and towards the cafeteria.

Her timing could not have been more perfect. His partner and Mrs. Sherman were almost at the door when Karla walked in.

"Whoa! I am really sorry. I am too late to share that cup of coffee with you guys. That is too bad because with these migraine attacks I get. Caffeine sometimes helps."

"Oh, you suffer from migraines? "Your partner here seems to think that it was something related to the colon," said Wanda.

"Well, he does not know; in fact, he does not know much about me at all. We have just been assigned to work together in this case for less than two weeks, because his partner is in the hospital. Besides, he likes to tease people, including me. He is one of those men who does not have an idea of what constitutes a joke and what could be offensive."

She said that with some rage that did not pass unnoticed by Wanda who said: "Well the important thing is that you feel better now, and you look better."

"Thank you. I have a pill that the doctor prescribed and, if I take that at the onset of the attack, it is possible to abort it most times."

"Thank God! You are lucky, a cousin of mine has migraines and nothing helps her. Sometimes she has to be in a dark room and totally quiet for two or three days before it goes away. You should give me the name of your medicine, so she could ask her physician for a prescription. Could you do that for me?"

"It is called Imitrex, but it is my understanding that are other newer medicines, as good or better than that one," Karla told her and started to think that the woman was not so bad after all. In fact she could be rather likable.

"Go have your coffee, dear. I am sure Mr. Garcia would not mind keeping you company. I have to go back to my office anyway. It was very nice to meet you both." She shook hands and smiled as she left.

"What was that all about?" asked Andy. "Is it true that you suffer from migraines?"

"Well, it is less embarrassing than having diarrhea, but yes, I used to suffer from migraines and still do, albeit much less often than in the past. And yes, I use Imitrex, and also yes, it does help most of the time. Oh, and a final yes, I do want a cup of coffee, and no, I did not appreciate you telling that woman that I have a colon problem."

"I am sorry, but I was the first thing that came to my mind. Besides, you did appear to be sick back there. And if my apology is not enough, I shall drink another cup of coffee with you even if I have to stay up all night between the effects of the caffeine in my brain and the bladder—the coffee by the way is rather good here," said Andy and added, "Now, going back to business, did you accomplish your goal?"

"Almost, but I tell you all about it in the car on the way back. I have the feeling that the walls have ears in this place," says Karla.

"Why do you think so?" Andy inquired.

"I would tell you that, too, in the car. Let's now have that coffee, ok?"

FIFTEEN

Kevin's plan was diabolically simple. All he had to do was contaminate the spinal fluid specimens that Melvin Bright was going to inject into patients during the next few days by mixing them with specimens from other subjects or even the animals that the laboratory had been experimenting with.

Of course, it was likely that the subjects would get very sick, suffer brain damage, or die. Still, Kevin did not care. After all, that was exactly the reason for his actions. Whatever happens to the subjects will be blamed on Doctor Bright's son.

Besides, who would care about those individuals who submitted themselves to be guinea pigs for money? They were either a bunch of illegal aliens or a few street dwellers who would be better off dead anyway.

As far as the illegal aliens was concerned, he thought that he may even be doing a favor to the United States of America by eliminating some of those leeches that not only came to his country illegally and took jobs away from full blooded Americans, but also cost the taxpayers billions of dollars in educating their kids and providing health care for them...

And the same for the homeless; everybody would be better off if they disappeared. Never, not even for a second, did Kevin stop to consider that all those were human beings, not much different from him, except for being less lucky and born in a different country or environment.

Kevin's only concern was being discovered, but so what? If he was found, he would play stupid and pretend he made a mistake.

If worse came to worse he would leave the blasted institute and look up that drug dealer he knew, because although it was evident that the man was only a tiny peon in the big chess game of drug dealing, he would know people up the ladder who would be interested in stopping these people from developing a cure for drug addiction.

They would be willing to pay really big bucks for such valuable information, but although he thought about doing both of those things, especially if he did not get the job he wanted, he would take care of one thing at a time; right now, his main goal was to ruin the young doctor Bright.

As Kevin had announced earlier—after most of the technicians left at five o'clock or shortly thereafter, to the Korean scientist who ran the laboratory—he remained in the lab.

Only a couple of scientists and technicians remained, and Kevin used his best charm to subtly obtain information as to the location of the incubators in which the fluids that were going to be used over the next few days were located.

He was unable to obtain information as to who the patients were or who was going to perform the procedures, but he knew that only Dr. Paul Bernstein and Dr. David Bright performed them. Since it was clear that Doctor Bright had brought in his son to substitute Dr. Bernstein in that area of their work, one of the two Doctors Bright would be doing them.

Kevin knew where some old specimens of cisternal fluid were stored and knew that those belonged to sick or dangerous individuals. He also knew where the fluids of animals from the veterinary department were stored. He just hoped none of those places were locked. If they were locked, he would have to wait another day or two for the opportunity to get to the keys and take molds of them.

He was lucky. Not only were the places he wanted to reach unlocked, but the lights had been turned off in the part of the laboratory where they were located. Additionally, the few people who were still there were busy on the other side of the room, and one technician was on her coffee break.

The video surveillance cameras were on, however.

Kevin did not even look at the names or labels. With the hypodermic syringes he was carrying, he withdrew fluid from several different vials and then moved to the area of the animal specimens and did the same. He capped the syringes and put them in the pockets of his lab gown. In his hurry, he did not think of placing labels on the syringes. There would be no way for him to tell the human and animal samples apart, but he did not care.

Next, he pretended to check the controls of all the machinery and incubators in the place. When he got to those scheduled to be transplanted into the human subjects over the next week or so, he randomly put half a cubic centimeter on each one from the syringes he had in his pockets. However, since the institute did not do those procedures on a daily basis, nor in great quantities, he was able to contaminate only three specimens.

Now, he needed to get rid of the syringes that he had in his pockets, but it was dangerous to do that right there at the Laboratory.

It was also not good that he left the lab right away without arousing suspicion, so he decided to hang around for a couple more hours after stuffing some Kleenex tissues in his lab coat pockets to hide the syringes. Later, he would throw those somewhere along the road on his way back home.

When the night watchman came around and announced that it was almost nine o'clock, the few people left decided to call it a night and go home. Kevin perspired heavily as he saw the supervisor examining the very same incubators where he had tampered with the specimens, but she did not seem to notice anything out of the ordinary. Turning the lights off, she said goodnight to Kevin, who actually walked out ahead of her.

He went into his small office just to get his car keys and jacket and walked out of the Institute still wearing the lab coat. Of course, nobody paid much attention to this because many employees did that to take home the gown and wash it—except that nobody had seen Kevin do that before.

Once in the street, at the wheel of his yellow Hummer, Kevin congratulated himself for his cleverness and anticipated what would happen to the miserable soul who would be injected with the specimens by his rival, Doctor Bright.

His confidence was slightly shattered when he detected that Melvin Bright had evidently also worked late and was getting in his car at the same time he did; he was not sure if Bright had seen him, and it really did not matter, but the fact is that he became a bit nervous.

Doctor Kevin Nelson would have felt even more confident if he had known that the young Doctor Bright's nickname was Doctor "Not-so" Bright.

At the time those events occurred, Andy Garcia and Karla Colles had gone separate ways. While Karla was feverishly working on her computer at home, Andy was watching *Lost* on TV.

The afternoon had been enjoyable, especially for him, because although Karla was at the moment pissed off at him –supposedly about the thing he told Wanda Sherman about her having a colon problem- but he was hoping it would be mainly because she was a little bit jealous. It was too bad that his nurse lover was on duty that night. He could enjoy her company, if anything, not to think so much about Karla Colles.

She had not been very talkative on their drive back to Fort Pierce; her conversation was limited to describing her ability to break into the woman's computer and transmit the data to her home computer.

And, no, she was not sure if she had been able to transmit everything because she had to stop running the program as he and Wanda were getting back. Still, yes, like Andy, she had the impression that Mrs. Williams knew exactly who the dead man was, and that he had worked at the institute because other employees appeared to have seen him there and then no more.

Andy told her about his experience with the soccer players, his curiosity as to what the initials R-S in their uniforms meant, and why Wanda prevented him from talking to the men.

They both commented on the institute's strict security and the presence of video cameras everywhere. She told Andy that she had visited the center of that security system and was impressed by its technology.

However, she did make sure that her tampering with the computer was not detected. She worked fast, away from the camera, and most of the work she did with her back turned toward the video camera.

Andy agreed on that point, as he thought that they would have been detained, cops or not, if that activity was detected.

The men at the video screens were probably more interested in watching her sexy walk than in anything else.

With little else to say, they drove back to the St. Lucie County Sheriff's office, where each one reported their return to their superiors; they walked toward their parked vehicles to head home.

As Andy was starting his car, Karla walked towards his window and said, "I am going to start looking at whatever information was transmitted to my computer. It probably will work all night, so I shall call you first thing in the morning. Please try not to be too crabby." Handing him a piece of paper, she said, "That is my address, and you know my cell number."

With this, she walked back to her car. Andy wanted to say that he would be glad to work with her all night, but he knew that she would know that working was probably not what he had in mind, so he started his car and drove away.

SIXTEEN

Andy Garcia, "The Cuban" was hoping that when Karla had said she was going to call early, it was supposed to be at least sometime after eight am, he was not pleased when the cell phone rang at barely quarter to six, and it was her.

"I know you won't appreciate my call this early, but I have been on this blasted computer all night, and there is a lot of important information that I must share with you before we can plan the next step."

As he answered by a caveman-like grunt, Karla continued, "Come on, do not be crabby, I promise that I fix you a good breakfast with lots of fresh black coffee to wake you up. Hope did not wake up your nurse friend", she ended with a giggle

Caught off guard, he grunted, "She is not here, she does not live here," and then he was going to add, "How in hell do you know about her?" But she was gone.

Reluctantly and swearing at everything and everyone, he got in the shower, which, to make things worse, dispensed only tepid, almost cold water. He cursed the landlord and promised himself that he was going to shoot the man if he did not fix the water heater. After taking the shower, he actually felt better and was surprisingly awake. He decided not to shoot the landlord after all, but if the heater was not fixed by the end of the month, he would hold the rent until he had it done.

He thought it might be a better idea to take cold showers when he had to get up early in the mornings, although he had always considered such a practice highly uncivilized.

Once he had showered, he dressed up quickly. He wore kaki Docker pants, brown polo shirt socks to match the pants, and brown letter shoes. Although he preferred to wear sneakers and T-shirts, the department's dress code called for more serious attire. He had to be thankful that it was not mandatory for him to wear uniforms anymore, not even the polo shirt with the Sheriff's Department logo.

Before Andy found the address on Second Street and Ocean Drive, he knew he was close because of the aroma of fresh coffee, fried eggs and sausage—or was it bacon—and fresh baked bread could be detected from at least half block away from the charming little house at the end of the street, a house, like the many around it, that spoke of times gone by, of fishermen and of times past and gone forever.

Like the homes around it, the house had been remodeled, and a new, freshly painted picket fence, with a gate of similar material, opened into a small but well-manicured flower garden.

He parked by the curve and walked to the gate, which, as expected, was not locked. Neither was the front door, from which the aroma of the food was coming stronger.

He opened the door, but then closed it again and rang the bell, Karla's voice responded to it, saying:

"The door is open, just follow the smell of the food, I am in the kitchen."

The house was as charming inside as it was outside, beautifully decorated in early American style, with two wooden rocking chairs at each end of a comfortable couch, in front of which a flat color television set, was hidden inside of a matching wood cabinet, shelves with old American and Native American knick-knacks and memorabilia decorated the small tables surrounding the room and the shelves around it, which also held many volumes of books which have been read perhaps more than once. An old musket was decorating the wall, and several guns and rifles were on a locked cabinet.

Separated from the living room by a wall made of bookcases, was the small dining room and kitchen, were breakfast was served on a wood table, also early American style, on it was the breakfast consisting of a basket of fresh backed biscuits, a container with white, creamy gravy, a large serving plate with half a dozen of fried eggs, sunny side up, a pitcher of orange juice, another container with bacon and sausage links and fresh smelling coffee, all served on fine china.

"Lovely place you have here, but I feel guilty that you had to go through all this for me. I am not used to this luxury, but thanks anyway," said Andy,

"Not to mention it, I usually have a big and hearty breakfast myself. I try to make it the largest meal of my day. You know what they say: breakfast like a queen, lunch like a princess, and dine like a pauper to be healthy. As for china, it was a gift from my mother when I moved here from Gainesville. I love it, and I like to use it often in order to remember her. But do not stand there, sit and eat because we have work to do before going to the office."

She was a very pretty sight that morning. Her hair was loose and down to her shoulders. A simple, no-logo T-shirt covered her chest, and yes—in spite of Andy's hopes—she was wearing a bra under it. She had low-waisted faded jeans and beach sandals on her feet. Andy thought she was as adorable as the morning. That was until he remembered that he hated mornings…but certainly not this one.

He ate with an appetite that he did not know he had, and before he knew it, he had gulped down three eggs, with several pieces of bacon and sausage and several more of the biscuits socked in the gravy, all of which he thought was delicious. She had been talking through the meal, and henceforth, she had eaten very little. She was very excited about what she had found in the computer, but Andy had been so fascinated watching her and eating the delicious food she had prepared that very little attention was paid to it.

When Karla decided he had eaten enough, she told Andy to grab his coffee and follow her.

She took him to a room that worked as a den and an office where she had two computers, printers, faxes, etc. She sat in front of one of the computers that was already on. She pointed to a chair, asked Andy to bring it close to the computer and invited him to sit down.

She had been very formal during the meal and continued to be so; it was obvious that she was very excited. "As I was telling you, detective." she said I did not go to bed until the wee hours of the morning because since I came home last evening. I have been in front of this computer. It was rewarding and very informative. Let me show you."

After pressing a couple of keys, she worked the mouse on the screen, and several faces of men and some women started appearing on the monitor.

"Look at these men, Detective," Karla said. "First of all, all the men who have died—including those who had the chemical 'Versed' in their blood— had been working for that Neurological Institute probably until the time of their deaths."

"Second, they did belong to a group of workers who do not have a job description. See for yourself, even the top executives have a job description or at least a title, seen there is Dr. Bernstein, the head honcho, here is Claressa Williams, and your friend Mrs. Sherman, and the gate security guard, Mr. Smith, and there are janitors, ground keepers, physicians, radiologists, technicians, lab techs, etc.., followed by a brief job description. But our guy and all the other dead ones—plus few more that I found—are only listed as R-S."

"Maybe that means "Rest his soul," Andy said jokingly

That did not amuse Karla, who continued, "There are still many more living men who also have R-S as a job description, but I have not discovered what that means."

"What are those other letters and numbers at the bottom of the files of the dead ones? I do not see the same letters, although I see the same numbers on the R-S ones who are alive. See there?"

"It says 25 pd on the death ones, but only 25 on the living ones, except on our Mister Torres."

"I did notice that, but I have not been able to figure it out yet. I was hoping that you could help on that one."

"I must certainly try, but right now I am so full, that I cannot think."

"Not my fault. I fixed the food. You ate it"

"*Mea culpa*, I assume full responsibility for my actions." He was close to her and could smell the fresh shampoo on her hair.

She moved away.

They had worked for almost two hours and it was time to report to the office; she was the first one to remind him of that, so he got up thank her again for the breakfast and walked out after a feeble attempt to give her a peek in the check, which she rejected pushing him away gently and saying with a million dollar smile: "let's keep this at a professional level, your thanks and enjoyment of the breakfast is more than plenty. See you at the office in a little while."

He drove away from her home flabbergasted. He could not figure out this woman and she was beginning to drive him crazy. There was a moment at her house where he was sure that she would respond favorably when he felt the urge to kiss her, but now, he was glad he did not try that. Most likely, she would have slapped him across the face.

He tried to forget about it. Who understands women anyway? Through the centuries, poets and writers have tried and, still, it is impossible to figure them out.

Much to everyone's surprise, he showed up early at the office and looked surprisingly cheerful. He started his computer, waited several minutes, checked his watch to make sure it was already nine o'clock, and started making phone calls.

When Karla Colles walked in at about 10 after nine, Andy barely waved at her and continued to stay busy on the phones and the computer.

He continued doing so all morning and through lunch hour. When everyone returned from lunch, he was resting with his legs on his desk and had a big, satisfying smile on his face when Karla walked back in.

One of the other officers commented to her: "Would you believe it, Colles?—the man said—"The Cuban not only came to work early but he has not moved from that desk in the whole morning. He did not even take a lunch break. I am not sure what is going on"

Much to her surprise, Karla answered somewhat rudely: "He is not Cuban. He is American. His parents came here from Mexico several generations ago, probably before your ancestors or mine came to the US. Check his file if you do not believe me."

The man brief response was simply, "Sorry. I guess I was just trying to be funny."

"You weren't", Karla said, walking to her desk. As she sat, her phone rang.

"Hi! It is your new partner across the room from your office. I think I have good news for you; would you like to walk over to my office or me to go to yours?"-He said

"Is it classified?" she asked

"Yes, it is somewhat classified, considering our computer caper of yesterday," Andy responded.

"Then I better walk to your office. It seems to have more privacy than mine. If you can call my little cubicle an office, at least yours has a door. I'll be there in a few minutes."

Even though she was modestly dressed and her clothes were not revealing, all the heads of the men at the office turned to follow her as she walked to Andy's office. The women's heads also turned to observe the men and to criticize them, not because they disliked Karla, but quite the contrary; she was well-liked and well-regarded by her women colleagues, but they felt offended by the men's attitude. Some of them murmured not too subtly the words: "all men are Pigs"

Andy got up when Karla walked into his office and offered her a seat, then he said: "I've been on the phones and on the computer all morning, but I think that I found out some things that may be of interest to you."

"First, I spoke with Doctor Raymond, at the Medical Examiner's office and he informed me that no one has reclaimed the body of Mr. Torres as yet, but that there was a call from the office of that Stuart lawyer requesting a copy of the death certificate. Thereafter the good doctor helped me to figure out what the initials R-S mean for those people who work or worked at the institute. He thinks it means RESEARCH SUBJECTS. In other words that those men are hired to participate in some kind of experimental treatment."

"That would explain the anesthetic and the secrecy of the institute, but if those people died accidentally during some experiment, why they did not just bury the bodies in some remote area or dumped them in the ocean?" Karla said.

"I asked myself the very same question many, many times until just recently when I received my credit card bill in the mail," said Garcia.

"Are you kidding? What the heck does your credit card bill have to do with a multiple murder case?" inquired Detective Colles.

"Nothing really, except that it opened my mind to a possible motive; remember the numbers at the bottom of the files of the Research Subjects?"

"Assuming that is what R-S stand for" corrected Karla

"Yeah, yeah, assuming that, but I believe the doctor is right on the money. Anyway there were the numbers 25 and in some of the death ones next to it the letters 'pd' that is where my credit card bill helped me to understand, 'pd' means paid... I believed those men were insured and whoever collected the Insurance money needed a body to be paid." – explained Andy.

"All that sounds great in theory, but who would take risks of being jailed for meager twenty-five thousand dollars? We already know that the law firm of Williams paid for the bodies to be shipped to their home countries and then probably paid an additional twenty-five grand to the families...I fail to see where the gain would be?" argued Karla.

"What if it is not twenty-five thousand but two hundred and fifty thousand? That is a quarter of a million dollars apiece, and we do not know yet how many of those people died."

"I do," Karla said. "It was in the computer. A total of eleven, perhaps twelve men died, or disappeared, or left. But only the last eight—actually, nine, if we count Mr. Torres—had the 25 numbers on their files."

"Don't you see? It is quite obvious. Perhaps accidents started to happen to those research subjects and after that someone had the idea of insuring them to profit from their deaths. It is also possible that once they were insured, their deaths were not so accidental."

"There is no question that you have a vivid imagination, Detective Garcia. Do you read a lot of science fiction novels?" Karla said in a joking way.

"Oh, but there is more," Garcia said. "Remember Mrs. Williams, Carlessa Williams, the head of human resources at the institute?"

"Sure, the one who did not remember that Torres ever worked there." And then she added the one with the very attractive secretary, what was her name? Oh yes, Mrs. Sherman, the one who thinks that I have a colon problem. Yes, I do remember them very well."

"Well, you be surprised to know that she has a record in Saint Lucie County," Andy told her.

"You kidding, the well-mannered, elegant Mrs. Williams has a criminal record? Whoa!"

"Well, it is nothing big, and the charges were dismissed, but she was accused of helping and protecting a fugitive criminal, who happens to be her brother," Andy said and added, "Remember when you stated that Williams was a very common name? Well, it is, but that is her married name. Her maiden name is Taylor, and she is the sister of Jerome Taylor."

"Jerome Taylor? The Jerome Taylor? The well-know leader of one of the most dangerous gangs of Fort Pierce?" asked Karla.

"That's right, that very same Jerome Taylor, who has been in and out of detention since he was 10 years old, the same one that was in jail for armed robbery and managed to do only two of the 10 years he was supposed to do, the one who is now free after being the suspect of killing a man in front of a bunch of people who suddenly lost their collective memory and could not remember how the shooter looked like, that Jerome Taylor who incidentally was a close friend of the man who shot my partner Frank."

"Whoa, isn't this a small world?" commented Sergeant Colles.

"That is the good news. The bad news is that we cannot use most of this information because we obtained it illegally. We cannot tell anyone about it, not even the sheriff; it may get us both fired," stated Garcia.

"You can use the part discussed with Doctor Raymond; after all, you saw the people wearing the uniforms with the R-S logo when you visited the Institute," suggested Karla.

"True, and perhaps I could tell him that the employees gave me a hint about the insurance. Perhaps we could obtain financial records and bank statements if the DA agrees that there is enough ground for being suspicious about those people," Andy said.

"Perhaps we should talk with the boss first and then see if he agrees to talk with the DA," said Karla.

"Let's not rush into it. First, let me type a report of our trip to Indiantown. I will put some adornments in it. Then, before I submit it to the boss, I shall run it by you to see if you have any suggestions. And not until after we do that will we show it to the boss. Agreed?" said Andy.

"Sounds good to me," responded Karla. "Perhaps we should also make another trip to that institute and this time talk to one of the head honchos. What are their names, Bernstein and Bright?" Colles said.

"I think so, and I also think it is a very good Idea, but we still have to justify another trip out of the county, so the sheriff has to see my report first," said Garcia.

"I am cool with that," ended Colles.

SEVENTEEN

Melvin "not-so" Bright was very worried, he was at the moment taking the blood pressure, pulse and Oximetry on his patient for –at least- the twentieth time, under the careful watch of his father and "Uncle Paul", who were also checking the neurological status of the patient for at least the fifth time in the last hour.

They were able to stop the seizures, first with Valium IV and then with Phenobarbital and Dilantin, but the patient required multiple and high doses before he stopped seizing.

Now the man was in a deep coma, and the doctors were not sure if it was because of the original insult to the brain or due to the effect of the drugs. They will have to wait and see; meanwhile, assuming that there was some degree of cerebral edema, they were injecting through the IV high doses of corticosteroids and lowering his body temperature with cooling blankets.

All that, they all hoped, would prevent "Homeless Tony" from developing permanent brain damage.

Several people were watching, primarily people from the laboratory and radiology; from the back of the crowd somebody said: "I am sure he hit some part of the brain, it is his entire fault."

Although nobody paid attention to the remark, some people heard it clearly, and they commented that it came from Doctor Kevin Nielsen.

At that very moment, another voice, a very thunderous one at that, resounded above the people gathering: "No, he did not. Actually, the procedure was flawless, and I have the CT films right here in my hands to prove it."

The voice belonged to the gigantic Doctor Raj Dramsjold, who was holding several films on his hand, while effortlessly making his way through the group while adding:

"Doctor Bright, do you think your patient is stable enough to perform an MRI on him?"

Melvin did not know what to answer, but he thanked the doctor from the bottom of his heart.

He knew that the voice from behind had said, before Dr. Dramsjold intervened, was the same thought that probably was in the minds of all those present, including his father and "Uncle Paul."

"We believe he is," answered Dr. Bernstein. "And I would really appreciate it if everyone returned to their duties. Only Doctors Bright and Dramsjold and two nurses will remain with the patient. "

Since the cisternal tap was done at the Radiology department, with patients resting on a stretcher and medications always at hand, in case of emergency, immediate care was administered to the man everyone called "Homeless Tony" and now only had to be moved few feet to be placed on the MRI machine. This procedure was done with some difficulty since the patient was not only sedated but an endotracheal tube had been placed in his throat. He was being artificially ventilated by a machine, which supplied additional oxygen to the intubated man.

"Mild cerebral edema, as you suspected. Otherwise, the MRI is normal," Dr. Raj Dramsjold told the physicians present. I think your patient is going to be okay, personally. It may take several days, but he will recover. "I would like to scan him with BANDI after a day or two," he said, adding, "Do you doctors know what happened to this guy?"

Melvin answered, "I do not know what happened. I just finished injecting the liquid that was brought to me from the lab by the technician, and the next thing I knew, the man started convulsing." Then, addressing his father, he said, "Does this happen often, Dad? "

Paul Bernstein answered: "We had some adverse outcomes in the past, but no one had seizures after the procedure before. We had anticipated that possibility and that is why the patients are sedated with Versed for anesthesia and Valium to prevent seizures."

The senior Doctor Bright added: "I want whatever residual material is on the syringe we used tested for everything, including DNA analysis. We shall stop further experiments until every sample in that lab is similarly analyzed. I will tell Doctors Cho, Ching, Mitt, and Singh to do so, in case they are not already starting to do it"

"Let's take your patient to the ICU, son. You are responsible for his care, and Paul and I will assist you as neurology consultants. Do not forget to order bacterial, viral, and fungal cultures to be done on all the fluids. Order a PCR on the spinal fluid to have a fast preliminary report to detect any possible infection. We shall start him on triple antibiotic therapy as well as antiviral and anti-fungal medications, until we get final results on those tests."

Melvin was feeling very much like a "Not-So-Bright." He was pale and shaking, but he felt a jolt of reassurance when his father patted him on the shoulder and said, "You did very well today, son. I also think that your patient will make it."

Melvin thought, "Yes, maybe, but in what shape?" Perhaps as a vegetable? But he was afraid to verbalize his concerns and just smiled while saying, "Thank you, Dad!"

He felt much better when he saw Jasmine Porter entering the hallway as he and the male nurse pushed the stretcher. Her smile was more reassuring than any word that any of the medical geniuses around him could be. She just came alongside him, squeezed his hand, and asked, "Are you all right, Melvin? Do not worry. Mr. Tony will be just fine. You will see."

Everyone—except Melvin—had been correct. "Homeless Tony" pulled the endotracheal tube that very same afternoon and could breathe well on his own.

By the following morning, he was sitting in bed and requesting breakfast, which he ate with a voracious appetite. By the afternoon of the second day, he was out of the ICU and back in his room, and by evening, he was walking with only minimal help from a wheeled walker. By the following day, he was walking without help and ran perfectly on the treadmill at the gym.

On the morning of day three, he was taken to be checked by BANDI.

Doctor Raj, Schneider, and other radiology experts analyzed the pictures and called the bosses to a private conference, almost three days to the hour since Tony had convulsed at that same place.

When Dr. David Bright and Dr. Paul Bernstein entered the radiology department's conference room, they saw concerned faces all over the room.

"Paul, David", the petite Dr. Scheneider started, "I am speaking in the name of all of us here present, because we are confronted with a situation that we never had before. See these films?" she said, putting a series of films on the X-ray screen. "They were taken from Mr. Homeless this morning, and these are the films taken from Mr. Homeless only few days before he was submitted to the injection."

The change was obvious even to those not trained in radiology. Red had taken over most areas of the brain where there had been blue, green, or yellow before.

Scheiner continued: "If we are to believe BANDI—and we do not have any reason not too because we ran test on other patients after this—instead of curing Mr. Homeless Tony of his drug addiction and mild schizophrenia, we have turned him into a furious man, with potentially serious aggressive tendencies, possibly even inclined to murder."

"What you are saying does not make sense. He received the serum of a very calm and centered man, a fluid that has been enhanced with nanoparticles programmed to make him even a better man than the donor," said Dr. Bright.

"Well," Dr. Dramsjold said, "The only thing we know is that what we see, and what you have before your eyes is what we see. Unfortunately, there is no question about it."

"Tony has made an almost miraculous recovery and—to the best of my knowledge—he has not shown any aggressive tendencies. Yet. I shall order security to put an additional video camera in his room and to watch him 24/7," said Dr. Bright.

"Speaking of cameras, has anybody checked the ones from the lab where the specimens are stored?"

I am also going to request Dr. Alice Rodriguez to interview him, see what she can learn from him," said Dr. Paul Bernstein and added, "Of course I do not have to tell all of you that what has been discussed here does not go anywhere else. Not a word about it even to your spouses and closest associates. I am putting my trust on you, ladies and gentleman."

After the two of them left the conference room, a concerned Dr. Bright asked his colleague:

"What about Melvin?"

"What about him?" Bernstein responded.

"Well, should've warn him? This guy could be dangerous and harm my son.

"Do not worry about Melvin, David. He is a big guy, not a kid anymore, and he is much bigger than this guy Tony. However, if you are concerned, I shall place a security guard dressed as a nurse to bodyguard him. Are you happy now?"

Doctor Bright was not happy, but he agreed with the older man.

EIGHTEEEN

Mondays were not good days for most people, but this particular Monday was especially bad for some people at the institute: Doctor Kevin Nielsen, Doctor "Not-so" Bright, and Carlessa Williams, each for quite different reasons.

Kevin was pissed off because his lawyer had called him earlier and chewed him up for wasting his valuable time—and he did remark the word "valuable." He had been at the institute and had interviewed the alleged witness of the brutality of the police against him, and he had gotten a totally different -but very similar story- from the two of them, relating to the events that occurred during his confrontation with the Saint Lucie County Detectives.

Both of the witness, , the security guard, and Ms. Gladys Franklin, had indicated that it was Dr. Neilsen the one who verbally and physically assaulted the detectives and that the two law enforcement agents had been extremely polite and nice towards the doctor "who had been an absolute jerk"—according to Ms. Gladys Franklin—and that the doctor had been fortunate that the detectives did not arrest him and press charges for assaulting a police officer, " and a lady police officer at that."

He finished by informing him that he would send him a bill for the time spent and travel expenses. Of course, Kevin knew that the lawyer's bill would be grossly inflated. He would have to refer to Mom and Dad to pay it. He knew they would.

He was also pissed off because after all the trouble he went through to try to make that pesky young Doctor Melvin Bright look bad, nothing had happened to him. His patient had few seizures, spent less than 48 hours in a coma, and now not only had he recovered, with no apparent damage to his brains, but Bright was being regarded as a hero by everyone at the institute who knew the history.

Lastly, Kevin was worried that no further patients have been subjected to injections or withdrawals since the incident and that a bunch of doctors and technicians were working on the fluid to determine what had gone wrong. What if his tampering was discovered? He could say he tripped over something and accidentally contaminated the sample. Still, even if they believed him, his stay at the institute would be over, and his hopes of working there after his residency would be gone for good.

If that happened, he would go back to do a residency somewhere and perhaps specialize in pain management. There were enough people addicted to pain pills around to make a doctor rich with little effort. And of course, if he got kicked out of the Institute, he could also look for a drug lord to sell him the information about the research to cure drug addiction. They would probably blow the whole dam place off to prevent that from becoming a standard treatment.

Still, he would miss the prestige of working at an Institution like this and the glory of one day becoming a discoverer of something that would make him famous…and rich, of course.

Melvin was also worried, on two counts, first because he had not yet recovered for the scare of the incident suffered by "Homeless Tony" and he had seen the changes in his BANDI scan, so he was not sure if he could say that everything was ok, even though Tony seemed fine, was acting fine, his neurological exam was regular and the fact that Doctor Alice Rodriguez, the psychiatrist had reassured him that Tony's mind was regular and normal. However, processes and reactions had been and had stayed normal.

But if it all was ok, why had Dr. Bernstein and his father assigned him a bodyguard?

The other person full of concern was Doctor Jasmine Porter; not only had she not gotten over the death of the Spanish-speaking chimp, but every day that passed, she became more suspicious and had more dislike of the work that the institute was doing. She expressed to Melvin her desire to quit her job at the institute and either go back to school or open a veterinary clinic to treat dogs and cats like most vets do.

So far Melvin had been able to persuade her to stay –he thought his world would end and his heart would be broken in tiny little pieces if she was not around anymore-; unfortunately when she learned about the incident with "homeless Tony" and the fact that Melvin was going around accompanied by a bodyguard, made her again wish to leave the Institute, this time she was trying to convince Melvin to leave as well. "Of course, not together," she had said, to which Melvin had answered, "Of course, not together", but of course, he would leave if she even hinted that they would go together.

He would follow her to the end of the world, but leaving this job was not the cool thing to do. He did not want to leave his father disappointed by quitting, especially not now that he was beginning to show him that he was not the good-for-nothing kid that he always had suspected his father considered him.

Equally concerned and upset were Carlessa Williams and her secretary, Wanda Sherman. Upon turning on the computer that morning, Mrs. Sherman discovered the new program installed, and doing what she did every Monday morning, she checked the list of programs installed on it.

At first it thought that Mrs. Williams had installed it, but with a nagging suspicious on her head, went to ask Claressa if she wanted her to have access to the new program: "PCANYWHERE," as soon as she look at the expression on her boss face, she realized that she did not knew anything about it. After she turned her own computer on, she discovered that the program was also in hers, as well as it was in all the machines in that particular section of the office that were interconnected; worse yet, she had the custom of leaving hers on while she was leaving the office for short periods, as she did few times the previous week.

She tried to keep her calm and asked Wanda if she could try to find out where that program had come from. Wanda had a suspicion but she would not let her boss know as she would most certainly would fire her on the spot, so she said that she would try but if she were not able to do it she would call a guy in the computer department, who supposedly was a computer genius – at least judging by the amount of salary that according to his file he was paid.

Of course, Wanda was not able to track down the source of the program, and the computer guru was called in; he worked over six hours. He left the office smelling of old sweat mixed with cheap Aqua Velva. Still, eventually, he yielded, "Eureka," and told them that although it was impossible for him to find the actual name of the person who had installed the program, information from their computer had been transferred by e-mail to the e-mail address kccsi@aol.com.

Carlessa was not a stupid woman and had the memory of an elephant, so she remembered seeing an address similar to that one recently. She went to her desk and pulled the cards of the detectives who had visited her the previous week; one of them had an e-mail address that read kccsi@stluciesherif.com.

Claressa mumbled to herself: "This is her work e-mail address. The little bitch probably transferred all my data to her personal computer, however that is illegal. Perhaps not all is lost yet."

Wanda asked her boss what she had in mind, but she simply dismissed her and took her cell phone out of her purse.

"Gary! It seems we have a problem. some detective from the Saint Lucie Sheriff's Department was here last week and somehow I believe she may have broken in to my files and transferred all data to her computer."

"To her office computer? that is highly illegal and cannot be used in a court of law; it would cost her job and her office quite few pennies," the voice at the other end of the line said

"I do not think she would use the information, not right now anyway. But the problem is, Gary, that we can afford that information to be known by anyone," Claressa said

"I know that she can share it with her superiors, not officially anyway, and if she still has it on her computer or made a disc, perhaps we can still retrieve them. You have a brother who is quite skilled in that sort of thing. Why don't you have him handle the situation, or better yet, in case something goes wrong, perhaps he can ask one of his buddies to do it? Offer him a cash reward, you know that you can afford to be generous," the person named Gary responded

"Me? What about you? I thought we were in this together," said Claressa.

"We are, sweetheart, but this is your mess, not mine. So you fix it and you pay for it. Got it?"

And he hung up.

Claressa was furious and wished she could kill that pesky police woman. Well, maybe she could. After all, people get killed during breaking and entries, even police detectives.

And she dialed another number on her cell phone, this one in Fort Pierce.

NINETEEN

The cute ten-year-old Afro-American boy walked into the main office of the St. Lucie County Sheriff's station carrying a dozen beautiful red roses and shouting, "Anyone here is Sergeant Karla Colles. Someone sent her these flowers." The receptionist clerk and a few others pointed to the desk where Karla was absorbed working on her computer, and it was not until she heard the teases and the exclamations of her coworkers that she paid attention to the little boy. He was cute, and although he was wearing his baseball cap backwards, as it was the fashion, he was not wearing baggy pants that dropped below the waist and showed the underwear, nor was he wearing an oversized t-shirt with some smart or offensive logo.

On the contrary, he was wearing faded but clean blue jeans, an orange polo shirt, with the colors slightly faded and a small Gator team logo on the breast pocket, his sneakers were in good wear, and he was wearing socks. All in all, the kid gave the impression of being ready to go to school first thing in the morning.

When Karla identified herself, the kid very delicately gave her the roses. In response to her inquiries, he only said that his grandmother owned a flower shop and that some gentleman had ordered the roses to be delivered to her. Karla visibly moved, took the roses from the boy, and proceeded to read the card that came with them. It simply said, "from a secret admirer."

She looked in the direction of the desk of Detective Garcia, suspecting that perhaps he was "the secret admirer," but he actually appeared to be upset over the delivery.

She gave the boy a few dollars as a tip and proceeded to find a vase to place the flowers in water; nobody seemed to notice that the boy took several pictures of her with his cell phone camera before walking out of the place.

After Karla found a vase to put the flowers in and looked for the kid, he was long gone. "This is a school day, right? Why was that kid not in school?" she said, going to the door to see if he was still around. All she saw was a white commercial van, without any lettering, speeding away down the road.

The man driving the van asked the boy if he had delivered the flowers and if he had been able to take a picture of the police woman; when the boy answered in the affirmative, the man pulled out his own cell phone and dialed a number: "Jerome, my brother! We have the pictures. Your little boy is a real pro; he really did a good job. Do you want me to send the pictures over to your cell? No? Then do you want me to take your son back to school or what? Oh, I see, brother. You want to see your son. Where? OK, we will meet you at the McDonald's on Okeechobee Road. Then you take him back to school, right, man?

Jerome Taylor, Carlessa Williams's younger brother, received the call at the pool hall on Avenue D in Fort Pierce, where he usually hung out with his friends. He put the phone in the case hanging from his waist, took a sip from the beer bottle, walked out to get his car, and drove to meet his son at McDonald's, where he planned to treat the boy to lunch.

Jerome was a handsome man in his mid-twenties. He was over 6 feet tall and very muscular, he dressed well but conservatively, neither with the flashy garments that some of his friends liked to wear, nor with the below the waist baggy pants. Most of the time he wore dark, expensive brand glasses, had a large gold cross hanging from his chest and two large gold, diamonds studded rings on his finger, only by those items people could guess that he was not a poor man. Those who knew him better knew for sure that he wasn't poor.

He drove an old model black with red stripes Chrysler that had been repainted, remodeled, and fitted with a powerful, silver-plated engine. The car had aluminum alloy hubcaps and red leather seats. He loved his car more than anyone else, except perhaps his son, and his son loved his daddy and his daddy's car just as much.

As he walked into the fast-food restaurant, he was greeted by several of the female attendants; he barely waved to them and went to meet his son. He gave several bills to the guy who had brought his son there and told him to go sit somewhere else to finish the soda he was drinking. he wanted to be alone with his boy.

Although separated from the boy's mother, to whom he was never married, he was as good a father to the boy, as his lifestyle—which was not one of the best—allowed him to be. He also gave the mother child support, and in his own way, he really loved that boy.

Of course, the boy greeted him with great enthusiasm and started telling him about his delivery of the flowers and how trill he was that Daddy had picked him out from school, taken him for a ride in his cool car, given him a job to do, and, on top of that, was now treating him to lunch at his favorite place: McDonald's.

Daddy would have preferred that the boy wasn't that loud but he listened with a smile and waited until he had finished his meal to ask for the cell phone which the boy gave back to him with a proud smile,

"J.D. said that I did a really good job, did I do a really good job daddy?" the boy asked.

"You did a fantastic job, in fact so great, that from here we are going to Walmart and buy you any toy you want," Jerome said.

"Can I keep the cell phone too, Daddy? It is really neat."

"I do not think you should have a cell phone, not just yet. It seems to me you are too young to have your cell phone. Besides, you would probably lose it, or some kid may steal it from you. And by the way, I do not want you to tell a word about anything we did today to your mommy, you know, those are things between men and she would not understand. Come on promise me that you would not tell her anything," Jerome said to his son.

"Can I tell her about McDonald's, Daddy?" Junior said.

"Of course, you can tell her about McDonald's, you can tell her about our ride in the car, and you can tell her about us going to Walmart. I just do not want you to tell her that I let J.D get you from school let alone to deliver those flowers. You know she does not like J.D. too much," Jerome said, being careful not to mention the taking of the picture part, as he preferred if the child would forget that.

"I know, Dad. Mom does not like any of your friends. I am not sure if she likes you that much," said the boy with a grin that pretended to be sad.

"That is too bad because I do love her very much, and she may be right about some of my friends, but J.D. is okay. Besides, he is family. He is my second cousin."

Then, the boy started to inquire about what a second cousin was, and Jerome tried to explain the family relation as best he could. By then, they had finished the meal and were off to the store.

His plan was to take the boy back to school so he could take the bus home, but it was getting late, and it would be tough to pull the boy out of a toy store.

Of course, if he missed the bus, he could drive him to his maternal grandmother's house where he usually stayed after school until his mother picked him up after work. But the old woman would probably yell at him for taking the boy out on a school day.

Of course, the boy's mother would do the same thing, but at least she would do it over the phone, and he did not have to face it. He cursed himself; he was glad to spend some time with his son, whom he shared custody with the mother, but he wished that he did not have to take him out of school and put him to do this errand for him.

If Claressa had not said the matter was urgent, and of course there was the issue of five thousand dollars, his boy could have bought many toys with that kind of money.

He let his son rummage through Walmart's toy department and made a call on his cell phone.

"Hey, Wanda baby, how are you doing, darling? Figure I call to ask how you feel about making a hundred dollars in less than thirty minutes? No, it is nothing illegal or dangerous, a friend of mine, has a girlfriend—she is a white—he thinks that she is playing the field, if you know what I mean. So all I need is for you to follow her and see where he lives, so my friend can watch and see if any men come in to her house. See, I told you it was easy. Sure, I send you the picture to your cell phone. She works at the sheriff's office on Midway Road."

The woman on the other side of the line was asking questions, so he continued, "What, no, I do not know if she is a cop. But what difference does it make to you? All you have to do is see when she comes out of work and follow her car. What? Now you want two hundred dollars and will only follow her to US 1 or Virginia Avenue. You are a thief, baby. I will give you one fifty and that is it because I will have to pay someone else to follow her from wherever you leave her."

After reaching an agreement, Jerome dialed another number, that of his second cousin J.D.

"This is your lucky day, man. I do have another hundred for you. All you have to do is wait for Wanda's call and follow the car she was following until you see where the woman we delivered the flowers lives."

This job was already getting expensive; he would ask Claressa for the five thousand plus expenses.

Karla left work at about five fifteen and did not pay any attention to the black Toyota Camry that pulled behind her and followed, she drove east on Midway road and before hitting the light of US 1. He pulled into a shopping Center, she needed to buy some groceries at the Win-Dixie store there.

Wanda parked nearby and dialed J.D.'s phone. He was there within ten minutes, while Karla was still in the grocery store.

When Karla left to take US 1 North to get home, JD followed her all the way home. Once he saw her driving her car into the carport of her house, he drove away.

Karla never suspected that she had been followed.

TWENTY

Karla left work the following morning in good spirits. She had spoken over the phone with Garcia, and they both discussed, for the hundredth time, the pros and cons of disclosing their findings and suspicions to her boss, Sheriff Ken Mascara.

While Karla favored going to him and telling him the whole story, Garcia was against it. He argued that what they had done was illegal and probably subject to prosecution because they had obtained the files based on a hunch rather than facts or evidence.

Karla counteracted by arguing that although the files contained no evidence against anyone in particular, they disclosed a motive for a series of crimes…insurance policies that together amounted to more than two million dollars for the beneficiary. All they had to do was find out who was the beneficiary, and they would have a suspect.

Garcia, on his corner, argued that even if they did find out who that person, or persons, were, it would be tough to prove that the individual did actually commit the murders. He failed to see how a company run by people with millions, probably billions of dollars in assets, would bother to whack some poor nobody Mexicans or Guatemalans to collect an amount of money that, for them, would be pocket change.

Karla counteracted with the argument, "What if the management does not know anything about the insurance?" "What if it is a deal between your friends Mrs. Sherman and Carlessa Williams, or perhaps someone else, maybe her husband or even her lawyer brother-in-law?"

Garcia finally agreed that such a theory sounded plausible and that it would be wonderful to be able to check those people's bank accounts. However, she was able to convince Karla that they did not have any evidence, and without it, no judge was going to authorize a subpoena for those people's bank accounts. Because of that, it would be better not to tell their boss anything about the files.

They both agree that they would need to go back to the Institute and talk, this time with the big men at the top command. For that, they needed another authorization from the sheriff, and they planned to get it first thing in the morning.

Neither of them slept well. Garcia watched the Sci-Fi Channel on TV until he fell asleep in front of the tube and dreamed of green ugly men sticking needlessly in the heads of people and making their heads swell until they exploded like an overinflated balloon. Karla played the files on her PC and spent most of the night transferring them to discs.

The next day, of course, Karla was the first to arrive at the office. The sheriff arrived shortly after her, so she went in to his office to inform him that they had some leads, that probably there was more than one murder, told him about the chemical Versed found in some of the bodies and their suspicious that the same, or similar substance may have present in other corpses, that this was not her opinion but that of the Medical Examiner, and that therefore someone at the Neurological Institute may be responsible.

The sheriff probably have had a bad night as well, as he was not his charming self that morning, so although he interrupted Karla's explanations with several remarks of his own, finally agreed that it was worth to investigate that angle, however, he needed her to go to the scene of a murder in Port Saint Lucie—"Something straight forward," he said. "An old gentleman shot his Alzheimer-afflicted wife twice in the chest and then put the gun in his mouth and killed himself." He had just gotten the call as she walked in, and since a CSI officer was needed, she got the assignment.

"Oh and one more thing, Colles," the sheriff said, since there seems to be no clear and present danger in going to ask question to the doctors that run that Institute, I see no need for you and Garcia to go together. It's either you or him and if you guys are busy today, go tomorrow."

Karla would have preferred to go that very same day, so she was a bit disappointed. She was used to following orders, so she took her bag with the CSI equipment and left for the car.

Thinking it over, she retraced her steps, went to her desk, took the disc where she had copied the files of Carlessa Williams from her handbag, and placed them in a locked drawer on her desk. She took an extra one, put it in a manila folder, and walked to Andy Garcia's desk. She left it there with a note informing him about the sheriff's decision and leaving it up to him to decide whether to travel to Indiantown without her today or not.

When Andy finally arrived at work, Karla was gone, and it took him at least half an hour and a cup of black coffee to fix his attention on the manila envelope; he read the note but decided that it was not his place to go because he was aware of how intensely Karla was taking the task of solving those murders. So, he thought letting her go by herself the following day was best.

Andy did not see Karla at the office in the whole day, evidently that double suicide—if it had been a suicide—had taken the whole of her day, and his day had been long, so he went straight home from the office shortly after five pm., took a shower and lied down for a nap.

He did not know how long he had been sleeping when his cell phone started ringing. He picked it up after several rings, and at first, he thought it was a prank or the wrong number because the voice on the other end sounded very excited, and whoever it was calling was sobbing loudly. He finally recognized the voice: "Colles? Karla? Sergeant? It is you. What is going on?"

The voice, a bit more composed, said, "They came in. They robbed me. They ransacked my home. I am locked in my bathroom and have my gun with me. I do not know if they are still here. Please come."

"I am on my way, and I am calling 911. Please stay where you are," Said Garcia.

"I already called the police, think they are on their way, I can hear the sirens now" –Karla's voice said.

"Great, calm down, and make sure you tell the cops that you are a police officer, and do not come out of that bathroom brandishing your gun, some of our colleagues are very trigger happy you know? And I guess I would be too if I see a disturbed woman coming out of a closet with a gun on her hand."

"You are an ass, but thanks for the advice, I shall put the gun away as soon as I am sure the cops are here."

When Andy got to Karla's house, several police patrol cars were already there and he had to show his ID for them to let him pass; He was shocked and saddened to see the status of the house, the furniture was either turned upside-down and some of the upholstery had been slashed open, pictures were in the floor with the glass smashed, some of the delicate China was broken in to million pieces and all the drawers were either wide open or on the floor. Karla was sitting on one of the dining room chairs talking to a policeman: "They took my computer, my stereo and all my CDs and DVDs, they left all the VHS movies, they even took all the empty discs.

They also took a 44 Smith & Wesson Revolver that belongs to my father. I do not have many valuables here, except for that China, which belonged to my great-grandmother, and that painting on the wall, which is an original Backus.

She got up when Andy approached and broke out in sobs, he did not know what else to do so he held her close to his chest and very tight until she calmed down and whispered almost directly into his ear:" They took the computer Garcia, my computer and the discs…do you know what that means Andy? It means it was them, Andy. I am sure it was them, but they did not get what they were looking for; they did get nothing!"

"Come on, you are upset now. Burglary happens all the time in this town and everywhere, actually, much more often than the murders we are supposed to solve. You are just nervous. I will stay and help you clean up this mess. If it is okay with you, I will keep you company. I can sleep on the couch once we put it upside down."

"Thank you, Andy, but that would not be necessary, my next door neighbor has already offered me her spare bedroom to spend the night, she be here in few minutes with her husband and teenager son to help clean up, you are welcome to stay and help. I can offer you a drink or a beer, I need a stiff drink myself." Karla said all that, this time acting transformed, the scared, sobbing woman of few minutes before had suddenly transformed herself in to a determined, controlled, strong person; she was also feeling very, very angry.

The cops left after going through the house for prints (they found none) and interviewing the neighbors. They found out that shortly after Karla left the house that morning, a white van from an air conditioning company (sorry, nobody paid attention to the lettering in the truck) pulled in. A burly white guy, accompanied by two black guys, came in and walked around the house. They left after about an hour (no, no one saw them taking anything from the house).

They could not give much information about the two Blacks, but the white guy apparently was the driver of the van and (the neighbors assumed) the boss of the others. He was a heavy-set guy with a reddish goatee and gold front teeth. He was wearing dark glasses and a Florida Marlins baseball cap.

"I am sure that awful woman Williams sent them. I bet they were looking for discs and information from my hard drive, I may even have been that brother of hers" Karla said to Andy in private, may be now we can tell the boss tomorrow and he may be able to do something about this mess"

"Come on, Karla. That is just a hunch of yours. The boss will not get a judge to subpoena the computer records of that huge institute, just based on your supposition. Even if you are right, we have no proof. Besides, you heard the cops. This sort of thing happens every day and everywhere. It just was your luck that it happened to you today."

Karla got terribly upset at the lack of sympathy she sensed from the man who was supposed to be his partner. Without a word, she turned around, picked up a bottle of scotch from her cupboard, and said, "I am going to the neighbors to spend the night and get drunk with them. You go home, too; your nurse friend must be lonely."

She disappeared into the next-door neighbor's house, closing the door behind her, almost on Andy's face.

Not even half an hour had passed since Andy left, and Karla had barely finished her second shot of scotch when her cell phone rang. It was an unknown number and an equally unknown caller. "Sergeant Colles, you probably do not know me, but I am a secret admirer—I hope you like the flowers I sent you—but now I am here to help. I know that someone has done wrong to you today, and I know who did it, but I cannot tell you over the phone because I will be in danger. Meet me in half hour at the convenience store at the corner of Orange and twenty Fifth Street and I shall tell you everything."

The man said all that in one fast sentence, only repeating the last part: "Meet me in half an hour at the convenience store at the corner of Orange and Twenty-Five."

It was the voice of a white man, and Karla's suspects were black—she conveniently forgot that the neighbors had said the driver of the truck that was parked on her driveway earlier that day was white.

She was furious at those who had robbed and trashed her home and would do anything to catch them. She thought of calling Andy for backup, but she was almost as mad as him for his lack of support as she was at the robbers, therefore she decided against calling him. However, the woman was not stupid, and she was not going to put her life in danger without taking some precautions.

She paused to think for a moment, amid the pleas of her neighbors not to go. After telling them that if she was not back in an hour, they should call the police, she dialed another number on her cell phone.

"Vince? Is that you?"; this is Karla Colles, yes, thank you Dad is fine, but I do need your help. Do you still do undercover in the hood? Do you? "Oh, you are working tonight, and you are bored because nothing is going on. Great, I need to ask a favor from you; it may be nothing, but I may need some backup tonight in a little while."

She told the man called Vince all about the robbery, the flowers, and the secret admirer, leaving out that she had obtained the files from the Institute illegally and telling him instead that someone had anonymously sent her a disc in the mail.

Karla continued talking on her cell; this time, she said, "Yes Vince, you are right. I have been assigned a partner. It is a temporary thing, though; we are working together on the same case. "Why did I not call him about this? Well to be honest we had an argument this evening but the main reason that I do not call him is because he is one of those cops who is trigger happy, he believes in shooting first and ask questions later. Yes, you are right, his name is Garcia, Andy Garcia, and they call him 'The Cuban,' that is the guy. See, now you agree with me, don't you Vince?"

Vincent Jones was an old cop, that had always liked to work alone, it had been a rookie under her father and although he was a Puerto Rican raised in the Bronx, he was dark enough to be considered Afro-American, which was a great asset when one works undercover in the middle of the Black and Spanish neighborhoods.

Karla went back to her house and changed into faded blue jeans, sneakers, and a loose shirt, under which she tucked her pistol. She did not carry her service pistol but a .35 that had been overlooked by the robbers because she kept it inside some dishes in the cupboard. Then she put on a windbreaker, and after consulting her watch, she drove away.

The place was easy to find and well-lit, but not too busy at that time. Even though it was not even 9 p.m., the neighborhood was not the kind that makes people wish to get out at night unless you are the kind of person who conducts business at night. But even for that, it was kind of early.

The place was open, and there was a small cafeteria at the end of the store. The Indian owner looked at her and took her money after she ordered a soda and a pack of cigarettes. Karla did not usually smoke, but she needed to calm her nerves, as the couple of Scotch drinks that she had early were barely beginning to take effect.

The place was well lit under the gasoline pumps, but on the sides, some of the lights had been broken by vandals, and some were just burned out and never replaced, so the store's side and back were quite dark. That was the reason nobody saw the old bum who seemed to be rummaging through the garbage and that was the reason the old Chevy Caprice parked there.

The old black man seemed to abandon his efforts to find something in the garbage and staggering approached the Chevy. He knocked on the window, and it was opened by an angry young black guy who, in not so nice way, sent him to perform an impossible sexual maneuver upon himself; there were other two black guys in the car, one on the passenger seat and one seating in the back of the car.

The one in the passenger seat told the driver to be nice to the old man and that "the way you are going, you will be like him in a few years." He gave the beggar a five-dollar bill and told him to go away.

As the beggar disappeared from sight, the man on the passenger side, walked out of the car and around the convenience store. He returned to the car and said to the men: "She is there, ok, and she seems to be alone. you stay in the car and keep the engine running, J.D., you come with me"

The two guys wore dark, obviously expensive glasses and jackets with hoods that they lifted and covered their heads.

"I go first. You stay by the door and bolt if you see anything unusual. Please do not do anything stupid. I shall go talk to the lady."

Meanwhile, Andy was feeling pretty stupid himself and pretty guilty. He had eaten the dinner that his nurse friend had prepared for him, and both were now sitting in front of the tube watching a movie while sipping Budweiser; then his phone rang.

"This is Vincent Jones. I do not know if you remember me, but I work undercover in the hood, and I think I have to tell you something about your partner Karla Colles. She may be about to let herself in deep shit. She could be killed, or worse. So you better get over here as fast as you can. I will handle the situation the best I can in the meantime"

Jerome Taylor walked slowly towards Karla, who was drinking her soda and smoking and had already spotted the two guys. She had not expected two, so she became nervous and prayed that Vince was somewhere nearby.

Jerome smiled and said, "You are a really pretty lady. No wonder you have secret admirers."

"Cut the crap and let's get down to business. You told me you would tell me who broke into my house and how to recover the belongings that you, or some of your friends stole from me." said Karla, pretending to be in control.

"Oh, I should have known that I was going to meet one though, ho. After all, you are a cop, not a lady. Or can a woman be both a cop and a lady? But you are right, let's cut the crapola, I will tell you all you want to know and see that you recoup your stuff but first you have to give me back something you stole from some friends of mine," said Jerome

"Oh, do you mean this?" she said, reaching into her purse, only to find her wrist grabbed with quite a bit of strength by Jerome, who said, "No tricks;

put the handbag on top of the table, please."

Karla saw J.D. standing by the door and reaching into his pocket, probably for a weapon, but then she let go as Jerome spilled all the contents of Karla's purse on the table. A CD was among them.

"Perfect cop lady, very good. I see you are a smart woman. The problem is that I am also a smart man. Therefore you would understand that unless I pulled a computer from my ass, I would not be able to see if this is a blank disc, a copy of *Pirates of the Caribbean* or *La Traviatta*, so you will have to come with us to a place where we can play the disc and also were you can tell us how many more copies you made and where are they, so please be a nice lady and come with us."

"The hell I will," Karla said without any conviction. Both of them were standing; she was standing behind the table, and there was no way she could give him a karate kick. Even if she could, Jerome's friend was standing nearby. She decided to do as the men said and hoped that Vincent or someone else would come to her assistance.

As they walked outside, J.D. opened the door and walked ahead; Jerome was behind her. He had already searched her and removed her gun, which he put in his pocket. "Great," she thought. "If this hoodlum did not have a gun before, now he has one, and it is mine."

They heard the engine running as they approached the Chevy and saw the man at the wheel. As they got closer, JD. Realized that something was wrong; the man at the wheel was not their friend, it was the old beggar. Not only that, but the old beggar opened the car door, and with a burst of energy that would not have seemed possible for an old guy, he jumped out, produced a big gun, and yelled, "Police, you guys are under arrest! Let that woman go!"

J.D. was the first one to react; he jumped to the side, trying to find a shield behind the post that supported the canopy that covered the pumps while holding a gun in his hand and trying to aim it at the cop. He never made it to the covered area. One single shot from Vince's gun pierced his heart; he was dead before hitting the floor.

Karla took advantage of the opportunity and, raising her right leg, she spun around to give Jerome a karate kick in the face. Unfortunately, Jerome had seen what was going on and his reflexes were faster. Although he did not pull a gun, he was able to grab Karla's leg and twist it, making her fall to the floor. Jerome took the opportunity to run away from the place.

He figured that there were more cops around. He was lucky enough that three cars were waiting at the street intersection for the red light to change and breaking the glass of the driver's side of the one closest to the middle, he made the driver leave the car at gun point and sped away towards Martin Luther King boulevard and his neighborhood.

When Andy got there, it was all over. Much to his delight, Vince was giving Karla a tough time. "I wish your father were here to give you a good spanking, young lady; this was a stupid thing for a civilian to do and the stupidest for a police officer."

Karla said he was right and she was sorry. After she kissed Vince on the cheek, the man's rage disappeared as if by magic.

Andy wanted to say something himself, but considering his earlier encounter with Karla, it was believed that it was best to keep his mouth shut. He went to check on J.D. just to make sure he was dead, in spite of Vince's assurances. "I seldom miss," he said.

On the other hand, there was no way he could follow the car driven by Jerome; in fact, nobody had seen what kind of car he took, and the driver, who was an illegal alien, had disappeared from the scene.

Vince called on the radio and few minutes later the place was crawling with cops; it was then that he informed them that there was another guy locked in the trunk, this one alive and well—at least that was what he assumed, after all the engine of the car had been running and carbon monoxide can kill same as a gun.

Luckily, or perhaps not so luckily for him he was alive and well, but the cops took him by ambulance to the Hospital ER to be checked before they book him.

Vince recognized all three of the men, and he was one hundred percent sure that Jerome Taylor had escaped.

The only thing Garcia said before leaving the scene was, "Now we have reason to go talk with the boss tomorrow. Just let me do the initial introduction, and you can take it from there."

"Oh, and I am very thankful to Sergeant Jones and happy that you are all right, Sergeant Colles. Good night you all!"

Karla went home accompanied by a police patrol car. She planned to spend the night at the neighbors', but she was sure she would not be able to sleep.

TWENTY-ONE

Jerome Taylor did not get scared easily; however, that night, he was more worried than usual, to say the least.

It was not enough that the job his sister sent him to do that morning failed to produce the disc she wanted—after ditching the air conditioning company van that they had stolen, he drove all the way to Stuart to meet her and after spending most of the morning and part of the afternoon going through all the disc taken from the home of the lady cop, Claressa had gone very pissed off because none of them had the files she wanted.

She had almost refused to pay him the five grand that she had promised and it was not until he offered to get the information from that woman cop herself, that Claressa paid him the money and offered an equal amount if they did the job right this time.

He had to remind her that they had done the job right the first time, because all that his big sister had said was that she wanted "the computer from that woman cop home and all the discs that you can find at the damned ho's place", He had done exactly that, it was not his fault that the woman had put the files elsewhere, actually Claressa should have been the one to think about that possibility, because he did not know shit about computers.

So after driving around the deserted streets of black town, he parked the stolen car behind a free-standing bar and called his sister on the cell. She was fuming, and this time, he could tell that she was very scared, so he took advantage of that and told her to wire him the money for the second job to Mobile, Alabama, because he was leaving town.

The second call was to a friend of his, to whom he only provided information about JD being dead and his need to get a car right now so he could get out of town. He offered to trade anything decent on wheels for his own hot rod. It took some bargaining, and he had to throw in the stolen car he was driving now. Plus, when his friend learned he was heading out of town, he requested that he take "a package" to a friend in Tallahassee.

Of course, Jerome was not stupid and immediately realized that such a "package" most likely contained drugs; therefore, he was able to extort an additional thousand dollars in cash for travel expenses.

Then Jerome called his child's mother and asked her to let her see him before leaving town, as he did not know when he could return to Fort Pierce. She gave him a tough time, calling him the worst names she could remember and scolding him for making their son an accomplice in his dirty dealings. Evidently, the boy could not keep a secret and had told his mother about the delivery of flowers to the policewoman.

Only after Jerome told her that JD was dead, she agreed to let him say goodbye to his son, but advised him that he would not be allowed in the house, the boy was already in bed, but she would wake him up and have him meet him on the curve in front of her home.

Because of the time, Jerome decided to drive to her ex's home first, even though he was risking that some cops could be there. He needed to say goodbye to his son.

Jerome parked the stolen car about half a block from his son's house and walked up to their meeting. He walked twice to ensure no cops were waiting inside the home. He knew that the mother of his child probably would like to see him behind bars, but he also knew that she was not going to let the cops take him in front of his son.

He did not dare to walk to the door; instead, he threw pebbles at the windows and whistled loudly to the song he knew his boy liked. After a few minutes, the door opened, and a woman holding a child by the hand appeared at the door.

They walked to the curve to meet Jerome and without responding to his greeting, she whispered on his ear, "Do not dare to take the boy with you because if you do I swear to God that I shall kill you"—and she opened her robe and showed a gun that she was holding. Then she stepped aside and said, "You have five minutes, tomorrow is a school day and your son needs to go to sleep"

Jerome held the boy tight and told him he had to leave on business and did not know how long he would be away. He told him that he loved him very much and that he would think about him and take care of his mother.

The boy, half asleep, was not sure what to make of that, but he was glad to see his father again and was sad that he was going away.

He mustered to say, "You are not going to jail, are you, Daddy? I do not want you to go to jail!"

"No, I am not going to jail, son. I promise I have to get out of town on business, and I shall be back for you and your mom. You have to promise me that you will not cry, will go to school and get only As and Bs, or straight As. Do you promise, son?"

"I promise, Daddy," the boy said as he and his dad were embracing each other. Then Jerome whispered in the boy's ear, "I am putting something in the pocket of your pajamas. It is something that I want you to give to your mommy after I am gone. You must wait until I am gone before giving it to her, OK?"

The boy promised, and the mother informed Jerome that the five minutes were up and that the boy had to go to bed. Jerome did not say anything else to the child; he just held him tight against his chest and, after letting him go, said to the woman as he walked to his car, "Take good care of him. I know you will, and I also hope that one day you find room in your heart to forgive me."

After driving away, it took Jerome less than one hour to trade cars with his friend and be on his way out of Fort Pierce. The car was an old Lincoln town car, but it was in great shape, and his friend apparently had the engine modified and put two carburetors on it. "This shit burns much gas. I do not care about stopping at every fucking gas station along the way to refuel. Can you give me something else?" said Jerome.

"This is all I have at the moment brother, take it or leave it. It also has two gas tanks and, if you do not want to drive too fast or burn too much juice, you can drive with only one of the carburetors, by simply turning that switch," Jerome's friend said. He added, "Because I knew you would be fucking bitching about the car, I am throwing an extra hundred for gas. Just make sure the package reaches the address. Have a good trip, brother."

TWENTY-TWO

The following day, at around eight thirty, Karla walked into her office at the sheriff's department. Contrary to her expectations, and probably because she had been so exhausted, and probably because the two scotch drinks also helped, she slept like a baby at the neighbor's house.

Andy walked in about ten minutes later, and after stopping for a few seconds at Karla's desk, he knocked on the door of Sheriff Mascara's office.

After the greetings he proceeded to inform his boss that the day after they had gone to that Neurological Institute pursuing a lead on the investigation of the murder of Mr. Torres, he had received an CD, from an anonymous source, which somewhat confirmed the suspicious of the coroner, the good Doctor Raymond, that several people, most likely workers or ex-workers of that Institute had been murdered in order to collect several hundred thousand dollars in insurance money. Apparently, the disc was not supposed to have been delivered to Garcia but to Detective Colles, and because of that, her home had been ransacked the day before, and she had been almost murdered and kidnapped the previous night.

The sheriff was aware of the last two events. He was about to talk to Detective Colles, because it had been outmost imprudent from her part to attend the meeting the night before without the proper back up, and that she had been lucky that a very experienced member of the Fort Pierce Police Department had been nearby to stop the kidnapping and probably subsequent torture and murder of Detective Colles. She would be reprimanded for her actions, even though she was off duty when those events took place, because they were linked to the investigation they had conducted with Garcia. She was theoretically still on service.

Garcia tried to soften things for her by telling the sheriff that she had actually called him for backup but that he got there too late, yet one of the suspects was dead, another was under arrest, and only one got away.

That one had been identified as Jerome Taylor, who—perhaps not too coincidentally—was the brother of Carlessa Williams, a big wheel at the institute and probably the main person of interest in the case. However, he respectfully requested permission to go back and interview the actual heads of the institute to see if they were involved in any way.

Actually, Mascara first mentioned the need to obtain records of the Institute's operation, as well as the financial records, bank accounts, etc., of the directors, most especially those of Mrs. Williams.

Yes, he knew that she was the sister in law of a prominent Stuart attorney and because of that it would be difficult to obtain a subpoena from a Judge from that county, but since not only murder was involved but also a kidnapping attempt, that made the case a federal one and he would go to a Judge in Palm Beach to get the subpoena that very same day, however, it may take the judge some time to analyze the facts before actually issuing the papers and that could take few days.

Meanwhile, a state-wide manhunt was being carried out to locate Jerome Taylor and bring him to justice. Some of the local law enforcement people thought he may be hiding, but the sheriff was of the opinion that he had skipped town.

And yes, Andy had his authorization to go back to Indiantown as soon as possible and see what he could find out. As for Sergeant Colles, it was best to remain at the office until he figured out what punishment her actions deserved. For sure, at best, a bad report on her record, at worst, perhaps a suspension without pay.

As Andy left, it was another beautiful day in South Florida and there were no signs of any change in the weather, in spite of the weathermen and weatherwomen forewarnings about a storm forming in the Gulf of Mexico; but there was no way yet to determine if it was to become a hurricane and if so whether or not it would hit the Treasure Coast.

As he drove, Garcia realized he missed Sergeant Karla Colles's company much more than he would have considered possible.

The drive to Indiantown was uneventful, and upon arrival at the Institute, he was greeted by Gladys, the receptionist. She was not only glad to see him again but was quick to inform him that both she and the gate guard had told the lawyer of that "weasel of Doctor" how nice he had been with the man and that he had been the aggressor of the "pretty policewoman lady."

Andy thanked her for that, and although he had not given any thought to that incident, it was nice to know that he did not have to worry about it anymore.

Apparently, the sheriff had called ahead of time advising of Garcia's arrival, and therefore, Gladys did not make him wait and conducted him directly to the office of Doctor Paul Bernstein, close to the end of the long corridor, past the cafeteria, and right in front of the part that the members of the Institute called the "resident clients area" and the patients called it, more properly perhaps, "the hospital."

Of course, the doors leading to that area were closed, and Andy, this time, like the first, could not get a glimpse of what it was like behind those doors.

After knocking and hearing a firm "enter" Gladys opened the door and ushered Detective Andy Garcia in to the office of Doctor Paul Bernstein the official Head Master of the Neurological and Medical Research Institute of the Treasure Coast.

Andy was unable to hold his expression of surprise, before the door opened he had guessed that such intense and mainly voice belonged to a tall, young, and well-built man, instead he was being greeted by a short, elderly man, almost completely bald, wearing Geppetto style glasses, behind which were a couple of vivacious blue eyes, a short, well-trimmed but completely white beard and mustache, below an aquiline nose that gave the man more the appearance of a prophet from the Old Testament than that of modern day world renowned scientist.

A not-too-clean laboratory gown covered what seemed to be a personally tailored and expensive dark blue suit, a white shirt, and a blue and gray striped necktie held in place by a small caduceus tie pin.

The man's office was as unexpected as his appearance, instead of finding an spacious and elegant office, Garcia was introduced in to a small, cluttered office, on which the mahogany paneled walls were covered by wall to wall book cases, full of obviously frequently read books, the spacious and elegant desk was almost covered by files, journals, books and magazines, which also covered the floor, chairs and every inch of space in the office of Professor Paul Bernstein, who was wearing a very warm smile, as he stretched a hand ——in which a slight tremor was evident—to shake the hand of the Detective he said "Welcome to the Neurological Institute Detective, I am Doctor Paul Bernstein, and I have been forwarded of your coming by Sheriff Mascara. A good man, and a good Sheriff Ken Mascara. In fact he used to be also a good Chiropractor it was in that role that we meet at a convention, where I was honored to be one of the speakers, some years ago."

Without stopping to catch his breath, Dr. Bernstein continued, "Sheriff Mascara informed me that you are investigating the death of a man and that somehow your investigations have led you to us, here at the institute. That Detective, as you will understand, is of utmost concern to us, particularly to me as a head of this institution, because we are involved in the most delicate work, and it would be tragic for mankind—and I am not exaggerating here— if something occurs that slows our work down."

"Please have a seat," he added while removing some files from a chair in front of his desk. "Would you like to have a drink? I have scotch and brandy under these papers, or if you prefer, I can order coffee, tea, or a soft drink from our cafeteria."

"Thank you, Doctor Bernstein, but I am fine now. It is an honor and very nice to meet you, I am Detective Andy Garcia of the Saint Lucie County Sheriff's Department, and as Sheriff Mascara informed you correctly, I am in charge of investigating the murder of a man, who used to work here, in fact, according to our information he was one of your R.S."

Andy dropped the "R.S." part to test the doctor's reaction, and sure enough, there was a subtle change in the doctor. His smile froze for a couple of seconds, and the tremor of his hands seemed to intensify, before he regained his composure and said, "I see, and may I ask Detective Garcia, how did you come to find this out? If it is okay for you to give that information, of course."

Andy was still surprised. This small, obviously bright, and charming old man, who looked more like someone's grandfather or a rabbi, could not possibly be involved in murder or in covering up murder, and although he hesitated, he decided that it was best to be honest with the professor.

"The man's name was Torres, Ismael Torres. We found his body in Saint Lucie County, with a bullet hole in his chest. Of course he did not have an ID with him but because of a tattoo on his skin of a bird called Quetzal, which is the National Bird of the Country of Guatemala, we suspected him to come from that part of the world and since there is a large number of Guatemalans in Indiantown we came here to see if anyone could identify him and we were lucky enough to find someone who recognized him"

"I am sorry Detective but still fail to see how did you associate him with our institution and, although I am very sorry to hear about Mr. Torres, I do not see the reason for you to request to talk to me, I believe the people in Human Resources, specifically Mrs. Carlessa Williams would be able to provide you with more information about Mr. Torres, if he ever worked here that I would be able to give you" –said Paul Bernstein, now in total control.

"Been there, done that," Detective Garcia responded. And proceeded to inform Doctor Bernstein about the data they had received on a disc sent anonymously to them and asked if the institute had insured its workers' lives.

The doctor answered in the negative but proceeded to inform the detective that he took care that every worker of the institute who died, for any cause, in or out of the premises, had the funeral expenses, or repatriation of the remains paid for by the institute, and also a small sum—about ten thousand dollars—was paid to the surviving family of the deceased. Bernstein said, he had personally suggested that even if an ex-employee who left the institute, within three months should die, his/her funeral was paid by the corporation.

Garcia proceeded to tell him that the data on the disc suggested that not only the deceased but others who may have died under less than precise circumstances did indeed have hefty insurance policies that were collected by someone other than the families of the departed, someone within the Neurological Institute.

After saying this, he saw surprise in the face of the old Professor Bernstein who quickly said, "Are you implying that someone here at the institute has murdered more than the one person and has done so in order to collect life Insurance? That is preposterous, detective, totally incredible. I sit on the Board of Directors of this institution, and I can assure you that no one is aware of this Insurance scam, if such a thing exists, provided that what you suspect is correct.

"Does Mrs. Claressa Williams sit on the board, Professor?"- asked Garcia.

"Is she the person you suspect, Detective Garcia?" responded the professor

"Please answer my question, if you do not mind, Professor, and I shall tell you why I am mentioning her name as a person of interest in this case," Andy said.

"No, Detective, Mrs. Williams is not a member of the Board of Directors, and I hope that your next question is not going to be for the names of the members of the board, because I am not in liberty to tell you that."

"And I suppose you are not at liberty either of telling me what kind of research you do here at the institute," Andy said.

Bernstein responded, "I can give you a general idea but not the specifics. We are researching new and innovative radiological machines –you know, x-ray-like machines- we are privately funded to do Stem cell research with embryonic stem cells, and we hope through such research to be able, in some not-too-distant day, to cure or at least control some diseases that are currently considered incurable.

"I'm sorry I can't tell you more, but I promise you that as soon as some of our work is completed and even before it is published, if you are still interested, I will explain everything to you myself."

"Thank you, Professor, I would in exchange try to be as honest as I am in liberty to be," Andy responded sincerely, starting to feel sorry for that fatherly man as he proceeded to disclose to him the ransacking of the home of Sergeant Colles and the subsequent attempt to kidnap her by no one less than the young brother of Mrs. Carlessa Williams. He then proceeded to inform the professor that, most likely, the records and files of the Institute would be subpoenaed within a couple of days.

Bernstein did not like the news and stated that he did not have any problem with surrendering the financial and operational records but that he and the Board would fight until the end to keep the research and medical records secret. In fact, he thanked the detective for that piece of information because he would contact the Institute's lawyers as soon as the detective was finished with the interview.

Garcia realized that he had gone too far and given too much information to the nice professor. Therefore, he indicated that he was finished and that he would see himself to the door. Bernstein insisted on accompanying him to the lobby, and Andy could not help but feel a warm feeling toward the patriarchal-looking man.

As they were shaking hands to say good-bye in the lobby, Andy asked one more question: "Do you use much Versed in your patients, Doctor Bernstein?"

Again, the old man's smile disappeared, and his hands shook more vigorously as he answered, "That is an anesthetic used by most anesthesiologists for light and/or fast anesthesia. Why do you ask, Detective Garcia?"

"Just curiosity, because in our victim's corpse and a couple of others, the coroner detected that chemical," said Andy as he stretched his hand to shake the already shaking right hand of Professor Paul Bernstein.

As he drove away, he could still see the figure of the professor at the institute's door, remaining there until he could no longer be seen.

As soon as Andy disappeared, Bernstein returned to his office and dialed Doctor David Bright's office, summoning him to his office.

As soon as he arrived, Dr. Bernstein, who had now lost all the previous composure that he had shown in the presence of Detective Andy Garcia, was now obviously frightened, and his tremor had intensified. Doctor Bright tried his best to calm him down, and after he had some success, he listened to the information that Bernstein had obtained from Detective Garcia.

The two men discussed the subject for over an hour, finally arriving to the only possible conclusion: the situation was serious enough that the people in New York, specifically Mr. Mellon needed to be informed.

Bernstein did not want to do it, so it fell upon Doctor David Bright to do it. After pouring himself a large drink of scotch from a bottle he found buried under the papers and journal that cluttered the office, he drank it in one gulp and dialed a number in New York City from a private phone.

The Russian answered, and after requesting a code number from the caller, he passed the machine to Mr. Mellon.

He listened to the information without interrupting. When Bright finished, instead of having one of his temper outbursts of late, he calmly said, "Ivan and I were bored to death today. It is gloomy here in New York, and I welcome some excitement. Tell Paul, as I tell you, do not do anything stupid, and do not answer any more questions, at least not without a lawyer present. Do not trust that lawyer related to the woman Williams. I shall call my New York lawyers immediately. They should be in Florida tomorrow. I really was itching for some action."

The Florida doctors did not hear the next conversation. If they did, they would be nervous.

"Ivan, you know what to do. Call Kurt, the head of security there in Florida, and ask him to investigate if that woman has really been profiting from the mistakes of the old professor. And remember, we can afford to take any chances with her going to the police."

"Aren't you pissed off at Kurt? He should have been responsible for disposing of the bodies produced by the goof ups of old Dr. Bernstein in a better way. Oceans, on both sides, surround Florida, and there are sharks in those oceans, lakes, and rivers with thousands of alligators. Why did he not dump those bodies in there?"

"True, we may have to deal with him later, but for now, we need his service. please call him."

As he finished talking, Ivan was dialing another number, this one a cell phone number, at the institute in Indiantown.

TWENTY-THREE

It made front page news in most of Florida's Treasure Coast newspapers and television stations.

For most readers and viewers, it was just another murder; some secretly rejoiced that one of the victims had been a lawyer, and except for those friends and relatives of the deceased, few took serious interest in the report.

The reactions of some of those familiar with the victims were quite different.

Sheriff Mascara read it in the "Fort Pierce Tribune" and immediately called in Detectives Andy Garcia and Karla Colles and asked them to read it.

Doctor Paul Bernstein read it over breakfast at his cottage on the institute's campus and immediately called Doctor David Bright to his home. Doctor Bright was reading it when Bernstein called, and he rushed to his colleague's place.

Curtis Max Kraft, the institute's head of security, had read it before anyone else because he had gotten up early that morning to pick up the paper with morbid curiosity.

All the articles coincided in reporting that two people had been murdered, a man and a woman. The murders took place at the elegant Palm Beach apartment of the man, who was a prominent lawyer in Martin County; the woman was the lawyer's brother-in-law's wife.

Both bodies had been found naked, hands and feet bound with duct tape behind their backs, and showing signs of having been tortured with cigarette burns and blows to the faces and bodies before being shot in the back of the heads, execution style.

The police already had a suspect in custody, a Mister Jonathan Williams, husband of the woman, who also happened to be the brother of the deceased lawyer, and who was nabbed at the scene of the crime, still with the murder weapon on his hand, apparently trying to decide whether to shoot himself. High levels of drugs were found in his blood.

Other details were sketchy, and there were some pictures of body bags coming out of the building and being loaded in the ambulance.

According to the "Post" reporters Mr. Williams wife, one Claressa Williams, who worked as a head of the Human Resources Department of a reputed Neuroscience Institute located in Indiantown, had been having an affair for some time with her husband's brother, Attorney Gary Williams, the apartment on which the murders took place was owned by the attorney, and was the lovers usual place of rendezvous.

The previous afternoon, as the lovers met, somehow, Mrs. Williams's husband became aware of his wife's infidelity and his brother's betrayal and went to the apartment building with the idea of ending the affair once and for all.

Most likely, he used drugs and alcohol to build up the courage to do the deed, and evidently, he mustered enough to tie the couple and torture them before going for the kill.

"The Post" being a serious newspaper, made clear that the history was based on information provided "by sources closed to the victims," as the police only had acknowledge that they did have a suspect in custody, the name of same and that "there was the possibility that drugs were involved," and regarding the torture they had only said that "there has been some speculation in that respect but we will not know until the Coroner examines the bodies."

The Tribune and The Port Saint Lucie News pretty much printed the same story. At the same time "The Stuart News" had almost the entire front page dedicated to the story, which was the same as that of "The Post" and others but dedicated a lot of space to the personal life and careers of the victims, as well as a small space to profile Brother Jonathan Williams, whom friends and relatives described as "a good man," "a man of the church," "hard to believe capable of committing such a crime." A local preacher was quoting as saying "I guess the love of a woman and her betrayal can drive a good man insane, look at the Bible, Eve, Delilah, Salome; men lost their lives and souls because of them."

The article duly noted several times that Mr. Williams had loudly proclaimed his innocence when arrested and that he claimed that there was no liaison between his wife and his brother, that he had never used drugs, and that he did not remember how he got to the apartment in Palm Beach. He claimed that he was drugged and being framed for a crime he did not commit.

Unfortunately for the poor guy, the police always suspect the husband first, especially if he is found at the scene of the crime, literally with a smoking gun in his hands.

At the Saint Lucie County Sheriff's office, the sheriff and the two detectives were less convinced of the guilt of the betrayed husband. To them, it was too much of a coincidence that the two people they suspected as involved in a plot to murder Hispanic men to collect insurance money had died violently. The sheriff was to leave immediately for West Palm to talk to the police there and to obtain the subpoena of the bank accounts of the deceased from the judge. At least now it would be much easier to get that subpoena.

Meanwhile, at the institute, the two head doctors had arrived at a somewhat similar conclusion: someone else was responsible for the murders, and Claressa's husband had somehow been set up. They both feel guilty and terrified because they know that their call to New York was linked to the murders, yet they did not know what to do.

They could not go to the police, they had no proof of anything, they did not know who the murderer was, and they knew that if they opened their mouths, they could suffer the same fate as Williams. Therefore, they both agree to remain silent and not to let anyone know about their fears and suspicions.

On the other hand, Max Kraft was having the same sensation that an artist or an architect has after completing a masterpiece: pride and satisfaction. He had committed the perfect crime. He had known for a long time where Claressa and the lawyer met; in fact, he had met with them there when they offered the ten thousand dollars apiece to dispose of the bodies of the Latinos accidentally killed by the good old Doctor Bernstein.

What he did not know until he tortured them before the killings was that they collected a quarter of a million dollars each time, while he only got lousy ten grand. Even if he did not have orders to do it, he would have killed them should he have known "the cheating bastards, he did all the dirty work while they were getting rich."

Max was also aware that Claressa kept a gun in her office; he had seen it once, and she mentioned that she had brought it there because her husband "had gone crazy on her and might do something stupid with the gun."

It was easy for him to text the three and ask them to be at the lawyer's apartment in West Palm. The woman had arrived first and he made her get naked at gun point, he still remembered her slender and well-formed body and how much he had to control himself not to rape her. It would not have been a rape, as the woman begged to let her go and offered herself to him in exchange. She looked so beautiful naked, her body was moist with sweat, and it gave her dark skin a shiny, very sexy look, yet Max's self-control prevailed—a fact that he was also proud of—even though he did it mostly because he knew that his DNA could be detected in the semen.

She was already tied down when her supposed lover arrived; Max heard him coming and quickly put a piece of duct tape over her mouth. The lawyer was not a big man but was well-built and muscular. Max was prepared to use his abilities with martial arts if necessary, but the man became was so terrified at the sight of the gun that he peed on his pants before Max asked to remove them.

Although Max was prepared for a much rougher session, he only had to hit them a couple of times and burn their arms in a couple of places before they spilled the beans about the insurance scam.

It was the lawyer, the one that came up with the idea after Claressa told him that the old professor Bernstein had accidentally killed two people in a row while performing some experiment on them. She had mentioned that the old professor should not be doing any more of those things, but that, apparently, he stubbornly refused to give up. He told him that the institute had hired him to take care of the funeral expenses and the repatriation of the bodies and had paid twenty thousand dollars to the families of the deceased.

He would appear publicly as a benefactor of those poor people, and the Institute would pay him a hefty fee for his services.

However, greed was a powerful incentive, and he asked Claressa to give him the names of all the subjects of those experiments, and he would insure them for several hundred thousand dollars. No physical examination was needed because Claressa provided copies of the extensive physical and laboratory tests those individuals underwent before being selected as candidates for the experiments. An accidental death added to the policies increased the amount to be collected by the beneficiary, who was also the premium payer, who was, of course, one Mr. Gary Williams, Squire.

It was because of that that they needed the corpses to appear to have died accidentally, in whichever way Max would consider proper, and they paid him ten thousand clams in cash for every person disposed of in these ways.

Of course, they offered him more money and apologized for not being forward with him. In fact, they begged him to let them go. He would have liked to take the money, but now he could not back off; he had orders to carry out, and he would be facing a gun to his head if he did not do as ordered. Then, Claressa's husband arrived. Max had instructed him to find a key to the apartment over the door frame and to walk in silently. He did all that and almost surprised Max, who was sitting backwards on a chair and facing the naked couple who were sitting at the edge of the bed.

Jonathan Williams was startled, and upon seeing his wife and brother naked and tied up, with a gun-yielding man sitting in front of them, he turned around and tried to flee the room, perhaps to call the police. Max had been too quick for him who getting up from the chair, tackled him to the floor and hit him in the head with the butt of the gun, the man did not lose consciousness. Still, he remained groggy, face down on the floor. Then, as he got up on his knees, Max, who had pulled a loaded syringe from one of the pockets of his jacket, injected the liquid into the man's neck, hoping to hit the jugular vein.

He probably was lucky in doing that because although the man got up, it was groggy,

Max pointed the gun at him and forced Mr. Williams to sit in the very same chair that he had occupied minutes earlier.

He waited a few minutes; the man was obviously not strange to drugs as he was still awake after about 10 minutes. Max injected him again, this time in the vein of the arm with another chemical, it was Versed this time and worked quickly.

After that, it was matter of cleaning up, making Jonathan Williams hold the gun to leave his fingerprints on it then shooting the couple in the back of their heads and replacing the gun on Mr. Williams hand, he forced the hand of the sleeping man to pull the trigger once more, so traces of gunpowder be found on his hands.

Thereafter, making sure that nobody saw him, he calmly walked out and took the stairs down—the apartment was on the third floor—as it was less likely to be seen there than if he had taken the elevator and then walked out of the building.

Then he called 911 to report hearing shots coming from somewhere on the third floor. He had hesitated about doing this, but he did want the police to find the betrayed husband at the scene of the crime.

The police know that husbands kill their wives all the time, even without a motive, and this guy had one. Once they found a suspect, they did not look any further.

Of course, he called from a paid phone.

A masterpiece indeed, the perfect crime! He was proud of himself. Mr. Richard Melon and the Russian would be happy, too.

TWENTY-FOUR

Although it was late in the season, almost November, it had been a big storm. It had caused quite a bit of havoc in the Caribbean and awful destruction in the Yucatan Peninsula, where it had lost most of its strength. However, upon entering the still warm waters of the Gulf of Mexico, it was predicted to regain some of its force, and it was heading northeast straight to the peninsula of Florida.

The weather experts had forecasted that it would enter about Sarasota, cut across the state, and come back out in the Atlantic at the level of Jacksonville.

The Treasure Coast would get heavy rain and gusty winds. Therefore, in Palm Beach, Martin, Saint Lucie, and Okeechobee Counties, only the schools were closed, while for everyone else, it was business as usual.

Except for the police, sheriff, and fire departments, which stayed on high alert "just in case." Of course, this made it impossible for Sheriff Mascara to take the planned trip to West Palm to obtain the subpoenas they needed.

On the other hand, back at the Neurological Institute in Indiantown, everything was on the normal, daily track.

All the employees had shown up for work, some with their children in tow. As Doctor Bernstein had told them the day before, they could bring their families to be sheltered from the storm at the Institute.

Whether everyone was there because they felt safer on the solid structure of the buildings or because they were loyal to their work was a matter of question, but Dr. Melvin Bright was betting on the former as he had breakfast that morning with beautiful young Doctor Jasmine Porter.

In turn, she informed Doctor "Not-so" that she planned to talk with Dr. Bernstein that very same day and inform him of her desire to resign from her position at the institute.

She had not totally gotten over the death—she insisted on calling it suicide—of the chimp, and she had observed some other things around there that she did not like and not agree with. She had been having heated arguments with her mother about the subject, with her mother pleading to her to stay.

Obviously, young Dr. Bright also pleaded with her to reconsider and reminded her of the unique opportunity that they had to contribute to the welfare of mankind, plus the prestige, the learning experience, and the money that they were being paid.

Jasmine did not buy those arguments. She said that her mind was made and ended with a coquette smile while saying, "I wish you go away as well."

She did not say, "With me," but Melvin felt like she meant to say it. It made his heartbeat 140 beats a minute, and he felt as if he was floating in the air as she left the cafeteria, leaving behind her the sweet smell of her perfume.

Kevin Nielsen had also shown up for work, but he was undoubtedly one of those who did it because he felt safer there; his Hutchison Island condominium was beachfront. He was afraid of being there during the storm, no matter how small the experts said it would be. The rising surf is usually the most dangerous part of those storms

Besides, weathermen were often wrong, and the storm could very well have hit closer than anticipated; he could have gone to his parents in Tampa, but that area was definitely in the path of the Hurricane.

He had not been at his office long, before he overheard someone reporting to Dr. Cho that the DNA report on the samples of the serum injected to the patient known to them as # 1344 were back and they were unusual in that not only it contained DNA of an individual different than the one planned to be the donor but it also contained traces of canine, feline and other animal species. And yes, the name of the person from which the serum had come was Ismael Torres, a patient who was no longer at the Institute, to the best of his knowledge.

Dr. Cho sounded alarmed, and he called his colleagues to share the report. However, this part of the conversation probably took place in the conference room, and he had not been invited to attend the meeting.

He also heard that the videotape recordings of those previous days had been taken to the conference room to be reviewed.

Kevin became concerned but not overly so, although someone might identify him as the culprit, he could always claim error or ignorance and although he would probably be fired from the Institute, especially for not reporting the mistake in time, that would not be the end of the world for him; he could always go tell about the cure for drug addiction and maybe create some problem for all those dammed professors.... No he was not overly worried, but he was nevertheless sweating even when the A/C was running at 70 degrees.

Outside, it had been thundering, and the wind was picking up strength. It was beginning to rain.

Doctor Alice Rodriguez knocked on the door of the room lodging patient 1344, known to most of them as "Homeless Tony," who was just finishing his breakfast; as the voice inside gave her permission to enter, she walked into the sparsely furnished room and sat on one of the two chairs available. "Good morning, Tony. How are you feeling this morning?" she asked.

"Pretty good, Doc. The headaches are completely gone, but the feeling that I am another person or that there is another person inside me is frightening at times. I even think that I am changing physically. When I sleep, I dream of jungles, and war, and dead people, like Vietnam, you know? Problem is ...I was never in Vietnam nor any jungle anywhere. I have traveled across most of the US though, mostly jumping on trains, but I've never been all over, the world I think."

"You told me yesterday that you could understand some of the things that the Spanish-speaking fellows were saying. How is that going?" the pretty doctor asked.

"Well, I have not heard anyone talking to me in Spanish lately, but last night, just by chance, I turned the TV in to Univision, the Spanish channel, and I believe that I could understand most of the stuff they were talking about. Is that weird or what Doc?"

A loud thunder was heard very closely, and the lights of the room flickered as Dr. Rodríguez asked in Spanish, *"Escuchaste las noticias de la tormenta?"* (Did you hear the news about the storm?)

Tony responded in perfect Spanish as well *"Dicen que no va a ser muy malo por aca, lo peor sera en Sarasota."*

As Doctor Rodriguez looked at him in amusement, a flash of bright light filled the room. The loud sound of thunder deafened her, and electric power went off throughout the building. This was followed by two more flashes and explosions in rapid succession.

Doctor Rodriguez's first thought was that lightning never hits twice on the same spot, but then, the smell of burning rubber filled the room. For few seconds she was blinded by the first lightning strike but as she was beginning to be able to see in the dark room, the second lightning strike occurred and by its light she saw that Tony was up from his bed and approaching her with an object in his hand, she was not sure at first of what it was but then she saw it. It was a kitchen knife.

She then felt Tony's breath on her neck and the cold metal of the knife against her jugular, as the man said in muffled voice: "Now that those dammed TV cameras are out, you are going to help me get out of this place, do not do anything stupid or I kill you. Understand that? Do you have a car? No? Let's go anyway."

As they walked down the hall towards the lobby, Dr. Bernstein's office door opened, and the old professor, accompanied by Dr. Jasmine Porter, emerged.

The hallway was dark, illuminated only by the emergency lights mostly over the exit ways. Still, Bernstein realized that something unusual was happening and step in front of Tony and Doctor Rodriguez, blocking their way.

"Do you have your car keys with you, old man?" Tony said to Bernstein.

"The hell with you. Even if I had my car keys with me, I would not give them to you. Let Doctor Rodriguez go right now."

"You have guts but no common sense, old man. Stay out of my way," said Homeless Tony. As he said it, he stabbed the old man in the middle of the chest. Jasmine was so terrified she did not even dare to scream. The man took her by the arm, cleaning the blood off the knife on her lab coat as he said, "You also are coming with us, cutie. The more, the merrier. I am sure you have a car."

Doctor Rodriguez, despite having the knife back against her neck, mustered enough valor to say, "No, she doesn't, not here, anyway. You see, most of us doctors live on campus, so we park our cars in front of our homes, which are farther than the parking lot. We are brought to the institute whenever we want by a shuttle bus."

"Ok, Doc, then let's go see who has a dammed car, before the power comes back and those blasted surveillance cameras go back to work," Tony said as he pushed the two women down the hallway.

As the three of them entered the lobby, they saw that Gladys was at her post behind the reception desk. However, she was rather shaky about the storm, the lightning, and the power failure. She was being comforted by security guard Joe Smith, who was obviously coming out of duty but was still wearing a uniform and weapons.

Neither the guard nor Gladys saw the arriving party until they were a few feet away. Joe was quick to notice that something was not right, and he attempted to draw his gun while shouting, "Stay right there, mister, and put your hands above your—"

Joe did not have time to complete the phrase that ended with "head" before the knife thrown by Tony "The Homeless" pierced his right shoulder through and effectively nailed him to the wood-paneled wall.

Gladys let a loud scream that made those who had taken refuge from the storm at the lobby turn their heads towards her. By then, Homeless Tony was on top of Joe Smith, who was screaming in pain while trying to pull the knife out of his shoulder and, with an almost incredible speed, took the belt off the security guard. The belt was the one holding Joe's gun, ammunition, and handcuffs.

Tony buckled it in his own waist while holding the Beretta and waving it across the lobby: "Whoever moves is going to get hurt. Get down on the floor, all of you! NOW!" He shouted, and everyone got down.

And then, facing the pale and shaking Gladys, who was trying to approach Joe, who was moaning and bleeding heavily, Tony said, "Now you cutie. I see you have a purse, so you must have a car outside, don't you?" After she nodded her head in the affirmative, he said to her, "Okay, grab it. We are going for a ride. You be driving."

He did not wait for Gladys to grab her purse. He did it for her and made the three women walk towards the exit door.

That was when the other security guard, who had left the gate earlier because of the lightning but had been outside under the main entrance's awning, took notice of what was happening inside and entered the lobby with his gun drawn.

Tony saw that and, with another swift motion, leveled the gun he had taken from Joe Smith and shot twice hitting the second security guard right in the middle of the chest. The man fell without a sound. After Tony ushered the women past the fallen man, he bent over to pick his gun and shackles. He now had two Berettas and three women hostages as they walked into the heavy rain towards the yellow Toyota Camry 2005 belonging to Gladys Franklin.

He made Gladys sit at the wheel, Jasmine on the passenger side and Doctor Rodriguez sit at his side in the back seat of the car.

It was still raining heavily, but the thunder and lightning were almost gone. All four were soaked with rainwater, and the three women were shaking. They were all shivering from being wet and also from being frightened.

Homeless Tony, with one gun in his hand and the other in the holster, told Gladys in secure voice, "Drive, and drive as fast as you can"

Gladys only mustered to respond, "which way?" and was further surprised when Tony said

"North, drive north, towards Okeechobee."

Doctor Rodriguez, who as a psychiatrist was used to dealing with dangerous delusional patients—although she had never been in a situation near as dangerous as this one—was the first one to partially regain her composure as she said, "Are you sure, Tony? The storm is probably worse that way. Remember that the weatherman said the storm was going to be heading northeast."

"For a doctor, you are not very smart in these matters, Doc. That is precisely what the cops will think—he is not crazy enough to go where the storm is—and they will look for us in the other direction. Besides, if we go where there is a storm, the cops would be busy with car wrecks, power outages, fallen trees, flooded streets and the more than average number of heart attacks to be looking for us," said Tony. He continued after a pause: "To good old Okeechobee we go ladies. By the way, I only know the Doc's name here. What are your names, cuties in the front seat?"

"It is Doctor Porter to you," said Jasmin in an angry voice, to which Tony responded scornfully

"Another Doctor, what an honor. I guess I do not have to be afraid of being shot, with two doctors around."

"That is right, I am exactly the kind of doctor you need. I am a veterinarian," responded Jasmin with anger.

"Well, well, a woman with a sense of humor. How nice; it looks like this trip is going to be much more fun than I had anticipated. How about you lady driver, do you have a name?" Tony appeared to be having a great time. He was not a bit worried about being caught or killed, and that worried the psychiatrist quite a bit, as Gladys answered with a shaky voice:

"It is Gladys, Gladys Franklin, sir. And what is yours?"

"They call me Tony. Actually, they call me 'Homeless Tony,' but my real name, heck, I am not going to tell you my real name. I do not think that

I even remember what my real name was. However, you can call me Ismael; Ismael Torres. Yes, that is it: Ismael Torres. What do you think of that name, Doc? Maybe Tony is better. It is more American. The other one sounds Mexican. Don't you think so Doc?"

Doctor Rodriguez thought that it was good that he was talking, and she started to speak to him, but she was not sure if or rather when he was going to snap and rape and kill the three of them.

TWENTY-FIVE

Normally it would have taken only couple of minutes to start the potent backup generators that the Institute had installed for emergencies like this, however, because the storm was still dropping buckets of rain, the winds were over 60 miles an hour and the lightening continued, with leaves and tree limbs falling all over the place, the remote control, that should have been able to start the generators from the central security office inside the building had been damaged. Therefore, the machines had to be started manually, which meant venturing out in inclement weather to reach the small building in the back of the institute where they were installed, so it took better than fifteen minutes to start the generators and have the power back.

Because of the same reasons, the security people, and in fact, no one else, had seen what had happened in front of Dr. Bernstein's office. On the other hand, quite a few people witnessed the events in the lobby. Some of them were trying frantically to assist the wounded security guards, while others called 911 on their cell phones, and still others ran inside the building yelling for help.

Even so, it took several minutes for the security and medical staff to become aware of what had happened.

Melvin Bright was one of the first physicians summoned by a nurse, alerted by one of the people running from the lobby. Doctor "Not-So" ran from the hospital guard into the hallway only to almost trip over the body of Doctor Paul Bernstein.

Melvin was not the most competent physician in the Institute, or even around Stuart and Saint Lucie, but he had seen few dead people during his training to tell that "Uncle Paul" was very dead. There was a pool of blood under the body, which was beginning to cloth

Melvin did not have much chance to hold his dear friend in his arms, as it was his impulse, because many other people started coming and yelling that there were other victims in the lobby, and they needed a Doctor. Melvin shouted to a nurse to summon his father and the other doctors and ran to the lobby, preceded by several people and followed by others.

The scene he found at the Lobby was chaotic, people were screaming, one of the security guards was pinned to the paneled wall by a large kitchen knife sticking out of his right shoulder. He had passed out and was being held by some of the bystanders so as to keep him from slipping down to the floor and allowing the knife to perhaps sever his arm from the shoulder. He was bleeding heavily, but Melvin thought that his wound was not fatal; there was a pulse, albeit faint on the guard's wrist, so probably the arteries at the arm pit had not been severed. He instructed the male nurse to pull the knife from the wall, but not from the man's shoulder, and called for someone to start an IV on the other arm.

Thereafter, he went to the other security guard; his condition was much more serious and, at first, he thought he was dead. Then he detected shallow breathing and pulsations on the carotid artery at the neck.

The man had two bullet holes on his chest, and his white shirt was soaked with blood, as was the raincoat that he was wearing, and his chest felt unusually hard. When someone brought a pair of scissors and Melvin cut the man's shirt open, To the surprise of all those present, they observed that the man had put a square piece of hard plastic under his shirt, whether he did this not to get wet or a as a homemade bullet proof vest, would be something that they all had to wait to learn, if the man survived his wound. Fortunately for him, such a thing may have served to slow down the speed and, therefore, the damage from the bullets.

Nevertheless, he was losing blood, and his chest was probably filling with it very rapidly. He would be dead in no time unless surgery was performed.

Unfortunately, the institute did not have a chest surgeon available. In fact, it was not equipped to handle that kind of emergency at all.

As they heard the sirens of the police and ambulance approaching, they all developed a dim of hope for the life of this poor man who was shot while performing his duty.

The rain and wind were still loud and heavy, so the approaching vehicles must have had trouble getting there fast enough.

Almost simultaneously, Dr. Bright, the senior, most other doctors, nurses, and the security team on duty arrived and started working on the wounded. Dr. Bright, senior, called for a chest tube, and in a couple of minutes, someone had brought one. By then, both guards had intravenous fluids going through their veins. After lifting the man onto a stretcher, Doctor David Bright listened to the man's chest with his stethoscope and then, without hesitation, made a small cut on the side of the man's chest and, with a gloved hand, inserted a plastic tube into it. Immediately, blood started pouring out, and the man's breathing became less labored.

Doctor Kevin Nielsen was standing nearby, but in the back of the crowd. He was not helping the others. Pale and terrified, he just stood there, afraid to move, afraid to be noticed, afraid that someone could start asking him questions.

Nielsen became more scared as he heard the people who had witnessed the events tell the story to the security team; his concern became panic when he overheard one of them telling another that the man known as "Homeless Tony" could not be accounted for, and neither was Dr. Rodriguez.

It soon became clear that" Homeless Tony" had killed Doctor Berstein and attacked the guards. He not only forced Doctor Alice Rodriguez to go with him but also took the Receptionist, Gladys Franklin, and another woman with him. Nobody was sure at that time who this other woman was because the power failure knocked the video cameras out of service.

Kevin, felt nauseous and was about to vomit right then and there, it was not that he was sorry for the injured men, in fact he was almost happy that "that s.o.b., Joe Smith received what was coming to him." But he realized that if someone found out that he had tampered with the serum that was injected in to Tony, he would be held responsible for what Tony had done.

Kevin was not stupid. After what he had heard that morning about the results of the DNA test, it would not take long for someone to blame him for what was perhaps soon to be three murders, possibly six if you counted the three women.

He looked out through the glass doors of the lobby. The rain and wind were still heavy, but he sensed that he would be in much more danger if he stayed at the institute than if he left in the middle of the storm, so he chose the latter.

It was then that the police arrived; unfortunately, they had brought only one ambulance with them, so it was a no-brainer to decide to take the most seriously injured man to the nearest hospital, which happened to be in Stuart. The senior Doctor Bright was not certain that the patient would survive the trip, and so he volunteered to go with him in the ambulance. The other Doctors on the staff of the institute would care for Joe Smith and struggle to keep him alive until another ambulance arrived.

The body of Doctor Paul Bernstein would not go anyplace or anywhere soon.

Kevin Nielsen looked around, saw that no one was watching him, and walked towards the door. A policeman was standing there and requested his name and address. He gave them to him, not too willingly, and responded to his question by stating that he had not seen anything because he was working way in the back of the building at his lab.

To the question as to why he was leaving while the storm was still raging, he lied that he had been "like a son" to the murdered Doctor Bernstein and he was unable to bear to see him dead. He told him he suffered from "hypoglycemia" and those strong emotions triggered it, and he was feeling sick already.

The cop let him go; it never occurred to him that if the guy was about to suffer an attack of hypoglycemia, he should not get behind the wheel of a car, not even in fair weather, much less during a storm. But the poor cop probably had more important things in his mind than to worry about a nerdy-looking guy crashing his probably expensive vehicle.

An expensive vehicle it was, for Kevin drove a yellow Hummer 2, to which he dashed under the heavy rain while pressing the remote control to open the doors. Once inside, he did not worry about getting the expensive leather seats wet, as he typically would have; his only concern was to get away from that place. He turned the car radio on and listened to the news as he drove away. The storm had entered Tampa as a Hurricane category I or II—the newscasters differed on their opinions—and it was indeed heading northwest, the eye of the storm was at that point exactly over Saint Petersburg. The consensus was that there would be no threat to the Treasure Coast and that the rain and wind over those areas would be slowing down within a few hours.

Therefore, there was no way he could go to Mom and Dad in Tampa, but he felt the urge to get further away than his apartment in Hutchison Island. He would have to go there to pack, get some money, a passport, and then drive to West Palm, Orlando, or Miami to take a plane to Mexico. He felt he deserved a vacation, perhaps after Mexico City; a few days in Cancun would be great.

Kevin took road 76 to Stuart and then got off at 95 to Fort Pierce. He figured that the Interstate would have less traffic and less chance of debris hitting his vehicle or getting in his path. He had to be careful on 76, though, because it was, in most parts, a two-lane road, and the wind was blowing leaves and small branches from the trees. He was almost about to reach 95 when he saw two more ambulances coming in the opposite direction.

After about a fifteen-minute drive, he reached the Fort Pierce exit, passing the first one and exiting on the one marked "Orange Avenue," which would take him more directly to the bridges connecting downtown Fort Pierce to Hutchison Island and his apartment on the fifth floor of the exclusive "Ocean Village compound." Hoping that the Police had not blocked access to the beach because of the storm, he continued heading east.

There were no cops on the bridge, and the rain and wind were slightly less in Fort Pierce than they had been in Indiantown. Kevin did not know if that was because the storm had already passed over there or because of the area's geographic location, which was more south of Tampa than the place where the institute was.

Once he reached the gated condominiums, he drove towards his building and, for the first time, felt the chill of his damp clothes as he got out of the car. Before packing for his trip, he decided to grab a bite, take a hot shower, and see what the TV had to say about the storm damage in Tampa and elsewhere. He turned to the weather channel as he made himself a ham and cheese sandwich on rye and gulped it down with the help of a Corona light.

After taking his wet clothes off and downing a white terrycloth bathrobe, he ate without hurrying. Then, he sat in front of the TV to watch the weather news.

A good half hour had passed before Kevin got up and walked into the shower, and he took a long one before coming out, fixing himself a cup of instant coffee, and opening the curtains of the balcony. He looked at the sea. It was a depressing but awesome spectacle. The ocean was dark grey, and the wind made the waves grow big and hit the beaches in areas much farther inland than normal. Still, the waters were quite far from the building.

Then Kevin, holding the cup of steaming coffee in his hands, walked to the opposite side of the apartment and looked through the window. The rain was still heavy, and no cars were coming in and out, so he stood there for a while looking at the parking lot.

Suddenly, something caught his attention: a black car had pulled into the parking lot, and it appeared to be about to park in front of his building.

He recognized the car, although it did not have any markings. It was just a black Mercedes, perhaps belonging to one of the neighbors.

He kept looking with curiosity and saw two men, wearing black raincoats, getting out of the car. The panic that he had felt earlier at the institute came back twice as hard, for he recognized one of the men as Max Kraft, the Chief of Security at the Neurological Institute.

Kevin was frantic; he knew they were coming for him. He did not know what they would do, but he was certain it would be nothing good. Perhaps they only wanted to ask him questions about what he had seen, but what if they wanted to hurt him? What if they hit him or roughen him up? What if they wanted to kill him?

"No, that is stupid," he thought. "They are only security people, and they are not killers; scientists run the institute, so they would not send assassins after him. But what about the real boss, that guy from New York and his bodyguard or whatever, the Russian fellow? He had heard some rumors about them, and none were very reassuring."

Kevin looked around the apartment for something to defend himself with. There was nothing. He lifted his phone to dial 911, and the line was dead. "Was it due to the storm, or did these guys do it?" He did not know, but he searched the pockets of his wet jacket for his cell phone. While doing so, his wallet fell, and out of it came a business card with the name "Saint Lucie County Sheriff Department," the name "Detective Andres Garcia," and the cell phone number.

Kevin dialed the numbers in a hurry, missing to dial correctly twice before he heard the dial tone and the voice at the other end: "Detective Garcia here."

"Thank God, Detective. You probably do not remember me but I was the jerk who trampled your lady partner when you came to the institute in Indiantown. I need your help. I believe I am in mortal danger. Someone is coming to get me, please, please help."

Kevin's voice was broken and hard to understand, especially since he was almost sobbing, but Garcia was able to get most of the message and responded, "Because of the storm, we are all working as regular cops. Right now, I am attending to a vehicular accident on US 1. Are you saying that your life is in danger? Where are you calling me from?"

"Ocean Village, in Hutchinson Island, apartment 505, please hurry."

At that moment, the door of the apartment swung open and Kevin dropped the cell phone as two men burst inside

Garcia still had a chance to say: "Hold on tight. I am sending a patrol car over, and I will be there as soon as I am through here."

TWENTY-SIX

At the Neurological Institute, between the medical personnel, the police, and the institute's own Security Corps, the pieces of what initially appeared to have been a puzzle started to fall in place.

It was determined by all those that one of the patients, the one known as "Homeless Tony" and whose real name was Anthony Malatesta, an Italian American born in Brooklyn N.Y., and who had left home as a teenager after dropping off high school and becoming involved with drugs and gangs. Most likely, the family, who was a well-known, hard-working, catholic Italian family had kicked him out after many failed attempts at rehabilitation.

It was also determined that the individual named Tony, had murdered the head doctor of the institute and had fled the place in a stolen car belonging to one of three women he had kidnapped. The three women had been identified; the last one was a Doctor Jasmine Porter, a young veterinarian physician.

Nobody but very few people knew that Tony Malatesta was two men in one. He was also Ismael Torres, a veteran, special forces, anti-guerrilla fighter from Guatemala who had fought a dirty war against the guerrillas in the jungles of Guatemala and had been trained to do so at "The School of the Americas" in the very core of the United States of America.

Doctor Linda Porter learned that her daughter had been kidnapped and almost fainted, blaming herself for making her stay at the Institute when Jasmine had expressed her desires to quit right after the incident of the death of the chimpanzee.

Melvin Bright did not learn about it until he left the OR, after doing surgery on the shoulder of Joe Smith, the wounded gate security guard.

As head of security, Max Kraft knew not only that he had a massive problem in his hands but that "The Homeless" behavior had something to do with the experiment to which he was submitted.

After questioning some of the Doctors involved, he was informed about the DNA report, and watching the video tapes, the name of Doctor Kevin Nielson came into the picture.

Since Doctor Bright Senior had not yet returned from his ambulance trip and Doctor Bernstein was dead, Max was not sure who was in charge. He quickly assumed the role by first calling Ivan Peters (aka Peter Ivanovich), the man who had hired him for this job and for whom he had previously done several jobs.

Ivanovich's instructions were clear: find out who had paid Dr. Kevin Neilson to sabotage the experiment and find Tony Malatesta. Neither one should be allowed to talk to the police, the press, or anyone else. They should be silenced forever. As for the women hostages, try your best to rescue them, but if that is not possible, they should be considered collateral damage.

Max was told that he should take care of the young Doctor Nielsen personally and may delegate the hunt for Tony for the time being.

"Homeless Tony" was sitting in the back of the car, playing with one of the two Berettas he had taken from the security guards. Dr. Rodriguez was next to him, and the other two women were in the front seat. Gladys was driving. They all cried and shook really badly. The rain was very heavy, and the wind was strong. Thunder and lightning were everywhere.

"What are you going to do with us?" and "Where are we going?" were repetitive questions, mixed with a surprised and irate reaction from Doctor Rodriguez after he directed Gladys to take 710 towards Okeechobee: "You must be mad. In this weather, we should be heading away from the storm."

"I told you my reasons, dear Doctor, and let me remind you that you are no longer in charge. I am the boss now. In fact, I am more than that because I have your bodies and lives in my very own hands," Tony said, sticking the gun on Doctor Rodriguez's ribs.

They thought that if this madman did not kill them, they were going to die in a car crash, especially since Tony had instructed Gladys not to drive below 70mph. However, a few seconds after Alice Rodriguez had spoken, he instructed Gladys to reduce the speed of the car to 60mph and to 40mph once they reached the outskirts of the town of Okeechobee.

Tony kept smiling and told Gladys to turn the car radio on; he wanted to hear some music, but only news about the storm was broadcast in most stations. He told her to turn it off, then he ask them if they had any money or credit cards; neither one of the doctors had any, because they lived on campus and were wearing uniforms, Gladys handed him her bag, which Tony emptied on the lap of Doctor Rodriguez. After finding a wallet, he opened it and got some dollars out. "Thirty dollars? Thirty lousy dollars, that is all you have?" Tony first sounded angry, and Dr. Rodriguez thought that he was about to hit her, but then his mood became festive, and he sarcastically said, "They do not pay you well at the institute. What a shame."

And then he continued in the same sarcastic tone: "Well, I see that you have a bankcard. Would you mind telling me what your credit limit is? We need to stop and get some mullah."

"Ah, ah, I am not sure. I never used my limit before, perhaps something like a couple of thousand dollars, if that," said Gladys in a tremulous voice, keeping an eye on the road. They were on the outskirts of the town of Okeechobee now.

"Slow down and look for a bank, and no one of you dare to scream for help, because I swear that I blow all of your fucking heads off."

It was the first time that Doctor Rodriguez had heard Tony use a curse word. She was not sure if he was getting more dangerous as time passed or if he was just trying to act rough to scare them. If it was the latter, he was certainly doing a very good job at it.

"There is a bank, pointed Tony, pull into the parking lot" instructed Tony and then he said "I'll be darn, Bank Atlantic is open for business, this is our lucky day, we may be able to make a larger withdraw and without using this poor girl's bankcard"

Tony Instructed Gladys to park the car as far back as possible from the road and to turn the vehicle around to face the main road in case they had to leave in a hurry. He pulled out of the belt that he had taken from the guard, two sets of handcuffs, and handcuffed the two girls in the front seat, one to another and then Gladys's right hand to the steering wheel of the car.

Thereafter, he removed the clip and the bullet from the chamber of one of the guns and handed it to Doctor Alice Rodriguez while saying, "Now you are going to have another really exciting experience, dear Doctor; you are going to help me to rob a bank. Because if you don't, I will rob it myself, but first, I shall blow the three pretty faces of you all to kingdom come. *Entiende Doctora?*" he finished in Spanish.

They exited the car under the heavy rain and walked to the door of the bank lobby. Since it was darker outside than inside where the lights were on, they could have a perfect view of the inside.

There were three tellers, all female, no customers and they were all watching the news about the storm on a giant plasma TV screen, located on the wall behind the counter. The women did not see the two persons coming in until they were inside and close to the teller's booths, which were actually separated from the main lobby by a glass about two feet tall.

"You stay here and just show the gun," Tony instructed the frightened Doctor Rodriguez, "and please do not do anything stupid. I promise you a reward if you behave like a good girl." And then he fired a shot to the ceiling which startled all the women simultaneously. Using the left hand to support himself, he jumped with ease over the teller's glass while shouting, "This is a robbery! Stay where you are, do not move, do not try to sound an alarm and you all will be fine. I will just take some money from here that is not even yours. Why risk your lives to protect it…right?"

He made the women open their drawers and turn the lights off so anyone outside would think the bank was closed. Then, he asked for a bag. As none of the women reacted, he told them, "Fine, one of you go get your purses. I want all your purses. Bring them here to me. You have one minute before I start shooting." And then he added, "Is there anyone else in the building?"

"Only Mrs. Krammer, the branch manager. I think she is in the bathroom," one of the women said.

"Okay, you go get her out, and do not try anything cute, or you will be responsible for the death of your friends here…and also yours," said Tony with extreme calm as he took money out of the drawers and placed it on top of the counter.

The woman returned in less than a minute, holding four female handbags and accompanied by a classy looking, middle-aged woman, wearing a professional looking navy blue pant suit, glasses and short hair beginning to gray at the sides. She had somewhat lost her executive appearance because she was struggling to pull up her pants and button then.

Tony smiled at her sight but did not make any comments. Actually, he was very polite: "Good afternoon, madam. I am very sorry to rush you, but you see, my friend and I are in a hurry, and we wanted to meet everybody from this fine financial institution."

"I am assuming that you hold the keys of all the doors of the institution, is that correct, ma'am?" he asked.

He just nodded while going around the bank, ripping the cords of all the phones off the walls and instructing Dr. Rodriguez to empty the contents of the bags on a desk in the lobby.

"Do not worry, ladies. I am not going to steal your money, and I am not an identity thief either. All I want is all your cell phones. So if any of you is wearing one, besides what is in the purse, better hand it to me now."

"They are not allowed to have cell phones while working," stated Mrs. Krammer.

That is excellent policy, Mrs. Krammer, how about you, would you be so kind as to hand me yours," said Tony with sarcasm—and then he added: "Now let's see. This is the most oversized purse. I think we can fit all the money and the cell phones, and oh yes, I almost forgot, all the car keys and remotes too. Now, what about those dammed keys to the premises, Mrs. Krammer?" Tony said as he pointed the gun at her, threatening to fire.

The woman turned around went in to a small office, followed by all three tellers, Dr. Rodriguez and Tony behind them all. She opened her desk and produced a set of keys and handled them to the man.

"Thank you, ladies. Now, please tell me which is the key to this room and which is the key to the front door."

Mrs. Krammer appeared to be ready to faint, but she selected two keys from the bundle and showed them to Tony.

"Ok, now we are going to end this beautiful reunion. You all stay in this room until I am gone. I am going to lock it and put some explosives in the door. So, if it is opened before one hour, the whole place will blow up. So be good girls and be patient."

"Oh, I forgot to tell you, my girlfriend Maria, here," Tony said, referring to Doctor Rodriguez. "As I discovered, she has not been faithful to me, so I will leave her behind here to keep you company." He said that as he took the unloaded gun from her hand and pushed her into the room, whispering in her ear, "I told you I would give you a price if you were a good girl."

Then he turned around, locked the door, and walked through the lobby. He grabbed the bag with the money, the cell phones, and the car keys and walked out of the bank, locking the front door as he did so. Then, calmly, he walked to the Toyota, where Jasmine and Gladys were shivering from cold and fear.

The whole thing lasted less than five minutes.

"I see that you've been good girls," he said as he approached the car and looked inside to ensure they were still handcuffed and secure.

"Just wait a bit longer, girls. We may need to change our means of transportation," Tony said very calmly.

As he walked away in the rain, clicking the remotes, opening the cars to see their condition and whether they had enough gas in their tanks, he left a one-hundred-dollar bill on the front seat of each vehicle.

All the cars had tanks full of gas in case of a shortage after the storm.

The two girls in the car were more frightened than ever. "Where is Doctor Rodriguez? She did not come back with him," said Gladys to Jasmine. "Do you think he killed her?"

Jasmine answered that she did not know, but she was sure that Doctor Rodriguez was all right; perhaps she got away, or he let her go.

Actually, Doctor Jasmine Porter only said that to reassure her companion, as well as herself, because she had seen that man kill three people back at the Institute without hesitation or remorse and both had heard a shot fired inside the bank.

Tony returned, "Ok, ladies, sorry you have to get wet again. This dammed rain does not want to stop and probably is not going to do it all night. We are transporting you to a late-model silver Chevy Lumina."

Jasmine mustered the courage to ask, "Where is Alice, I mean Doctor Rodriguez?"

"She decided to leave the party early," Tony said as he made them board the Lumina. Gladys was again the designated driver.

Tony spoke: "There is a gun shop about three or four blocks from here, on this same side of the road, almost exactly opposite where the Walmart is. Stop there, I need to buy some things."

After passing the handbag and removing the cell phones from it, told to Doctor Porter to, "Please count our assets, I think we are a bit richer than we were half hour ago."

The woman doctor grabbed the bag and started taking bills of different denominations out of it and placing them in bundles according to value. There were many singles, fives, tens, and twenties, a few fifties, and at least twenty-one hundred-dollar bills. After a few minutes, she returned with the number and said, "You stole exactly nine thousand seventy-four dollars and fifty cents; there are two quarters here."

He laughed and only said, "Good, there is the gun shop, and if our luck holds, it is open for business. We are going to repeat the same thing we did at the bank. Be good, ok? And I shall bring you a present."

After handcuffing them again in the same fashion he walked into the gun shop, emerging few minutes later with a shotgun and several packages that the threw in the front seat, while telling them: "There, my pretty ladies. Those are some dry camouflage clothes, which I hope will fit; heavy rain ponchos for all of us. I also bought myself a couple of toys." He said this while loading the shotgun with large buckshot shells and showing them his other purchases: a hunting knife, several replacement clips for the Berettas, ammunition and a couple of duffle bags, into which he proceeded to put the guns.

Tony did all that while continuing to talk: "That guy in there is a thief; someone should report him to the authorities. He took almost a thousand dollars of our hard-earned money for this junk." And he laughed, a laugh that made the girls even more afraid and nervous.

Yet Gladys found enough nerve to ask: "Can you tell us where you are going to take us, please?" asked Gladys in a tremulous voice.

"Right now, I need to find a place to eat. I am famished, and I doubt a restaurant will be open where we will be heading."

"And where will you be heading?" asked Jasmine this time.

"Way into the storm," answered Tony as he removed the handcuffs from the girls, and then added, "Now let's find the drive thru window of the nearest McDonald's, Burger King, Taco Bell or Wendy's. You girls tell me now what you will have and I order it for you. Sorry, perhaps latter I could treat you to eat at a fancier place. Now, you each will have five minutes to enter the restaurant if you have to pee or change clothes."

"I suppose that you are as hungry as I am. In any case you girls better eat, because I do not know when we will be able to eat again today. If you girls want to use the toilet, go one at the time while I will wait in the car with the other one. If the one inside fails to come out in five minutes, or if I see you talking to anyone, I shall kill the person who stays with me and do my best to kill the other one as well." Then, realizing that if he terrorized them too much they may be willing to take their chances and do something stupid, Tony added: "On the other hand, if you girls behave, I promised that I will set you free, safe and sound, as soon as I feel it its safe for me to do so. Is that understood? Ok, let's roll."

They did find a McDonald's nearby, and both did as requested. Neither one dared to contact anyone there, which actually would have been impossible because there was only an old couple sitting far away from the restrooms and the people at the counter, who were more interested in watching the rain falling still heavily outside than in anyone coming in or out of the premises.

The girls found that they were actually hungry; they had not had anything to eat since breakfast, and it was almost two in the afternoon. So they ate the burgers and fries and drank the coffee which, much to their surprise, tasted good.

Tony spoke again "Ok, lady –what is your name? Oh yes, Gladys. You have been an excellent driver, so far, so see if you can get us out of this town, take route 42 to 98 and then 17, those will take us, hopefully to the town of Sebring, and then to Avon Park. You do not have to go too fast, it is going to be raining cats and dogs"

The road was a two-lane road, and it was raining so hard that even with the windshield wipers at full speed, it was very hard to see more than a few yards away from the car. "Keep your eyes on the right side of the road, that way you will neither go off into the shoulder, nor in to the upcoming traffic lane. Although it appears that nobody is as daring as we are to be driving in this kind of weather" Tony said again with that dry sense of humor of his and the same cynical smile.

Indeed Route 42 was deserted and as it turned into 98, continued to be so until, suddenly, a silver pickup truck passed them at fast speed, the passenger window open and a young head with a cowboy hat about to be blown away by the wind stuck out of it followed by a hand holding a can of beer. The two occupants of the truck were yelling something, probably vulgarities. They threw the finger at the passengers of the Lumina as they passed it and showered water from the road, causing Gladys to almost lose control of the car, which skidded on the wet pavement and nearly spun out of control into the opposite lane. Still, she skillfully controlled the spin and continued to drive at a slower pace.

Jasmine screamed and turned pale, and Tony, although did not lose his cool, said in a soft voice: "God, how do I hate rednecks!"

They kept driving for several miles, as both of the girls continued begging him to turn around or let them stop because they all were going to be killed if they kept driving in that kind of weather. Especially since the wind had increased, tree branches were falling everywhere, making visibility more difficult. Also, from time to time, they had to steer to avoid large tree branches that had fallen in the middle of the road.

Then, they saw the blinking red rear lights of a car parked on the right shoulder. As they approached, they realized that it was the same silver, double-cabin Toyota Tacoma pickup truck that had passed them before. The passenger-side door was open, and one of the guys was spilling his guts into the shoulder of the road.

Tony instructed Gladys to stop behind them, and after putting the handcuffs back on the girls, he got out of the Lumina. He was hiding the shotgun under his rain poncho until he got really close to the truck. "Did you guys run out of gasoline?" he asked while peering through the open door to check the gasoline gauge. Seeing that the car had a tank full of gas, he pulled the shotgun out of the poncho. He pointed it at the driver, while commanding him to get out. Then turning around to the other guy who was still vomiting, he kicked him hard in the butt, making him lose his balance and fall forward into the canal at the side of the shoulder.

The drunken, young cowboy struggled to get out of the water and get up, and by that time, his friend the driver was out of the truck and being shoved into the trunk of the Lumina. The young redneck was shaking like a leaf and pleading for his life, while Tony was saying, "That is the problem with you rednecks. You are brave when in groups or with weapons in your hands, but when confronted by the real shit you pee in your pants."

Tony had said that as he was looking at a wet spot that was rapidly enlarging between the legs of the young cowboy. "I hope you got wet in the rain, over there," Tony said to the young man while pointing to the enlarging wet spot in the man's pants. He laughed as he continued, "But as I recall, it was your buddy the one who fell into the water. So, let's go get him, I think the trunk of this car will be big enough for the two of you. Oh, and I hope he does not need to barf again. Otherwise, between that and the pee, you will need to take a bath before Saturday night, cowboy."

"Oh, that is a nice cowboy hat. I always wondered how I would look wearing a real Stetson. I think I am going to borrow it from you, boy. I hope it is okay." Tony laughed again while putting the young man's hat on and then went to address the girls: "It really fits well. How do I look, girls? I look like Clint Eastwood for sure."

With the two men inside the trunk of the Chevy Lumina, Tony closed it and proceeded to remove the handcuffs from the women sitting in the front of the car, commanding them: "Come on, girls. It is time to change vehicles and, perhaps, after driving a few more miles, find a place to wait until the storm gets better. This rain and wind are beginning to get on my nerves."

After they all moved into the Tacoma, Tony instructed Gladys to continue driving at a much slower speed; she obliged by driving between 40 and 30 miles an hour, and even at that speed, the driving was extremely dangerous as rain, leaves, debris, and tree branches continued to fall in their path.

Eventually, the party reached the Town of Sebring, where many of the traffic lights were down, some streets were flooded, and most of the signs at the intersections were leaning forward, perilously pushed by the wind. It was not until they reached the opposite side of the town that they saw the red neon lights of a small motel, with the sign "Vacancy" flickering in and out, as if ready to turn off at any given moment.

Gladys pulled the Toyota truck in front of the motel's check-in office, and Tony told her to get down with him so they could register as husband and wife with a sister-in-law in tow.

At the reception desk was a middle-aged fellow with the features typical of an individual of Asian Indian origin who looked scared and appeared to want to be anywhere else but behind that reception desk.

Tony fashioned his best and most charming smile and told the Indian fellow that they were trying to reach Ocala because "his wife's" grandmother, who lived alone there, had fallen sick before the storm hit. However, as hard as they had tried, it had become increasingly dangerous to continue driving under such difficult weather conditions, so they sought shelter until the storm got better.

Tony was aware that family was very important in Indian culture, so if the fellow who turned out to be the motel's owner seemed suspicious at first after hearing Tony's history reinforced by a hundred-dollar bill with instructions to keep the change, the man's attitude changed, and he was even able to produce some coffee and doughnuts for them; after which he gave them the key of a room on the second floor of the motel.

Tony pushed the girls ahead of him to climb the stairs to the second floor, their heads covered by the rain ponchos, and he climbed the stairs carrying the two duffle bags that he had purchased along with the weapons at the gun shop in Okeechobee, one of the bags contained the weapons and ammunition, the other his wet clothes, as he had changed in the car in to the camouflage fatigues. In contrast, the girls had put the ponchos over their damp clothing. He also had the bank's money and the teller's belongings in the other bag.

Then they entered room 205 at the "Best Rest Motel", owned and operated by Mr. Ragnatar Patel, originally from Calcutta, India.

TWENTY-SEVEN

When Detective Andy Garcia and his temporary partner, CSI Detective Sergeant Karla Colles, arrived at the elegant beachfront apartment complex "Ocean Village," they saw that two patrol cars had already arrived.

After they identified themselves, the young patrol officer waiting in one of the cars directed them to an apartment on the fifth floor of one of the buildings.

Upon entering the apartment, a strong fecal odor hit their nostrils, and they saw that the three officers in the room kept the door open and held handkerchiefs to their noses. One of them said to them, "There is a dead guy in here, hanged himself from the balcony, shitted in his pants while doing it. Appears to be suicide. He left this note"—this while holding with a globed hand a handwritten note.

The detectives examined the note, which, in large, bold letters, said, "I am sorry I did it; I am the sole responsible for all this tragedy. Please forgive me." The letters appeared to have been written hurriedly and with a shaking hand as the lines were not even and the letters distorted.

After looking at the note for few seconds, Karla walked to the balcony where Doctor Kevin Nielsen's lifeless body was hanging by the neck with one end of a curtain rope around it and the other tied to the rail of the balcony. The strong wind made the corpse swing grotesquely from one side to the other and against the lower part of the balcony. The heavy rain was soaking its clothes, and as it mixed with the product of defecation, a brown liquid was dripping down onto the balcony of the apartment below. Fortunately for those who may be living there, the rain was also taking care of washing it away.

Because of the stronger wind near the ocean, it was impossible to keep the sliding doors leading to the balcony open. They tried once, and the wind almost blew them, along with some of the furniture, off the balcony.

Karla, braving the rain, and the wind, remained on the balcony for a while taking pictures of the body and surrounding areas with the digital camera that always accompanied her. Actually, the smell was almost imperceptible at the balcony and the officers nearly ran one over the other when Karla requested some help to lift the body up to the balcony. In the end it took the two officers and the two detectives to pull the body over the rail and place it on the floor of the balcony, for which they had to untie the rope from the railing.

Karla instructed the officers to leave the corpse there while she covered it with a blanket that someone found in one of the closets. Then she went to inspect the front door, paying particular attention to the doorframe, of which she took additional pictures. Then she got in all fours and with a flashlight inspected every inch of the area around the door, finally picking up a small golden object from under a sofa. Thereafter, getting up, she announced: "Gentlemen, this man did not commit suicide. He was murdered. We are treating this as a murder scene. Let's call an ambulance to take the body out of here."

Detective Garcia, was not impressed and calling her away from the other cops, he said in a low voice, "It is true that this guy called and sounded scared, but it could be that he was scared because he was about to kill himself and perhaps wanted us to prevent it. Why do you think he was murdered?."

Karla answered the question of his temporary partner with some irritation. "I was under the impression that you were a heck of a good detective, Garcia. I am disappointed"

He did not answer, by now being used to her snotty remarks, besides he was curious. The dead guy was a prick, and Garcia was not feeling particularly sorry for him. But he liked the idea of suicide better, even though he was thinking about the phone call that the departed had made to him and he also thought that Nielsen was the kind of fellow that loves himself way too much to commit suicide, so he simply asked: "Ok what did you see?"

Karla responded, after a pause: "First of all, or number one, if you wish, the smell. Although it is well known that people crap when they are strangled if this guy hanged himself OUTSIDE the apartment, there would have been little, if any smell INSIDE , especially with this wind and rain.

"Second was the length of the rope. If he hung himself out of the balcony, he had to climb in the chair there, go over the rail, and jump; the rope was way too short to allow him to do that. Third, if he was strangled inside, and then carried to the balcony, and pushed over the rail, a short piece of rope would do fine. Fourth and final clue: the deceased had a bolt chain lock in the door, and someone cut it to get inside, then he took the time to remove the bolt from the door. However, a small link from the chain fell under the couch." She said this while showing Garcia, the small bright object that she had found.

Garcia was impressed. All he could say was, "That is a very impressive detective work. Thank you for the lesson." At that point, his cell phone rang, and he went out to answer it. The call was from Doctor David Bright of the Neurological Institute, who sounded very distraught, almost hysterical.

He told Karla after hanging up, "Some guy, last name Bright, from the Neurological Institute wants me to drive down there. There has been some big trouble. There has been a murder, and it seems that the murderer kidnapped some women. One of the women appears to be this Doctor's son's girlfriend, and it sounds like the son wants to go after the kidnapper. He is promising to tell me about our case if I help with that mess."

"Then go," said Karla. I still have some work to do here, and I may catch up with you later."

Garcia was relieved to hear her saying that because Dr. Bright had actually requested him to come alone.

After Doctor Melvin Bright came out of the operating room. Having fixed an almost severed brachial artery on the arm pit of Joe, the security guard, he was confronted by a tearful, hysterical Doctor Porter. In between sobs and screams, she was able to inform him, that the man who killed Doctor Bernstein and wounded the gate guards, had also taken her daughter, hostage, along with the front desk receptionist and Doctor Alice Rodriguez.

Melvin did not take the news well. He became almost as frantic as Doctor Linda Porter and then announced that he was going to go after the kidnapper while requesting to borrow a weapon from someone, anyone. Never mind that he had never handled a gun in his entire life.

Fortunately, at that time, the senior Doctor Bright returned from the ambulance trip, after delivering the other guard at the hospital in Stuart. He was able to calm his son down, while realizing that the kidnapped young woman must represent much more than a mere infatuation for his offspring.

Dr. Bright senior in moments of crisis usually did honor to his name, and this time it was not an exception. In the mist of all the turmoil and tragedy that was taking place at the institute, with his own son begging tearfully for him to do something about the missing Doctor Jasmine Porter and with the mother of the girl crying hysterically in front of him, it was simply amazing that his brain was able to remember that the late Doctor Bernstein had mentioned to him that he was very favorably impressed by a young Detective who came to ask questions about "one of the failed cases, whose body ended up in the street in Fort Pierce." He had kept couple of business cards with the man's name, one of which gave to him "just in case."

So he stepped into his office and with the business card of Detective Garcia in hand, he dialed him on, then went in to a small room adjacent to his office were aligned along the wall were several numbered boxes, like those found at most banks for safe depositing. After selecting a key from a group of several that he got from a locked desk drawer, he opened one of the smaller safe boxes and withdrew from it a device that looked very much like the remote control of a TV set, except that it was thinner and bit shorter than most of the devices.

Then Dr. David Bright returned to his office and tried to do his best to console and reassure his grieving son and the grieving mother of the kidnapped Doctor Porter.

They had to wait over half an hour before someone announced that a detective, Mr. Andy Garcia, had arrived and was requesting to see the senior Dr. Bright.

Max Kraft was also back at the institute and he was able to hear the announcement as well. So he went to the surveillance room and turned on the TV camera on Doctor Bright's office, as well as the volume of the listening device located in that office.

Actually, Dr. Bright went out to meet Detective Garcia in the corridor and found him halfway from the lobby. After shaking hands, he informed the detective of what had occurred at the institute over the last two hours. Garcia very politely indicated that although he was more than willing to help, the crime had happened in another county and he did not have authority to mingle with that investigation. As for the kidnappings, that may be something that fell in to the jurisdiction of the FBI, and he could be asking for trouble if he got involved in that.

Doctor Bright took him into his office. After introducing him to his son and Doctor Porter and assuring him that he may be able to help find Jasmine, he requested that the two of them leave the office so he could speak with the Detective in private.

"Listen, detective, I am desperate. The woman you saw is the mother of a girl who was kidnapped from these premises and could be murdered. The local police have their hands full with the storm, and they are looking for the man and the girls south of here, in West Palm. They said that only a fool would go west and into the storm that is or will be really bad there. But I have confirmation that they went that way, towards the storm."

"How do you know that?" asked Garcia.

"First our Chief of Security suspected it. He said to me that the local police were stupid, that if it had been him the one with the girls, he would have gone in the direction of the storm where the cops would be busier and much less likely to go after them. Second, we just got a call from one of the kidnapped women, our psychiatrist, Doctor Alice Rodriguez, she has been arrested and is at the police station in Okeechobee."

"Arrested? For what? I thought that she was a kidnapping victim," said Garcia.

"I am afraid that I do not have all the details, detective, but apparently, she is being accused of being an accomplice of a man who held up a bank in that city," responded Dr. Bright.

"Anthony Malatesta for sure," concluded Andy

"For sure," answered the doctor.

"But Doctor," added the Detective, "almost every cop in this and the surrounding counties knows 'Homeless Tony.' He is a drifter, a small time thief, shoplifter, cheap drug user and dealer, a drunk. But he does not have the spirit to pull something like this. Not killing two people, wounding another, kidnapping three women and now robbing a bank. This sounds almost impossible unless you guys did something to him here to change his personality."

Doctor Bright blushed at the detective's remarks and, unable to look him in the eye, lowered his head and said, as if talking to himself, "I hate to say it, and God forgive me, but that is exactly what has happened. And, if you agree to go after him and take my son along, I will tell you all about it."

"I'll do it, but you better start talking, Doctor," said Andy

"I cannot tell you exactly what type of work we do here because I do not have the authority to do so, but if you are going to do this, you need to know, even if I risk my job and perhaps my physical integrity," continued Dr. Bright. "Some years ago, Dr. Bernstein and I, with the cooperation of a team of scientists, from all over the world, discovered that it is possible to actually see patterns of behavior in the brain of living animals and that such patterns of behavior can be modified with certain treatment. The possibilities were enormous: treat Parkinson's disease, cure mental illness, Alzheimer's, drug and alcohol addiction, correct criminal behavior and much, much more. Unfortunately, we had some accidents, and some of our patients died. Your case, Mr. Torres, was one of them. However, we were not supposed to present them as murder or accident victims, and we always compensate the families generously."

"Then someone else took advantage of the situation and made quite bit of money by insuring your patients," interrupted Andy.

"Yes, but none of us were aware of that. In fact, you were the first one to inform Dr. Bernstein of that irregularity," said the doctor.

"And now both of the responsible parties are dead. Don't you think that is a very convenient coincidence, Doctor?" Andy interrupted again

"It is my understanding that it was a crime of passion, but you are right to be suspicious. In fact, I find the coincidences very estrange," Doctor Bright added. He continued, "The fact is that we were supposed to treat 'Home–....' Mr. Malatesta to correct his substance addiction, but another unfortunate event occurred; someone sabotaged the treatment, and Mr. Malatesta was injected with the altered serum of someone else, and that someone else, Detective, was nobody else but the man whose murder you are investigating...Ismael Torres."

"Are you saying what I think you are saying, Doctor?" Andy inquired with surprise.

"Yes, Detective, our "Homeless Tony," whose real name, as you well know, is Anthony Malatesta, is no longer Tony Malatesta, or at least part of him is not; he is Ismael Torres, a much, much dangerous man." As Doctor Bright said this, he turned and punched a few keys on his computer keyboard, and the picture of a man appeared on the monitor screen, as the doctor continued: "This is Mr. Torres, or was Mr. Torres, the man whose death you are investigating. I would encourage you to read about his background, and you are welcome to do it. However, for the sake of time, I shall summarize it for you"

"Mr. Torres was born in Guatemala. You do not need to know much about his childhood, except that he was one of several kids, no father, was destitute, lived in the streets most time, skipped school, and eventually became a small thief and the leader of a bunch of small boys who would steal from vendors, other kids and old people, at some point he was arrested and sent to a juvenile detention facility, where he learned to read and write and was regarded as very bright.

"After he was released, he got a job working as a messenger for a military officer, but he did not last and returned to the streets and to robbing people. The mother could not control him. Knowing that he was to end up in jail or dead, she talked to the military officer. Through him, Mr. Torres was forced to enter the Guatemalan Army. Although at the beginning he got in trouble, he finally submitted to military discipline and began to like it. So, he rapidly ascended in the ranks and was made corporal; apparently he was an excellent marksman. At first he was trained to become a sniper, but he found the job boring and requested to become part of the special forces, an elite Army group, called 'Los Kaibiles,' a unit with a reputation for ruthlessness and cruelty, but also able to survive under the worst circumstances and having great expertise in jungle warfare.

At the time, there was a civil war in Guatemala, and the guerrillas controlled the jungles and most of the countryside. The army was certainly not winning. The Guatemalan military, with many of them US-trained at the school of the Americas, in Fort Benning, Georgia, decided to adopt the same technique we used in Vietnam, that is destroying the support, eliminate the suppliers and then terminate the guerrillas."

"So, they sent this Kaibiles to do the dirty work?" –interrupted Garcia.

"Indeed, they did, and the Kaibiles carried their orders with utmost efficiency. They would drop from helicopters over a village and proceeded to massacre every living soul in it, babies, women, old men—but mainly young men whom they saw as possible present or future guerrilla recruits. Not only they killed, but did so in the most brutal and cruel ways, often using machetes to cut limbs or heads and raping the women. There are credible histories of pregnant women's bellies being but open and the babies inside chopped with machetes, or woman's stomachs opened and the severed head of their husbands, fathers or boyfriends placed inside their open bellies. And apparently Mr. Torres was in command of a Kaibil unit that was particularly efficient in performing those deeds. In fact so efficient that, when the Army and the Guerrillas finally signed a peace accord and part of it was to grant amnesty and immunity to those, in both sides, who had committed war crimes, Mr. Torres did not feel that it was safe for him to remain in Guatemala. He came to the United States, apparently with a tourist visa and decided to stay."

"How did he end up here, at the institute?" inquired Garcia

"As far as I know, he learned that there was a large Guatemalan community in this area, and like most others, that drew him here; unfortunately for him, apparently someone recognized him, and he decided to laid low and perhaps eventually move on, somehow he knew that we were looking for volunteers for our scientific work and that the pay was excellent, plus he would live inside the walls or the Institute and decided to volunteer."

"And you guys hired him knowing that he was a sadistic criminal?" asked Andy.

"No Detective, we did not know that at first. Our radiology experts have developed a machine, let's call it an X-ray machine, which can look at the brain of a person and tell about his or her feelings, emotions, and inclinations. We scan all our volunteers with it before doing anything, and Mr. Torres was terribly bad. The rest of the history was obtained by our people in New York, from sources in Guatemala, and last but not least by our psychiatrist, Dr. Alice Rodriguez," said Bright.

"The same person that he took as a hostage. And being aware of all that you guys still took him in as a patient," Garcia said critically

"Yes, we did take him as a RS, 'Research Subject,' that is," said the Doctor. "But Paul and I were hopeful we could reverse all those awful trends and make him a different person. Unfortunately, when we were drawing some fluid from his brain, he died on us. It was not a murder. It was a tragic medical accident."

"That would be for a jury to decide, don't you think Doctor? Anyhow, how that is the spirit of a really bad death man is now in the body of a druggy and small-time thief?" –asked the detective.

"That is the second part of the story. As I may have said before, we were preparing to treat Mr. Malatesta in the hopes of turning him into a better man and curing his drug addiction. You see, Detective Garcia, Tony's scans were not bad at all, and there was much hope for that boy. Unfortunately, someone changed the serum he would receive, and Tony got Torres' serum."

"And you know who did that, I suppose?" Andy asked.

"We suspect that an intern, a Doctor Kevin Nielsen was responsible for that," responded the Doctor.

"Well, my dear Doctor Bright, if that young man was responsible for turning Tony into Frankenstein, he would never be able to tell us. He was murdered in his apartment a couple of hours ago," informed Andy and fixed his gaze on Doctor Bright to see his reaction. The doctor appeared to be genuinely shocked.

"Oh my God, no, not another one, please tell me it is not true, you are playing police games with me?" asked Doctor Bright, almost crying.

"I wish that were it. Whoever did it tried to make it look like a suicide, written note and all. But it was pretty clear to us that he was murdered, especially since he called me on the phone and reported that he was in danger a short time before it happened. Unfortunately, we were too late to prevent it," informed Garcia.

"Oh God, oh God!" he continued loudly, lamenting Dr. Bright, and then in a murmur too soft to be totally heard by Garcia. "Kraft, it probably was Max Kraft who did it," he said.

"What did you say Doctor? Do you know who did it? Do you know who killed Doctor Nielsen, Doctor Bright?"

"No Detective, I do not know…at least not for sure, but let me tell you something else." Everybody here thinks that Doctor Bernstein and I run this place, and that is only partially true because those who build the facility and provide the financial support are the real bosses. They have here several men that run and control the institute's security system, who spy on all the rest of us, report directly to the higher boss, and respond only to them."

"The Chief of Security is one Mr. Max Kraft. You could ask him about the murder of Doctor Nielsen. However, Mr. Kraft is not going to go anywhere, at least not until Tony Malatesta is found and killed. And that is the main reason I need your help. I am afraid that if Max and his henchmen find Tony before the police do, they will start shooting first and ask questions later, with little or no regard for the lives of the women Hostages," the senior Bright informed.

"And why do you think I am better qualified than the local police to locate Tony, Torres or whoever he is now?" – inquired the detective.

"Several reasons, Detective Garcia. First and foremost, I think you are a good man and a competent law enforcement agent; second, you are already involved in this case; third, my son Melvin is going crazy about the woman he thinks he loves being in the hands of a paranoid murderer and he wants to go alone to find them –which you would agree is totally nuts-, fourth, as I stated before the security people are going to go after this guy and if they find him with the girls they may easily become 'collateral damage'; and finally, and most important, I have a tool that would allow you to pinpoint exactly where Mr. Torres is." Dr. Bright said this while handling the device that he had retrieved earlier to Garcia.

"A TV remote will help to find Torres?" inquired the detective scornfully.

"It does look like a TV remote, but in reality, it is a device that would lead you to Mr. Torres. You see Detective, Dr. Bernstein and I foresaw that some, if not most, of our patients would eventually leave the Institute and return to their normal lives. In most of these scientific research projects, some of the people who participate fail to return for follow-up, and it was of outmost important to follow these people for many years in order to see if the changes were going to be permanent or if there were going to be complications, etc. So we implanted a microchip under the skin of each one of them and developed this device to track them down," explained Bright

"Very clever, Doctor, and why are neither the police, nor Mr. Kraft now using one of those?" asked Garcia.

"Two reasons, first this is the only device, we only have one per patient. And second, only Paul—Dr. Bernstein, that is—and I knew about these devices for the reasons I explained to you that it would be dangerous for Mr. Kraft to be in possession of this device."

Garcia was beginning to find Doctor Bright's habit of putting his explanations and arguments in order a little bit annoying, but at the same time he was fascinated with the man's personality. He considered himself a good judge of character and was convinced that Bright was a good and honest man who, like Dr. Frankenstein, got carried away by his own brightness.

Garcia inquired, "Where is Tony Torres at this time?"

"Well, that is another little problem, the range of detection for the devise is only about fifty miles and it appears that the climatic conditions affect its functioning, so it is impossible for me to tell you that at this time. However, I am convinced that if you get closer to the man, and especially if the weather improves, you will have no problem finding your man," Bright said.

"The weather conditions are not too bad around here. But if you assume that Tony is going towards the storm, it would be impossible to track him until the weather clears," argued Garcia.

"We know he was in Okeechobee and from there he, most likely traveled north. "Please, Detective, you may help to save the lives of the women but also that of my son, because he is determined to go after this guy, with or without you. And he does not even know how to fire a gun. He would be killed on the spot; he has only agreed to wait until after I get your answer. I am a wealthy man, Detective. Give me your price. My son's life is worth any amount," said Bright.

"You are offering me a bribe, Doctor. I should be offended, but I am not because I do understand your position. I am sure my father would do something like that for me. I will do it because it is my case and it is my duty. Would you please call the sheriff and explain the situation for me. I am only carrying my service pistol, and I have a shotgun in the trunk of my car. I will need some ammunition and, if your son is to go with me, is it possible to provide him with, a revolver—since those are the easiest weapons to handle—and perhaps a bulletproof vest?"

"I am sure security can provide us with those items. I talk to them."

Actually, that would be totally unnecessary, Max Kraft had been hearing the whole conversation through a listening device from his office.

"The son of a bitch doctor. Mellon will be informed about this and, hopefully the pesky detective and Junior could become "collateral damage" as well" Kraft said to himself, as he ordered one of his men to go place a tracking and listening devise of his own, on Garcia's car.

TWENTY-EIGHT

Tony Malatesta—aka "Homeless Tony", aka Ismael Torres—sat in a chair, leaning the back against the motel's room door. He placed his bags under the chair. He reclined back and went to sleep almost immediately, while the terrified young women lay in the only bed in the room.

At the beginning they were afraid that the bandit would try to rape them or molest them. Still, he showed no interest in them as females, at least not for the time being, so neither one of them dared to take off their clothes or even go to the bathroom to shower, a task that proved difficult as the two were handcuffed together.

Gladys, who was still wearing high heels, took off her shoes and soaked her feet in the tub, all this with Jasmine in tow. She, in turn, had to wait while Jasmine used the toilet to pee, and then she took her turn there, too. As they did, the room lights flickered off and on and finally went off. The storm outside appeared to be getting stronger, but in spite of the roaring wind, they could still hear Malatesta's loud snoring. The women huddled in the bed, shaking, not knowing if they were more afraid of their captor or of the hurricane blowing outside the door.

Several hours went this way and Tony did not move, if it wasn't for the snoring the women would swear that the man was dead; they could not comprehend how could someone be sound sleep in the middle of storm like that and with all the cops in the state of Florida, probably looking for him…or were they? In that weather, the woman wondered.

The women may have eventually dozed off because they were awakening by the rough hands of Tony on their mouths. At first they thought that was it, the man was going to take turns to rape them, but then, he just took off one hand, grabbed a shot gun, and listened.

It was eerie. The wind had died out, and after all the howling, there was silence. Yet Tony kept listening, and opening the drapes of the window, he looked outside. "It is a goddammed helicopter, and it is going to land right here. Let's go, girls. Let's go."

And without much ceremony, he pulled both by the handcuffs and dragged them out of the room.

There was indeed a helicopter about to land in the parking lot, and there was also a car coming into the place. Two men jumped off the Helicopter even before it landed and dashed towards the motel, one in each direction in an obvious attempt to cover both sides of the hallway, while he assumed the people in the car were going to cover the front.

Tony realized that he was in big trouble, but he also had the slight advantage that the men did not know exactly in which room he was staying. Or did they?

How in the darn world did those people know where he was? He never imagined that the cops of the State of Florida were that clever and efficient. Moreover, the helicopter did not have any police or Sheriff Identification. Those guys were not wearing any police uniforms, and they were carrying automatic weapons, AK-47s, as far as he could tell. When a third guy jumped off the chopper, Tony recognized him. He had seen that fellow back at the institute, yes, now he remembered; he was the Chief of Security there. Why were these fellows coming after him? And who were the guys getting out of the car now?

The chopper's lights were blinding him now, but he could distinguish the shapes of a fat guy and another guy getting out of the car.

The guys were not moving in Tony's direction. The last guy to get out of the chopper went into the registration office, which was closed, and the manager probably had gone to sleep. Tony heard the registration office door being broken, and he knew the man would find out in a minute or two where he was, so he decided to act.

The chopper light was blinding him and probably also the guys who came from it, but at the same time, the lights made the field almost as clear as daylight, so Tony told the girls to get down on the floor of the upper corridor and crawl towards the stairs, at the end, same as he did.

As he reached the top of the staircase and started coming down, the guy with the AK-47 standing on that side of the building spotted him and raised his weapon, however Tony had seem him too and he was faster, with a pistol in one hand and a shotgun in the other, he fired the latter as the surest and deathliest of the two, hitting the man in the upper chest, neck and face, he was death before he even hit the ground.

Tony pulled the girls by handcuffs to make them come down, but they were frozen with fear and tumbled down the staircase, almost taking Tony down with them. He, however, avoided the fallen women by standing up, and that gave time to the guy who was on the other end of the corridor to climb the stairs and come running towards them, AK blasting as he ran the corridor of the upper level.

This was a rather stupid move on the man's part, as by then, Tony and the women were several steps down and protected by the staircase from the gunman's fire. All that Tony had to do was to lie down on the stairs and shoot the second shot from the shotgun towards him, he was hit in the legs and fell, then Tony, with deathly accuracy, fired one shot from the pistol and hit the man in the middle of the cranium.

Tony proceeded to get down when he saw the man who had gone into the registration office standing at the bottom of the stairs with his automatic weapon pointing right at them and ready to fire.

The man was Max Kraft, the Chief of Security of the institute. Tony was about to drop his weapons, but first, he addressed the man. "If you fire that thing, you will kill the girls also," he said.

"They be collateral damage, I am afraid," Max answered, ready to pull the trigger, which he did, but the hail of bullets went up in the air as the fat man who had come in the car charged him and knocked him off balance and down to the floor.

"You are not going to kill my friends if I can help it," the fat man shouted as he was getting off the floor himself and tried grabbing the AK-47 that Max had dropped.

Tony, of course, took immediate advantage of the situation, and in two laps, he was down next to them and with his foot on the fallen weapon, while pointing his gun to the two men on the ground.

"I know that there are two more of you around here, drop your weapons or I blow the heads of these two right off! Turn that dammed light on the chopper off, leave the car lights on and both of you come with your hands up." Since he could not see because the lights blinded him, he went back two steps into the staircase, just enough to protect him from any shots fired at him.

Somewhat to his surprise, the helicopter's spotlight went off, and even though his eyes took a few seconds to adjust to the semi-darkness, he could distinguish that two men were approaching with their hands up. One of them was wearing a helmet and was obviously the chopper's pilot. The other was a plainclothes man who looked somewhat familiar.

"Hello Tony!" the approaching man said. "It has been a while since I had the pleasure," Detective Andy Garcia said.

"Come closer so I can see you better. Is there anyone else in the car or in the chopper? Are you guys expecting more company?" Tony asked.

"Negative to both," responded Garcia, "but then again, we did not know that these guys in the chopper were following us."

"Well, well, well! Detective Garcia! Nice to see you again! But I think you are way out of your territory. Do you work for these guys now?" asked Tony.

"As always, Tony, I work to enforce the law, and all I want is to bring those two girls back home to their mammas and catch the person responsible for several felonies, including murder. And I know that that person is not Tony Malatesta," said Garcia.

"You are breaking my heart, Garcia, but I am already in a too deep pool of *caca* to get out of it easily, so I must keep riding." Tony said. Then, addressing the men still lying on the floor, he said, "You, the fat one, get up. Let me see your face. I want to know to whom I owe my life."

Doctor Melvin Bright got up slowly and raised his hands after getting up. "Please let the girls go, Tony. Let them go, please," he said to the gunman.

"Holy shit, if it isn't the good Doctor Bright. It appears that I owe you my life twice, Doc. Once you cared for me after they injected me with that shit that almost killed me. Now you saved my hide from this bastard." As he spoke, he kicked Max hard in the face with his hunting boot, knocking off several teeth and making the man fall unconscious.

"I guess I owe you, Doc. So I am going to do something nice for you. I am going to let you and your cop friend here take one of the girls. Who would that be? Take your pick, and please hurry. I do not have much time."

Melvin hated to make that decision, but his heart made it for him. Before he could think, he whispered the name of his beloved one: "It be Doctor Porter, Dr. Jasmine Porter."

"Very well, you can take the Doctor with you, but first you have to tell me how you find me so quickly, and tell me fast before I change my mind, take the girls and kill you all," Tony threatened with a grave accent.

In his anxiousness to rescue his beloved Jasmine and take her out of there without harm, Melvin answered before anyone else could respond, "You have a microchip implanted somewhere in your body—I swear that I do not know exactly where—that permitted us to track you down with a device."

"Very clever, Doc. Now, we are all going to walk slowly back to your car. You will hand me the tracker for that device, and then we will all go our separate ways. Let me just make sure this bastard will not have any other surprises for me." And while saying so, Tony searched the unconscious Max with one hand while pointing the shotgun at the three men and the two women. Once he pulled a pistol from a holster in the man's chest and threw it into the darkness, and after kicking the guy in the face few times more, he commanded the party to start walking towards the cop's car. As they walked, he asked the helmeted helicopter pilot guy, who was scared shitless, "You are one of them, are you?"

"I am only the pilot for the corporation's chopper, sir. You can see for yourself. I do not even carry a weapon," the pilot responded.

"Fair enough, pilot of the corporation, you came like an angel out of the sky, and you are going to fly me out of here. That is if you want to live beyond this night, of course, mister pilot of the corporation. Tony used that menacing voice that the detective knew was not his, but the Guatemalan special forces guy's.

Once they got to Andy's car, Tony instructed Melvin to retrieve the tracking devise and handle it to him, once he did so, he got the keys of the handcuffs, and freed Jasmin while saying, "Feel free to go with your prince charming, it is too bad that we did not have more time to get to know each other better, farewell princess Jasmin." He spoke while pushing the woman in to the back seat of the car. Then, after frisking the doctor to make sure he did not have any weapons, he told him to get in the back seat next to Jasmin.

Finally facing the detective, "You may be the tricky one. I do not want to kill you, but remember, I am still pointing the shotgun at you and your friends in the back seat."

Andy knew the man was serious, that he was a killer, that he was desperate, and that, as he had shown in the last few minutes, he was also an excellent marksman.

"I carry a small revolver in my leg holster," he told Tony

"Very clever, Detective. I am enchanted to meet an honest cop. Ok, handle it over"

Andy reached down to his leg and handled the man a small two-shot derringer.

"A girl's weapon, but a very effective one; I prefer something of higher caliber, but this would do in an emergency," Tony said as he put the derringer in his hunting vest pocket. Then, reaching into the front of the detective's car, he fired two shots from his beretta into the radio of the car.

"Sorry about that, Detective, but I can't afford you calling the local cops on me before we are far away from here. Please stay right where you are, in front of your car, until we take off. I know that cops carry shotguns and stuff in the trunks of their cars." Then, addressing the now more frightened than ever Gladys and the chopper pilot, he told them to get in the flying machine and to take off.

The detective stood helpless by the hood of his car as the chopper lifted off the ground and started to rise above the dark shadows of the trees.

Jasmine was sobbing in the back, and Melvin tried to console her. She was grateful to be alive and free but felt guilty about the fate of Gladys, who had been her companion and support over the worst several hours of her life.

The detective tried the radio, but the bullets had done their job. The radio was dead, and so was the engine, as the bullets had probably damaged something inside. He, however, had his cell phone and proceeded to call first the local 911 and then Doctor Bright at the Neurological Institute in Indiantown, requesting another chopper and an ambulance.

The senior Doctor Bright was elated to learn that both his son and Jasmine Porter were alive and well but was shocked at the news about the casualties, the kidnapping of Gladys, and the loss of the company's helicopter. As to the detective's request for another chopper, he informed him that he did not have another one at his disposition; however, he could get one in several hours.

The detective responded that it was better late than never; however, his hopes of chasing Tony's chopper would dim as the hours passed.

The local police and sheriff's department would not be able to help either; one of their choppers had been damaged by the storm, and the other was being used in a rescue mission.

Tony was a lucky bastard; there was no question about that.

For. the first time, he noticed that Gladys was barefooted.

"Where are your shoes?" he asked

"Back in the motel, they were high heels, they were bothering me, I took them off and then you did not give me time to put them on as we had to run out of that room," Gladys answered.

"Well, I am sorry, but as you probably saw, those men wanted to kill us all, you, the other girl, and me. We had to run, and I'll get you another pair."

"Yes, I know," she simply answered and somehow, for the first time, she felt reassured that this man was not going to kill her.

TWENTY-NINE

After the helicopter lifted off, and he made sure that Tony was no longer aiming his weapon at them, Detective Garcia left the side of the car and ran to the side of the fallen men. Max Kraft was lying face down on the pavement of the motel parking lot, in a pool of blood and rainwater, unconscious but alive, the blood was coming from a cut on his scalp and another one on his face, both caused by the blows that Tony Malatesta had given the guy.

Garcia summoned Melvin, who was still in the car, comforting and holding the still-sobbing Jasmine in his arms. Garcia had to yell couple of times and then actually go to the car and open the door to tell the doctor, at that point in not too kind words to get his ass out of the vehicle and tend to the wounded man.

Somewhat embarrassed, but reluctant to let go of the woman he loved, Melvin finally comply and knelling by the wounded man, tore us his shirt an use it as a bandage to try to stop the bleeding, by then the detective had returned from checking on the other two guys and confirming that they were completely, absolutely and forever death, he decided best not to move them until the local police arrived.

"I think we should take him into a room; the door of the one Tony and the girls were occupying is open. There should be towels to help stop the bleeding and maybe some ice to apply to his head. I already called the cops and the ambulance, but because of the storm, it is going to take some time. We should try to keep this guy alive until they come," informed Garcia.

Melvin was a burly guy but not in the best shape. The German was lean and slender. Still, all muscle and at least six feet tall, the room was upstairs, so taking him up was not easy despite the detective's strength—who he soon realized was doing most of the work of carrying the unconscious man.

Of course, neither the owner of the place nor any of the other guests had yet dared to open their doors. They did not know for sure what had been going on out there and probably did not want to be involved in any case.

Jasmin, not wanting to be left alone in the car, came out to help and eventually placed Max Kraft in the room's bed between the three of them. He was still unconscious but beginning to utter a very weak moan. Jasmine, with a wet towel started to clean some of the blood from the man's face and matted blond hair. But the gash in the scalp was too large and blood kept coming out of it. Despite the efforts of the two doctors to put pressure on the wound to stop the bleeding. After couple of more weak groans, the guy sank back again in to stupor.

Detective Garcia realized that the two physicians were far more capable

166

than him to help Max Kraft, who, in his opinion, was a goner unless the bleeding was stopped soon, the blood replaced and the swollen brain controlled. So, he stepped back and announced to the couple: "There is nothing much I can do here. You are the doctors and know what to do. I am going to go back to the car to see if I can make it start. However, Doctor, there is something that is been bothering me since I saw that helicopter. How those guys did know where we were? Does your daddy have another tracking device he did not tell me about?"

"I been asking myself the same question, Mr. Garcia," lied Melvin, "and no, as far as I know, Dad did not have another tracking device, but they may have had one."

"That is very unlikely, or they would have gotten here ahead of us and Tony and the two ladies would be the death ones, rather than those out there; They must have put a tracking devise in the car, after all we are driving a vehicle that belongs to the institute," Andy said that while praising God for it, because otherwise it could have been his car the one pocked with holes from a relatively powerful firearm.

He went back to inspect the car, tried to start it, and opened the hood, just to close it rapidly. Gasoline and other fluids were leaking from everywhere inside.

Using his cell phone, The Detective called Karla at the Sheriff's office in Fort Pierce to report the events of the day.

She could not believe that the well-known "Homeless Tony", the harmless drunk and druggy that had spent many nights at County Jail, off and on, during his summer visits to the Treasure Coast of Florida, had turned into such killing machine, a monster capable of killing four people in one single evening.

She was, however, glad to hear that Garcia was ok and that Tony had been nice enough to spare his life and release at least one of the girls he had kidnapped.

Karla laughed hearing the story of the bank robbery in Okeechobee and how Tony had so cleverly implicated the lady psychiatrist while at the same time letting her go free. She laughed even more when learning the story of the two young men that Tony had kept inside the trunk of the stolen Lumina and whom Garcia and Doctor Melvin Bright had found and set free while driving along Route 42 in pursuit of the infamous Tony.

And, oh yes, she made fun of him, he was there because the father, of the doctor who was now stranded in the motel with him, and the mother of one of the kidnapped woman; had trusted more the famous Detective Garcia as more capable of rescuing the women than the security men of the institute and the local police combined.

Garcia had to explain that Doctor David Bright had feared that the security men from the Institute would kill Tony and the two women hostages as well, and the local police were busy as heck at the moment helping the victims of the Hurricane.

Karla apologized to him and showed concern about him having been in danger of being shot; She almost cried while promising to ask Sheriff Mascara and everyone there to call for an ambulance.

Garcia next called Dr. Bright at the Institute to report again that his son and his beloved one were safe and sound but that they were stranded in a Motel in the middle of nowhere with a man who may die soon if help did not arrive "Pronto." Plus one of the women remained hijacked, along with a Company Helicopter and its pilot.

Dr. Bright was elated to hear the news, and he promised to send a Helicopter to bring them back, but they had to wait because the only other helicopter at their disposal had gone to the Palm Beach Airport to pick up someone very important. He requested to speak to his son, and the detective went back upstairs to give the phone to Melvin, who, after expressing his content of having been able to rescue "Doctor Porter", now was facing the problem of trying to save Max Kraft's life.

Doctor Bright told his son that facial and scalp wounds have a tendency to bleed heavily because of the many blood vessels present in those areas and that the only way to stop the bleeding was to close the wounds. Since he had no surgical instruments he best improvise, see if the manager of the Hotel had some needles and tread, the largest and heaviest of each or either, the better and try to suture the wounds the best he could; as for the head injury, to keep the brain from swollen, he had to keep the guy cool, so he needed to put ice to his head, most motels have an ice machine, so there, actually the ice may help to stop the bleeding as well.

Garcia heard those instructions and headed downstairs to bang on the door of the motel manager's room while the doctors continued putting pressure with towels over the wounds.

THIRTY

Once the helicopter was airborne, Tony simply said to the pilot, "Go west." The man responded, "Do you mean towards the ocean?" It would be dangerous; there are still strong winds from that direction from the remnants of the hurricane."

"You go west and will see what happens, unless you want to be thrown from here now, do you?"

"No sir, I sure don't. It is west we fly, as you wish," the pilot said while correcting the aircraft's course and making it go in the desired direction. He very well knew that this was a perilous man, who, just in the last few hours, probably had killed six men, and he certainly was going to do his best not to become the seventh.

For several minutes, they flew without saying a word, the silence only broken by the silent sobs of a most terrified Gladys and the noise of the rotors and the whistling of the wind, which somehow found a way to enter the small cracks in the doors of the vessel. Then Tony spoke more to himself than to the other two people, but the pilot probably used to read lips in order to hear his passengers talk among the roar of the helices.

"I wonder how the hell those goons were able to track us down so fast. I better find out. Otherwise, we may have more problems down the road."

The pilot, in an attempt to make brownie points with the man in whose hands his life was at that very moment, volunteered his opinion. "The man in charge told me to follow the car that got there just ahead of us. They had placed some tracking device in the vehicle."

"Is that so?" Tony said, "But then how in the world that cop and the doctor were able to find me?"

The Pilot spoke again: "I am not totally sure, sir, but from the way they were talking, it seems that the people on that car had some tracking gadget to find you. I think they said that you have a microchip implanted somewhere in your body."

Tony could not hide his excitement at learning this. "That son of a bitch doctor. I am glad I killed him. He marked me like a pet so I won't get lost. Hold this a second and will you please shut up," he said to Gladys, who was still sobbing while handling the bag with the ponchos and weapons.

Tony instructed Gladys to run the tracking device over his legs

He remembered that he had a cut in there that he could not account for, but now he was not sure which leg he had on.

As Gladys did as instruct, the device beeped loudly when she scanned Tony's left thigh.

Opening the zipper of the bag, he pulled out the large hunting knife that he had purchased at the Okeechobee weapons shop and made a cut on his pants at the mid portion of this left leg and palpated the area until he found what he was searching for.

With the same knife, he made a one and a quarter inch cut on his skin and in spite of the pain and blood he pocked his pinky finger in to the wound, until he felt something metallic. After poking more with the knife, he was able to extract a small piece of metal, which he held in front of his eyes and then opening the door of the helicopter he tossed it out to the ground; then tearing a piece of his own shirt, he put pressure on the wound and then wrapped it around the leg.

Gladys had stop sobbing horrified by what she had just seen and by the motion of the helicopter that seemed to advance few meters only to be pushed back by the wind gusts, never the less she helped to wrap the piece of cloth to cover Tony's wound. She could not help herself having a feeling of admiration for this strange and stoic, real life Rambo.

Tony Malatesta did notice that emotion and smiled.

At that point the Pilot announced: "although is dark and windy, we will be flying over the beach in few minutes; where you want me to land sir?"

"No landing, go straight ahead," said Tony.

"Do you mean into the ocean sir? There will be no place to land once we have left the shore," said the pilot.

"I do not plan to land anywhere, go ahead, fly across the gulf to Mexico," said Tony.

"With all due respect, sir, that would be impossible. We do not have enough fuel even to make it a third of the way across. If we run out of fuel, we shall plunge like a rock in to the ocean. See for yourself, sir, that is the fuel indicator. We have less than half a tank. We left with a tank full, but with the weight of those people and flying at times against the wind, she burns twice as much fuel."

Tony look at the gauge and realized that the man was not lying, he was mad and disappointed but since he was no fool, after uttering several curse words, told the pilot to keep flying North, until the chopper ran out of fuel and then to put it down in any open field away from major highways.

After a little more than an hour, the gauge started to point to empty and there was an occasional sputtering of the blades. Although by then it was pitch dark below, the experienced pilot pointed to a cow pasture about two hundred yards from a country road. The lights of a small town could be seen from the air about three or four miles away.

As the pilot was landing, Gladys grabbed Tony's arm and whispered in his ear, "You are not going to kill this poor man, are you? Please, please for the love of God, don't do him any harm." And she started crying again.

Even the most ruthless men have a soft spot, and for most, that soft spot is women, especially crying women, and most especially beautiful crying women.

Besides, Tony was really two men in one and—so far—Ismael Torres has been in absolute charge, so perhaps the mild natured Tony Malatesta was in control at that particular moment, therefore he simply said, "Do not worry I won't."

"I think we filled our quota of killings for one day." He tried to say this jokingly but he sounded very serious, even sad.

Once the bird was on the ground, Tony handcuffed the pilot to the steering bar and told him that he was leaving a time bomb that would go off if he abandoned the helicopter before six hours had passed; it would automatically deactivate after six hours. Of course, Tony did not have such bomb and all he left under the pilot seat was an empty ammunition box with a wrist watch inside; of course that was enough for the man to believe him.

Next Tony told the pilot to turn the search light on for a few minutes, so he could see where they had landed. He only needed few seconds to access the situation; they had indeed landed in a cow's pasture, but the place was flooded ankle deep with the downpour of the hurricane, he was the first to jump and fired a shot to blow the search light away, then he told Gladys to jump out.

"You be crazy if you think that I am going to jump in to that mess. I rather you kill me with a bullet than drawn me in there to be bitten by a poisonous snake, or eaten by an alligator, especially since I am not wearing shoes, I left them back at the Motel remember?" said Gladys with a voice so firm that surprised herself.

Tony noticed again that the woman was barefooted, she had tiny feet and the hunter's rain poncho was much too large for her, so it did come down below her ankles. Tony also noticed that she had very nicely formed calves and, there for a second, he pictured on his mind the gorgeous legs that she must have higher up.

Tony did not say anything, just grabbed her by the wrist and pulled so strongly that she fell off the vehicle and into Tony's arms. He tossed her over his right shoulder, and carried her, while with the other arm he carried the bag with the weapons. With the additional weight of the girl, it was very difficult for Tony to walk across the flooded field; at times he sunk to his knees in the muddy water; at others he almost lost balance and drop his precious cargo down, but he always managed to straightening up, until they finally reached the road having to break through a barbed wire fence, which, much to their good luck had been already weakened by the wind and water.

After gently putting Gladys down on the paved road, he took one last glance at the chopper to make sure that the pilot had remained there; he was satisfied with what he saw and started to walk holding the girl by the hand.

Gladys could not help herself from feeling a certain degree of admiration for this strange man on whose hands and wishes her life still was. She was not used to walking barefooted and walking on the pavement was uncomfortable, she knew that it was impossible for her to walk too long before her feet started blistering or bleeding.

Tony was not unaware of her discomfort and he almost wished he could let her go, but now, even if he wanted to it was impossible, He was not going to leave this pretty girl alone, in the middle of the night in the middle of nowhere.

After walking in relative silence (she was moaning and complaining to herself) about a mile, he said to her, "I think that I saw a traffic light ahead of us, that means that quite few cars travel this road even at night, I can carry you again and then we wait there for a ride."

In spite of the pain she was feeling, she proudly responded, "No thanks, I think I can walk there."

Tony did not insist, and no further words crossed between the two, once they reached the traffic light, they crossed the road to be on the side of the northbound traffic, they sat on a rock near a ditch and waited.

Very few cars passed southbound and a couple northbound, but they all hit the light on green, and ignored their signaling to stop.

Tony spoke. "I am sorry, miss, but we have to change tactic and you will have to help, unless want to spend the night here or walk barefooted to the nearest town. You have to show some flesh to the next driver. If it is a man, it will stop, I assure you."

Gladys was not sure if feeling insulted or flattered, but she refused to help…until it started raining again.

THIRTY-ONE

The private jet plane landed at the West Palm Beach International Airport even though the place was not officially open for flights after the storm, the authorities did not seem to object to the landing.

Several men and two women got out of the plane. Then they awaited making parallel lines on each side of the ramp with open umbrellas that were almost blown away by the still somewhat strong winds until a man in a wheelchair came out pushed by a tall middle-aged and muscular man with hair graying on the temples that gave him a distinctive look, all of them were wearing dark sunglasses despite the overcast rainy and windy weather.

Of course, they were Mr. Richard Mellon, his inseparable friend Peter Ivanovich, aka Ivan Peters, and their entourage. They boarded two helicopters that were waiting with the rotors already in motion and took off immediately. Only minutes later, they landed at the Neurological Institute in Indiantown. Dr. David Bright was already expecting them near the landing patch.

"I knew you be coming, but did not expect you to do it this soon and almost in the middle of a storm, which, thank God, is over now," Dr. Bright said as a greeting while shaking hands with the man on the wheelchair and the Russian. He acknowledged the others with a hand wave, which was barely responded with a head flexion by the men, while the two women shook hands and introduced themselves as the secretaries of the two important men. Then the three men walked inside the building to talk privately in the conference room.

"I am not very happy and frankly quite concerned about the news that I hear from here, Dr. Bright, please tell me what went wrong?"- asked Mr. Mellon, although he already knew about most of the events that had taken place that day.

"Well, Mr. Mellon, it all started because a disgruntled intern sabotaged one of our experiments and we ended up with a Frankenstein type of monster in our hands." The doctor explained and went on to tell the whole story in detail, including the most recent events about the shooting in the motel north of there and the killing of two, possible three of his men.

Mellon was unaware of that last part, and his face contracted in fury after the doctor finished telling the story. "So, you are saying that this punk, this homeless piece of shit, took down three veterans and well-trained men after killing your friend Dr. Paul and seriously injuring two of our security guards? And then hijacked one of our helicopters? What the heck did you guys put in this guy's brain? Rambo's DNA or something?

173

"Well, we do not know what else this intern mixed in there, but for certain he got spinal fluid from a guy that had been a sort of a green beret down in the jungles of Guatemala. For all we know, he may have gotten some animal fluid as well. I am sorry to say, Mr. Mellon," Dr. Bright said.

"And where it is now, this fucking intern who caused us so much trouble?" asked Peter Ivanovich.

"Oh! So this is the game you guys playing. That is very good!" thought Dr. Bright to himself. "Pretending that you do not know that the poor bastard is dead when you probably ordered him killed." And then speaking to them out loud, "It appears that he killed himself by putting a rope around his neck and jumping out of the balcony of his apartment. However, this Andy Garcia, the Detective that I told you about, thinks someone from the institute murdered him."

"Interesting, and this is the same detective Garcia that went after our Rambo and got away without a scratch while three of my men are dead?" asked Mr. Mellon with sarcasm.

"Well, if you allow me to express a personal opinion, I think it was perhaps because the Detective did not go there to kill the guy at first sight and ask questions later. also, perhaps it was because he knew him before, under his other personality," said Bright.

"Ok, whatever. The point is that all these events jeopardize tremendously the work at the institute and, as you are very well aware, my very own life," said Mellon.

"Do not worry, Richard, I can go after that man myself with a couple of the guys. It would be fun, like in the good old days" –Intervened the Russian.

"Unfortunately, my dear friend, these are no longer the good old days, and I cannot afford that you put yourself in danger. Not now, not at this stage of the game when we are ready to take the final step, and we are going to do that right now."

"With all due respect, Mr. Mellon, Looking at the positive side of this unfortunate event, it proves that the nanoparticles mixed with DNA actually work and that individuals receiving the transplant can actually maintain both the new and the old personality"

"I was under the impression that the vet doctor had proven that theory," said Richard Mellon

"Yes, but only on monkeys, and one of them killed himself rather than become monkeed," answered the Doctor.

"I can hardly blame the poor bastard for doing that, but we have more pressing issues to address.

"Peter, the next, thing that we are going to do is to move this operation out of this building, out of this town, out of this state. But first, send one of the helicopters to get those people stranded at that motel. Make sure that, if any of my men is alive, they are brought here so that the doctors can take care of them. And when you come back be ready. Also you, Doctor Bright, because you are going to perform the transference this day, right now." "I am sure that you, my good Doctor, already suspected that the transferee was going to be my good friend Peter"

It was more of an order than a statement, and the doctor did not have the strength to argue. Although he was not really responsible for the events of the day, he felt extremely guilty and very, very exhausted.

Then Mellon added in a low voice, almost to himself, "I know that I do not have much time. Every day this shit gets worse, more weakness, more pain. I do not want to live like this any longer."

"You do realize, Richard, that because of the storm, we are only working with a skeleton crew, and the electricity we are using comes from our own generators." The doctor tried to find a good argument to postpone the procedure that he was not sure he could perform in the state of mind that he was in at the present time. He also knew that refusing was out of the question and failing…well failing may very well cost him his own life.

"You are here, David, and you knew all along that you were the one that was going to do this for me. I knew that Paul had Parkinson's disease and you both had discussed what to do when this moment finally arrived. If you need extra nurses, those two girls and two of the men who came with us are trained RNs. There is also a neurosurgeon since I knew you do not have one here on staff. And yes, indeed, I am aware that the circumstances are less than ideal, but the current events are forcing our hands. And Peter will tell you in person that he is willing to take this risk. He and I have faced much worse over the years. so, therefore, I am afraid that you ran out of excuses Doctor Bright."

Mellon said these words in a somewhat menacing tone, emphasizing "Doctor Bright" at the end of his sentence to indicate that he had not been too thrilled by his familiarity with calling him by his first name instead of Mr. Mellon, as he was accustomed.

The doctor understood and responded: "Ok, Mr. Mellon, you are the boss. I just want to hear it from the mouth of Mr. Ivanovich, if you do not mind, sir."

"That is fine with me, Doc," concluded Mr. Mellon. "In fact, here is Peter back, and you can ask him how he feels about this."

Ivanovich walked into the room, calm and straight walking as if he was marching on a military parade in Moscow's Red Square. Evidently he had overheard the last part of the conversation between the Doctor and Mr. Mellon and he said: "I am as ready now as I have been ready for months. It was you Doctors that were dragging your feet." And then, without awaiting a response, added, "The helicopter is on its way to the motel. It should be back in a couple of hours or less. Doctor, I am at your disposal. Whenever you are ready, I certainly am."

"Fine then, I just have to go to the lab and run some last-minute test on your specimen, on which—in case you want to know—we have made sure that it was not tampered with or suffered any type of contamination. I can guarantee that it is two hundred percent yours and as pure as your soul." This was said with disguised sarcasm, a sarcasm that did not pass inadvertently by Mellon, but it made him laugh aloud, hard enough to make him cough and request a glass of water.

After the Doctor left the room and the coughing spell subsided, Mellon held Ivanovich's hand and looked at him directly in the eyes with a soft, almost paternal expression. He said to him, "Peter, you know that I love you like a son, and therefore I do not wish any ill to you, so please do not feel obligated to do this. You still have time to retract, and we will remain friends as always."

Peter Ivanovich said: "Do not be ridiculous, Richard. The only reason you and I put millions into this project was for this moment. I do not know if people have a soul. Still, if no doctor has been able to save your body, I can try to help save your mind, soul, spirit, whichever it is inside us and make you live as long as I live. Then, who knows, maybe I will have a son or a daughter to pass your soul and mine in to. And if I die trying, well, so be it. After all, you and I have cheated death so many times that probably we owe her."

This was one of the longest speeches and, certainly, the most touching and sincere Mr. Ivanovich had given in a long time, and Richard Mellon was moved.

Doctor Bright came back a few minutes later, dressed in green scrubs, followed by Doctors Damsjold and Scheider and a female nurse wearing similar attire: "Everything is ready, Mr. Peters. Are you?" one of the doctors asked.

"I was born ready, Doctors, let's go," said the Russian.

"I would like to watch," said Mellon. "Let me call one of the nurses to wheel me in."

They all understood that he wanted to witness the procedure to ensure nothing out of the ordinary would occur. They had no choice but to agree.\

"You and your nurse have to wear scrubs, masks, and hats if you want to be in the room unless you want to watch through a glass from the next room"

"We want to be in the room; where are the scrub suits?" Mellon said firmly.

"Fine, then follow us, please."

Doctor Bright was now calm as a cucumber for some unknown reason. He was relieved that soon it all would be over. Now that his son and the daughter of the woman he loved were safe, he was once again the skilled professional he always had been.

THIRTY-TWO

The big car was about half a mile from the intersection, and the light was green. It had remained green since the driver first saw it and had not changed colors. Perhaps it was one of those lights that remain green all the time in one direction and red in another, just to indicate caution to the drivers. Yet, as he was only yards away from it, the light turned yellow.

His first instinct was to speed up and beat the red light. He knew that the car was powerful enough to do that, and in the worst case, he did not see any cars approaching from any direction at the intersection. However, he thought it was best to be careful. A cop car could be hidden nearby; these small towns have a reputation for setting traffic traps.

So, he slowed down and came to a full stop, awaiting the red light to change. Then, he saw her. It was a petite, well-formed blond woman wearing a miniskirt, no shoes, and big hooters. She seemed to be in distress as she signaled him and approached the passenger side of the car.

The driver lowered the electric window, and although she appeared to be alone, he put his hand on the gun that he had hidden between the driver and the passenger seats. The woman started to say something that started with "please," when he saw the shape of the man.

He grabbed the gun, and as he tried to raise it, he heard a loud bang, his head exploded, and he was no more.

Had he lived, he would have heard the woman sobbing and yelling, "I thought you said you were done with killing for this day…you bastard."

The man held the woman in his arms to calm her sobbing and said, "I honestly thought that I was, but he had a gun. Didn't you see it?"

Then he opened the back door of the Lincoln Town Car and gently put her on the back seat. Then he opened the front door, pushed the dead man's body to the passenger side, and drove away.

After a few miles, he pulled into a deserted dirt road, turned the car lights off, and pushed the dead man out of the car. In the back seat, Gladys had stop sobbing and was now sound sleep.

Tony emptied the man's pockets, taking his wallet, which, even in the dark, he could tell was full of cash. He searched the glove compartment and found a flashlight, which he lit only for a second to confirm that there was a lot of money in that wallet. Also, there was a credit card and a driver's license.

He did not want to call attention by keeping the light on, so he opened the trunk, removed two small pieces of luggage from it and put them in the back seat being careful not to awaken the sleeping woman, then put the dead man's body inside the trunk, with a rag he found in the trunk, he cleaned the blood from the windshield and the seats of the car. Thereafter, he drove back onto the main road and continued going North.

Luck was with him: the car also had a GPS, which, even if he was not familiar with those modern devices, it did not take long to find out that they were approaching the City of Tallahassee. Now he wished he could find a store open all night, and he knew that there should be a Wal-Mart in that city; he needed to buy her shoes and clothes, and he was hungry.

Feeling out of danger and driving at the speed limit, he turned on the car's interior lights and noticed that the GPS had a bottom that apparently allowed the driver to ask for directions, as it said, "voice activated."

It did not take long for them to find the Walmart that the device had guided them to. He parked the car in the darkest spot he could find but not too far from the store to look suspicious. He did not know if the car had blood spots that could be seen from outside, and he did not want to take any chances.

He gently woke Gladys and asked her if she wanted to go shopping for shoes, clean, dry clothes, and some food. He did not mention that they were carrying a dead man in the trunk, and when she asked why there were pieces of luggage in the car and not in the trunk, he avoided giving her an answer. Besides, he had moved the luggage to the passenger seat, so she would be comfortable in the back seat.

Tony knew they would look odd and was concerned about people asking questions, but after looking at the people who shop at Walmart at that time of night, she felt sure no one would notice them.

Gladys got shoes, jeans, several T-shirts, a dress and more shoes, sneakers and sandals and high heels. Tony got two T-shirts a pair of jeans and boots, and plenty of junk food. After paying, they informed the cashier that they were going to change in the restrooms, Tony told her that they had car trouble and got caught in the storm down south, the woman was very talkative and informed him that there was nothing but some rain and slight wind in these parts of the state, but she had heard that it had been bad down south and, of course it was ok for them to go change in the restroom, do it after you show your ticket to the woman at the door.

After that, they walked back to the car and drove north again. He was tired, so he did not object to her suggestion to stop at the first motel and spend the night there. However, she added, "Do not get any ideas, mister. Get a room with a double bed or sleep on the couch." Something had changed between the two, and she now felt secure with this murderous man, who seemed to have a soft and tender side.

They did have more than enough money now to stay in a Holiday inn or some even fancier place. Still, Tony realized that in those places, they requested ID and to present a credit card, and although he knew that Gladys had one in her purse, he did think it was foolish to leave a paper trail for the cops to follow. Therefore, he chose a cheap motel.

Gladys had fallen asleep again, so he almost had to carry her into the room—thank goodness, the motel only had one story—then he came back for the two pieces of luggage, the bags of clothes from Wall Mart and, of course, the bag with the weapons and ammo.

When he came back to the room, Tony found Gladys sound sleep in the middle of the only bed in the room, so he decided to sleep in the couch, but first he wanted to search the luggage belonging to the defunct, dispose of his clothes and place the ones they had purchased on it.

He noticed that the clothes were expensive but too big for him and some were too flashy for his taste. So he placed them on the Wal-Mart bag, keeping only a couple of T-shirts, it was then that he noticed the double bottom on the luggage, it had been cut. Then closed again, so using his knife, he cut the cloth and, after removing some bags containing coffee beams and grounded Coffee, found two packages bound in mailing paper and wrapped in plastic; with the knife, he made a hole in one of the bags and a white powder came out of it. He found the same in the other piece of luggage, four bags in total, containing, he estimated, a kilogram of cocaine each.

Tony put a bit of powder on his tongue to confirm that it was pure cocaine, and at that time, he felt a sensation that he knew he had experienced before but not for a long time. It was a well-known feeling to Tony Malatesta, aka: "Homeless Tony," but one not yet, ever experienced by Ismael Torres. It was a craving for the drug.

Up to that moment, Ismael Torres had completely controlled Tony Malatesta's body and mind, but this feeling was so strong that Torres felt he was about to give control to Tony. Torres, without being fully aware of what had happened to him back at the Neurological Institute, since the last thing he remembered was being put on a stretcher and being wheeled into a room that smelled like a hospital, and then someone stuck a needle in his arm, and that was all he remembered.

After waking up, he had a super, duper headache that lasted a couple of days. He was informed by the fat doctor back there and the lady doctor Rodriguez that something had changed about him. He noticed that his skin was of a lighter color and that he had freckles on his hands. and he had seen his reflection in the glass windows of his room back at the hospital, but he never had the opportunity to look at himself carefully in a mirror; he thought that they had performed some plastic surgery on him.

But then, there were those other things, like his speaking English, true that he had received some training at the School of the Americas, but he hardly learned anything more than few words and his accent was awful.

Not that he had been sent to the School of the Americas to be trained on anything but the best and fastest way to kill human beings.

But suddenly, he realized that he had been speaking perfect English and understanding every word of it.

With the pack of cocaine on his hands, he went to the bathroom and looked at himself in the mirror. He was blondish, almost red-haired, and growing a beard of the same color. Being a Guatemalan of Indian descent, he seldom needed to shave, and then, it was just fine hair above the upper lip and on the chin. No, this was a totally different person, and whoever this person happened to be wanted to have cocaine fast.

Torres realized long before today that "they" had changed him, but he did not fully realize the extent of it until that moment. He also knew that he had to fight the demons of whoever he was he was sharing this body with. Because Ismael Torres was a sadistic murderer, but he had never used drugs and despised those who did. To him, they were weak people or rich kids who did not know what else to do with their parents' money.

But he was not ignorant of the value of his finding, and he was not going to waste it poisoning this body, which now belonged to him.

The fight went on for the rest of the night; Tony, speaking in English, begged to have the drug, and Ismael, speaking in Spanish, refused to give it to him. Finally, the exhausted body of Tony Malatesta and the weary but stronger mind of Ismael succumbed to fatigue and fell asleep right on the floor of the room, in the part leading to the bathroom. Tony did not get the drug.

When Gladys woke up, she found him snoring on the floor. She had to walk around him to get into the bathroom, and then she did not flush the toilet in order not to wake him up. She looked for the car keys but did not find them anywhere, she assumed that Tony had them on his pocket, so she grabbed her purse and without putting her shoes on, walked slowly to the door, as she was about to open it she heard Tony's voice:

"You are not trying to leave, are you?" And she heard the sound of the pistol being loaded.

"No, no, of course not, I was just going to go see if they have coffee at the office." And then trying to distract his attention she continued, "Did you have a visitor last night? I was so tired that I fell sleep right away but I seem to remember you talking with someone in Spanish. Was I dreaming or something?"

"Yes, you were dreaming," said Tony now up and close to her. "Let's get out of here, have some breakfast and shop for a car."

"Shop for a car...what about the one you..." She did not finish the sentence.

Tony said: "It is very hot. Let's get going"

He failed to inform her that there was a body in the trunk of that car and that the owner was not only perhaps sought by the police but soon would be also by some drug cartel guys.

Tony loaded the luggage consisting of one suitcase packed with cocaine, another with a few clothes, and a big bag filled with firearms; he returned the room keys to the manager and drove away.

"Do you prefer The International House of Pancakes, the Waffle House, or a more fancy place?"

THIRTY-THREE

It was about two o'clock in the morning when the two helicopters that went to pick up the people stranded at the motel had returned to the Institute. Of course, the two poor devils that had perished in the shootout were left behind for the local sheriff's Department to take care of.

Max, still unconscious, was being taken care of by Dr. Melvin Bright and the Neurosurgeon that Mr. Mellon had brought with him; they were performing an MRI while replacing blood in the vein of one arm and infusing large doses of Phenobarbital and Corticosteroids in the other, this to keep the brain from swollen or minimize the damage if edema had already occurred. Ice was put around the body to maintain hypothermia, with the same purpose.

Dr. Bright, a senior, was taking care of Mr. Ivan Peters, who was also unconscious and being treated in a similar fashion, minus the hypothermia, which Dr. Bright considered unnecessary at that point.

Mr. Mellon, who had been at Peter's bedside up to that point, left for a few minutes in order to meet Detective Garcia in person, to whom he expressed his personal gratitude for bringing both Drs. Bright Jr. and Jasmine Porter back safe and sound, this while sharing with him a warm cup of strong tea. The hot infusion hit the spot as the Detective's clothes were wet and blood-stained, and the pants thorn at one of the knees; he was also hungry and tired. He was not looking forward to the long drive back to his apartment in Fort Pierce, so he welcomed the invitation that Mr. Mellon extended to him to spend the rest of the night there, thereafter ordering one of his men to take him to one of the bungalows in campus, were he would find clean, dry clothes, a warm bath and a comfortable bed, these while stressing his wish to have a long conversation with him the next morning, however, he indicated that he was going to remain at the Institute for at, at least the next day, possibly longer if the criminal responsible of the murders was not caught soon.

Before letting the Detective leave, he inquired: "As an experienced Detective, where do you think our man is heading? I am told that you know him from before."

"I knew a guy called "Homeless Tony", a drifter and small timer, borderline retarded, born in New York City, with family connections both in the 'Big Apple' and New Jersey. So, if I had to guess him I would think he was going to go on that direction if he was in trouble; however, your doctors here have been playing with his mind, and now someone else is inside his head and probably controlling and directing his actions; that somebody, would be trying to get to his country of origin, Guatemala, probably via

Mexico. That is probably where your Helicopter is heading now, sir, towards Mexico." "Good night, sir," Detective Garcia said, while leaving the room, following the entourage to guide him to his room.

It was well past noon the following morning when the Detective opened his eyes. He was still feeling sleepy, but the noise of people moving around and talking somewhere in the house, plus the smell of fresh coffee and food, helped to wake him up.

At first, he did not know where he was. Then he remembered that he had spent the night in one of the cottages reserved for guests of the Institute. He noticed that his clothes had been washed and ironed and neatly placed on top of the other bed in the room. There was a bathrobe and sleepers that he put on and walked out of the room.

The bedroom led to a short hallway, and across the hall, there was another bedroom similar to his, which was unoccupied. At the end of the hallway, he came to a spacious living room, partially divided by a wall that separated it from the kitchen and dining room.

Mr. Richard Mellon was sitting comfortably on a large sofa, drinking a cup of coffee, his wheelchair at the side, the Russian was nowhere to be seen; another man, dressed in a dark suit with shades before his eyes, was standing on guard behind the man.

Someone was preparing food in the kitchen, but Garcia could not see who it was because of the wall dividing the room. The smell coming from the kitchen was wonderful and the detective did not need to remember that he had not eaten for almost 24 hours, except for the small sandwich he had with the tea the night before.

Mr. Mellon received him with a wide smile and signaled his bodyguard to pour coffee from a silver pot into a cup of fine China. "I trust you sleep well, Detective Garcia; please drink some coffee here. I hate to brag, but this is the best coffee Colombia produces; it is harvested specially for us and shipped directly. it is one of the small advantages of having some money and connections at the right places."

"I bet that is not the only thing that is shipped to you from Colombia," thought the Detective. He said, "I am sorry, Mr. Mellon. I think I overslept. Please tell me what time it is."

Mr. Mellon raised his arm with some difficulty and looked at his very expensive wristwatch, then said" "it is a little after one o'clock, but you do not worry, my dear fellow. You had a very rough day yesterday, and you did a great job for us, for me and for the Institute, that is."

"I am supposed to be working this morning; I already lost half a day," said Andy.

"Do not worry, my dear Detective, your office has been notified, and by the way, your boss, Sheriff Mascara, is a really nice fellow. I understand that he is doing a great job in Saint Lucie County since he took office. He told me you can take all the time off you want." Mellon told Andy and continued, "I do not know if you prefer to refresh yourself before eating or if you want to eat in your pajamas; either way, it is fine with me. I had my French chef prepare one of his most delicious omelets. Then we have to talk."

Detective Garcia was not particularly impressed by the charm that the man sitting there was expressing, and he knew a little about him to realize that he was in front of a dangerous and cunning man, nevertheless that he was partially crippled by whatever disease he was suffering from. So, he did not feel being particularly polite. Besides, he was really starving, so he admitted it: "If you do not mind, I will eat now. I am really starving, and the smell of that food is making me hungrier."

"Very well then," said Mellon, who in a louder voice gave some instructions, in French to the French chef, whose name evidently was Pierre. He appeared with a dish full of great-smelling omelets, followed by two maids, one bringing plates and silverware and the other a cart full of dishes with different kinds of fruits and pastries.

Mellon continued talking while the chef served him a small portion of the omelet, and the maid put some fruit on a small plate. "I love good food, it is one of the few pleasures left for me to enjoy, but I have to be careful as to how much I eat; my stomach is not what it used to be; this darn malady seems to attack all body systems."

"Sorry to hear that, sir. However, you do not look that sick, if I may say so," said Garcia, thinking, "He is probably bullshitting; maybe he wants me to feel sorry for him."

"I am dying, Detective, and this is why I must do things fast; I do not have much time. But enough about me, I really do not like to talk about my problems. Believe it or not, I rarely do, but I wanted you to be aware of my condition because I have a proposition for you. It is something I would have done myself in the good days but not now...."

"First the good news, they found the Helicopter and the pilot is alive and well, they landed on a cow's pasture near Homosassa Springs on the West Coast. The Sheriff of Citrus County was nice enough to personally call to inform us. Another good news is that you were right when you said that our man wants to go to Mexico. That was where he asked the pilot to take him before they chopper ran out of fuel. Now for the bad news, our man Tony, was nowhere to be seen and neither was the girl. The Pilot heard something sounding like a shot, so this poor girl Gladys may be dead by now."

"With all due respect Mr. Mellon, I do not think so. If he wanted to kill the girl he would have done it where they landed the chopper, and your pilot would not be alive either. I am pretty sure that that poor bastard, your pilot, probably is alive because of her.

"She probably pleaded for his life, and Tony listened.... That is actually a good thing," Garcia said while taking another serving of the omelet—which indeed was the most delicious he had ever had—followed by another cup of coffee and a glass of orange juice. Then they tackled the pastries and the fruit.

"I hope for the sake of that girl that you are right. And the more I think about it, the more sense that possibility makes. You certainly have a remarkable power of deduction."

"It goes with the territory. It is part of the job, and I pray to God that I am right on this one," Garcia added.

"That is why we need you on board, Detective. You know this man, and you clearly seem to know how he thinks. I, we, everyone at the Institute, would appreciate it very much if you could be the one going after this criminal," said Mellon.

"Me?" responded Garcia. "Mr. Mellon, I would love to catch that fellow and put him behind bars, but first of all, I do have a job that I like. Second, I am not sure if I want to play the role of bounty hunter on your behalf. Third, even if I wanted to do it, I am a detective with a County Sheriff's Department. I do not have jurisdiction anywhere outside Saint Lucie County."

"That last one would not be any problem. I took the liberty of calling some friends in Washington, and from this day on, you have become a United States Marshall; you will continue receiving your salary from St. Lucie County, plus a paycheck from the Federal Government, In addition, once you have rescued the girl and brought her home safe and sound, I shall pay you the reward that I am offering for her rescue." Mellon said it all in one breath, taking advantage of the fact that the detective had his mouth full of fruits.

Garcia almost choked on his food, and his face became red not only because of that but because he was really pissed off at the arrogance of this fellow.

"I know, Mr. Mellon, that you are used to buying people and lots of things with your money, but I am not for sale, and what the heck gives you the right to speak for me to the Government? I certainly like the same as you, that is to grab this guy and make him pay for his crimes, but I am sure the FBI and the local police can do the job better than me."

"So, thanks, but no thanks, final answer"

"Sorry, Detective, I did not expect for you to take the matter in this way. You see, for me is very important; Dr. Paul Bernstein, one of the persons he killed, was a personal and dear friend, besides being my doctor. I suggest you think about it and reconsider my proposal. You won't be alone on this, other people will assist you and they will be under your command. Please do it, for me, for Paul, for the institute, for justice, for the law and order that you have sworn to keep. Good afternoon, Detective. Should you change your mind, call me on this cell phone anytime, day or night. "Mellon got up on his wheelchair with the help of the bodyguard- put a cell phone on the table -and left the room.

Garcia went back to his room to shave, take a shower and get back to Fort Pierce, as he was showering, he calmed down a little but not enough. He had barely finished dressing choosing his own clothes when there was a knock on the door of the cottage.

"Come in, the door is open," he yielded from the bedroom.

After the door opened, he heard a familiar voice: "Are you decent, Garcia? Can I come in?"

Garcia was shocked to recognize the voice of his temporary partner, Karla Colles, who, without waiting for an answer, continued talking from the living room. "I guess you know the good news: We are now U.S. Marshals and have full jurisdiction to enforce the law in all the territorial United States, as well as Puerto Rico and the Virgin Islands."

Garcia came running out of his room and planted himself a few inches from her face and confronted the pretty detective, whose smile faded upon seeing the expression on Garcia's.

"Uh, hu, I take it that you do not believe that is good news, ha?"

"No, and of all the nerve of that sneaky son of a bitch, I never expected that he would go as low as to use you as a tool to make me do his dirty work for him."

"Are you Insane Garcia? What the heck are you talking about? That poor man is the most charming, generous, and sincere guy that I have met in a long time. Do you know that he promised that he would turn himself to us and assume all guilt and responsibility, not only for the murder, or murders we were investigating, but of all the events that took place here yesterday, provided that we—that is right partner, you and I—capture this crazy man that our old friend Homeless Tony has turned into."

Garcia felt even more enraged, and he may have realized jealousy snapped at her: "Oh, there you go, women, so dumb that a few nice words and a show of richness can make you do whatever. "Did he offer you French Champagne, a new car, or perhaps an expensive piece of jewelry if you were able to talk me into accepting his offer?"

Karla's face became pallid as a ghost, and she fought hard to keep tears from flowing in to her eyes. Instead, she slapped Garcia's face so hard that the man took a couple of steps back, then, she slapped him again in the opposite cheek and turned around to leave while saying: "That was just in case you wanted to turn the other cheek.... You men are so stupid. I thought for a second that perhaps you were different." She left, slamming the door as hard as she could behind her.

When Garcia left the building, he saw her car still parked in the Institute's parking lot. He felt terrible about what had just happened, but his cheeks were hurting a lot, and he was angrier than ever against Richard Mellon.

However, with every mile, he drove back towards Fort Pierce, the sorrier he felt about what he had said. He tried to call Karla back on her cell phone, but she did not answer. He knew that she had seen his name on her caller ID and would not pick up.

Since he knew he had the rest of the day off, he went to a bar and got drunk, returning to his apartment by cab early that evening. His nurse friend was not there, and even though he tried to call her, was somewhat relieved when she did not answer either.

Andy slept until about 2.30 am when he woke up with a severe headache and puked out about four times before he could keep an Alka-Seltzer down and go back to sleep.

Then he slept until about 9 a.m., had only one cup of strong black coffee and another Alka-Seltzer for breakfast, and decided to head to the Sheriff's office and go to work. In reality, he was hoping to see Karla and apologize to her.

Upon entering the office, he was surprised by everyone's congratulations on his being made a US Marshall and then learned that Sergeant Colles had not been to work.

Garcia went as far as knocking at Sheriff Mascara's office and found out that Sheriff Mascara was quite surprised to see him there, as he was supposed to be working on a manhunt across the southeastern States as a U.S. Marshall. He was informed that exactly that was Sergeant Karla Colles was doing at that particular moment and, it was the opinion of the Sheriff, -expressed in a not very friendly way- that Garcia should be doing the same thing.

He had not only received an order as a Marshall but also had a duty as a partner of a fellow officer.

Andy became alarmed and felt much more guilty than he had been since the confrontation with Karla Colles.

He had no choice but to return to Indiantown and join the hunt for "Homeless Tony."

THIRTY-FOUR

When Jerome Taylor left Fort Pierce, he would have preferred to drive along the busy, large highways, where his car would have been less conspicuous among the thousands of vehicles on the highway. However, to make the delivery that she was paid to make, he had to go across the State, forcing him to take the 70-two-lane roads towards Okeechobee and then to Arcadia, where he was expected to bring the goods.

He did not know what he was carrying as his friend had taken his own two small carry-on suitcases, and his clothes had been stuffed into a large plastic garbage bag. Jerome praised himself for his good taste in clothes, and most of his garments were expensive, but he was in a hurry to leave Fort Pierce and was being paid well to make the delivery. He knew he would need money until he could get established in another town, out of the State of Florida.

As Jerome was driving along, the car radio gave alarming reports of an incoming storm that was supposed to hit the area he was heading for. However, the forecast indicated that the storm would probably not be near the West Coast for at least another twenty-four hours. As usually, the weathermen did not know precisely the point where the storm was going to make landfall, but it was coming from the Gulf of Mexico. It could hit anywhere between Naples and the Florida panhandle.

Jerome was not a coward, but he had seen storms before, and he certainly did not look forward to driving a car during a hurricane. Since his first stop was going to be in Arcadia, which is not along the coast, he figured he would pass the storm there.

On the other hand, the people of "Big John", or "Daddy John" as he was also known in the drug trade, were not the kind of people you fool around with, and those were the people to whom he was to deliver the goods. Perhaps it was not actual story, but rumors circulated that "Big John" himself had killed more than fifteen men, and probably some women, in the most painful and cruel ways when he felt that someone had betrayed his confidence. On the other hand, the name "Daddy John" was given to him by people he had helped through hard times, and those, apparently, counted in the hundreds therefore he had thousands of people who were grateful to him and that small army helped to protect his trade and his men from the cops. Through that network it was said that "Big John" was kept informed about everything that went on from Arcadia to Tallahassee.

And, of course, "Big John", who had played some high school football in his youth, was a six foot-and-a-half man who weighed over 400 pounds naked.

Obviously, Jerome did not have the slightest intention of alienating the big man or any of his men of trust, even though, as a man who was born to be a boss and as a man of more class and sophistication, he sincerely despised "Daddy John" and was hoping that this was the last time he had the need to deal with such a character.

Jerome drove carefully, staying no more than 10 miles over the posted speed limit and passing other vehicles only when necessary, safe, and legal. He kept the radio volume reasonably low, and he made it to Arcadia in about three hours.

Jerome knew the town and the place where he was going; it was an auto mechanic garage in the black area of town. He pulled into the auto shop and dialed a number on his cell phone; obtaining a response he drove further inside and a large panel in the wall of the garage, large enough to allow a semi-truck to pass through opened and then closed after he drove inside, into a very large, but apparently empty warehouse. There was an office upstairs and another room, or rooms along the walls from where three men came out.

None of them was "Big John," but Jerome recognized his right-hand man, a tall black man with a shiningly shaved head. He was dressed in expensive clothes, smoking a cigar, and several thick gold chains hung from his neck.

Jerome thought to himself, "If this mother fucker does not look like your typical drug dealer, I probably look like Mother Theresa. How can the Cops be so stupid?

One look at this guy, and you can tell what kind of business he is in. Of course, "Big Daddy" probably has all the cops of this town on his payroll. Instead, he only said "Hi" as he got out of the car.

Two of the guys approached the car while the man with a shaved head stayed at the same spot where he was; one of his hands was inside his jacket. None of them showed any weapons, but Jerome knew that they had them and that there were probably other guys pointing weapons at him. The two guys frisked him, asked if he had any weapons, Jerome did not see any point in lying, so he told then that he had a gun in the car, which one of the men fetched and after taking the clip off, and giving it to the bald man, put it back on top of the car's passenger seat.

Jerome gave the trunk keys to the other guy, who opened the trunk and retrieved the two suitcases. Then, they all went upstairs to an office, where the massive figure of "Big Daddy," who had been observing the scene, was seated on a supersized couch that seemed about to break in half with the weight of the man's body.

"Big Daddy" spoke with a squeaky voice, very much in contrast with his massive frame, and in a very friendly way apologized to his visitor for the inconvenience while adding that "one cannot be careful enough these days, too many enemies, too many competitors, it is not like in the good old times."

The men opened the suitcases, which happened to be stuffed with high-denomination bills. After a man and a woman grabbed the cash and placed it in two different machines that counted it, Jerome became nervous at this point. "What if the money, whatever the amount was, was not complete?" he thought while a file sweat pearled his forehead.

After about fifteen minutes of silence, only interrupted by the money-counting machines, the man first and the woman next wrote something on a piece of paper and handed it to "Big Daddy," who, after reading it, put the paper through a shredder and, with labored breathing due to his size, said to Jerome, "Good job, my boy. Do you know how much was there?"

"No sir, I did not even know that I was bringing cash."

"Good man, Jerome…it is Jerome, right?"- Said "Big Daddy", "Good man, now I am going to treat you to the best meal you ever had, and whatever else do you need or desire; we need you to do one more thing for us, you are going to take a package to Tallahassee."

"Thank you very much, sir. I'll be glad to do it. However, I am sure you heard about the storm that is coming over from the Gulf. Do you think it is a good idea to drive along the storm with the valuable cargo that you probably would put in my care?"

Big Daddy did not respond, but reaching into a compartment on the arm of the couch, he pulled a remote control, switched on a giant TV concealed behind a panel on the wall, and turned to the Weather Channel. The news was indeed alarming.

"I see, there is really no hurry; when do you think would be best for you to leave Mr. Taylor?"

"If we could wait for the worst of the storm to pass around here, probably then would be the best time because the small roads would be deserted, and the police would be busy directing traffic and helping people hurt by the storm."

"I like your idea, Mr. Taylor. My men will take you to the Hotel. Do not be afraid to run the bill, and by the way, you do not need to give your name there. You will be registered as my nephew. Your clothes and your luggage will be taken to your room promptly and your car can be available to you."

Thank you, Mr. Jerome Taylor, "Big Daddy is in debt with you."

With this, he was ushered out of the office and into a car that drove him to the Holliday Inn, which was indeed the fanciest hotel in Arcadia.

All was done as Big Daddy had said, and although he did not see him anymore, the person who brought his car and luggage to the hotel instructed Jerome to leave as soon as he thought it was safe to do so and without rushing.

Jerome's plan was to drive from Arcadia along Route 70 to join I-75 in Bradenton. However, upon watching the news, he realized that the Interstate was being used as an evacuation route, and it was already bumper to bumper with cars of people trying to get away from the storm. He was sure that even after the storm had passed, the people returning and those stalled on the highway would make it difficult to drive along that route.

Therefore, he considered it would be easier and safer to drive along the small country roads, probably 70 to 675, to 301, follow it until it changes into 98, and then take 41 and 491. Those would take him to about Homosassa Springs, and from then, perhaps he could safely take I-75 to Tallahassee.

Jerome, in the comfort of the Hotel room, watched television most of the night and until the wee hours of the morning, knowing well that he was going to spend most of the following day confined to his room.

When the storm passed, which was not as bad as predicted—it was nightfall, so he got in his car and drove away.

Jerome had been driving for several hours. There had been some rain, and the roads were littered with debris. On a couple of occasions, he had to drive around a fallen tree or a large tree branch, but the whole trip had been as smooth as planned.

He was getting close to Homosassa, and apparently, the storm had not really reached that area, as only some light rain remained. He could almost see the glow of the town's lights when he came to a traffic light.

"These stupid small-town people, why in the world did they have to put a traffic light in the middle of nowhere?" Jerome said to himself.

The light was about to change from yellow to red, and although he could easily beat it, he did not know if that was a traffic trap, and a cop could be hidden somewhere waiting for someone to do exactly that…run the red light.

Of course, he could not afford to take that chance, so he stopped at the light.

Then he saw the woman. It was a petite, young, and pretty woman wearing a rain poncho over a miniskirt that showed a well-formed pair of legs. She signaled the car to stop, but Jerome did not see her until after he had stopped at the light; she approached the car on the passenger side, Jerome lowered the window, and acting on instinct, he put his right hand on the gun resting next to him.

She said something, and then the shadow of a man came out of nowhere and was very close to the driver's window.

Jerome grabbed his gun, but before he could lift it, something exploded inside of his head.

And Jerome's head was no more.

ˋTHIRTY-FIVE

Andy Garcia was still very pissed off when he returned to the Neurological Institute, he did not see more than a couple of cars in the front parking lot of the building, but he recognized one of them as that belonging to his temporary partner, Sergeant Karla Colles.

Upon entering the building, he noticed that the lobby was deserted and yellow tape left there by the local police still marked the crime scene, in fact, near the door, he still could distinguish the chalk-drawn silhouette of the slain guard near the front door, and mentally tried to count the number of people that had been killed and were in one way or another connected to that building. He worried about Karla.

The building halls were empty, as were all the offices usually occupied by tens, perhaps hundreds of employees. Of course, that should not have surprised him, after all, and there had been a storm and two murders just about twenty-four hours earlier at that very same place.

Andy started shouting as he walked the hallways until, apparently out of nowhere, two men in black suits appeared behind him. One of them said, "Can we help you, sir?" and the other added, "Please keep your voice low, sir. We have patients here, you know?"

The two were polite but somewhat menacing, and one did not need to be a detective to realize that the men were someone's bodyguards and both were packing heat.

"I'm sorry," Andy said. The place looks deserted, and I am looking for my partner, Sergeant Karla Colles. "

"I believe Miss Colles was waiting for you, but since you did not show up, she left a while ago," one of the men said.

"Gone? Where?" asked Andy.

"That we do not know, sir, but if you would like to talk to Mr. Mellon or with Doctor Bright, they are here and may be able to tell you," the other man responded and signaled Andy to follow him.

As they were walking, Andy noticed that the doors of some of the places where laboratories should be were half open, and he could see that the rooms were empty. He refrained from asking what had happened because he knew he would not get an answer; besides, he figured it out for himself…the rats were leaving the ship, and there wasn't a thing he could do about it!

The saying that there is calm after the storm could not have been more accurate in this case; as they reached the end of the building and came to the well-manicured gardens, he found Mr. Richard Mellon sitting on a lounge chair next to a swimming pool, which was feverishly being cleaned by a couple of Latino-looking men. A couple more were around picking branches and leaves while straightening and supporting with poles and twining those plants and small trees the storm had damaged.

Those were menial workers. Andy did not see any of the other Latinos who were there during his first visit, those who had the labels of RS and uniforms. Those were all gone.

"Well, hello, Detective Garcia! Or should I call you Marshall Garcia? Welcome back to the Neurological Institute! As you see, we gave our employees a few days off on account of the tragedy that took place yesterday," greeted Mr. Mellon, "Would you have a drink with me?"

"Scotch on the rocks, please," said Andy, with some sarcasm. "You could have fooled me; I could swear that you are moving out of here."

"Smart observation, detective. In fact, we are doing some early spring cleaning and moving some equipment that would be needed elsewhere." However, if this is what you want to know, I am not going anywhere; I am staying here until my friends are well, and, believe it or not, that includes the wounded guard; plus, Paul Bernstein was my friend, I want to attend his funeral. Oh, and last but not least, I am sticking to the deal I proposed to you —the one your lady partner accepted: if you capture or kill the man responsible for all of these, I will make a full confession taking responsibility of those accidental deaths that the institute had," said Mellon.

"What about Clarissa Williams and her lawyer friend and Doctor Kevin Nielsen's murders? Would you be willing to take the blame for those?" asked Andy.

"You are going too far, detective. Remember that I was not even here when those murders occurred—if murders they were, but if that makes you happy, I may be willing to take some indirect responsibility for those as well.

"What else? You want me to confess to the Holocaust or the 9-11 attacks?" said Mellon sarcastically and then added:

"You may be surprised if I tell you that I met Osama bin Laden years ago, way before 911, when they were fighting the Russians, and we were helping their side, so, I guess I could take some blame for the attack on the towers…. I should have killed the bastard then…. But enough of that," Mellon said while both men were sipping their drinks.

"I am assuming that since you came back, you are willing to help us hunt for this criminal. Your lady partner is already on his track. She contacted us a few minutes ago indicating that they have found the tracker chip that the Docs had placed on your friend Tony's body. Of course, he removed it and tossed it in the middle of a parking lot near the motel where my men were killed. Clever boy, that Torres dude is. Very clever, but hopefully no more clever than you."

As Andy showed discomfort, the man continued, as if able to read his mind: "Do not worry about the young lady. She is fine, and two of my best men are protecting her. Now we know what this criminal is capable of, so he is not going to take us by surprise. Still, if you want to join the chase, I would appreciate it a lot, Detective Garcia."

Those last words, "Detective Garcia," disarmed Andy. Besides, even though he would not like to admit it to himself, he was worried about Karla. Perhaps she had been right about this guy, Mr. Mellon. He seemed a likable person to him right now.

"I cannot let my partner do this alone, Mr. Mellon; I am going to try to assist her," said Andy

"Perfect Detective," said Mellon "So, unless you want another drink— which I doubt you do because by accepting this mission—you are now officially on duty. I shall tell my people to take you by helicopter to the place where your partner is right now."

Once in the air, Detective Garcia could see much better the outline of the Institute and the fact that there were no trucks or moving vans around it. Still, the grass over the places where this helicopter had taken off was flattened; therefore, he deduced that several other helicopters, much bigger than the one he was riding on, had probably landed and taken off from that area.

The helicopter landed next to Route 491 near Homosassa Springs in less than one hour. From the aircraft, he could see the ocean, and it was a beautiful sight.

Several patrol cars and a limousine were parked on the shoulder of the road, and Andy could see Karla, three men in dark suits and dark shades, and several deputies from the local Sheriff's department carefully inspecting the area.

The only greeting he heard from Karla was: "It was about time you showed up." She did not bother to introduce him to any of the people around.

"I am very glad to see you, Sergeant Colles!" said Andy, proceeding to introduce himself to the Sheriff and Deputies of Citrus County and to the three black suits.

"Our man got off the helicopter over there," she said, pointing to the pasture where the institute helicopter had landed the night before. "It ran out of fuel," Karla reported.

"He was lucky Tony did not kill him" Andy responded.

"Apparently, that lady he kidnapped, Gladys Franklin, interceded for his life," Karla informed. "However, he may have killed someone else, probably at this very same spot, because the chopper pilot is certain that he heard a shot, some short time after they left him."

"Any trace of blood or glass?" asked Andy

"None whatsoever; we have been looking for that, so we are not sure if they went south or North," said Karla.

"I'll bet my Marshall salary that they went north" said Andy.

"Most likely because Tony wanted the pilot to fly across the gulf into Mexico. Thank God he realized that it did not have enough fuel to make it across the gulf," Karla said.

At that point, one of the deputies approached and said to her: "Sergeant

Colles, would you come over for a second? We found the jacket of a bullet almost buried in the mud, and if you look at the shoulder of the road in that spot, where a car would have stopped to wait for the light to change, there are tracks of something being dragged."

Karla walked over to the spot that the officer had pointed at and, bending over, she picked up a bullet casing that, as the officer had said, was almost buried in a mud puddle. She picked it up carefully, with tweezers, and then put it on her gloved hand.

"It is a 9mm., probably from a semi-automatic pistol. I bet the same one that killed the guard of the Institute." Karla stated.

Andy looked at the casing and nodded in agreement. As he did not want to look stupid or pompous in front of Karla, he avoided saying anything else to her and instead asked to talk with the officers who had been first at the scene and talked to the helicopter pilot, who had been taken by ambulance to the local hospital to be checked.

"What else did the pilot said to you?" he asked the officer.

The deputy seemed more than willing to help and, pulling a small notebook, he told Andy: "Apparently, the girl did not want to get off the helicopter, the field was partially flooded, and she was afraid of snakes and alligators. Especially since she was not wearing shoes. So the man carried her to the road. That man must be a powerful guy, because he was also carrying a heavy bag containing the weapons he used to shoot those people at the motel in Pasco County."

Andy could not imagine Homeless Tony as a man capable of carrying a woman and a bag across a flooded cow pasture; he knew him as a fragile, skinny guy. But again, those guys at that institute may have created a true Frankenstein, or better yet, a Dr. Jekyll and Mr. Hide. He could not help but admire the kind of science involved and grew more concerned about Karla Colles's safety.

Now more than ever, he realized that the man on the loose was a public menace and had to be stopped at all costs. He was determined to do it himself.

The deputy continued, "Marshall Colles knows about this, and she thinks that they should probably stop at some place to buy shoes for her. "Our Sheriff agreed, and since the only stores open all night are the Wall-Marts, our people are looking into it, from here to Tallahassee, and hopefully, we'll get a videotape of them. "

Andy felt stupid once again and promised himself only to observe and keep his mouth shut.

Karla asked why anyone would want to place a traffic light in the middle of nowhere, and the deputies, who were obviously impressed by her, volunteered that the road to the left led to the ranch of a powerful and wealthy man with lots of friends in public places. Because there had been a couple of traffic accidents at that intersection, he had the county commissioners authorize a light for that place.

THIRTY-SIX

"Homeless Tony" and Gladys Franklyn were now driving along the streets of Tallahassee, the Capital of the State of Florida. It was about noon, and although they had a heavy breakfast, Gladys indicated she was hungry again.

Gladys tended to eat a lot when she was nervous, and nervous was she; indeed, her condition was more than understandable under the current circumstances. Yet, even though she herself did not quite understand the reason, she did not have the earlier desire to run away as fast as she could from that murderous man.

In a strange way, Gladys felt some admiration mixed with attraction towards that individual. She was even beginning to feel some thrill and excitement about being in a stolen car, bellowing to a man who had been murdered by the man who was sitting next to her. (She did not know the man's body was in the trunk of the car.).

Tony insisted that Gladys continue at the wheel because she had a valid Florida license to show in case the cops stopped them.

Tony asked the GPS for a used car dealership, and after following the directions, they found a long street with several new and used car lots. Tony parked the car at a "Pollo Tropical" restaurant, and they went inside to eat.

While in the restaurant, Gladys observed the guy's face. He did not look like a vicious killer nor a dangerous man. Besides his slightly reddish hair, he was an ordinary-looking man whose skin was darkened and roughened by exposure to the sun and the elements. Gladys could not see his eyes, as he had them covered by dark shades, which she was not sure if he got at the Wal-Mart store or belonged to the death man, thinking that gave her a shivering sensation along her spine, yet mustering some courage she dared to ask:

"Why did you want to find a used car lot? You did not pretend to sell the car you...we are driving now, right?"

"That would be very stupid. Do I look stupid to you, Miss?" Tony said in a tone of voice Gladys had never heard before, sending another chill down her spine.

After swallowing a few bites of chicken, rice, and black beans, Tony continued in a different tone and very low voice: "You are going to buy a car, and we are going to leave the one we borrowed right here.

We are going to walk to the used car lot, right at the corner, and look for a car. "You'll be the buyer since you have a license and ID. I'll give you the money, and you tell them that I am your mechanic who will make sure the car is okay for you to buy. No tricks, please. I will be carrying a piece, and a lot of people, including you, could be hurt."

Tony locked the car, leaving most of their belongings in it, except for one of the pieces of luggage with the cocaine packs.

Once on the street, they walked about half a block and then crossed the street into a used car lot that did not look as reputable as the most reputed in town. Gladys pointed that out to Tony and also asked if it would not be better to rent a car. Tony responded that in a shabby place like this one, few questions are asked, and cash is welcomed, whereas, at a rental place, they even take your picture.

A man dressed in a red shirt with a yellow tie, plaid pants, and yellow shoes came out and was obviously eager to make a sale. He showed several models, which Tony, who indeed was well versed in automobile mechanics, looked inside the hood, turned the engine on, and checked the tires; finally, he selected a four-seat Toyota Corolla 1998, and Gladys was able to make him cut the price about five hundred dollars, but Tony insisted that they have been charged at least one thousand over the car actual value.

He did not care; he did have enough money and much more to come, so they drove back to the "Pollo Tropical" restaurant, moved the rest of their luggage into the trunk of the Toyota, and drove away. It would be at least twenty-four hours before someone detected the smell or noticed that the car had been left there for a long time.

They drove west along Interstate 10 and reached Mobile, Alabama, by nightfall. They had a light dinner, and after allowing Gladys to go to sleep in the back seat of the car, Tony continued driving in the same direction. They reached the outskirts of New Orleans around midnight, where they checked in to a motel.

Once again, they slept in separate beds, and Tony fell asleep right away since he had not slept well since leaving Indiantown. He did tie his right leg to Gladys's left, but left enough slack in the cord for her to move around and go to the bathroom. They slept until after nine in the morning.

Tony woke up first, showered quietly, and left the room, returning several minutes later with two cups of hot coffee, bagels with cream cheese, and some pastries. Gladys was already in the shower and came out to share the meal with Tony. Both of them felt much more at ease around each other.

For some reason unknown to him, Tony felt like he had to tell Gladys, at least part, of his plans for the day: "I am sorry, but you will have to come with me to see some people in the French Quarters. You would like it there. I am only going to do some business, and then hopefully, I can check you in a decent hotel and then be on my way, and you never will see me again. I promise you that."

Gladys was flabbergasted. She could not believe her own ears. Was he really saying that in a few hours, she would be able to go free? She felt a strange mixture of joy and sadness, and she was not even sure why she felt that way. She only managed to babble: "Oh, oh, okay, thank you, Tony."

This was the first time she called him Tony, and it made him produce a sweet smile while responding: "You are welcome. Of course, I shall give you enough money to pay for a plane ticket back home."

Was it the Stockholm Syndrome?

Gladys said, "Thanks, Tony," one more time.

After that Tony loaded the trunk of the car with their belongings and drove on in silence until they reached the area of the French Quarters. and after looking for a place to park, they walked together a couple of blocks until they reached a store that sold novelties and souvenirs to tourists, anything from T-shirts to stuffed alligator heads, and, under the table, many types of recreational drugs.

A bald man in his fifties, sporting a flashy shirt decorated with flowers, alligators, and flamingos, was behind the counter.

Tony greeted the guy: "Hello Francois, remember me? Tony?"

At first, the guy did not seem to recognize him, but after a few seconds, he reacted: "Tony, of course, Tony Malatesta, you son of a gun, I almost did not recognize you...you look so, so..."

"Clean, perhaps, is the word you are looking for," Tony said. "Yes, I am clean in and out now, and I have some business for you if we can go to where we can talk."

The man named Francois looked suspicious and hesitant, so Tony reached into his pocket and produced a thick bundle of greenbacks that fanned in front of the store guy's face. This made him change his whole attitude, and Tony was invited to go behind a curtain at the end of the store.

Gladys was left alone in the shop, this being her first time away from Tony and her first unique opportunity to run away from him.... But she did not run.

Once in the back of the store, Tony told Francois that he needed a driver's license and a passport, to which the man responded that it would cost him at least fifteen hundred dollars.

Tony counted one thousand and told the man that was half the money, that he would get an equal amount if he could get the documents ready no later than two o'clock in the afternoon.

After that, Tony took a small plastic bag from his back pocket and put it in the palm of the hand of Francois while saying, "This is for you, at least another two hundred dollar's worth of the good stuff, hundred times better than the shit that I used to get from you.

"I know that you sell small amounts to blokes like I used to be, but you know the big guys. I have four Ks to sell because you are my friend. I give them to you for two hundred and fifty thousand dollars. You know that is worth at least five times more in the streets. "

"Gee, I do not know Tony. The business is not like it used to be. There is a lot of competition. You know the Colombians, the Jamaicans, the

Cubans, the Mexicans. They all want a piece of the pie, and the DEA is always behind us, smelling our behinds," the Frenchman said.

"Ok, you are not the only person I know who is in the business. I can go elsewhere with my snow, but you have treated me well in the past, so I let you make some mullah on my account. Sorry, you don't have the money."

"I will be back at two to pick up my documents," Tony said and pretended to leave.

"Wait, wait. We need to take your picture. Besides, there is something about that too. You know the guy who used to do that kind of work is spending time in jail now, and the new guy is not that good. He is okay with passports but not that great with driver's licenses, especially the new ones. They are very hard to reproduce," said Francois.

"What if I have someone's license already?" asked Tony while holding in his hand the license that once belonged to Jerome Taylor

"I think that could make matters simpler. Let me see. Well, I guess we have to make you white. That name is Jerome; what about Jeremy? That would sound more white and more southern. Oh, one more thing, please do not do any business with the other product. I shall try to contact some people and will have an answer for you when you come back for your papers, and it would not hurt if you bring then another small sample," the Frenchman said.

"Be back at two o'clock sharp; see you then." Tony left the back of the store after having his picture taken and did not seem too surprised to see Gladys still browsing in the shop.

"Let's go, pretty lady," Tony said. "I will take you to buy some nice, expensive clothes and then have lunch at the best restaurant in New Orleans: Antoine's.

Gladys tried to say something, but Tony, gripping her gently by the arm, walked her back to the car, which he had locked with a bar on the wheel beside the standard lock of the doors. One could never be too careful, he explained to Gladys, New Orleans is almost as bad as Miami, thank God the car was an older model and somewhat beaten.

Nevertheless, He opened the trunk just to see if everything was still there, even though he had hidden the cocaine inside the back seats of the car.

Then they drove to the largest shopping mall in New Orleans and spent the rest of the morning shopping.

Tony had been very gracious all morning and even allowed Gladys to choose a suit, a couple of shirts, and an extra pair of trousers, as he was now wearing the same pants he had purchased at Walmart days before.

He had never shopped with a woman before, so he did not know that shopping for a few items would take a woman so long, but in truth, he had enjoyed it.

Lunch at Antoine's would have to wait. After they went to the car, Tony removed the four packs of cocaine from inside the back seat and placed them in some of the shopping bags of their purchases. Afterward, asking Gladys to wait for him, he returned to the mall, rented a locker, put the bags inside there, and returned to the car.

It was after one in the afternoon that they left the Mall and drove back to the French Quarter.

People in the "Big Easy" take life easy. So many shops and businesses close for lunch and do not reopen until two p.m. It was ten minutes past two, and the shop of the French man was still closed, and it did not look right to Tony.

Tony drove around the block a couple of times, and after finding a parking space about half a block from the store, he walked alone to the French man's shop.

Meanwhile, Gladys went into a jewelry shop to browse and spent some money that Tony had given her.

It was not until much later that she realized that the money she was spending was the money they stole from the bank and from a man killed by Tony, but back there and then, she was enjoying herself.

Tony walked past the Frenchman's shop window and saw it was dark inside. Then, he tried the door and found it unlocked. Looking around to see if anyone was observing him, he pulled the gun that he had tucked in the back of his belt and kicked the door open as hard as he could. Sure enough, there was a growl of pain as the man behind the door was hit in the face by it, then before he knew it, Tony grabbed the hand that held a gun. As Tony pulled him forward, he bent over, the gun fell on the floor, and Tony kicked him in the balls.

The Frenchman and another guy who were behind the counter did not have time to react as Tony jumped over the counter and put his gun on the temple of the unknown man while pointing the gun he had taken from the man at the door at the head of the Frenchman who looked more surprised than scared.

Tony did not fail to appreciate the Frenchman's surprise and smiled and said to him, "Didn't I tell you that I have changed? I am a new man now."

The French was not a coward and figured that he still could make good of a bad situation, so he said: "Ok, Ok, I misjudged you, and I am sorry, we were just trying to make sure that you were not a DEA confidant or something like that. We can still do business; we can still be friends." And addressing the man beside him said: "We can still do business, right Pierre?"

The man named Pierre was more nervous than Francois and he was fast to answer, "*oui, oui*, yes, yes, we do business with you, yes, *monsieur*."

"Ok, but this funny business will cost you an extra hundred and fifty grand, and believe me, three hundred thousand dollars is really a cheap price for four k's of good coke."

"In fact, if you have the money, here is a bag or dope that is probably worth that much or more, but I want the ten thousand now, or there is no deal," Tony said while placing a zip-lock bag on the counter.

Then added, "And Francois, do not forget that you are supposed to have some documents ready for me."

Francois moved to the store to fetch the documents, but Tony stopped him and said, "I think the three of you go ahead of me in the back of the store and keep your hands where I can see them."

The guy behind the door was barely getting up. Tony told him to close the door and walk ahead. He was still groaning and walked bent over... Tony realized that he was not going to be a problem.

Francois did produce the documents and after examining them Tony handled him one thousand dollars while saying: "This is just to show you that I do keep my word. Now let's see those ten thousand."

The Frenchman opened a safe and extracted the amount required while putting the bag of coke inside and saying, "It is always a pleasure to do business with you.... When do we get the rest of the dope?"

"You alone should bring the money this evening at six to the old cemetery. I heard there is going to be a funeral this evening. We shall exchange briefcases there," Tony said, pointing to one similar to the one he had stolen from Jerome Taylor. "Please, no tricks. People could be hurt badly."

Then he walked away to meet Gladys and drove to have a late lunch or early dinner at Antoine's, where even without reservations, a fifty-dollar bill was good enough to guarantee the best table.

After eating, they strolled through the French Quarters. At about four, Gladys checked in to a fancy Hotel near Antoine's, with Mr. Jeremy Taylor of Florida paying the bill in cash.

Tony accompanied Gladys to her room just to say goodbye and give her an envelope stuffed with cash, but as they were saying farewell, Gladys could not help crying, and Tony could not help but kiss her.

They made love about three times before five thirty when Tony definitely said goodbye and drove away.

He returned to the mall to retrieve the packs of cocaine from the locker and then walked casually with two innocent-looking shopping bags, one that said: "Macy's" and the other that said "Dillard's." He drove to the old cemetery to close the drug deal.

He felt a strange sadness. He had lost something very valuable, someone he knew he would probably never see again, someone who had awakened something good inside of him. As he sighted, a single, solitary tear came to his eye.

Although he had planned ahead for the exchange, he was counting on being early and searching the area before showing himself to the buyers. He did not trust these French guys before, and much less now since the events of earlier that afternoon. However, he had not included the love-making session in the equation, and now he was going to be late.

Late—it had advantages, too. The men would be nervous, perhaps even gone, if they had a lookout. He or she may be bored and less careful. And there was indeed a funeral, with the band, the music, and the tourists, many of them with suitcases, in his favor.

So he walked through the opposite entrance to the one where he was supposed to meet the guys, mixed with the funeral crowd and pretending to contemplate the mausoleums, he walked slowly between the tombs until he found himself behind the French guys.

Only two of them were on sight. He carefully searched the tops of the nearby mausoleums and the doors of those that were open. He failed to see anyone else except the two men, so he approached with his hand on the gun and the gun inside the shopping bag that he held on his right.

Tony got close enough that anyone trying to shoot him would hit one of the two Frenchie's. He showed the contents of the shopping bags, then told them to walk into the doorway of a Mausoleum, whose door was easily open, and the three men walked inside.

The rest was easy, the French had the money, Twenties, Fifties and hundreds and after they opened a hole in each of the packs of coke and tasted its content, they exchanged packages.

Tony's hand had come in contact with the white powder, and when he put the hand near his nose, he felt the same urge that he had felt at the Motel in Florida a few nights earlier. But, once again, Tony Malatesta was just the body, the voice, the spirit, and the man in control was one Ismael Torres, whose body was buried somewhere in Fort Pierce, Florida.

Tony drove away looking for I-10 to leave New Orleans and head west towards Texas. He may spend the night in Baton Rouge or keep driving into Texas.

He expected to get into Houston by noon the next day, dump the car there, and buy another one to drive along Route 59 to cross the border in Laredo, or else take Route 77 at Victoria, Texas, and cross at Brownsville.

With luck, he would be in Mexico in less than twenty-four hours, and then he would spend a few days in luxury and relax before taking a plane to Guatemala City.

THIRTY-SEVEN

"This case should be in the hands of the FBI."

"At first, I thought that those guys in black suits and dark glasses were FBI agents; now I find out they work for Richard Mellon."

"What the heck is going on here, Sergeant Colles? Or, I guess you'd rather be called Marshall Colles... right?"

Andy Garcia was angrily talking to Karla Colles while both, at different screens, were searching through hours of video tapes obtained from about 17 different Walmart stores in the nearby areas.

"I never said anything to make you believe that those men were FBI; yes, they work for Mr. Mellon, but they are nice, they are efficient, it seems they have experience, and I LIKE THEM. If I was you, Garcia, I would not talk too loud; they may overhear you, and believe me, you do not want to antagonize those fellows.... trust me on that," responded Karla.

Just then, one of the men they were talking about, who was looking at tapes on another screen, yelled: "BINGO...here they are! I believe these are them, the man and the woman we are looking for."

Karla and Andy, along with the other two suits and a couple of other people from the local sheriff's Department who were sitting in front of screens doing the same task, jumped out of their chairs and converged behind the man who had announced the finding.

It had been almost a day and a half since the morning after the storm, and the delay was due to the fact that some Wal-Mart stores gave their tapes to the cops willingly and voluntarily, while others, alleging that they could not breach the privacy of their clients since no crime was committed on the premises, had to obtain a court order.

"This tape came from one of the stores in Crystal River, which is only a few miles from where we found the Helicopter," said the guy in the suit who responded to the name Ralph.

"Let's go check it out. See if you can contact the local police so we can get the names and addresses of the people who were working at that Wal-Mart at the time," Karla said with an authoritarian tone as she got up and started walking out of the room towards the cars.

Garcia realized for the first time that Karla was definitely the person in command of this operation. He felt relegated, and that made him somewhat angry. Even while realizing that it was his own fault, he had refused to participate in this, while Karla agreed from the start.

To make things more frustrating, after about three hours of interviewing about fifteen Wal-Mart associates, they did not learn anything that they did not know by watching the videotape. Except that the cashier who checked Tony and Gladys out said, "They seem to be a nice couple. The poor lady told me she lost her shoes in the storm because got stuck in the mud."

Nobody had seen what car they were driving and it was not recorded on tape.

Everyone agreed that "the lady looked tired and was wet, but did not appear to be scared."

"Perhaps another case of the Stockholm Syndrome," ventured Garcia.

"Or, perhaps she was so scared and tired that she could not feel anything anymore," Karla responded.

"So, what is next?"

"They took a car from someone, and that someone was likely shot. So, we will wait until a body or a car turns out somewhere. Meanwhile, since I agree with Garcia that our man would want to cross the border into Mexico, we must warn the border authorities on both sides of the fence."

"I hope we'll get him before he crosses the border; I do not wish to have to go through the process of extraditing him from Mexico. Besides, if he crosses and then, assuming that we can bring him back, he won't get what he deserves."

"What do you mean, Garcia?" asked Karla.

"Well, everyone knows that Mexico does not have the death penalty and that if they bring anyone back from there, it is only if the authorities on our side of the border promise not to seek the death penalty. And you know what the worst part of it is? In Mexico, they kill people in the streets every single day," Garcia responded

"I guess that is what you call hypocrisy."

"I would call it worse than that." Garcia was about to continue when Karla's cell phone rang.

After listening for few minutes, she announced, "It seems that Gladys Franklyn bought herself a used car in Tallahassee."

After getting the description of the vehicle Gladys and Tony were driving, they boarded their own, a large van with enough space for seven or eight people; the five sped off toward the given location. The car, driven by another one of the suits, this one, Andy learned, responded to the name of John, and Andy hated guys named John and also hated being driven, especially at high speed by someone else besides himself. However, he kept his mouth shut and fastened his seat belt.

The five of them made it to the place in record time; by the time they arrived, the local sheriff had already arrived and was talking to the owner of the car lot.

The owner was wearing the same flashy clothes that he had on when Gladys and Tony purchased the car, but he was acting humbler and more scared. Karla and Garcia immediately guessed that he was into something more than selling used cars.

The sheriff, an obese man in his fifties, wearing the obligatory dark glasses and sporting one automatic pistol on each side of his waist, introduced himself to the newcomers and told them that a woman fitting the description of Gladys had been there accompanied by a man, whom she presented as her mechanic. She bought a Toyota from him. It was a clean car. He had the papers, and she—the girl—had shown him a valid Florida Driver's license.

He did not know that the cops were looking for those people, and no, the girl did not look scared.

According to the sheriff, when the shop owner reported the sale to the local registration office the day after it took effect, the purchaser's name was entered into the clerk's file as Gladys Franklin.

When she saw the mane of the purchaser, she notified the Sheriff.

As they were interrogating the salesman, there seemed to be a commotion at a restaurant across the street. Then, seeing a sheriff's car nearby, one of the patrons crossed the street and approached the sheriff. He said that the commotion was caused by some restaurant customers complaining about a foul smell, and many either left without eating or paying for their meal. The owner insisted that the smell was not coming from the restaurant, and he was correct as some people had traced the smell as coming from a Lincoln Town Car parked in the back of the place.

Karla and Andy thought the same thing, and almost at the same time, they said, "That may be the car we've been looking for," and dashed across the street.

Their surprise increased when they saw the car had Saint Lucie County license plates.

THIRTY-EIGHT

"It is a small world after all. Who was going to think that Jerome Taylor was going to drive this way and find his death at the hands of Tony Malatesta? His prints were all over the car, and he used the same gun that he took from the guard and killed the others with," Karla commented several hours later as they were driving west along Interstate 10.

Garcia, instead of answering her comment, said almost to himself, "I still find it hard to believe that they did not call the Feds. I am willing to bet that Mellon did not want the FBI involved because he is afraid, they will investigate his dealings."

"Who are you talking about now?"- Karla asked. "The FBI is in it now."

"Sergeant Colles, you very well know who I am talking about. Sure, after three days, and I am sure he tried to bribe everyone from Washington, Quantico, and the locals, so the Feds stayed away from this mess. I would not even be surprised that he paid big bucks to make us Federal Agents."

"Enough of that, you, Detective Garcia," she responded with the same caustic tone. "You know very well that the Martin and Okeechobee County law enforcement offices were busy enough with the storm and the murders that it is understandable that it took them a while to notify the Feds. Besides, you, of all people, know that the police and sheriff departments everywhere in this blessed country of us, prefers to solve their crimes before involving the Bureau."

"True, Sergeant. Still, perhaps if they called them early, this guy Tony would have been caught by now, and we should not be here, driving around the Southern States like maniacs."

"You, Detective Garcia, could have stayed in Fort Pierce, but you probably think that a Macho man like you should be at the side of a poor, weak damsel like me, to protect her from those devil criminals around."

"Or perhaps, Detective, is it that you, with your famous thirst for revenge—which probably made you very happy that Jerome Taylor met a tragic end. And you probably hope that the German Security man meets the same fate. I, on the other hand, feel sorry for that guy Taylor, because he left a young boy orphan, and also hope that the German guy—whose name, by the way, is Max Kraft, comes out of coma and gets well."

"What you call 'thirst for revenge,' I call justice, and there is no question that the Lord works in mysterious ways, first that German guy; ok, Max, and now Jerome. I think they got what was coming to them, nothing more and nothing less."

"If I were a man of faith, I would start to believe that whichever experiment they did in the head of Tony Malatesta turned him into the Angel of Death and Justice."

"That is blasphemous, and you know it, Garcia. Those men may be bad, and we do not know for sure if Max Kraft, killed Doctor Nielsen, and as far as Jerome is concerned, I do not think he was going to hurt me. He was probably just trying to protect his sister," argued Karla.

"See, that is another case of divine justice. Carlessa Williams and her lawyer lover; they were not only profiting with the deaths of those people, if not doing something we do not yet know about to precipitate their deaths, but she was cheating on her husband with his brother. They made me sick, all that high-class lady pose. Of course, I am not a bit surprised about the lawyer. They are all lowlifes. Sorry, but, as far as I am concerned, they both had it coming. I wish all the criminals ended that way. What a big savings for the courts that would be."

Karla did not respond directly, even though she could present several valid arguments against those of her partner. Still, before doing that, she decided to gather the opinions of the three men in dark suits (they had changed into outfits exactly identical to the ones they wore before, and responding to Karla's questions, they told her that most of their wardrobe consisted of similar clothes, except when off duty).

"What do you guys think about Mr. Garcia's ideas?"

The men hardly ever talked to them to engage in small conversation; they limited themselves to making suggestions or giving information about the case they were following. So, there was not an immediate answer, and Karla had to be more direct, questioning the driver first: "What do you think, Ralph?"

The man named Ralph, took few seconds before responding and then politely said: "I am sorry, Marshall Colles, but I was not paying attention to what you two were talking about."

"Do not give me that kind of shit, Ralph, you guys are well-trained to listen to conversations, and I know you were listening and paying close attention; please do not take me for stupid."

"Ok, I'm sorry, Marshall Colles. Yes, I did hear some of it, and, with all due respect, I tend to agree with the opinions expressed by Marshall Garcia."

"You don't have to be sorry, Ralph; this is a free Country; a lot of people have given their lives throughout our history to make sure that each one of us is free to say what they think. I do appreciate your honesty, but I do not appreciate that you patronize me; I want you guys to consider me your equal, and you all can call me by my last name or my first name, forget the titles, OK? So, what the other two in the back think about this subject?"

It turned out that the guy named John and the other one whose name was Roy, all three agreed with Garcia on the matter, which made Karla a bit sully for the rest of the trip.

It was about noon when the phone of one of the suits, the one named

John, rang, he picked up the phone and after listening for few seconds gave the phone to Karla who after listening said to all: "The Feds got the girl, Gladys, at the New Orleans Airport; it seems she was alone."

"We will be getting there soon," said Ralph. "We must find out where they will hold her."

John got on the cell phone and started making calls to that effect.

THIRTY-NINE

"She is in the Hospital right now," said the fat woman sitting behind the information desk at the New Orleans FBI office. You can talk to Agent Clark. I believe he was the one who brought her in. His office is the second one on the left." She pointed to a hallway at the right and behind her desk and added, "I think he may be expecting you all. "

Karla and Garcia walked in the direction that she had indicated, and soon they found the door that read "L. Clark, special agent"; they entered without knocking, finding the Agent, in the process of interrogating no other but Francois, the French guy that had arranged for the false documents and the sale of the cocaine for "Homeless Tony."

After the formulary introductions and handshakes, the G-man wanted to check the "Marshall's" IDs, ordered Francois out of the room, under custody by another agent, probably of lower rank, and then proceeded to report to the couple.

"We picked up that girl Gladys at the airport as she was buying a ticket to fly back to Florida." "We had her picture at every Airport, seaport, river port, and bus station, so it was not hard to find her. Besides, she had called her mother in West Palm to pick her up at the Airport."

"Was she hurt...or..." interrupted Karla

"No, we asked her in many ways; in fact, she gave me the impression that she was trying to protect the man who kidnapped her." "He checked her in an expensive hotel in the French Quarters, where he spent yesterday afternoon with her." "He also gave her money for the airfare and more." "We found almost ten thousand dollars on her.

"She did not offer any explanation for the money, so we assumed that it is stolen money, so we confiscated it. By the way, she knew that the guy Tony shot a man to steal his car back in Florida, but she insists that it was self-defense, that the guy Taylor had a gun and was about to shoot our suspect. Also, she became hysteric and almost went into shock when we told her that she had been driving around for almost twenty-four hours with a corpse of the guy in the trunk of the stolen car.... She claimed that she did not know anything about it."

"Do you believe her?" asked Garcia

"Yes, I do. That is why they took her to the hospital," said the FBI man.

"You just said 'they,' not we,' took her to the hospital. Who are you referring to?"

"Well, that doctor, a psychiatrist, a female, who also claimed having been being kidnapped by the same guy along with this Gladys. Her name is Doctor

Alice Rodriguez, and she works at a famous institute in Florida. They flew her here by private jet. I checked, and it is all true."

Garcia said, "Shit!"

"What is the matter, Marshall? Do you not think she is legit? Is she involved with these crimes?" inquired Agent Clark.

"It is not that she is OK, it is just that my partner here has some paranoid fears about that Institute. His psychiatrist thinks it is because doctors traumatized him when he was a child," joked Karla.

Garcia said: "Funny, very funny."

"Can we see her now? which hospital is she in?" Karla inquired

"You certainly can"—and he wrote the hospital name and some directions in a memo pad and handled it to Karla while adding, still fixing his gaze on her. But before you go, you may be interested in talking to the guy that was seating here when you all came in; it seems he did some kind of a business with our friend Tony." The agent said this without looking toward Garcia; it was like he was not even in the room.

One more time, Garcia felt relegated to a secondary role. He rationalized that it was all because Karla was cute, sexy, and hot. Things would have been the opposite if the FBI guy had been a female.... Deep inside, he blamed himself for having refused to take part in this investigation when Mellon first offered it to him.

The French man's interrogation did not last long. He admitted only to helping Tony obtain some ID documents, and even for that, he claimed only to be an intermediary and did not know who made the documents.

Of course, he did not mention the cocaine, as he immediately realized that the agents knew nothing about that part. Yet, since he was not very happy about Tony's behavior at his shop, he told them that he did bring over a driver's license with the name Jerome Taylor, that the person who made the documents had changed the name to Jeremy Taylor, and that he also obtained a passport with that same name.

"So, you were right, he still plans to cross the border," Karla said, noticing the sour mood of her partner

"Big deal, we already knew that, remember? The helicopter pilot told us that," Garcia said with sarcasm, returning to his previous sour mood.

They drove in silence until they reached the hospital, and Garcia had the chance to get a smile from a petite blonde behind the reception desk. He felt a little bit better; she had ignored Karla's presence.

Neither one of them noticed being observed by a tall, handsome man with prematurely graying hair sitting in the waiting room reading a newspaper.

A pretty brunette wearing a short, black skirt that would have shown a pair of well-formed legs if she was not also wearing a long, white lab coat over it; the unbuttoned coat permitted her to show part of her well-formed breast, which were only partially hidden by a tight-fitting white silk blouse, which was casually but elegantly, unbuttoned just above her bosom. Of course, none of these could be fully appreciated until the woman stood and walked, for at the moment, she was sitting next to the bed where Gladys lay, apparently sleeping peacefully, as the woman was holding her left hand on both of hers and talking softly into her ears.

It took a few seconds for the woman to realize that visitors had come into the room, but then, she stood up, stretched her hand, and greeted the pair: "Hi, I am Doctor Alice Rodriguez. I am the Chief Psychiatrist at the Neurological Institute in Indiantown. You must be Karla Colles and Andy Garcia, the Marshalls. It is a pleasure to meet you. I heard that you saved Jasmine's life and rescued her from that horrible man. As you know, I was his psychiatrist. I should have been able to detect, at least, some criminal traits in this man."

"Perhaps I could have stop him before all of it happened. I really feel awfully bad and guilty."

"Well, according to what we been told you had your share of suffering, first the kidnapping, then he made you look as his accomplice in a bank robbery, that I am sure was not much fun" –Karla said while smiling at the woman and shaking her hand.

"Glad to meet you likewise," said Andy while admiring the woman's beauty, in such a blatant form that she blushed and buttoned her lab coat. "What is Ms. Franklyn's condition? Can you tell us?"

"I am here in an unofficial role, as a friend, not as a doctor. As you are probably aware, a physician, even one with a valid license and solid credentials, cannot simply walk into any given hospital and take care of a patient unless one is part of the staff of such hospital, and I am nobody here," Dr. Rodriguez said and added, "Thank God, outside of here it is another matter so, I was able to administer a strong sedative to this poor woman who became hysteric at the FBI office, that is why she is sleeping calmly now, she will sleep for few hours, the doctors here will check her make sure she did not suffer any physical injury—although she assured me that she not was hurt in any way. And I am pretty sure that she was not. The doctors here probably will perform a physical and a gynecological exam—if she allows that one. Then they probably will run some blood tests for HIV, Syphilis, Hepatitis B and C, etcetera."

"How long do you think they will keep her here?" asked Karla

"Most likely just through tonight, perhaps tomorrow morning, I am sure that we will be able to fly her home by tomorrow afternoon at the latest. "Meanwhile, I will stay with her so she sees a familiar face when she wakes up."

"So, that pretty much means that we cannot talk to her?" said Garcia in a somewhat sarcastic tone that did not go unnoticed by the psychiatrist.

"Of course you can, Detective Garcia; she may be able to hear and respond right now, although I cannot guarantee that her responses will be accurate, or, you can stay and wait for her to wake up; which could be in a few hours, or you could wait until the morning when she probably be one hundred percent lucid –unless of course she becomes frantic during the night and the doctors here find necessary to sedate her again" – responded Doctor Rodriguez with a million dollar smile which melted Garcia's mind as he babbled to her.

"That, that, that would be fine, Doctor. Unfortunately, we can't afford to wait till tomorrow, the man who kidnapped you, we think, is heading towards the Mexican border, and I do not need to tell you that once he goes across, arresting him would be a lot more difficult."

Karla intervened by asking the Doctor some questions, the answers to which confirmed what the FBI agent had told them.

So, they thanked the doctor. Karla shook hands with her again, and Andy, obviously embarrassed, could only mutter, "Thank you, Doctor. It was really nice meeting you."

Once out of the room and while walking the hallways of the Hospital, Karla smiled, "I thought you were a sort of Latin Lover. I never saw you blush and be embarrassed in front of a woman before."

"I was not embarrassed; besides, she is not only a woman, and she is a Doctor and a Psychiatrist on top of that."

"She is a woman, all right, a real one, and do not tell me you overlooked that. Besides, I told you a while ago that you needed a therapist," Karla said with a laugh.

"It is not funny Karla," –said Garcia and trying to change the course of a conversation that was becoming annoying, he asked: "You think she is telling the truth, I mean about what this Gladys told her, perhaps she gave the sedative so she could not talk to us, and all this concern" . "I never knew of a real Doctor spending the night with a patient that is not even hers –if you believe what she said about the hospital privileges and all"

"I believe her, in fact I liked her a lot, and she seems to care about this woman sincerely." Besides, let's not forget that she was kidnapped along with this Gladys, and if you would have paid attention to what she told us – instead of contemplating her legs - about feeling responsible for what happened, that is not something a Physician would admit in public, it may leave her widely open for a Malpractice suit." "Oh yes, I do believe her, in fact, at this juncture, I am so happy that the three hostages Tony took are free, alive and unharmed, that I do not care much if we catch him or not."

"Do not forget that he is a bloody killer and will keep killing if we, or somebody else, do not stop him." "I am so glad that the FBI is on the case, and they seem to have found the trail." –Garcia said while ignoring her remarks.

"Well, as far as they, and us, is concerned the trail ended here in New Orleans, where we go from here?." "I am open to suggestions" –Said Karla.

"If you do not mind my suggestion, I would say we keep driving West, towards Texas. I am sure he is heading that way, and he probably would try to cross the border at the closest point, either Brownsville or Laredo or any point in between."

"He may think that we are expecting him to do that, so he may go further, perhaps Eagle Pass or even further," Karla said.

"I doubt it; he probably knows that by now we have the girl, and she has told us about the car he is driving, and although we were told that she does not know about the false papers, he will figure that she told us about going to the shop where he got them and that the FBI questioned the Frenchman."

"Ok, I like your reasoning, and I agree with it. Let's drive down to Texas," Karla said while getting in the car, whose door was opened for her by one of the suits, who, like the other two, seemed to appear from nowhere.

"How about some lunch before we go? I am starving. " Does anyone know a decent restaurant nearby?"

This last part of the conversation took place inside the car. The man at the wheel asked the GPS for instructions, and they were directed to a fancy restaurant nearby.

Upon entering the restaurant—which looked rather expensive—John, the man at the wheel, told the other two to sit with him at a separate table, which gave the two Detectives some privacy. When it was time to pay the outrageously high bill, they were informed that John had taken care of that.

When they thanked him, he simply said, "Do not thank me, the Mellon Corporation pays all our expenses."

Garcia wondered if it was legal for a US Marshall to accept an invitation to an expensive meal.

FORTY

Mr. Richard Mellon was sitting on a comfortable "Lazy boy" chair with his feet slightly elevated. He looked pale and was perspiring despite the room's temperature being 70 degrees. His breathing was slightly fast and labored, but nevertheless, he was occasionally puffing on a Havana Cigar.

The wheelchair was at his side, and he was holding a glass half full of scotch, while a half empty bottle of Johnny Walker Black label, rested on a table next to his right side. There were two men in the room, both sitting across from him and listening to his every word.

"So, Peter, you are telling me that you are feeling all right and well enough to go about and take care of business as usual. Is that right, is that really right, when you were in semi-coma less than twenty-four hours ago? .

"Could that be so, Doctor? As you well know, both I and Mrs. Peters have always pushed ourselves beyond most human limits. Mellon said this in such a simple way that everyone in the room realized that he was stating a well-known fact, not bragging.

Doctor David Bright responded, "Well, Mr. Mellon, all I can tell is that I have performed a complete physical and neurological examination on Mr. Peters after he regained consciousness, all of which was perfectly normal.

Besides, we also ran an EEG and it was scanned very carefully by Doctor Dramsjold, and everything seems to be fine…you know, except for the expected changes, which are fine too." "Mr. Peters even had less headache than most of our subjects after he awoke and, he tells me it is gone away after only four hundred milligrams of Ibuprofen."

"And that is good news?"

"That is remarkable good news Mr. Mellon; in fact, I think he is one of the subjects that have shown the fastest recovery period and one of the best takes." "By the way, Richard," –Doctor Bright added this time in the type of tone that physicians use when talking to their patients- "You should neither smoke nor drink alcohol; you know it is not good for you"

"Shit! David, you know I am about to become extinct, and these minor mundane pleasures would make no difference"—he lifted the glass and the cigar in the air, then filled his glass with more Scotch and continued—"What about that fellow Tony Malatesta, didn't you say that he was remarkable too?"

"Yes sir"—they returned to the roles of boss and employee—"He was, but in a totally different way; he was in a coma much longer than Mr. Peters, and thereafter, his recovery was slower. What was unique about him is that he did not die or suffer severe brain damage after the cocktail that we unknowingly injected into his brain"

"Did that make him smarter?" This time, it was Peter Ivanovich, the handsome Russian, inquiring.

"That I do not know, we do not know; I speak for myself, my son Melvin, and Doctor Alice Rodriguez, who cared for him after the inoculation, but it does appear that he became smarter."

"So, he was smart enough to fool the four of you, two of the brightest MDs and the best Neuroscientists in the world, another doctor, this one with a Doctorate and a PhD in psychiatry, and your son, a rookie Physician but a doctor, nevertheless. I think that makes him smarter." "Smarter and very dangerous for what I have seen" – Said the Russian.

"Well, if you want to look at it that way and if we combine the street wiseness of Malatesta, who was used to survive in the streets, travel across the Country for free, and on top of that support a drug habit, with the abilities of someone who was trained in guerrilla warfare at the school of the Americas and is a veteran jungle fighter, I would say that one gets a pretty dangerous and explosive combination"- Responded Dr. Bright.

"Do you hear the doctor, Richard? That is why I think you should let me take care of this matter myself…I am not sure that those detectives you 'marshalized,' even with the assistance of our guys, would be able to handle this problem."

"Ok, we just got word that our girl Gladys has been liberated. The FBI found her when she was about to board a plane to come back home. She appeared to be unharmed and actually quite happy.

"Our friend Tony was nowhere to be seen. They are taking her now from the airport to the FBI office in New Orleans. If you go, you will act only as a coordinator; take the lady psychiatrist with you. I have contacted one of our lawyers in New Orleans, one of the best of course, and he is now on his way to the FBI."

"You may go, Peter, but you have to promise me that you will not get into any dangerous situation, even if necessary. You are now more valuable to me than ever. Remember that."

"Okay, Daddy," the handsome Russian said jokingly, but he did not smile.

"One more question for Doctor Bright,"- continued Mellon. –"How is my friend Max doing?"

"Well, sir, Mr. Kraft had massive post-traumatic brain edema. He was in a deep coma when we brought him here, and he is still the same despite treatment with hypothermia, hyperventilation, massive doses of Phenobarbital, and cortisone. He is on a respirator now."

"What happens if you take him off the respirator Doc?"

"Right now, he will probably die because the machine is hyperventilating him, and between the brain swelling and the sedation, he may not be able to breathe on his own."

"How long would he stay like this?"

"It is hard to say. The brain swelling would probably subside in couple of days, and when that happens, we will be able to reduce or cut the Phenobarbital and then see if he can breathe by himself"

"Then what, would he awaken? Would he recover consciousness? Would he be able to remember? Would he be the same as he was before?."

"I do not know the answers to all those questions, Richard; in fact, I could ask those very same questions myself. All I know is that he had pretty extensive brain injuries; some patients awake after few days, others after few weeks, others after few months, and others never wake up. As for the other questions, same thing, he could recover and be pretty normal; he may have only memory loss—usually they do, at least for the events before the accidents—or he may face some major functional incapacity.... Only time can tell."

"What about those machines of Doctor Raj; you all seem to think they are the greatest thing since the invention of lemonade? And what about a transference, David? Max has been with us for many years and has always been a loyal man."

"I am afraid that even the best machine cannot help us on this. The machine has shown how his brain is now –and it is not good- but it is unable to predict the future. Regarding the transference, if we do that now, we most certainly kill him. Perhaps we could try that latter, once we see how much he recovers and how much residual damage is there, but I am afraid that the procedure has never been tried on someone with traumatic brain injury....it actually be something exciting to try."

"In the future, right, David?"

"Yes, in the future, Richard."

Mellon took another sip of his Scotch and stopped to think for several minutes, then said: "Well, thank you, David, and thanks for the information."

"Are you sure you do not want a drink; it is 18 years old scotch"

"Thanks, Richard, but it is too early for me. Besides, I have to go back to my patients, so if there is nothing else you want to know, I shall leave" – Bright said this while getting up from his chair.

"So, are you sure that Mr. Peters is healthy enough to travel, Doctor?."

"I believe so, and Mr. Peters believes so too," Bright said, leaving the room.

Once the two men were alone, Mellon asked Ivanovich "How far back can you remember?"

"Remember what?"

"Oh, come on, of my life, how far back can you remember?"

"It is hard to tell, things pass like shadows across my mind, but they seem to become clearer every minute.... let's see," Peter Ivanovich said, closing his eyes and pausing to think for several seconds before starting to talk.

"It is snowing outside...the fireplace is lighted, there are lights....I think it is a Christmas tree…a child of about nine or ten years old is crying… there are no presents under the tree…suddenly the door opens, and snowflakes and a chilling wind get into the room, but the child is no longer crying; a woman has come through the door and has brought something with her….something that has a red bow on it…I think is a bicycle…the child is jumping with joy"

Richard Mellon poured half a glass of liquor into his glass and gulped it down like it was water while an indiscrete tear came to his eyes.

"That was me at age ten; my dad was a cop; he had been killed in the line of duty a year or so earlier. We received a small pension, but mom had to work as a waitress in order to make ends meet. She had to work late on Christmas Eve, and I thought that she was still sleeping on Christmas morning when I got up.

"I stopped believing in Santa Claus a couple of years before but had wished for a bike while realizing that the chances of getting one were slim to none, for we had so little money. So, when I came downstairs on Christmas morning, I was not surprised not to find a bike under the tree. Nevertheless, I could not stop myself from crying; then, suddenly, the front door opened, and there was my mother pushing a bicycle, with a big red bow on it . It was a used bicycle that the guys at the police station had found and fixed for me, but it was the most beautiful bike in the world."

When Mellon finished telling the history, Ivanovich felt moved. That was a rare and almost new feeling to him, so he coughed, grabbed a glass, poured himself a drink, and said, "Merry Christmas, Richard."

A moment of silence followed, on which Mellon decided not to ask his friend to bring up any more memories and Ivanovich decided to get back to business.

"I am sure you realize, Rich, that Max Kraft could be a serious liability to us if he regains his conscience and decides to talk to the police, the press, or even those doctors."

"Max has always been loyal to us, right now he is in serious state of coma and if he regains full consciousness, he has a lot to lose if he opens his mouth and a lot to gain if he keeps it closed."

"We both know that Richard, but you heard the doctor; he said that he could recover partially, that perhaps he would not be able to control his functions. What if, in the midst of some incoherence starts saying things that are not good for the corporation?"

"Are you suggesting what I think you are suggesting, Peter?"

"We could be doing the man a favor; I am sure that if I were in his shoes, I would not want to live being semi-retarded or semi-paralyzed. We both had seen enough of those in the many wars that we have been involved with and certainly, it is not a pretty life, at least for me I would not be"

"You be the boss soon, Peter, then you would be able to make all the decisions, but as far as I am concerned, at this point in my life, I do not want another murder on my conscience."

"Ok, Ok, but, as of now, poor Max's life depends upon a respirator. What if he is disconnected…legally?"

"How, how can we do it legally? David Bright would never go along with it."

"Well, I understand he has a daughter in Germany, he walked away from her and the mother years ago, but I heard him mention once that if he died, he was going to give everything he had to her"

"So?"

"Well, perhaps good old Max, in addition to a testament, has a Living Will on which he has written specific instructions forbidding that his life be prolonged by artificial means…such as a respirator."

"And if there is no such document, we can certainly write one, you speak and write German and are not bad in forging signatures."

"Plus, I am sure the daughter does not have a very strong love for a father who abandoned her as a child. Besides, she is bound to inherit some decent money if her daddy dies."

"Regardless of what he would give to her in the will, we will increase that amount substantially in order to make it more tempting."

"That is brilliant, Peter"

"Brilliant, legal, and the extra money also will make us feel less guilty."

"Fine, I tell some of the men to search Max's apartment, I personally would get in touch with his lawyer to see if he has those papers. - You know that there is no lawyer that money cannot buy, in fact they are a lot cheaper than the politicians."

"I will work on the Living Will while on the plane. I understand you can download one from the Internet, and then I would just translate it into German."

"Maybe he will expire before you get back"

"Maybe he would be nice enough to do that for us… You know, loyal to the death."

FORTY-ONE

Mr. Richard Mellon was still sitting on the comfortable Lazy Boy chair, sipping on his Scotch, He had been sitting in there for four or five hours since the Russian had left, he had been thinking deeply, at times sighting, and at times moving his lips, as if saying a silent prayer or, perhaps rehearsing a speech.

With quite some difficulty, he put the chair on a straight position and with yet more difficulty and not a good deal of pain, he rose on his feet. He was feeble, and his feet barely sustained him, so he had to lean on the lazy chair and then grab onto the arms of the wheelchair, almost swinging himself until he finally could sit on the wheelchair. He was pale, his lips became blue, he was sweaty and perspiring heavy, but he smiled.

Stopping several minutes to catch his breath, he first moved towards the table where the scotch, the glasses, and a pitcher were and poured himself a glass of ice water, then, after he accomplished the task and another couple of minutes to breathe easier and actioned the chair to move to behind his desk, pulled some papers from a drawer and started writing.

At that very moment, the phone rang.

"Yes…who? Big John, Who the hell is Big John? He says he did some work for me in Colombia and Mexico…and he has something very important to discuss with me, or Mr. Peters, he said that? He is in the lobby and has several men with him?; ok, put him on the screen and send the images to my office here."

Richard Mellon turned on the series of TV monitors hidden behind panels in the wall and took a look at the lobby and the institute's parking lot. It took him a bit to recognize the guy, but then he remembered: He was a guy who years before, when they were "on the business," helped to control the "mules" and other shipments arriving from South America via Mexico.

He remembers that after Peters retired and became a legitimate and respectable businessman, this man had gone into business alone. What possibly he would want from him after so many years and why he came with armed men? – He had three men with him and two waiting outside in the parking lot- Mellon did not like that but became curious nevertheless, so he picked up the phone and told his man to escort "Big John" alone in to his office and if he refused then tell him that he would not see him.

Mellon knew that he had less than a handful of men in the premises, as two were death, one was unconscious, three were assisting Karla and Garcia and two more had gone with Peters to New Orleans, yet those guys were well trained either ex-special forces or ex-CIA men, so he ordered them to be armed an on alert, just in case those people wanted to create problems.

Fortunately for all, Daddy John accepted having the meeting that way, only, very politely requesting that the only woman in the group came with him. She had very little in the way of clothes and was quite shapely, so Mr. Mellon did not have any objection, yet, he put a semi-automatic on his lap, just in case. He had enough experience with women to be able to trust any of them.

When Big John, his female companion and Mellon's man came into the room, the lights were dimmed over the area where Mellon was sitting and well lighted over the two chairs that he offered to his visitors.

"You have to excuse that I am unable to get up and greet you, especially the lady here, but as you can see, I have not been well and find myself confined to this wheelchair. Please sit down, and make yourselves comfortable…there is a good Scotch on the table if you care for some, if the lady prefers a soft drink, I can order some for her"

Big John poured himself a tall drink while giving the woman just water and saying, "She has to watch her figure you know?" then she drop his massive humanity on the chair.

"Understandably, she is very pretty" – Mellon said "Now Johnny, Johnny Watkins, - if I recall correctly, to what do I own the honor of your visit to my humble office.….I hope we did not forget to pay you for the little work you did for us over twenty years back; and if you came in with a business proposal, I am sorry to tell you that we retired from that kind of business many, many years ago."

"I am here for some answers, Mr. Mellon.… Something was stolen from me, and I and other people want it back."

"Now you lost me, what in the world that has to do with me, or my organization?"

Big John had lost his bossy attitude and he was once again, the old employee talking to his chief " Well, as it happened one of my men was carrying a shipment valued in about two million dollars, and according to the information I got from Tallahassee that man was killed and the shipment stolen, his car was found with his body in the trunk and the couple who did it came from this Institute."

Mellon was offended but did not lose his cool, as he was used to dealing with this kind of individuals, and he knew that he had him outclassed and outsmarted, besides, how could the stupid ball of grease think that he was going to go to the trouble of stealing dope worth two miserable million dollars; therefore Mellon decided to be honest with him and told him the whole history, starting from the fact that this was the first news that he had about the dope, and that, as far as he knew neither the police nor the FBI were aware or that either.

Mellon did not want any harm to come to Gladys, therefore he emphasized that the girl was not in cahoots with the man, that she was a victim, the last of three women that one Tony Malatesta had kidnapped and that she did not even know that there was a corpse in the trunk of the car on which she was riding.

He finished the story by warning "Big John" that the girl, Gladys was an employee of his and that if anything happened to her, he was going to forget about the old times. Nevertheless, he promised to let him know if he found anything else that could help him find out what happened to the drug.

"He is afraid of the Mexicans. They had paid him already for that shipment, and now he does not have the dope or the money....they may want to kill him. Help him please" -the girl who came with Big John speaking.

"I promise I do what I can my dear Lady, we shall keep in touch" ....

"But Johnny, remember, this is a medical facility, if you come here again with a bunch of armed goons, I shall have you killed and your fat parts scattered over the three county area...is that clear?"

"Yes sir, Mr. Mellon. I am sorry sir, I am really sorry," said Big John

"It is ok Johnny; just do not let it happen again, ok?" "Good by now Johnny and my dear Lady, whose name I did not catch"

"I am sorry sir...it is Daniela"

"Goodbye Daniela, it was nice meeting you" and with this Mellon signaled to his man to open to door and escort them back out, then the grabbed his private cell phone and dialed a preprogrammed number.

"Peter...how are things there in New Orleans? You are heading back, great"

"There has been some small complication, remember Johnny Watkins, yeah, the heavy set black guy that helped us for some time....no, not in Afghanistan, or in Asia, in South America and Mexico...well you wont' believe how fat he has become, he can hardly move and guess what, he was here a minute ago claiming that we had something to do with a shipment of some type of drug, coke, that apparently that guy Tony stole"

He told Peter Ivanovich the whole conversation and ended with "see if that girl Gladys knows something about it, perhaps Doctor Rodriguez can get that information out of her"

"The doctor stayed with her all the time while in the hospital and accompanied her to the airport and is here with her in the plane, let me see how can I tell her to ask without giving the pretty Doctor too much information about the dope."

Peter Ivanovich, always had an special charm with women and the two on board were not immune to it, so he went over to them carrying cups of tea and some pastries for both of the women; Gladys still looked sleepy and her eyes were red from crying,

"I am sorry about your ordeal, I do now know if you remember me but I was also with the doctor at the hospital, my name is Ivan, Ivan Peters, I am Mr. Mellon's partner; I thought you may want some tea and pastry, or a sandwich perhaps?"

Gladys was obviously impressed, not only by the masculine beauty of the man but also because the man was the second in command to one of the richest and most powerful men in the world, and her boss…and there he was offering her a cup of tea….whoa!

To Gladys, this was better than the time she thought she saw Brad Pitt and Jennifer Aniston at Disney World….. It turned out they weren't there, but Gladys always believed the story.

"It most had been awful….you must have been terrified, especially since that man is heavily addicted to cocaine. He must have bought lots of it with all the money he stole from the bank and that poor black man he killed."

Gladys visibly shaken by the memory of the killing and the though of having been driving around with a death body in the trunk of the car, could hardly hold more tears and her hands shook so violently that Ivanovich had to support the hand with which she was holding the teacup with both of his powerful but well-manicured hands.

"I am so sorry, pardon me, I am so clumsy, I should not talk about your experience, I am sure you have already talk a lot about it with Doctor Alice…. Isn't that so, Doctor Rodriguez?"

"Yes, we have talked about that but, evidently he did not use any drugs during the time they were together"

"No that I seen and he did not let me out of his side during all those days. There was only one weird thing though. It happened the night before we got to New Orleans, we stop in a small Motel, I honestly do not know exactly where and I feel sleep right away, however he stayed up, as he usually did to make sure I did not escape, then I heard him talking with another man, but they were talking in different languages, Spanish and English, yet, I am sure there was nobody else in the room. And I am pretty sure they mentioned the word Cocaine, snuff and dust, several times, however, I must have been having a nightmare because, like I said there was nobody else in the room"

Peter looked at her and asked: did the man he killed have luggage with him?"

"Yes, and I told the police that he –that man Tony- put the man's luggage in the back seat, and I never suspected that he did do so because there was no room in the trunk"

"Did you look inside the suitcases?"

"He put my clothes in one….you know the ones we bought at Wal-Mart, and probably put his in the other…I did not look there."

"Thank you, and again, I am sorry to have disturbed you, please drink your tea…..and whatever else you remember, tell it to Doctor Alice….try to get some rest"

Ivanovich went to the front of the plane, locked himself in a small office there and dialed Mellon.

"Richard, this is Peter, the girl is clean, she does not know anything about the dope; however, I am convinced that our subject found it and probably sold it in New Orleans somewhere….what should I do?"

"Nothing…it is not really any of our business, but I do not want any more problems that the ones we already have, so, I am going to give good old Johnny Watkins a courtesy call, for old times sake. Of course I am not going to do it myself—he would think that I am scared, or at least concerned; I shall have one of the boys do it and I am going to tell him that we suspect that the subject Tony did find the merchandise and that all the law enforcement agencies think that he is heading to Mexico."

"Has Johnny become stupid enough to believe that the merchandise is going to Mexico, when actually the Mexicans are the big exporters?"

"No, but he can send his hounds after him that way"

"That may not be in our best interest boss, what if they get to him before we do…they would want him alive to make him talk."

"I realize that Peter, all we have to do is get to him before they do; and in the remote possibility that they do get him first…well we have to make absolutely sure that he does not talk."

"One more thing, boss. If you would not mind telling Johnny that this girl Gladys had nothing to do with it and knows nothing, it would be a shame if she gets hurt any more than she already has"

"You are getting soft in your old age, Peter, or perhaps it is my own softness that is in you, I bet the girl is cute…. Am I right? Do not worry, I already told Johnny that if she is harmed, I would have his head on a platter…of course it would not hurt to repeated…. I enjoy seeing his face when I threatened him"

"I guess we both are getting old and soft boss"

"It has been a lot of years, Peter, and remember, I am almost old enough to be your father"

"You have almost been my father, Richard."

They ended the conversation, and the Russian sipped on a cup of tea that was already cold from sitting on his desk.

FORTY-TWO

Meanwhile, Tony Malatesta was already in Texas. He had driven along Interstate 10 to Houston, and then, he made what he later thought was his biggest mistake; he spent a whole 24 hours there, drinking and being entertained by prostitutes.

Waking up in a hotel room with two naked and drunk women at his side, he realized that a day of celebration could make a big difference between getting caught or staying free and alive; therefore, he decided to make a dash for the border right away.

At this time, he was not sure where he was going to cross. He would prefer to find a tunnel or a break in the wall that separated the two Countries rather than going through the check-out points.

Tony decided to explore the area between Brownsville and Laredo, so he got off at I-10 and took I-35 to Laredo, working his way close to the borderline trying to find the perfect spot. The area, as he soon realized, was a lot bigger than he had anticipated, and after spending most of the next day without finding a breach where he could pass with at least one of the automatic pistols and the money he was carrying.

Of course, He was not going to go with one and not the other, for he knew the Mexicans very well, especially the Mexicans in the border towns.

So, he turned to plan B.

It was late in the afternoon when Tony drove into the town of Brownsville. He had some very late lunch or an early dinner at a place that was a mixture of bar, restaurant, and pool hall. The customers were obviously not the high society type, and most were probably very well known by the local law enforcement.

So, while eating a cold sandwich and drinking a beer, Tony was sizing up the clientele, as he was sure they were observing him. He engaged the waitress in a conversation, stating loud enough that he was a traveling salesman and this was his first time in Brownsville, but the trip had been highly profitable, and to prove it, he gave the waitress a twenty dollar tip, pulling the bill out of a large roll of money. Following this, he ordered two more beers with shots of tequila, inviting the waitress to drink with him and enticing her to drink most of it, then claiming that it was late and he needed to deposit the money at the bank, he walked out of the place acting like he was quite drunk.

Two young men who had been playing pool followed him as he went out and walked into an alleyway, where he again pretended to be drunk and in need of pee while claiming in a loud voice, "The john in that dump was too dirty for a decent folk like me to pee in there."

With the corner of his eye, he saw the two young guys coming into the alley.

Tony pretended not to have seen them and faked fear and surprise when both approached him with jackknives in hand.

"Ok, old timer, hand over the money and we won't harm you, otherwise we cut you open like a pig on Christmas."

The two young guys did not even know what hit them; with a karate kick, their knives went flying, and next, they were down, holding their faces in pain, while the man they were supposed to rob was standing above them, pointing a gun to their heads.

The young punks were surprised and terrified as they looked at the barrel of the gun and the man holding it.

"So, you wanted to cut me up, eh? For that, I should put a hole in the stupid heads of yours"—and he acted like he was going to fire.

The punks begged, "Please, sir, no, please do not kill us, we have a mother, and we have kids; please, please do not shut," – both of them said in unison.

"So, you are brothers…. yeah, I see the same stupid ugly expression on both of you."

"You look Mexican. Are you legal here in the US?"

"Yes sir, we are American citizens. Our grandparents came from Mexico."

"Guess this is your lucky day. I do not kill American citizens on this day of the week; however, if it was Thursday, I could blow your kneecaps off or perhaps your dicks."

They continued shaking and begging until Tony ordered them to shut up and sit on some boxes stockpiled by the large trash bin, which was the only other thing in the alley.

Let's see if you deserve to get out of here with your dicks still in place, please answer the following questions and be true with your answers, because if I think you are lying, I can blow away both your kneecaps and your dicks; as you can see, there are more than enough bullets on this clip and I do not often miss."

The two young men nodded their heads in a yes motion, and Tony started talking:

"Here are the questions: One, do any of you have a car? Two, do you have a valid, current, non-suspended driver's license? Three, are you allowed to go back and forth across the border? Fourth, are the cops looking for any of you?"

They looked at each other in bewilderment now a bit less frightened and almost positive that the man was not going to shoot them and responded: "Yes sir."

"Yes, sir to what; question one, two, three or four?"

"Yes, to the first three, no to the last one of them sir"-

"That sounds Great, although I find it hard to believe that the answer to the last one is no, I am positive you punks have rap sheets longer than those stupid short pants you are wearing."

"Well, we did have some problems as juveniles, but we are clear now."

"I knew you were stupid, if you are clear now why were you trying to rob me at knife point? You can get 10 years to life for that, here in Texas or the death penalty if you would a kill me"

"We have a problem finding jobs sir, and we thought you were a person we could scare easily; we swear that we had no intentions to harm you"

"You fucking sons of a bitch are lying through your teeth now; you think I am stupid enough to believe that...I think I blow your kneecaps now."

"Ok, sir, perhaps my brother lied a little, but it is true that we do not do this for a living and are out of work."

"And do you expect to find a job in a pool hall drinking beer all day?"

"Our cousin owns that joint, and we were just hanging out there after lunch."

"So, you do not have jobs, need money, have a car, can go across the border as you please, and are not sought by the police." "Perfect, perhaps I could do business with you; let's go to someplace other than your cousin's joint, where we can talk money, and do not forget that I still have the gun."

They walked a couple of blocks to where Tony had parked the Corolla, and after making sure that there were no cops around, he told the boys to get in. He gave the car keys to the older of the two while the other sat in the passenger seat and then just told the driver to drive around.

After driving for about five minutes, Tony asked, "How would you boys like to own this car and a couple of thousand dollars in cash for gas on top of it?"

"That would be great, but is the car hot?"

"No, the car is mine. Actually, I bought it for my fiancée, but when we did split up, she did not want anything that I had given her, so she signed it over to me" Tony said this and showed them the bill of sale, where Gladys had written and signed trespassing it to him.

"The thing is that she wants child support for a kid that I do not think is mine, and I got a little rough on her, so she has got the cops after me for spousal abuse and demands child support. This is why I would like to go to the other side for a while until things cool off a little. Do not look at me like that; she came after me with a knife, and all I did was defend myself. I probably should not have hit her that hard...hope I did not break his pretty nose." –at this, he pretended to become a bit tearful. -

"I still love the woman, men, I still love the woman, but I want to stay away from her.... she was seeing other guys ...and I did not know about it; but I still love the bitch men, I still do"

"Okay, we are in. What do you want us to do, and where is the money?"

"Here is the money" – and he showed them a big wad of one-hundred-dollar bills. "First, we will get your car. One of you will drive my car across the border, and the other will go with me in your car. I will give whoever drives the Toyota the papers of it and one thousand dollars. I shall give the other one of you, a thousand dollars as soon as we are safely in the other side. Of course, if you even dream about crossing me, I shall put a bullet in the middle of the forehead of whoever is with me and come back to cut the head off of the other one.... Is that clear boys?"

The young men agreed, and they drove to get their car, a double-cab pickup truck, parked near the bar where the whole affair had started a couple of hours earlier.

One of the brothers, the one on the passenger seat, was going to get out and go get their own car, but before doing that, he turned around on the seat and, facing Tony, said: "I think it would be best to drive a little further, take 83, and cross the border at McAllen. Not only is it a little less busy and less fuzz in there, but we have a second cousin who works evenings at one of the booths. If we are lucky, he may be working today."

"You are not trying to bullshit me, are you boy? Remember that I would not hesitate to blow you away, part by part.

"No sir, that is true; what my brother is saying is true...we do have a relative who works at a McAllen border booth, we can call him now."

"Ok, lets drive there, and it better be true, but no phone calls."

"We will need a little extra money for gas," –the older brother ventured to say timidly.

"You guys are real hustlers, ok, we fill the tanks, and there be an extra five hundred if it all goes well."

"Ok, sir....that is fine with us"

"Let's then get going... Mexico, here we go!"

It was late afternoon, and it was beginning to get dark when they reached the McAllen border pass. The rush hour traffic was over, and most of the Mexican people who worked on the North side of the border during the day had already crossed to go home. Yet, the traffic was heavier but faster going south than for those coming from Mexico into the USA.

Only when they were less than a mile away from the border did Tony ask the boy driving with him in the pickup truck to call to see if his cousin was working and at which booth.

The cousin was indeed working, and once they knew which booth to use, they signaled the Toyota to stop and told the driver to take one of the booths on the side of that particular one. Tony told the driver of the Toyota to try to get a couple of cars behind them and blow the horn as if he was in a hurry or as if he had a problem with the horn being stuck.

Everything went according to plan; the truck went across the booth with minimal problem, and the boy's cousin just waved them to pass without looking at their papers.

On the other booth, a car was blowing its horn in a rather annoying manner, making everyone pay attention to the driver. One of the guards came to talk to the driver. Then the horn stopped blowing, and the Toyota went through without a problem.

At the Mexican side, two fifty-dollar bills opened the gates wide for the truck and a twenty for the Toyota.

Once on the other side, they drove until they passed the sign that said, in English and Spanish, "WELCOME TO MEXICO—*BIEN BENIDOS A MEXICO.*

They continued driving until they passed another sign reading, "*BIEN VENIDOS A TAMAULIPAS*—WELCOME TO TAMAULIPAS." Tony asked the brothers to continue to the nearest town of REYNOSA, where he could find a hotel, take a bus, rent a car, and set up the account with them.

They reached Reynosa well after ten, and it was dark. Up until the time they crossed the border, Tony had not said anything in Spanish, and it was not until he tipped the border guards that they realized that he was fluent in both languages.

The Toyota and the truck pulled up at a truck stop, and they went inside for something to eat and a couple of beers. Tony paid them as promised and asked them to drive him to the bus station, which they did very happily as their business with this dangerous stranger was nearly finished.

Tony warned the brothers not to tell anyone about him under penalty of death. Taking a small suitcase with a few clothes and the money, Tony walked into the bus station and waved goodbye to the brothers.

Tony waited until he was sure that they were far away and walked out of the bus station. Then, he went down the street looking for a Motel to spend the night. However, he was careful not to go into the first or second one near the station but rather one of the farthest ones from it.

He was beginning to feel at home in Mexico. For one, everyone took cash in these Motels, and no one asked for credit cards or questions.

He was exhausted, so as soon as he got in the room, he took a cold shower. After that, he got dressed again, minus the boots, and then it did not take him too long to fall into a deep sleep.

FORTY-THREE

Karla Colles, Andy Garcia, and the three Mellon's men had been in Texas all day and had contacted the authorities of all the Counties and towns between Brownsville and Laredo. Nobody had seen the man they were looking for, although the FBI had determined that he had been in Houston the night before at a strip club.

They also found the prostitutes that had spent the night with him, and the Motel where they had spent the night with Tony, and all, including the front desk clerk, had identified him … but after that … he had vanished entirely.

The area to be combed was much larger than it looked on the maps, and even with the added assistance of INS agents and helicopters, they could not even begin to guess where Tony was, whether he had crossed to the other side or whether he was still in the United States.

So, tired, hungry, and dirty, the five checked into a hotel in McAllen. Andy had said it would be the most likely place for Tony to cross, while Karla insisted that Brownsville would be the most logical place since it was the closest to Houston.

Earlier that day, they received a call from Mr. Richard Mellon, who informed them that there might be another interested party for Tony's whereabouts, the members of a drug Cartel from whom the man had stolen some merchandise.

Mellon said: "This, of course, is only a rumor that somebody heard from some blacks in Fort Pierce and repeated it to someone else until a member of his staff heard about it. So he was passing it to them, so they are aware just in case."

And no, he had not informed the police or the FBI because—as he had said—"may be only a rumor."

Garcia tended to dismiss the information as "as he said, it is only a rumor," but Karla insisted that if Mellon had taken the time to call, it was because he was concerned enough to think it was true; therefore, Karla decided to pass the information on to the FBI.

That evening, they had a light dinner of soup and sandwiches at the Hotel's restaurant and then went to bed, falling asleep almost immediately.

She thought that she had been sleeping for only a few minutes, but actually it was over three hours, when the phone in Karla's room rang. It was the local Sheriff's Department. The Highway patrol had located the Toyota Tony was driving and had two people in custody.

Since the arrest occurred in Hidalgo County, on road 83, between McAllen and Brownsville, they were bringing them back to McAllen, an

228

event for which Karla thanked God because she would not feel like driving a street block more that night.

She called Garcia's room and told him she did not feel it necessary to awaken the other three men; she would call them later if needed. She took a cold shower and was out of the room. Garcia was not out in the parking lot yet, so she called him on her cell.

When Garcia came out, she had already opened the door of the car and hotwired the ignition to start the engine.... she was sure that the men would be appreciative of her letting them sleep and probably would not mind that she started the car in that way.

Garcia did not say anything; he was too sleepy to talk, so they drove silently to the Sheriff's office, guided by the GPS on the car's dashboard.

The two Mexican boys that had helped Tony cross the border were sitting on a bench, guarded by two burly Deputies and a fat man, obviously the Sheriff, was talking to them, as well as two plainclothes agents, from the bureau.

After the routine introductions, handshakes, and ID exchanges, the Sheriff informed the Marshals that those "two local boys, from Brownsville" had told him that some man they met at a bar owned by their cousin in Brownsville had paid them big money and gave them a car to get him across the border. Of course, realizing that the money they were paid with may have been stolen, they did only admit to receiving a total of five hundred dollars.

Further interrogation by all the parties involved only helped to identify the fugitive as Tony Malatesta and confirm that the prey had escaped the hunters... Again.

He was already safe and sound south of the border, probably on a bus out of Reynosa. The only thing left for them to do was to notify the Mexican police, and hopefully, they would arrest him somewhere and extradite him.

Opening his mouth for the first time since leaving the Hotel, Garcia said, "What if he is still in Reynosa?" Buses do not leave stations constantly; people usually sit and wait for one. "Is there any way we can find out if any buses have departed since these boys left him there?"

"We can try calling the station and finding out, but do not hold your breath. Things do not work in Mexico the same way they do here, and of course, neither one of us has any jurisdiction there; however, as a sheriff of this county, I am well known by a lot of people in Reynosa. See what we can do."

After about half an hour of waiting and contacting several people, including the chief of police in Reynosa, the answer came in.....only one bus had left the station since 9 pm, and it was going to El Paso. And no one by the Name or description of Tony had bought tickets or was waiting at the station; two buses, one heading to Mexico City and another to Monterey, were expected around midnight at the station and programmed to depart about half an hour later.

"Can you ask the Sheriff or Chief of Police, or whatever they called there, in Mexico, to arrest the man?" asked Karla.

"We can try asking to go to the station and see if the man is there to arrest him. In fact, I will fax him a picture of the subject and see what he can do"

After only fifteen minutes of waiting, the Police from across the border called. He was sending two patrol cars to the bus station.

After another fifteen minutes, the news came back. The guy was not there, and no one in there appeared to have seen him. Good night. They will check around again before those midnight buses leave and also in the morning.

Garcia and Karla left the Sheriff's office planning to return to the hotel, but after they had driven only a couple of blocks, Garcia stopped the car and said, "We are so close, I am not willing to let it go like this. This man is a serial killer, a real danger to society; I do not care if he is a danger fo the American Society, the Mexican society, or the Guatemalan society, this guy must be stopped now"

"You heard the sheriff, the man is across the border; we have no jurisdiction there, we have no authority there, and it is all in the hands of the Mexican police now."

"Listen, miss, I am from Texas, my family comes from Mexico, I have been in Mexico many times, as a cop, I also had to deal with the Mexican cops. You know what are they going to do? Nothing, that is exactly what they are going to do, especially if the guy has some money with him; he will buy his way out...or the cops will kill him and steal whichever he has on him and we will never know what happens anyway."

"Are you suggesting what I am afraid that you are suggesting?"

"If you are afraid that I was going to say that I want to go after that bastard across whichever borders he crosses, you are right; that is exactly what I am going to do."

"But that is crazy, Detective Garcia, besides being against the law."

"Fuck the law! There is no law in these border towns, Karla; I am going across; you do not have to go; in fact, I want you to stay here. I am driving you to the hotel, and then I will go."

"I think that you are crazy and stupid, but I am your partner, and if you go, I go with you."

Karla and Garcia argued for several minutes, and as is most common, the woman won the argument. Andy turned the car around, and the couple headed for the crossing.

FORTY-FOUR

Karla Colles and Andy Garcia crossed the booths on both sides of the border without any incident and drove towards the City of Reynosa, which was only about 13 miles away, about a 25-minute drive via 23rd Street; the Detectives got there in fifteen minutes, and it took them another ten to find the bus station.

They had to wait outside because the two police patrol cars were still parked in the front. Karla entered and looked around at the few people waiting for the midnight buses. No one seemed to resemble Tony Malatesta, even if he wore a disguise, as most were young couples or women with small children in tow.

Garcia went to the bathroom and checked all the stalls, and Karla did the same in the ladies' room, just to be sure. There was no trace of Tony.

The frustrated detectives, meet again in the car and Karla said "Now what, I think we should go back to the USA, take a shower and go back to sleep."

Garcia acted like he did not hear her. "He is here, I know he is still here, and he is not far from this place. You know what, let's check all the motels and hotels nearby; I bet he realized that if the US police were going to ask the Mexican police to look for him, they would first look at the bus station. We know that he was there earlier because those brothers who drove him here saw him enter it, but unless he took that earlier bus to El Paso- which, as far as we know, he didn't- I am willing to bet that he just walked out of the station."

"Walked is right; he did not have a car, he did not steal one that we know of, and so are you saying he is still walking?"

"I am saying that he is around here, perhaps in a bar, he must have had something to eat at a restaurant, or perhaps he felt safe enough to check in to Motel for the night."

"That is a lot of perhaps Garcia; it is almost midnight…may be we should guard this bus station in case he arrives at the last minute to board one of those late buses."

"I do not think he will do that, but it is a possibility. If you want, you can stay here, and we can keep in touch via cell phone. "Just promise me one thing: You are not going to try to take him by yourself. This guy is too dangerous even for the two of us, not to mention one."

"Trust me on that one, I seen him shooting, he is very, very good."

"I am not too bad myself," Karla said proudly

"I know, you learned to shoot from your dad and all that, but you have to promise not to do something stupid, so your dad would be really proud of you."

Karla sat inside the bus station and waited; she was so tired that after a few minutes, she was sound asleep. She was aroused by the noise of people coming from one of the midnight buses that had arrived, and she checked on the passengers; none was Tony. The other bus arrived a few minutes later, and it was the same situation.

She was informed that no other bus was expected until 6 a.m., so she fell asleep again. This time, the ringing of the cell phone woke her up. She looked at the time showing on the luminous face of the phone: 3.35 a.m.

Garcia's voice sounded cheerful and alert despite the fact that the man had not had any sleep—"Bingo! I am happy to inform you that our man is staying at one of the Motels, sound asleep as we speak. "I am coming over to pick you up; we still have a long wait ahead of us until sleeping beauty wakes up."

Karla thought to herself that his partner was being overconfident. Tony was far more dangerous than the man they once knew, and, for what Garcia himself had told her, he took on three heavily armed men at another Motel in Florida, only a few days earlier. So, although she knew that Mellon's men were going to be mad at them for taking their car, she dialed the cell phone of one of them, the one named Roy…..there was no answer, in fact, the voice said that there was no connection. The same thing happened with the phones of the other two, John and Ralph; she sent them text messages just in case.

It was almost four o'clock in the morning when the now fully awakened Karla joined her partner in the car; she did not tell him about her attempt to contact their assistants but asked him if he had done so.

"No need. We will catch him when he gets out of the Motel, perhaps while having breakfast or while walking back to the bus station. We just have to look at the door of room 222, right above there. Said Garcia, pointing to the door of a room on the second floor of the Motel.

"I doubt that he would go back to the bus station. He is not stupid; he would know that we may know he is around here and that the police would be patrolling the bus station"

"Ok, he may take a cab, or steal a car, we will get him when he gets out in the open."

"That easy uh!?"

"Yes, hopefully that's easy, Sergeant Colles!"

"It is Marshall now, Marshall Colles."

"Ok then, Marshall Colles," and he did not say anything else, even when Karla, feeling guilty for the time she had slept at the bus station, offered to take the first watch while Garcia took a Siesta.

Garcia could not sleep with the adrenaline rushing in his blood—plus he had drunk several cups of coffee—but, in spite of that, they were both so weary that they dozed off on and on.

Karla opened her eyes first when the sunlight hit her in the face. Garcia's eyes were still closed when she looked up to room 222 and saw that the door was open and the cleaning maid was about to enter. Her heart sank, and rather than waking her partner up, she went upstairs and peeked into the room; it was empty.

As she did not speak Spanish, she could not ask the woman any questions about the guest in that room… so she went back to the car and got Garcia.

As expected, Garcia yelled at her but then realizing that it was his fault as much as hers, he went and questioned the Maid. Who said that the man had left on foot about five minutes earlier and yes he had asked her where he could find a cab. She thought he had gone to a restaurant down the street to have breakfast and perhaps call a taxi.

Garcia and Karla, drove slowly to the restaurant, leaving the car where it could not be seen from inside, opening the trunk, he got a straw cowboy had, and put on sun shades, while Karla put a scarf on her head and shades also, then both walked towards the restaurant, holding hands as a loving young couple would.

They spotted Tony sitting alone at a table at the far end of the restaurant, right next to the restrooms and not far from the emergency exit.

The couple sat in a booth, unnoticed, and Garcia ordered "*Huevos Rancheros*," toast and coffee while they discussed a plan of action.

There were not too many patrons at the restaurant, but still the detectives did not want to start a gunfight where some innocent bystander could be hurt.

They came up with two plans: plan A was to sit there, eat their breakfast and wait until Tony left the Restaurant, as he had to walk right beside them, then they could arrest him, or plan B , one of them could go to the bathroom, then come behind him and put a gun to his head.

As new patrons were entering the place, they decided on plan B as the safest for the good health of the bystanders. Next was to decide who would go to the restroom. Both wanted to do it: Karla because Tony had barely seen her before and Garcia because he was the person who had the idea of doing this, and therefore, he should be the one taking the greatest risk.

As usual, the female won the argument, which was settled very democratically by tossing a quarter in the air. The winner went back.

She walked straight, pretending to adjust her shades to hide her face, but Tony seemed more interested in looking first at her cleavage and then, after she passed him, at her perfectly round gluteus maxims, which were so well outlined by the tight jeans.

Once more, women probe to be men's perdition because if he had looked only a bit higher, he would have seen the outlining of the automatic that she wore tucked inside her belt but was a bit translucent under her white blouse.

Garcia did notice and he almost got out of his seat, gun in hand, until he realized that Tony had missed it and Karla disappeared in to the ladies room.

Karla texted Garcia from inside the restroom and told him that Tony was looking very interested out of the window at something in the parking lot, and his back is turned towards the bathroom. Then she came out, gun in hand, pointing to Tony's back while shouting, "US Marshals, you are under arrest; put your hands on top of the table and do not try anything funny, or I will blow your head off."

Andy Garcia jumped off his seat, and gun drawn, he came towards them saying, "You heard the lady, do not move."

Tony was obviously surprised and did as told; the detectives instructed him to remain seated with his hands on top of the table, both guns pointing at him. The patrons started leaving the premises in a hurry, most without paying their bills.

Garcia commanded, "Now, very, very slowly, move one leg at the time out of that booth, and be sure that should you try anything funny; we will shoot to kill. Please lift that right leg....good, boy" and Garcia reached inside the man's ankle boot and retrieved his old Derringer. 'I will take this back, it is mine."

It was then that Tony recognized him.

"Well, well, well, if it isn't Detective Garcia. I do not know what you are doing here, Detective, but this is Mexico, another country; I do not think you guys have any authority to arrest anybody here."

Garcia lied, "Yes, we do; we have special government privileges and full authority to come and get you, so start to get up slowly and do not try any tricks."

"You know Garcia, I should have killed you that day back at the motel."

"And we should not have saved your life that day back at the motel, but neither you nor me, can change the past"

Tony had gotten up slowly, with one of the detectives pointing a gun to his back and the other to his front, he knew that he did not have much chance, he also knew that neither one of them was going to shoot to kill him in cold blood. So he decided it best to do what they said and look for a chance to get away later.

Karla pulled out the 9mm automatic that Tony carried tucked on the back of his belt and pointed it at him, so now three guns were pointing at him.

Garcia threw a pair of handcuffs on top of the table on told Tony to put them on. Tony did as instructed even jokingly saying that he thought that they handcuffed prisoners with their hands to the back.

Karla corrected him by telling him to put his hands on his back after he had put one handcuff, and Garcia handcuffed the other wrist together on the back.

Garcia was very happy, smiling, "Didn't I tell you that this was going to be a piece of cake?"

Karla was not sure; Tony did not seem to be too concerned and they still have the problem of how to smuggle him back in to the US.

Tony was all smiles as they started to walk down towards the exit of the place; Garcia put a hundred-dollar bill on the counter and said to the owner, "This is for those who left without paying and for the three of us." And then to Karla, "remain me to ask Mellon to be reimbursed for this"

"You guys may want to take the bag that is under my seat with us....may come in handy."

Karla went back and retrieved the large duffle bag that Tony was carrying, she open the zipper and saw several bundles of one hundred dollar bills, among few garments and a shaved off shotgun, she uttered a vulgarity in the form of an exclamation and said without really expecting an answer. "Where did you get all this money? Did you rob another bank?"

Sure enough, Tony did not answer but instead said, "You detectives are so happy now, but you are fools because now we are all going to die here."

Karla and Andy did not understand and pressed their guns into Tony's ribs as he walked more slowly and continued talking, "Did anyone of you notice those black cars pulling into the parking lot? Better look now; there are four cars and about four guys in each car; that, if my first-grade teacher was correct, makes sixteen men, and each one seems well-armed. I am willing to bet that they are not with you and that they are not the police."

The detectives stopped walking and looked out the window. They could see very well because the sun was shining now, and inside the restaurant, it was darker. Realizing that Tony was right, they asked him… "Who are those people, Tony?"

"Oh, they may tell you that they are the Policia Judicial, either before or after they shoot you; perhaps some of them really are police- here in Mexico, you never know for sure mostly they probably work for the local drug cartel."

"What do they want from us?"

"They want me, but the problem is that I do not want to go with them; in fact I would rather go with you"

"All that money you are carrying there, you stole from drug lords?"

"Well, let's say that I found some merchandise that I later sold to an interested customer. Except that I believe these people do not believe in good old American enterprise." "Listen guys, you let me go; you can get out of here through the back door, give me my guns and I'll deal with them the best I can"

Karla was moved but also scared as she saw most of the men carrying high-power weapons like assault rifles, AK-47s and UZI machine pistols; two of the sixteen were blacks they wore bulletproof vests. The one who appeared to be the leader was now talking with the restaurant owner, who had somehow left the premises.

"Maybe we should do as he says; there are too many of them and our weapons are no match for theirs."

"Do not believe this rat, Karla. He would do anything to get away. They may be Mexican police," Garcia said in a not-very convincing tone.

"Do they have black people in the Mexican police?" –asked Karla

"It is too late anyway"-, Tony said, as he saw the men taking positions all around the building.

The man who acted like the boss sent three men into the restaurant. One of them said in broken English, " We are Police. Give us that man, and you can go free."

"*Ensename tus credenciales de policia.*" (Show me your police credentials.) –said Garcia in perfect Spanish.

To this the man responded in Spanish –"*Ustedes Policias Gringos no tienen nada que hacer en Mexico, nos han ordenado traer a este hombre, vivo, pero ustedes pueden venir muertos, si prefieren. Aunque la guerita yo la quisiera llevar para mi uso personal y bien vivita.*" (You Gringo police don't have anything to do in Mexico, we have been ordered to bring this man alive, but you guys can come dead, if you prefer it, although that blonde, I would like to take alive for myself)

"*Pos como que eso no se va a poder Buey*"- Garcia said (That is not going to be possible, Ox (–a common Mexican expression like pal in English)

At this, one of the guys who was next to the one talking raised his weapon, ready to fire, but he never did, as a shot from Garcia's weapon hit him in the right shoulder; the other two jumped out of the door for cover, and thereafter, it was a pandemonium.

Karla released the handcuff of Tony and gave him his gun back; they were all in the floor while the window of the restaurant, as well as everything inside was being blown to pieces by a hail of gunfire.

"Let's call the local police," Karla said, trying to dial 911 on her phone.

"They won't come, but it is worth trying," said Andy as he and Tony crawled towards the duffle bag to retrieve the shotgun and a box of shells, knowing quite well that even with that, they could not possibly hold on for more than a few minutes.

Someone tossed a smoke grenade, and two men jumped into the restaurant through the broken window, but since the booths were the closest to it, they had to roll or stand on the tables and were an easy target. Karla proved that she had not been boasting about her shooting skills, and Tony's shotgun proved equally deadly.

Andy had gone to barricade the back door, and Karla and Tony did the same with the emergency exit; that helped very little because the broken window and the front door were now a huge open space from which a rain of bullets was coming.

Tony told them to go behind the counter, as it would strengthen their shield against the bullets, but some of these guys were using armored-piercing ammo.

Nevertheless, in the few instances where they could stick their heads over the counter or on the side of it, they fired only when they had a sure target to save bullets, and going by the cries, they probably hit at least another two guys.

After only a few minutes, the place was full of smoke, and the defenders were down to one clip each.

"Do not waste all the bullets; save the last one for yourselves. Trust me; you do not want to be caught alive by this kind of fellows; they can get very sophisticated," Tony said.

Instead of answering, Karla let a loud scream –"Oh my dear God, they have a bazooka and are getting ready to fire it"

"It is not a bazooka; it is a rocket launcher," –contradicted Andy, and as he raised his head above the counter to look, a bullet hit him in the head, and he fell back to the floor.

Karla was over to try to assist him but Tony pulled her away, -"probably there is nothing you can do about him, at list he does not have to use the last bullet on himself. I need you to fire several shots in a row because I am going to try to hit the guy with the fucking grenade launcher before he fires."

As she was getting ready to do that, the noise of gunfire intensified, but something weird happened: the bullets stopped coming inside the building.

The Helicopter circled once, with two men firing heavy machine guns from the doors; a third man had a rifle with a scope and, with one shot, hit the man with the rocket launcher, who then was pointing it towards the helicopter.

As the man fell dead, the rocket went straight up and then, following the ancient law of gravity, fell back down, this time on top of one of the vehicles of the assailants, which blew in a burst of flames, injuring some individuals who were nearby.

Then, with the machine guns still firing, the chopper circled close to the ground, and several men, all wearing black, and faces covered by masks, came down from ropes and with AK-47s, spitting fire in every possible direction.

Some of the Mexicans decided to leave the battle and took to their Hummers, but only one made it out of the place; the other three suffered a similar fate to the first one from hand grenades tossed by the men who had come down from the helicopter.

It was all over in just a few minutes, and it was obvious that the men who came in the helicopter were enjoying the fight and also the killing because as they went around collecting weapons, they gave the coup de grace to those who were wounded.

The helicopter people had no casualties and no injuries.

Karla saw the figure of the tall, slender, handsome guy dressed in black but wearing a white long-sleeved, well-ironed shirt covered by a black vest. It was not a bulletproof vest; it was a tailor-made vest, and the man wore it with utmost elegance.

The two, semiautomatic silver handguns that he was holding, one on each hand made him look even more interesting. At first he thought that she was been part of a 007 movie, but looking at the man again, moving with such feline grace, the thought of an Angel, the angel of death, came to her mind and gave her a chill.

As he was approaching her with a smile on his lips, and saying: "My name is Ivan Peters, Mr. Richard Mellon's assistant; I am grateful to have been of service to you." She stretched her hand to him even though they were several feet away from each other, but suddenly she remembered that Garcia was on the floor, possibly dead or dying, and felt a grip of remorse as she bent down towards her fallen partner.

It was then that she felt the barrel of a gun on her temple, the arm of Tony Malatesta around her neck and a voice on her ear that said: "I do not know who these guys are, and I am very grateful to them for saving our skins, particularly mine, but I can afford to go to jail, so tell them to back off and let us go, or I blow your pretty brains off" and he took her gun also..

Neither Ivan Peters nor any of the other men now walking into the almost destroyed place was expecting that, so he hesitated and then ordered his men to put down their weapons, as he did put his two silver-plated 9mm Berettas on top of one of the tables next to him.

Tony and Karla started walking towards the end of the counter and he ordered Karla to carry the duffle bag. Karla knew that if everyone did what he said, Tony was not going to kill her; the problem was, that she did not know if any of these guys gave shit for her live and also Tony could get nervous and pull the trigger or shoot her accidentally.

No one was moving, but everyone was on alert for Tony to make the slightest mistake, and he would be a death man. Tony, of course, knew it.

Then, another unexpected occurrence: Garcia, with his face covered in blood, which was coagulating in front of his eyes by now, moved, and although he was unable to see his gun that had fallen on the floor when he was hit, He was able to pull the Derringer out of his boot and shoot it in the direction of the shadow that he knew was Tony.

Of course, the shot missed, but not totally. It hit Tony in the left leg near the knee, making him bend sideways slightly, losing a small portion of the cover that Karla's body offered. That was the opportunity that Peter Ivanovich was expecting. Grabbing one of his two guns, he fired a single shot.

That was enough; it hit Tony Malatesta right between the eyes, and he was dead before hitting the floor.

Karla was still shaking when Peter Ivanovich came to her, held her hand and kissed it

"I'm Sorry this little incident interfered with our introduction. I am Ivan Peters, and I am honored to be at your service. I believe your partner, Marshal Garcia, is going to be fine."

Then he walked out of the place, saying as he walked: "I suggest we better get into the helicopter and leave this place; the local police probably are on their way now that it is all over. Let them pick up the bodies; I do not want to answer any questions; let them think this was a war between drug gangs, cartels or whatever."

"What shall we do with the body of this guy Tony?" asked one of the guys

"What about the car these two cops came in?"

"Tony wanted to come to Mexico, so let him stay here; we will report the car stolen. Now hurry; we must take Detective Garcia to a Hospital on American soil.

FORTY-FIVE

Detective Andy Garcia woke up with a severe headache, dizziness, slightly blurred vision, and somewhat blurred thoughts. It took him several minutes to adjust his eyes to the light and to realize that he was resting on a hospital bed with his head covered by heavy bandages and intravenous fluids being injected into his left arm.

Since he was hooked to all kinds of monitors and electronic gadgets, evidently some type of alarm had made the nurse aware that he was awake. Seconds later, a very pleasant and rather efficient, heavy-set Afro-American nurse came into the room and, with a big smile, greeted his regaining of conscience: "Well, well, well, good morning, Mr. Garcia. I trust you had only nice dreams."

"Is it morning? Of what day? what year? and where is this place?"

"Oh, so many questions. Well, yes, it is morning, and it is the 20th of October, a Tuesday, of the same year that you got hurt, and this is Mercy Hospital in San Antonio, Texas, and you have been sleeping for almost two days."

"How did I get here? Who brought me to the Hospital?"

"That I do not know, sir. I heard they brought you here by helicopter, and there are some people, especially a pretty young lady, who had been here with you most of the time."

"Are they here now?"

"I believe so; they would be thrilled to know you are awake…they seemed quite concerned about you."

"I have a killer headache. Could you give me something for that? And please tell whoever can see me now to come ….or can't they?

"Of course, they can; but you have to promise to take it easy; you are not well yet"

"I promise, Miss Randall, and thank you very much."

"You are welcome, and your eyesight must be getting better since you can read my name tag." She left with a big smile after rearranging the pillows so Andy could be more comfortable.

Karla Colles walked into the room. She was no longer wearing jeans; instead, she was wearing a red and white dress that made her look prettier than usual.

"Welcome back to the world of the living," she said.

The nurse returned shortly and gave Andy a pill for his headache, and then she announced the arrival of the Doctor. It was a young Indian physician who introduced himself as Dr. Raj Lawande, a neurosurgeon and who, after stating to Andy the fact that he was a very, very lucky man to be alive, proceeded to inform him that a bullet had just grazed the side of his skull at the left temporal-parietal region only had lacerated the scalp –which is very rich in blood supply, bleeds a lot- therefore he had lost much blood and also the bullet had made a minor groove on the parietal bone. Still, it did not break it, and it did not injure the brain. Yes, he had a concussion, either from the impact of the bullet or from hitting his head against a dishwasher, or perhaps both. Still, there was no internal injury, and he was expected to recover one hundred percent.

"Thank you, Doctor. Does that mean that I can go home now?"

"No, not right now, but probably after a day or two."

"Doctor Lawande is trying to tell you that you have a thick head, but they had to make sure that the little brain you have inside it is fine and stays fine." –That was Karla Colles talking.

"That is about it," -said Doctor Lawande, smiling and shaking hands with both detectives before leaving the room.

"I am so delighted to see you are well. Do you remember everything that happened?

"No, what happened? Last, I remember we were about to die in the middle of a rain of bullets."

"Mr. Peters and a bunch of his men, including Roy, John, and Ray, literally dropped out of the sky and saved our skins"

"But how did they know?"

"Well, it seems that although they did not hear us taking the car from the Motel in McCallen, John woke up to go to the bathroom and happened to look outside. When he did not see the car, he came out and saw that we were gone, so he assumed we had taken the car and woke up the other two."

"All the company cars have a tracking device, so all they had to do was call a number, and they located us after only a few minutes. At that time, we were at the Sheriff's office talking with the two young Mexicans who smuggled Malatesta into Mexico, so they called a taxi to take them to the Sheriff's. However, that taxi took his precious time to get to the Motel, so when they got there, we were gone, but again, they tracked us down and knew that we had crossed the border."

"The cab driver could not, or would not, take them across the border, so they contacted the Mellon Company headquarters and were told that Mr. Peters was flying over on the Company's jet leaving Palm Beach airport."

"By then, you had located Tony's whereabouts, came to get me at the Reynosa bus stop, and went to stalk Malatesta. But I could tell we were going to need help, so I called Roy and the others; unfortunately, I could not communicate directly with them, so I sent them several messages that they somehow received.

"So, it was arranged to have a Helicopter waiting for Mr. Peters' plane right at the McCall airport, and they arrived right at the time when we thought we were going to die.

"They were absolutely wonderful, you should have seen Mr. Peters himself taken place in the gunfight ...he was, like...well, marvelous!" –Karla concluded.

"I see; well, I guess we have to be thankful to all of them,"—Andy responded without trying to hide the fact that he was a bit jealous and then continued—"Whatever happened to Tony?"

"I guess you do not remember, do you? I owe my life to you and Mr. Peters; between you, who shot him in the leg with the Derringer, and Mr. Peters, who put a bullet in the middle of his forehead, keep him from taking me hostage or killing me." "Tony is dead, Garcia, the case is over."

"My foot it is. Remember, this started as a murder in Fort Pierce. We have not yet solved that case."

"Yes, we indeed have. Mr. Mellon has made a full, signed and recorded confession, and he did assume full responsibility for all the murders."

"And where is he now; did the FBI take him in custody?"

"Mr. Mellon is dead also, Andy; he killed himself, shot himself, right in front of the camera, and it is all over the internet." "Here, you can see it yourself when your head clears off" – and she put a laptop computer on the night table beside Andy's bed.

"Rest now, you need it," she said, kissing him on the forehead before leaving the room.

Curiosity was stronger than pain; as soon as they left the room, he turned the laptop on and watched.

Mr. Mellon appeared sitting in a wheelchair in front of a video camera and spoke to the world.

FORTY-SIX

"My fellow Americans, and citizens of the world. Most of you probably never heard of me, some of you may have, and I am certain that the members of the media know me rather well.

"I stand corrected on this last statement: the members of the media know who I am and, for many years, have tried to know me rather well; because I have never given an interview to the press, they know me as the mysterious or the reclusive Richard Mellon.

"So, this is the interview I never gave, a way to apologize to everyone who has ever been harmed or hurt by my actions and to confess my sins, all in one.

"As I said before, My name is Richard Mellon, I was born over 65 years ago to a wonderful woman who died too young for me to remember much about her and my father, a military man who also died serving this Country in one of the many wars that we have been involved with, either directly or indirectly.

"I was only 7 when Dad died, but having grown up mostly on military bases around the world, it seemed only natural that I become a soldier, which I did. "I joined the Marine Corps at 18 and served in active duty in Vietnam and then as a CIA agent in Afghanistan and other parts of the world. For this, I earned the Purple Heart and other decorations.

"Eventually, I decided to go on my own. I was fortunate enough to be in the right places at the correct times and to find a loyal and intelligent partner who has been with me along this journey, so between the two of us, we were able to amaze a sizable fortune, perhaps what you my dear fellows of the press would call "an Empire", since, I believe that is a term you use to qualify people who have business interests in several corners of this planet.

"I have been married three times and divorced as many; I have six children –that I am aware of- and they all hate my guts, same as do their mothers, this even considering that they all received a sizable fortune after me and their mothers parted in different directions. The first woman was rich, and I was poor, so I married for money; the other two married me for my money.

"I dare mention these events of the past, only because, at the time, you guys and gals of the media made a big circus of all of it, even though you were getting the part of the history from the other side.

"Of course, that is water under the bridge, and I admit that I was at fault there as well, not only because I failed to be a good husband and a good father, being away in business most of the time, but also by doing something that I am not a bit sorry about, and that is not presenting my side of the stories to the public…even at this point I am not going to do that, so I plead 'Mea Culpa'; guilty as charged, on all counts.

"The next thing that I am going to say, is that while I was busy making money, even after fate and disease made me slow down, I always honored my firm belief that the wealthier one is in our society, the strongest the obligation we have to help those less fortunate members of the world's population, therefore, and again without any fanfare, during all these years we have contributed to many causes and to many charities about which I have chosen to remain anonymous and will continue to do so today.

"Nevertheless, it was on that philanthropical vein that shortly after I was diagnosed with a serious neurological disease- for which, I soon found out, not treatment was available-; and as I was going from one Medical Center to another; in this Country and abroad, that I decided to build a place where people with all kinds of diseases, but especially those of the Nervous System, could be treated with the latest technology, and drugs, available to Medical science. I pledge to focus especially on the type of research that our government refuses to fund, citing some ill-defined and, I dare say, hypocritical religious excuses. You know that I am referring to research with human stem cells.

"To that effect, I gather the best of the best in the scientific world from every corner of the globe, and soon I realized that although those scientists were able to accomplish things beyond my most optimistic dreams, they were unable to help me, because despite their successes they were unable to find a cure for my condition, but their findings and their discovers offered great help for others afflicted with similar and also a variety of medical conditions and illness.

"So much so, that is no longer a dream that we could one day, very soon, treat and cure. Yes cure, not only diseases like Alzheimer's, Parkinson's, Multiple Sclerosis and many others, but also mental illness and drug and alcohol addiction.

"This is why we came here, to Indiantown, Florida, to build and open the Neurological and Medical Research Institute of the Treasure Coast. We gave the keys and direction of the institute to my dear and good friend, Doctor Paul Bernstein, who has now departed. and to his associate Dr. David Bright.

"This fabulous team of physicians, veterinarians, chemists, radiologists, physicists, and researchers achieved the most fabulous results in treating and curing many patients.

"Unfortunately, as it is the case in most situations where new treatments and procedures are being tried, there were some treatment failures, few of them fatal.

"As you may know, I live far from here, in New York, but nevertheless made a strong commitment to staying in contact with the Institute and being informed about everything that occurred here." Also, I committed to visit the facilities as often as my health and occupations permitted me to do so, which, believe me, it was frequently.

"However, as I learned by these dreadful events, frequently was not often enough, and – although unfortunately too late- we found out that there was a saboteur, a physician, in our mist who caused these fatalities to occur and had a direct hand in the tragic events that took place here a few days ago. These tragedies included the murder of my dear friend Doctor Paul Bernstein, whose funeral I attended only two days ago.

"You may ask who the saboteur was and why he did it; I am not going to disclose his name here out of respect to his family, but also because that is a police matter; and as far as his motives are concerned, I am afraid that we would never know, as this young individual took his own life, possibly out of remorse, or fear of the law."

"Also, I learned from the police that there were individuals employed by the Institute, who either took advantage of the situation or worked in cahoots with the saboteur, and collected hefty insurance payments from the unfortunate patients who fell victim to these adultered treatments.

"Needless to say, the Insurance payments have since been directed to the families of the victims, and the Institute has added a substantial amount in the form of compensation.

"As to the person, or persons involved in this scheme, the old saying that 'God works in mysterious ways' could not have been more true in this case, as they also received punishment at the hands of a betrayed, jealous husband.

"Unfortunately, the most serious events were yet to come, as one of the patients being treated here, a psychotic and drug-addicted individual named Tony Malatesta- about whom you all have been hearing in the written and televised media-, went into a killing rampage, slaying not only my dear friend Doctor Bernstein, but a Security guard, while seriously wounding another, - who is fortunately out of danger as we speak – and, in addition, this deranged person got away taking hostage three fine ladies members of the staff of the Institute.

"Fortunately, I am now extremely happy to announce that all three young women have been rescued unharmed by two brave US marshals, Detective Miss Karla Colles and Detective Mr. Andres Garcia.

"Regrettably, before these fine Detectives took over the case, my security personnel tried to assist the law enforcement agents in their task of rescuing the hostages, and three of them were cowardly slain by Mr. Malatesta. Two of these brave men died in a shootout at the site of a Motel North of here, where the kidnapper had the hostages. The third one was brutally beaten and died yesterday—without waking up from a coma—he died of complications of pneumonia.

"I am, however, also happy to give the good news that although Mr. Malatesta was able to cross the border into Mexico, closely escaping from the hands of Miss Colles and Mr. Garcia with the apparent intention of joining a Mexican drug Cartel, upon crossing to the other side, he was killed in a confrontation with the Mexican Federal Police, who was able to locate him .The death of this criminal has been fully confirmed.

"I could tell you that none of this was my fault; that I was not aware of what these bad people were doing behind my back, that indeed neither the Doctors nor the staff knew about it until it was too late." If I said all that, I would be telling the truth, but I also know that I am the boss, therefore responsible for everything that happens in each and every one of my businesses.

"As they say in the Navy, 'The buck stops here,' and indeed it does; everybody has been properly compensated; my lawyers had reached to make reasonable and just agreements with all those harmed, and none of my employees or associates is to be held responsible for any of this....I am the only one to be found guilty."

"This is why I said at the beginning that this was a confession; it is, I confess to the police that I am the only person responsible, and I know that most of you are already thinking, "This son of a bitch rich bastard has to pay, we hope they would not let him get away with murder just because of his money.

"And do you know what?...... I agree with you, and I deserve to go to jail. However, I am too old and too sick and too used to the good life to spend whatever is left of the rest of my life in a cell. Therefore, I am choosing my punishment, I am going to kill myself with this pistol you see here.

"Those with a sensitive heart or queasy stomach do not have to worry, I am going to spare you the gross picture of me shooting myself in the head or my mouth. No, that would be too messy and not proper for kids to watch.

I am going to put this pistol it right here in my chest, right where my heart is, and pull the trigger.

"Oh, and the last couple of things. Feel free to use the confession I made on this disc in any way you please. Show it on the Internet or on YouTube for everyone to see, and you members of the media, feel free to copy it, comment on it, reproduce it, broadcast it, or whatever else you may think of doing with it.

"Also, I want to be cremated, and my ashes placed in a crypt in the small cemetery that we have in the garden of my home in White Plains, New York...unless one of my ex-wives or the law decides otherwise, of course.

"Last but not least, my best and loyal friend and associate, the person who has been with me through thick and thin and had considerable influence in the success of our many enterprises, Mr. Ivan Peters, is going to take over all my business and holdings. this wish is in a will, properly drawn and executed and is in the hands of my lawyers." "Mr. Peters, of course, will continue handling not only the business but the work in behalf of the sick and the poor." "Even though we have been forced to move the Institute, temporarily to a, for now, undisclosed location, to permit the scientific staff continue their work undisturbed by the memories of the recent events, as well. as you know, the curiosity of the media"

"So, having nothing else to say or confess, I bid you all farewell. May God forgive my sins, and God Bless America."

The pistol went off, and the body of Mr. Richard Mellon became limp without falling off the wheelchair where he was sitting during the recording.

Frank Allison old-time partner of Garcia turned off the laptop computer and commented: "He is actually going to be buried in D.C., at Arlington"

Frank was almost fully recovered from his wounds and ready to take Andy home from the hospital and return to work at the Sheriff's department.

"That is not a confession, Frank; that is a lot of bullshit and a fucking piece of propaganda."

"He wrote everything down and signed it, with a copy for each one of us and also a check for two hundred and fifty thousand dollars apiece," said Karla, who was sitting on a chair nearby and also watching the video.

"What for?.... I understood that we were government employees and received our checks from the Federal government" –said Garcia.

"Mellon had put a half-million-dollar reward for Tony Malatesta, death or alive," said Karla. We earned it.

"I do not want it; I think the son of a bitch got away with murder....all that he said in that confession is pure and simply stinking bullshit. The man knew about Max killing Doctor Neilsen; he probably ordered him to do it; maybe he killed him too, so he would not talk to us." "And I am willing to bet that he, or that handsome Russian you like so much, would not have hesitated to kill us if we got too close to the truth or interfered with his plans," said Garcia.

"Suit yourself, Garcia," said Karla, "I thought you were smarter than this; besides, if I recall correctly, the lecture you gave me about the death penalty, remember?" "So, if you feel that way, you should be very happy because whoever else was guilty, they are all dead now." "They all paid with their lives....as far as I am concerned, I am going to take this check –which by the way, my lawyer said it is ok to cash- and take a vacation in the Caribbean as soon as Hurricane season is over, then I am going to return to work for good old Sheriff Mascara. Yes, I have resigned from this US Marshall thing."

Karla left, and Frank helped Andy to get dressed and pack.

"You are not serious about not taking that check are you, Andy?"

"I do not know yet, Frank,"... but just in case, Have you exhausted all your sick and vacation time? I always wanted to take a tour to Europe."

"That is my friend Andy speaking....I am still on workers comp.. The Doctors I am seeing said they were going to release me probably next week, but I can always pretend that I had a relapse, "

"That is my man Frank talking.....how do I resign from this US Marshall Thing?"

"I do not know, but I am sure the Sheriff can tell us"

"Did she go to the funeral, Frank?"

"Who?"

"Do not give me that shit; you know who I am talking about"

"The Russian flew her back and forth to Washington DC"

"Shit....I think I will take that European vacation; you are cordially invited, we can go check the Spanish and Italian girls. Or you can take your wife and I can invite my nurse friend."

"Let's go then.....I am already beginning to limp again, and the pain is unbearable."

Laughing loudly, the two detectives left the hospital in Texas.

THE END

EPILOGUE

Ok, we would not know if Garcia and his partner Frank were serious about collecting the reward money and taking a long trip overseas with it. Still, the reader may be curious about the fate of other characters who participated in this adventure.

Having always considered myself a gentleman and a faithful admirer of most persons of the opposite sex, let's start with the Ladies, other than those about whom we already know their fate

Sergeant Karla Colles did take the money and the Caribbean Vacation…she went alone with her parents.

Gladys Franklyn supposedly developed Post-Traumatic Stress Syndrome and hired a West Palms Beach Law firm to sue the Neurological Institute; the lawsuit was settled out of court for an undisclosed amount, probably quite large since it allowed her to buy a waterfront home. Between her, her mother and sister spent almost all the money, so Gladys had to return to work at a Car Dealership and ended up marrying the owner's son and having seven kids.

Doctor Linda Porter left Florida along with all the other members of the scientific team. She continued doing research for them at a new facility in a "safe, undisclosed location" somewhere in the Caribbean.

Doctor Porter's daughter, Jasmine, refused to go with her mother and moved to California where she became Professor at Berkley's school of Veterinary Medicine.

Doctor Alice Rodriguez took a year's sabbatical at the Institute's expense, and after that, she rejoined the staff at that "safe undisclosed location" in the Caribbean.

Doctor Melvin Bright refused to go with his father and the others to the Caribbean and instead followed Jasmine Porter to California, only to learn that she did not want to become romantically involved with him and only offered him a sincere friendship and her moral support if he continued improving himself in the Medical Field.

Heartbroken, he failed the Medical Boards in the State of California, but having met a young medical student who returned his romantic advances and encouraged him to persist, Melvin returned to Florida, studied hard, and passed the Medical Boards with high grades. The two of them practiced Medicine for a couple of years in Miami.

However, during one of his father's visits, he offered him a job at the old Institute in Indiantown, indicating that "The Corporation" considered that enough time had passed since the tragic events related here occurred. They considered re-opening the place with Melvin and his fiancée as Medical Directors. Melvin put as a precondition that it should be re-named and open as the "Paul Bernstein Neurological and Medical Institute", with half of the services being free for those without insurance or money.

The Corporation agreed, and the Institute opened its doors again almost five years after the tragic events that led to its closure.

Joe Smith, the security ward wounded by Tony, recovered without complications and retired after receiving hefty compensation. He became a Minister at a Presbyterian church and eventually became a TV evangelist, making millions.

Max Kraft never recovered consciousness and indeed developed pneumonia and died from complications of it. As far as we know, neither Richard Mellon nor Peter Ivanovich had anything to do with it.

Also, they probably were not extremely sorry about this ending.

All the other Doctors and Scientists were moved out of Indiantown few days before the date on which Richard Mellon committed suicide, and they are working very happily for the "Corporation" at the new Neurological Institute at the "Undisclosed location."

Ivan Peters, aka Peter Ivanovich, is the President and major shareholder of "THE CORPORATION." Most people think that his ways are strangely extremely similar to Richard Mellon's. He never called Karla Colles again.

Doctor Dramsjold and Doctor Schneider got their Radiology machines patented, and "The Corporation" offered to manufacture, distribute, and sell them for a mere 25 percent of the profits. They became millionaires quickly but never abandoned their research work. Right now, they are working on a new machine and an upgrade of the first one.

The shipment of cocaine that "Homeless Tony" sold to the Frenchmen in New Orleans was never recovered.

"Big Daddy" refused to pay the Mexican Cartel the two million dollars that they wanted for the lost merchandise because it was not his fault and that he had lost three men (Jerome; and two others in the Reynosa shootout) in that particular business. Therefore, it should be him the one receiving compensation from the Mexicans.

He did not get precisely the kind of compensation he wanted because, about four months later, while coming out of a nightclub in Miami's "Little Havana," he, his driver, and his bodyguard were shot to death. The coroner recorded that there were 17 bullet holes in his body, and he still arrived at the hospital alive, only to die while being transferred from the ambulance to the ER.

THIS IS REALLY THE END

www.ingramcontent.com/pod-product-compliance
Lightning Source LLC
Chambersburg PA
CBHW060913250626
47159CB00008B/2991